A NOVEL

BRIAN FREEMAN

SILVEROAK
New York / London

SILVEROAK

New York / London

An Imprint of Sterling Publishing Co., Inc. (New York)
and Quercus Publishing Plc (London)
387 Park Avenue South
New York, NY 10016

ISBN 978-1-4027-9812-2 (hardcover)
ISBN 978-1-4027-9838-2 (ebook)

Distributed in Canada by Sterling Publishing
c/o Canadian Manda Group, 165 Dufferin Street
Toronto, Ontario, Canada M6K 3H6

For information about custom editions, special sales, and premium and corporate purchases, please contact Sterling Special Sales at 800-805-5489 or specialsales@sterlingpublishing.com.

Manufactured in the United States of America

2 4 6 8 10 9 7 5 3 1

www.sterlingpublishing.com

For Marcia

TO THE ATTENTION OF

MR. FLORIAN STEELE

CHIEF EXECUTIVE OFFICER OF

MONDAMIN RESEARCH

I KNOW YOUR SINS

YOU SACRIFICE THE INNOCENT

YOU SEVER FAMILIES WITH YOUR EVIL

YOU BELIEVE YOURSELF A GIANT IN THE EARTH

BUT YOUR HEART IS FILLED WITH VIOLENCE AND

CORRUPTION

NOW RETRIBUTION IS COMING

DESTRUCTION WILL RAIN DOWN

ON ALL THAT YOU HAVE CREATED

NO ONE WILL BE SPARED

I AM A TORRENT WITHOUT MERCY

I AM THE VENGEANCE OF GOD

MY NAME IS

AQUARIUS

PROLOGUE

Hobbled by a flat tire, Ashlynn's fire-orange Mustang convertible limped to a stop on the main street of the abandoned farm town.

It was nearly midnight, but moonlight gave the ruins of the town a silver glow. Dirty shards of glass from whitewashed storefront windows littered the gravel. Dead weeds traveled like snakes along broken sidewalks. Beside her, the façade of a deserted building boasted the name of the Southwest Farmers Mercantile Bank chiseled into its red brick, but the bankers had long since gone bust, along with the farmers and shop owners. Across the street, a rusted 7Up sign dangled from the worn metal banner for Ekqvist Foods. When the wind blew, the lone screw made a tortured, twisting squeal, like a captured animal.

Officially, the town didn't exist anymore. It wasn't on maps. Only the local teenagers came here now to break the windows and paint graffiti on the walls. A hundred years earlier, the street had awakened each morning with the throb of machines and the perfume of corn and gasoline. Not anymore. The town had dwindled year by year, family by family, and finally disappeared. Even the ghosts had moved on now, because there was no one left to haunt.

Ashlynn was marooned. She checked the signal strength on her phone, but she was in one of those great swaths of rural land where the mobile towers didn't reach. You could drive for miles among the corn and soybean fields of southwest Minnesota, cut off from the world, going back in time. She sat in the expensive car that her father had given her last year, when she turned sixteen, and wondered what to do next. Where to go. How to get there.

It had been a mistake to take the detour onto the lonely dirt road, but she hadn't wanted to pass through the town of St. Croix as she neared the river. These days, if you were a teenager from the town of Barron, you avoided going to the town of St. Croix alone. It wasn't safe for anyone to see you there.

Particularly Ashlynn. Particularly when your father was Florian Steele.

She got out of her car and stood like the last girl on earth in the center of the old main street. She studied her stricken Mustang, which was covered with a film of dust. The flabby rubber on the left rear tire looked like melted ice cream. On either side of her, the remains of a half dozen decaying buildings loomed behind boarded-up doors and No Trespassing signs. The buildings were interspersed with weedy, overgrown lots, like missing teeth in a rotting smile.

She called, "Hello?" Then louder: "Hello!"

Ashlynn didn't expect an answer. The road saw little traffic during the days, and at night, no one came here. It was a tiny, forgotten corner of the vast plains of the Spirit River valley. When she shouted, a raven squawked back at her. The towering trees rattled their bare branches with a gust of wind. No one else replied.

With nowhere to go, she wandered to the end of the street, where the town dissolved into a landscape of dormant fields. She saw the gray superstructure of a corn elevator, which was grimy with disuse. A children's park nestled in the open space near the farm machinery, underneath soaring oak trees. The ground was muddy and winter brown. She spotted an old swing made of thick rope with a warped wooden seat hanging from one of the low branches of the largest tree. She kicked through the soggy grass and sat down. With the heels of her leather calf boots in a puddle, she pushed herself gently back and forth and hung on to the scratchy twine.

It made her feel younger and innocent again. It made her want to stay there forever. She closed her eyes, listening to the roar of the wind and inhaling the scent of pine. She lost track of where she was. She thought about her father when she was just a girl, and she found herself humming a lullaby that made her smile. He'd sung it to her in the old days. She tried to pretend for a while that things were different, but pretending didn't erase what she'd done or change what she had to do. Sometimes life gave you unbearable choices.

When Ashlynn opened her eyes again, she was still in the ghost town, but she was no longer alone.

Two silhouettes had seemingly risen out of the dead ground. They stood, watching her, on the dirt road near the park. Ashlynn clutched the rope swing, keenly aware of how vulnerable she was. Her instincts told her to flee, but she couldn't run. The three of them stared at each other, thirty feet apart, frozen and cautious. No one moved; no one spoke. Then the taller of the two strangers ventured closer, and the second followed behind. Ashlynn recognized them. They were girls from her high school.

St. Croix girls.

The taller girl swaggered toward Ashlynn until she was practically in her face. She carried a beer bottle in her hand, and when she spoke, a hoppy aroma wafted from her mouth. "Ashlynn Steele. I don't believe it."

"Hello, Olivia," Ashlynn said calmly.

Olivia Hawk was a year younger than Ashlynn. The girl was five feet ten, bony, and pretty. Her legs were long matchsticks squeezed inside ratty jeans, and she wore an untucked flannel shirt over a white T-shirt that let an inch of her flat stomach peek through. She had long chestnut hair and intense brown eyes. She was smart and fiery, and Ashlynn could see naked emotion on the girl's face.

"What are *you* doing here?" Olivia demanded. Her voice cracked, more with misery than anger. She was obviously drunk.

Other girls resented Ashlynn because of who she was: the daughter of Florian Steele; rich in a town where everyone else scraped by; blonde, small, beautiful. That was enough, but with Olivia, there was more. Even if there had been no feud between the towns, no ugly secrets, the two of them would never have been friends.

"I got a flat tire," Ashlynn said.

"So where were you tonight?"

"Nowhere," Ashlynn replied.

She heard the unspoken accusation from Olivia: *You were in St. Croix, weren't you?* It wasn't true, but she had no intention of sharing what had really happened. That was her own secret.

"What about you two?" Ashlynn asked. "Why are you here?"

"You wouldn't understand," Olivia said.

"Try me."

"We're here for Kimberly, okay? The three of us used to hang out here."

Ashlynn closed her eyes and felt Olivia's grief and anger wash over her. She understood. She'd intruded on something sacred.

"Kimberly died two years ago tonight, Ashlynn," Olivia went on. "You probably don't remember."

"Yes, I do. Of course I do."

"She was my best friend."

"I know that."

"She was bald, and she weighed seventy-nine pounds when she died."

Ashlynn winced at the image. She hadn't known Kimberly well, but she remembered the girl's death. Kimberly. Vince. Crystal. Drew. Gail. She remembered each of the St. Croix teenagers who had died of leukemia in the last five years. Every ghost cast a guilty shadow on her.

"It was a terrible thing, Olivia," Ashlynn said. "Awful."

Olivia jabbed a finger in her face. "Don't pretend you understand. You have no idea what it's like to lose someone close to you."

Ashlynn couldn't stop herself. She laughed, which was the worst thing she could do. It was a strangled, tragic laugh that made her face twitch and made Olivia red with anger. She tried to compose herself and defuse the situation before it got out of control. "I'm sorry. Please, Olivia, let's not do this now."

"Fuck you," Olivia told her in a slurred voice. "I hate you."

Ashlynn simply wanted the confrontation to be over. She wanted to be alone to cry. She turned her attention to the other teenager, who stood off to the side of the swing, staring at the ground. If anyone would help her, it was Tanya Swenson.

"How are you, Tanya?" she asked.

Tanya was a moon-faced, curly-haired redhead. She was shy and withdrawn, a girl who trailed in the wake of a smart, outgoing friend like Olivia. She was a Barron girl, but she'd wound up in the St. Croix clique because of her friendship with Olivia and Kimberly—and because of her father. Tanya's father was the attorney who had led the charge to take down Mondamin Research in court.

That was how it had all started. That was how the blood feud between the towns had begun.

Tanya squeezed her hands in her pockets. "I'm okay."

Ashlynn wanted to see the girl's eyes. She wanted Tanya to acknowledge the silent bond between them. *You know I'm not the enemy.*

"Do you have your car here, Tanya?" she asked.

The heavy, short girl shuffled on her feet. "Um, yeah."

"I could use a ride home."

"She's not taking you anywhere," Olivia interrupted them. "No way."

"Is that true, Tanya?" Ashlynn asked. "Really?"

"I—I don't know. I guess I can't."

Ashlynn sighed in frustration. She had no strength to fight. "Fine. Whatever. I'll sleep in my car, Olivia. Will that make you happy?"

"Happy? You think we're here for laughs?"

"I know why you're here, but this has nothing to do with me. I've been driving for hours. I'm tired. I'm leaving."

Ashlynn got off the swing, but Olivia shoved her back hard. She spilled off her feet, grabbing the rope for balance. The swing jerked in a crazy circle, and her knee slipped into the mud. Cramps knifed through her abdomen, so sharp that they took her breath away. She tried to get up, but she couldn't, so she bent over with both hands in the dirt.

"Please don't," Ashlynn murmured, breathing raggedly.

Olivia was crying. She shouted through her tears, "Do you have any idea how scared Kimberly was? She was fourteen, and she was dying. Do you think that's right? Do you think that's fair?"

"No. It's not."

"People like you don't have a clue how horrible it is. You sit there with your perfect life while the rest of us go through hell. You know what I want? I want you to suffer like Kimberly did. I want you to be as scared as she was."

Ashlynn thought about screaming back at her—*You don't know anything!*—but none of this was Olivia's fault. She looked away to hide her own grief, but Olivia misinterpreted her reaction. She thought Ashlynn didn't care, which wasn't true. Not at all.

Olivia dug inside a large purse slung over her shoulder and came out with something in her hand. Ashlynn's heart turned over with a thump in her chest. Her stomach seared with pain. Olivia held a revolver, grimy and old, with a three-inch barrel.

Tanya's eyes widened into full moons as she saw the gun. "Livvy! What are you doing? Where did you get that?"

"Quiet," Olivia snapped.

The gun squirmed in her young fingers. She used her thumb to drag the hammer back, cocking the weapon. She aimed the barrel at Ashlynn's face and held it so close that the metal almost touched her forehead. Her finger slid over the trigger.

"Scared?" she asked Ashlynn.

"Yes."

"Terrified?"

"Yes."

"*Good.*"

Tanya's voice squeaked. "Livvy, cut it out. Quit it!"

Olivia stared at Ashlynn. Inches separated their faces. The two girls were both unsure where the line in the sand was drawn between them. How far would it go? How bad would it be? Ashlynn felt something wet in her jeans; it was either urine or blood.

"Please, Olivia, put it down," she whispered.

"Do you think I don't have the guts? Do you think I won't do it?"

"Killing me won't change anything."

Olivia swung the gun at the squat tree trunk, took hold of the butt with both hands, and jerked on the trigger. The gun exploded with a roar that made all of them jump. Bark burst from the trunk in a dust cloud as a bullet tunneled into the meat of the tree. Tanya screamed. Olivia blinked and stared at the gun in shock, as if realizing that she had actually fired.

"Livvy, my God!" Tanya screamed.

Ashlynn held up her hands. The burnt smell made her sick. "This isn't like you, Olivia."

Tears streaked Olivia's pink face. "You don't know anything about me."

"I know you're better than this. You're drunk, you're upset. Let's just get out of here. I won't tell anyone."

"I don't care what you do."

Olivia opened the cylinder of the gun and shook gold cartridges onto the wet ground. She caught one cartridge in her palm, reinserted it, and spun the cylinder. Despair was etched in her face.

"Do you know what Russian roulette is?"

"Stop," Tanya begged her friend. "Livvy, no!"

"I want you to see what it feels like to have somebody play a game with your life, Ashlynn."

Ashlynn pleaded silently with Tanya, *Do something*. Instead, without a word, Tanya bolted away from them. She wasn't graceful, and she looked even younger than she was, like a panicked child running from a monster. Ashlynn wanted to shout after her and tell her to come back, but Tanya was scared to death and out of her league. Her last hope for rescue fled.

"Now it's just you and me," Olivia said.

The revolver with the single cartridge loaded somewhere in its cylinder stared into Ashlynn's face. Its barrel wisped smoke. Ashlynn looked into Olivia's desperate eyes and understood exactly what was going on between the two of them. All of the hurt, loss, jealousy, bitterness, humiliation, frustration, and anger of the past three years had converged on this moment. It was Kimberly dying. It was the lawsuit failing. It was the tit-for-tat violence that had erupted between the two towns over the past year. Olivia had found someone to take the fall for everything she'd suffered. She blamed Ashlynn.

But it was more than that, too.

"I know what this is about," Ashlynn told her.

Olivia's hands shook like autumn leaves. "On three," she said.

"Don't you want to talk about it?"

"On three," the girl repeated, ignoring her.

"Olivia, listen, I need to tell you something," Ashlynn said.

"Shut up."

"Please, it's important."

"*Shut up!*"

Ashlynn closed her eyes and said nothing more. It didn't matter now. She had a one-in-six chance of dying as the other girl squeezed the trigger, but she didn't care. She really didn't. Part of her was already dead.

She heard Olivia breathing. Crying. Counting.

One.

Two.

Thr—

PART ONE

UNBEARABLE

CHRISTOPHER HAWK DROVE WEST ON HIGHWAY 7 INTO THE EMPTINESS OF rural Minnesota, leaving civilization behind him with each mile away from the city. Staring at the horizon between his windshield wipers, he could have sworn the world was flat, and he hoped there was a sign ahead to warn him before he sped off the edge of the earth. Long, empty miles loomed between towns. There were no buildings, other than the occasional desolate farm. He drove beside endless fields ruled by King Corn, but it was too early for planting, and the land resembled a rutted moonscape. He didn't feel welcome.

The weather made it worse. March was going out like a lamb, freakishly warm and wet. It had started raining almost as soon as he cleared the western edge of I-494, and the dreary spattering had continued nonstop for nearly two hours and a hundred miles. He passed swollen drainage ditches where the water looked ready to spill across the lanes of the highway. The bumpy gray clouds were like a thick hood thrown over his head.

An amateur billboard mounted in the midst of farmland caught his eye. The message had been painted in bold black letters on a plain white background. It said:

I AM COMING SOON. ARE YOU READY?

The message was signed, "Jesus."

Chris didn't think he belonged in a place where God felt the need to advertise. Even so, when he asked himself if he was ready, the answer was easy. No. He wasn't ready at all. He was nervous about this journey, because he was on his way back into the lives of two strangers.

The first was his ex-wife. The second was his daughter.

That morning, Hannah had called at six o'clock, waking him up. He hadn't spoken to her in months, but he could see her face as clearly as if she'd been sleeping beside him. There were still days when he reached for her in bed, hoping to take her hand, hoping to fold her against his body. He still had dreams in which the three of them lived together as a family. Chris. Hannah. Olivia.

She didn't give him a chance to dream.

"Our daughter has been arrested for murder," she announced.

Just like that. No small talk. Hannah never wasted time. She had a way of cutting to the chase, whether it was in college when he wanted to sleep with her (she said yes), or three years ago when she wanted a divorce (he said no, but that didn't change her mind).

Olivia.

Chris didn't ask for details about the crime she had supposedly committed. He didn't want to know the victim's name, be told what happened, or hear Hannah reassure him that she was really innocent. For him, that wasn't even a question. His daughter didn't do it. Not Olivia. The girl who texted and tweeted him every day—*Send me a pic of a Dunn Bros latte, Dad. I miss it.*— was not a murderer.

"I'll be there this afternoon," he replied.

The silence on the phone told him that his answer surprised her. Finally, Hannah said, "She needs a lawyer, Chris."

"I'm a lawyer."

"You know what I mean. A criminal lawyer."

"All lawyers are criminals."

It was an old joke between them, but Hannah didn't laugh. "Chris, this is serious. I'm scared."

"I know you are, but this is obviously a misunderstanding. I'll straighten it out with the police."

Her hesitation felt like a punch to the gut. "I'm not so sure that's all it is," she said. She was silent again and then added, "It's ugly. Olivia's in trouble."

Hannah sketched out the facts for him, and he realized that she was right. It was ugly. In the early hours of Saturday morning, a pretty teenage girl had been shot to death, and Olivia had been at the scene, drunk, desperate, pointing a gun at the girl's head. It hadn't taken long—it was Tuesday now— for the police to conclude that his daughter was guilty.

"What did Olivia tell you?" he asked. "What happened between them?"

"She won't talk to me. She said I should call you."

"Okay, tell her I'll be there soon."

Hannah didn't protest further. "Fine. You're right, she needs you. Just remember that you don't know this girl, Chris. Not anymore."

"We talk all the time."

"That's not the same thing. Believe me. You see the girl she wants you to see."

As his ex-wife hung up, he'd wondered to himself if that was true.

A lifetime had passed—three years—since Hannah left him to go back to St. Croix, the small farm town where she'd been raised. He saw his daughter every few months, but to him, she would always be a girl, not a woman. He didn't know much about the mix-up of emotions a teenage girl faced. She hadn't said a word to him about what was in her head She talked about meaningless things. Easy things. He should have realized there was much more to her than a girl who missed her father.

It didn't change what he had to do. Olivia needed him, and he had to go.

Now, hours later, he was deep in the western farmlands of Minnesota, with the rain coming down, with Jesus on a billboard asking if he was ready. It could have been Antarctica; it could have been Mars. Every mile here looked like the next. This part of the world was terra incognita to him. He was a creature of the noise, asphalt, and people of downtown Minneapolis. He owned a two-bedroom condominium near Loring Park, which he used mostly to sleep. He didn't cook, so he ate fish and chips and drank Guinness at The Local and ordered take-out *pho* from Quang. He spent his days and nights negotiating contracts for industrial parks and strip malls. Steel and concrete—those were things that were real, things he could touch and measure.

In the city, he was an insider. Not here. Out here, he was an alien.

Ahead of him, through the sheets of rain, Chris saw a highway sign for the Spirit Dam. The town of Barron, where Olivia was being held in the county jail, was on the river side of the dam, three miles to the south. He drove his decade-old silver Lexus onto the roadway, but he stopped in the middle of the bridge. For some reason he found himself hesitating. He got out of the car and shut the door behind him. Rain lashed across his face, and he squinted. He didn't care about getting wet.

Chris looked down at the wild water squeezing into whirlpools through a dozen sluice gates. Downstream, the Spirit River settled into a mucky brown calm as it wound toward Barron, feeding a web of narrow streams, including one that flowed behind Hannah's house in the tiny town of St. Croix a few miles to the southeast. On the north side of the dam, the water sprawled like a vast octopus into miles of man-made lake. The river pushed toward the valley, and the dam pushed back and said, *Stop*. That was exactly what he had to do. That was his mission. Olivia was in the path of a flood, and he had to stop it.

Still, Chris lingered on the bridge, staring at the water.

He was a tall man, almost exactly six feet. At forty-one, his hair was still thick and brown, without any gray to remind him of his age. He wore contacts over his dark eyes; years of poring over real-estate contracts had killed his eyesight. Since the divorce, he'd had no excuse for avoiding the gym. He'd dropped twenty pounds and added several inches of muscle to his chest. He looked good; the various women who chased him told him that. It wasn't just his lawyer's wallet that attracted them. Even so, he hadn't agreed to a date in seven months, and he hadn't had sex in over a year. He told himself that it was his busy schedule, but the truth was more complicated.

The truth was Hannah. He'd never stopped loving her. Her voice on the phone was enough to awaken the old feelings. She was what was holding him back.

Ready or not, Chris got back in the car, drove across the dam, and turned south toward Barron. The river followed the highway, winking in and out behind trees that grew on the shore. Houses appeared. A school bus pulled in front of him. The city sign advertised the population: 5,383. Out here, that was a metropolis, a hub for the whole county. As he neared the town, he felt as if he had crossed back into the 1950s, as if decades of progress had hopscotched over this section of land. Maybe that was a good thing. Maybe this place would not be as intimidating as it seemed.

Life in the city was fast and complex; life in the country was slower and simpler.

A mile later, he realized that he was wrong.

On the outskirts of Barron, he passed an agribusiness facility built on the western bank of the river. It was one story, white, clean, and almost windowless. The plant looked more like a prison than an industrial site, because it was protected by a nine-foot fence wound with coils of barbed wire to keep intruders from reaching the interior grounds. The single narrow gate in the fence, just wide enough for trucks to pass through, was guarded by two uniformed security officers who were both armed with handguns.

As he drove by the plant slowly, he noticed their eyes following him with suspicion.

He noticed something else, too. Outside the fence, he saw a dramatic marble sign ten feet in height, featuring the company name in brass letters. Mondamin Research. Its logo was a golden ear of corn inside a multicolored helix strand of DNA. Two workers in yellow slickers labored in the rain to sandblast graffiti that had been spray-painted in streaky letters across the white stone. Despite their efforts, he could still see what had been written.

The graffiti read: You're killing us.

Chris found the Riverside Motel a quarter mile beyond the Mondamin headquarters. From the parking lot, he had a perfect vantage on the plant's barbed-wire fence glistening in the rain. Ahead of him, he saw the main street of Barron. Between the two landmarks was the chocolate-brown ribbon of the river.

The motel was a U-shaped, single-story building with two dozen rooms. The white paint had begun to peel away in chips, and the gutters sagged from the shingled black roof. The doors were cherry red. After parking and retrieving his bag, he ducked through the rain and opened the screen door of the motel office. The interior was humid and a fan swiveled on the desk, which was unusual for March. On the left wall, he saw an ice machine and two vending machines selling snacks and pop. He approached the check-in counter.

"I'm Chris Hawk," he told the man seated behind the counter. "I called this morning about a room."

The motel owner nodded pleasantly. "Welcome to Barron, Mr. Hawk."

Chris guessed that the man was in his early fifties. He had an olive, Italian cast to his skin. His hair was black and gray, buzzed into a wiry crew cut. He had a jet-black mustache, a mole on his upper cheek, and a silver chain nestled in the matted fringe of his chest hair. He slid out a reservation form, which he handed to Chris with a pen.

"I'm looking for the county courthouse," Chris mentioned as he filled in his personal details.

"Yes, of course. Well, you can't miss it. It's downtown, beautiful old building, red stone."

Chris stopped writing and looked up. "Why 'of course'?"

"Oh, everyone knows who you are, Mr. Hawk, and why you're here."

"Already?"

The motel owner shrugged. He was short and squat with bulging forearms. His T-shirt, which fit snugly, advertised Dreamland Bar-B-Que. "This is a small town. If you fart in your bedroom, your neighbors start gossiping about what you had for dinner."

Chris laughed. "That's good to know."

The man extended his hand. His handshake was a vise. "My name is Marco Piva."

"Since you know why I'm here, Marco, can you tell me what people are saying about what happened on Friday night?"

The motel owner snuffled loudly. He wiped his bulbous nose above his mustache. "Trust me, you don't want to hear that."

"They think my daughter murdered Ashlynn Steele."

"Oh, yes, everyone says she did. No one thinks it was an accident or a game. I'm very sorry. I have to tell you, I knew something like this would happen. Violence begets violence, and someone dies. It's a shame two young girls were involved."

Chris handed the registration form back to Marco and turned as the screen door banged behind him. A teenage boy, the kind of fresh-faced Scandinavian Lutheran that Chris expected to find in this part of the state, stood in the doorway. He had wavy blond hair that was plastered on his head from the rain and the sturdy physique of a football player. His eyes were sky blue. He wore a form-fitting white T-shirt that emphasized his muscles, crisp jeans, and cowboy boots. Chris figured he was seventeen or eighteen years old.

"Johan," Marco called. "This is Mr. Hawk."

The boy didn't look surprised. "Hello," he said.

"Johan lives in St. Croix," Marco added.

"Oh, really?" Chris said. "So you know my daughter."

"She lives across the street."

Chris found it odd that his teenage daughter lived so close to a boy who looked like a Norwegian god and she had never mentioned him. Not once. He thought about Hannah's warning: *You see the girl she wants you to see.*

"Marco says a lot of people think Olivia is guilty, Johan. What do you think?"

The boy looked pained. "I guess nobody really knows what happened," he replied, but his face said something else. *We all know what happened.*

"I'm here to help her," Chris told him. "Maybe you can help me."

"How?"

"By telling me about the bad blood between the kids in Barron and St. Croix."

Johan frowned. "I try to stay out of it. It's like a poison."

"That's smart."

"Yeah, that's what I told Olivia, but she didn't listen."

"No?"

"No, she's stubborn. She couldn't let go."

Marco interrupted them, as if he didn't want the feud carried inside his walls. "Is Mr. Hawk's room ready, Johan?"

The boy nodded.

"Put his suitcase inside, all right?"

Johan grabbed the suitcase, swinging it as if it were practically weightless. He nodded at Chris as he left the office, and his sculpted face was pure Minnesotan: polite, handsome, but yielding no secrets.

"Johan is a good boy," Marco said when he was gone. "He cares for your daughter."

"He looked at me like I was from another planet," Chris said.

"Ah, but you are, Mr. Hawk. You're an outsider."

"Is that a crime around here?"

"Oh, no," Marco chuckled. "It's worse. Most people here would happily choose a local criminal over an honest outsider."

Chris smiled at the man's jowly Italian face. "You look like an outsider yourself."

"Yes, you're right about that. I bought this place in December. What a shock, all that snow and cold! I hate winter, but I needed to get out of San Jose. My wife passed away last year, and all I had was my city pension and a house full of memories. I asked a realtor to scout motels for me, and this place looked like a nice business in a beautiful area. I figured, that's for me."

"Have the locals accepted you?" Chris asked.

"No, I could be here twenty years, and I'd still be a newcomer. The people are perfectly nice, but that's as far as it goes. I don't mind. I didn't come here to make friends, just to get a little peace. It will be worse for you, Mr. Hawk."

"Why do you say that?"

"Because a man who tries to stop a dogfight usually gets bitten for his trouble."

"I'm just here for Olivia," Chris said. "I don't care what's going on between Barron and St. Croix."

"It doesn't matter whether you pick sides. You will not be trusted. People will not tell you things you need to know. They will want to see you gone. Be careful, okay?"

"I appreciate the advice," Chris said.

Marco shrugged. "No charge for that. It's free from one outsider to another. If you want to know more, talk to Johan's father. Glenn Magnus is the minister at the church in St. Croix. His family was among the plaintiffs in the lawsuit against Mondamin Research."

Chris felt a heaviness in his heart. He knew what that meant: death.

"Who did they lose?" he asked.

"Johan's sister," Marco said, shaking his head. "Her name was Kimberly. Johan has shown me pictures. A lovely girl. Grief leads to some dark places, Mr. Hawk. When you get a cancer cluster in a place like St. Croix, especially among young people, it can't help but cut out the heart of the town. It makes people crazy. It makes people want revenge."

2

THE MAIN STREET OF BARRON LOOKED LIKE HOLLYWOOD'S IDEA OF A SMALL town. Chris drove by nostalgic storefronts, like the pharmacy with an oversize mortar and pestle stamped on its sign, the hardware store advertising lawn mower repair, and the Swedish bakery displaying racks of fresh kringle cookies. The brick walls were bright and clean; the paint on the stores was fresh. He saw none of the economic decay he expected. In a time when rural areas were bleeding young people into the cities, the streets of Barron bustled. The smell of money was everywhere, and most rural towns hadn't known that smell in a long time.

It was easy to see why, to the people of Barron, the ten-year-old biotechnology company on their borders felt like a godsend. Their prosperity had a name: Mondamin Research.

Ten miles south along the highway, in the neighboring town of St. Croix, families had a darker view of Mondamin. They blamed the company's pesticides for the deaths of their children. They'd sued to prove it, but the litigation had been thrown out of court, and in the year that followed, a wave of violence and vandalism had spread into the streets. Teenagers in St. Croix attacked the town of Barron. Teenagers in Barron struck back. The two towns, which were near enough that most of the people who lived in St. Croix worked or went to school in the larger town of Barron, became enemies.

Now it was worse, because a line had been crossed. Blood had been spilled.

Even among the primped store windows and flower baskets hanging from the streetlights, Chris saw evidence of the feud. A concrete statue of a founding pioneer in the street's roundabout had been beheaded. The doorway of a clothing shop showed the black scars of a recent fire. He saw tiny starbursts popped through the glass of second-floor windows. Bullet holes.

The bullets had targeted one building in particular. The white lettering stenciled on the pockmarked windows above the street advertised the

Grohman Women's Resource Center. The center was housed in Barron, but the woman who ran the organization lived in St. Croix, where her parents had lived, where her grandparents had lived, where her great-grandparents had settled after emigrating from Uppsala, Sweden. Chris knew her. She had a master's degree in psychology from the University of Minnesota. She had a freckle in the swell of her left breast that he had kissed a thousand times.

Hannah, Hannah, what are you doing here?

But Chris understood. Hannah was where she always wanted to be. In the center of the storm.

He drove two more blocks to the end of Barron's main street and found the county courthouse. Like a cathedral out of the middle ages, it looked oddly elaborate for its rural surroundings. It was a majestic three-story building with brick gables and a massive central clock tower. He parked and climbed terraced steps leading up from the street. Outside the oak doors, he turned to overlook the town from above. The river flowed immediately behind the downtown shops, and he saw a pedestrian bridge stretching across the water to a swath of forested parkland on the far shore. Away from the main street, he saw a neatly organized grid of houses built between the water and the rocky bluff that bordered the river valley.

From up here, Barron looked peaceful. Not violent at all.

Chris went inside the courthouse, which glistened with lacquered oak. He checked the directory. The sheriff's office and the facilities for the county jail were buried in the basement. He headed downstairs, where the surroundings were institutional, not ornamental. Security was modest. It wasn't a place that housed hardened criminals.

He told the uniformed officer at the desk, "I'd like to see Olivia Hawk. I'm her lawyer."

Her father. Her lawyer. It didn't matter which hat he was wearing. The policeman, like everyone else in town, knew who he was.

Chris gave up his driver's license, had his picture taken, and walked through a metal detector. The officer led him through a metal door and into a conference room that wasn't much bigger than a phone booth. Chris sat down on one side of a narrow conference table, and the policeman left him alone. The door lock clicked as the officer left. He waited.

Two minutes later, the door opened again.

Chris told himself he was prepared, but he wasn't. He'd steeled himself for this moment, but his heart raced, his stomach climbed into his throat, and his eyes stung with tears. Olivia walked in, her long brown hair dirty and tangled, her wrists bound in handcuffs as if she were praying. She wasn't in prison gear; she wore a flannel shirt with the sleeves rolled up and faded jeans. He'd seen her at Thanksgiving, but even since then, she'd changed. She was growing into her adolescent features. She was more graceful. She was taller. She'd always joked about getting her looks from him, not Hannah, and if anything, she looked more like him than she ever had before. His sharp nose and high cheekbones. His mouth. His expressions.

For all that, he was afraid of what he saw in her face. Her brown eyes were as deep and unrevealing as a black hole, and he thought he could search in them for days without finding her. The daughter he knew, the girl he remembered, could never fire a gun at another human being, but this was someone else. A woman. A stranger.

The policeman undid the handcuffs, and Olivia rubbed her chapped wrists and shook out her fingers. The officer left, the lock clicked on the door, and it was just the two of them. Father and daughter. Silently, he pushed his chair back and came around the table to embrace her. She hugged him back fiercely, and he clung to her, stroking her hair. When he helped her into a chair, she stole a look at him and then hooded her eyes, her hair tumbling across her face. The shame in her beet-red cheeks was like a ten-year-old who'd broken a figurine she wasn't supposed to touch. That was the Olivia he knew.

"Guess I really screwed up," she said.

He sat next to her and stroked her face with the back of his hand. "First things first. Are you okay?"

Olivia squirmed in the chair. "I've had the Hersheys for two days. Yuck."

Chris smiled. "I'll make sure they give you something."

"Other than that, I guess I'm okay."

"Good."

"Jail sucks."

"Yeah, it does."

His daughter pushed her hair back behind her ears. "So how was Matt's?"

"What?"

"We texted on Saturday, remember? Didn't you go to Matt's Bar that night?"

"I did."

"I could really go for a Juicy Lucy," she said.

He didn't say anything. Olivia was in jail, and she was talking about cheeseburgers like she needed a new Facebook status. He wondered if she didn't realize the gravity of her situation or if she was simply stalling. He also thought, *She texted me on Saturday.* That was the day after the murder.

"Why didn't you say anything?" he asked.

"What do you mean?"

"You texted me on Saturday to ask what I was doing that night. Ashlynn was dead. You'd just been through one of the worst nights of your life, and you didn't say a word about it, Olivia. Why not?"

Her lower lip quivered. "I don't know, Dad. I couldn't believe it was real, you know?"

"Your mother says you wouldn't tell her what happened."

"I couldn't. I can't deal with Mom right now. It's easier to talk to you."

Or maybe it was easier to lie to him. He put that thought out of his mind.

"Okay," he told her softly. "Here I am. Let's talk."

Olivia sat frozen.

"I don't know what to say, Dad," she told him finally. "I don't know what happened."

He was afraid she would give him an excuse. An apology. A plea for forgiveness. *It was an accident. The gun went off. I didn't mean it.* He waited for her to go on, but she didn't.

"Just tell me what you know," he said.

"What's the point? No one will believe me."

"Not true. I'll believe you."

Olivia swung her head, and he saw those dark, pretty, mysterious eyes again. "I'm not so sure, Dad. You're already scared of what I'm going to say, aren't you? That's why you haven't asked me the big one. Whether I did it. Whether I killed her. You think I'm going to say yes."

She was good. Chris had sat across the table from dealmakers who spent their whole careers perfecting their skills at psychological warfare. These were lawyers who conducted opposition research like politicians, knowing what buttons to push, figuring out every weakness they could exploit. He'd built a suit of armor for those confrontations that had never failed him, but against this teenager, he was defenseless. She saw through him as if his heart were opened up on an autopsy table.

"Lawyers don't usually ask their clients whether they did it," he said. "That's not how it works."

"Because you assume I'm guilty, right?"

"No, because I assume you're innocent."

His daughter pushed back her chair, stood up, and folded her arms. "If I did it, what difference does any of this make? They should just lock me up."

"It makes a big difference," Chris explained. "You're sixteen years old. You were drinking. You were mourning the loss of your best friend. There are a lot of mitigating circumstances. If a jury understands what was really going on, they may conclude you weren't responsible for your actions."

"If I killed her, I'm responsible."

"Not necessarily. Not legally."

Olivia stared at the ceiling, as if to hide that her eyes were filling with tears. She shook her head in despair. "See? You think I'm guilty, too."

"I didn't say that at all."

She looked at him, bereft. "Don't you get it? I don't want a lawyer to play games for me. I want a father who cares whether I did this."

"I do care, Olivia. I just want you to understand that nothing you tell me will change how I feel about you. No matter what you say, I'm here to help you."

"Ask me," she said.

"What?"

"*Ask me*," she repeated, her voice breaking. "Please."

She needed to tell him, and he realized that he needed to hear it. He got up and put his hands on her shoulders. "Olivia, did you do this? Did you shoot that girl?"

She sucked in a long, loud breath. "*No.*"

As if she assumed he would doubt her, as if she thought he would wonder in his heart if she were lying, she wiped her eyes and nose on her sleeve and repeated herself calmly, so he could hear every word. "I didn't do this. I swear to you. I didn't. You have to believe me."

She cried again and threw her arms around his waist. It didn't matter what he didn't know about the girl in his arms, because he did know one thing. She was his daughter, and she was innocent.

"Tell me what happened."

Chris had his briefcase open and a fresh yellow notepad in front of him. He had given Olivia a tissue and asked the police officer outside for a bottle of water, which his daughter sipped in small swallows. She had composed herself, and when she spoke, he was reminded of how intelligent and passionate she was. Physically, she looked like him. Emotionally, she was Hannah's child.

"Tanya and I met at the ghost town on Friday night," she said. "She drove from her dad's house in Barron. I drove from St. Croix. The ruins are west of both towns, maybe five miles out. It must have been about ten o'clock when we got there."

"Your mother says you used to go there with Kimberly."

Olivia stared at the wall as if seeing a ghost. Her grief over her friend was near the surface. "Yeah."

"I know it was the anniversary of her death," he said. "I know you two were close."

"I'm not sure you really do, Dad."

"Okay, tell me."

A tiny frown sprouted on her face. "Look, it sucked when Mom and I left three years ago. Right? Sucked big-time."

"I'm sorry. It sucked for me, too, kiddo."

"I was pissed at Mom. I was pissed at you. I hated this place. I wanted to get out. If I hadn't met Kimberly, I don't know what I would have done. I mean, I was thinking some bad things, Dad. She saved me."

He hated to think of his daughter feeling like an outcast. "I'm glad you found her," he said. He added softly, "Had she already been diagnosed with leukemia?"

Olivia struggled with her emotions. "Yeah, she was going through chemo. She was sure she was going to beat it, even though three other kids had already died. It was really awful, Dad."

"I'm sure."

"Kimberly sort of became my mission, you know? Mom says I have to have missions, like her."

He smiled again. "I know."

"Anyway, the first few months, when she still had the energy to go out, we did a lot of exploring. The ghost town was one of her favorite places. She loved how creepy it was, all the ruined buildings. She said she heard the echoes of the people who lived there, especially at night. That's what she called them. Echoes. I think that made her feel better, you know? She liked the idea of ghosts and hauntings and stuff like that."

"Okay."

"Tanya hung out with us, too," Olivia went on. "Mostly, it was me and Kimberly, because we lived so close to each other, but Tanya was over at the church a lot in those days. Her dad was filing the lawsuit, and Kimberly's dad was one of the plaintiffs. Tanya hooked up with the two of us."

Chris waited.

"When Kimberly died—" Olivia stopped. She wiped her eyes again. "I go back there sometimes. Like maybe I'll hear the echoes, you know?"

Chris covered her hand with his own. "I get it."

"It's stupid."

"No, it's not." He understood her state of mind that night, but he was afraid that a jury might think a girl in that fragile state of mind would take revenge when it was offered to her. "How about we go back to Friday night, okay? What did you do?"

"Not much," she said. "We dug inside a couple of the old buildings. We walked along the railroad tracks."

"Did you see anyone else?"

"No, it was just the two of us."

"The police found beer bottles. Were you drinking?"

"Yeah, Tanya snuck some Miller Lite out of her Dad's house."

"How much?'"

"A six-pack."

"Did you finish it?"

"Yeah. I had four. Tanya had two. I was pretty buzzed. I don't do it a lot, but I was really upset."

"I understand."

"Ashlynn showed up around midnight. We hid when we heard another car, because if it's Barron boys, you don't want to be around, you know?" A hardness came over her face. "But it was her. That blonde bitch."

Chris stopped writing and put down his pen. "Olivia, listen to me. Ashlynn is dead. She was a teenager like you, with people who loved her. She had her whole life ahead of her, and someone stole it away. It diminishes you to talk about her that way."

Olivia looked upset with herself. "Yeah, I know. I'm sorry."

"What was it about Ashlynn? Why did you hate her?"

She pulled a messy strand of her chestnut hair through her lips. "Mondamin," she said. "What else? St. Croix is dying, and no one will do anything."

"Mondamin is run by her father. Why did you blame Ashlynn for that?"

"She was there."

"Is that all it was?"

"Look, Dad, I'm not proud of it. I was drunk. I was stupid. I just wanted to scare her."

He waited for her to say more, but she looked down and fiddled with the buttons on her shirt. He could feel her withdrawing. There was a disconnect between what she said and what he could see in her face. For the first time, he felt as if she were hiding something from him.

Lying.

"They tell me you had a gun," he said, changing the subject.

She nodded. "Yeah."

"Where did you get it?"

"One of the boys in St. Croix gave it to me. I've had it for months."

"Why?"

Olivia gave him an exasperated look. "You don't know what it's like around here, Dad. I mean, yeah, the kids in St. Croix did some stupid things, but the Barron boys ratcheted up the violence. They started to treat the feud like it's a gang war. I wanted protection."

"Have you ever fired the gun?" he asked.

"A couple of times out in a field."

"Did you fire it on Friday?"

She bit her lip and nodded unhappily. "Yeah."

"Why?"

"I don't know. I was showing off. I fired into the tree."

"The police say you put a bullet in the gun in order to play Russian roulette with Ashlynn. You were terrorizing her."

"I guess so. It all happened so fast. I was yelling at Ashlynn, and I fired, and yeah, I started messing around like in Russian roulette. Tanya freaked and ran."

"What did you do next? After you and Ashlynn were alone?"

"*Nothing.* I swear."

"Did you point the gun at her head?"

"Yeah, I did, but—"

"Did you pull the trigger?"

"*No.*"

"Did you play the game, Olivia? Did the gun go off?"

"I didn't pull the trigger," she insisted, her voice rising. "I didn't."

Chris let his daughter sit in silence, her chest rising and falling. He scribbled notes on his yellow pad, but he was really thinking about Olivia on a witness stand and how her story would survive on cross-examination.

Answer: Not well.

"Okay," he asked softly, "what did you do next?"

"I dropped the gun. I left. I was really upset with myself. I couldn't believe what I was doing. I just left."

"You didn't take the gun with you?"

"No, I never wanted to touch a gun ever again. I mean, I almost did it, Dad. I was this close. That was too scary."

"What about Ashlynn? What did she do?"

"Nothing."

"Did you talk to her?"

"No, we didn't talk to each other. I left her there. That was it."

Chris watched the darting motions of her eyes. She was lying to him again. There was something more going on, something that Olivia was determined to hide. If it came to that, a jury was likely to think she was hiding the fact that she had fired the revolver.

"Okay," he said.

He deposited his yellow pad in his briefcase and closed it. Olivia stared at him with a nervous half-smile, and he knew what anyone in the world would think, studying her expression.

She looked guilty.

"So what now?" she asked.

"There's a detention hearing in the morning, and I expect you'll be released. I'm going to talk to the county attorney about the investigation and the charges. They're moving fast. We need to slow them down."

"I didn't pull the trigger, Dad," she repeated. "I didn't kill her."

"You said that already. I know you didn't." He thought of a question he hadn't asked. An important one. "Do you know who *did* kill Ashlynn? Do you know what happened to her?"

"I left, Dad. When I left, she was alive."

"That's not what I asked you."

His daughter met his eyes, and he wished he could believe whatever she said. "No, I don't know what happened."

"Okay." Chris got up and kissed her on the head. "Take care, and don't be scared. I'll be back in the morning."

He turned to flag the guard, but Olivia stopped him by grabbing his sleeve. "Have you seen Mom yet?"

"Not yet. I'll stop over there tonight."

"There's something you should know," she said.

"What?"

Olivia hesitated. "I told her she should tell you, but she didn't."

"Tell me what?"

"Mom's got it."

He stared at her, and he didn't understand. Or maybe the truth was that he simply didn't want to understand. He stood in frozen silence, as if he could postpone forever the next words out of his daughter's mouth. She felt it, too, and she kept his arm tightly in her grip.

"Mom's got cancer," she said.

3

"Mr. Hawk?"

Chris heard someone calling his name, but the voice wasn't enough to rouse him. He sat on a wooden bench on the first floor of the courthouse near the outside door. The tapping of rain had a hypnotic quality, and it lulled him out of reality. He thought about his ex-wife. Hannah, the ferocious athlete, a runner, a tennis player. Hannah, obsessed with organics and gluten-free foods. Hannah, whisper-thin, all muscle, healthy, passionate.

Hannah did not have cancer. That was not possible.

"Mr. Hawk?" the voice repeated.

He dragged himself back into the present. An older man in a black trench coat stood in front of the bench. Water dripped from the fringes of his coat onto the oak floor. The man wore a gray fedora, which he removed to smooth his thinning silver hair. He wore rain-speckled heavy black glasses. He had a beard trimmed so neatly that he must have used tweezers to keep the lines precise. He was short, no more than five feet seven.

"I'm sorry," Chris told him. "Yes, I'm Christopher Hawk."

"Michael Altman. I'm the attorney for Spirit County. I believe you wanted to speak to me."

"Mr. Altman, yes, I do. It's about Olivia."

"Of course. My office is upstairs. Shall we talk there?"

Chris trailed behind Altman, who was a compact, efficient engine. The county attorney was easily sixty years old, but he marched up the courthouse steps like a soldier, without losing a breath. On the second floor, he guided Chris to an office on the south corner of the building and closed the door when they were both inside. The office looked out toward the river.

Altman removed his trench coat and hung it on a hook behind the door. He wore a solid navy suit, not expensive but perfectly pressed, with a starched white dress shirt and paisley tie. His dress shoes weren't new, but they had a shiny polish. The county attorney pointed to the chair in front of the desk, and Chris sat down. The older man slid a handkerchief from his pocket, which he used to dry his wet glasses. He repositioned them on his face, then sat, checked his watch, and folded his hands together. His desk was empty of clutter.

"You haven't asked for my advice, Mr. Hawk," Altman began, "but do you mind if I offer you some?"

"Not at all."

"I did my homework on you. You're smart. Smart enough to realize you don't belong anywhere near this case. My advice is that you hire a good lawyer from the Twin Cities and let him or her do the heavy lifting."

"I appreciate your candor."

"I'm a father, like you. Four girls. If it was one of my daughters, I know that I couldn't separate my emotions from my legal judgment. Neither can you. You are not a defense attorney, and even if you were, you'd be making a mistake representing your own daughter. Frankly, if you persist in representation, I may ask the judge to have you removed as counsel."

"I understand your concerns, Mr. Altman," Chris replied. "I haven't made any decisions about outside counsel yet. Right now, I'm just trying to figure out what happened on Friday night."

"Unfortunately, the chain of events is pretty clear," Altman said.

"I'm not so sure."

Altman swiveled in his leather chair. He pinched his gray beard. "You're a negotiator, Mr. Hawk. I've learned that much about you. Are you looking for some kind of deal here? Are you already thinking about a plea agreement?"

"No."

"Then what are you saying?"

"I'm saying that you and the sheriff's department already have your minds made up about Ashlynn's death, but I think you're wrong. My daughter says she's innocent."

"Innocent?"

"She didn't pull the trigger. She didn't shoot Ashlynn Steele."

Altman's head snapped back and forth in a sharp dismissal. "Your client is lying to you. I don't need to tell you that defendants lie all the time, do I? Clients lie to attorneys, and daughters most certainly lie to fathers."

"I believe her."

"Of course you do, which is another reason to bring in counsel with no emotional attachment to the accused. Look, Mr. Hawk, any attorney you hire will do a dance about your daughter's age, and her consumption of alcohol, and her emotional state, and about whether a game of Russian roulette—if in fact there was any such game, rather than a cold-blooded execution—demonstrates a depraved mind. Fair enough. Those are questions for a judge and jury. But if you don't believe we have overwhelming evidence that Olivia Hawk caused the death of Ashlynn Steele, then you are fooling yourself."

"No one saw her pull the trigger," Chris pointed out, "and you didn't find the murder weapon at the scene."

"Your daughter tested positive for gunpowder residue."

"Tanya Swenson saw Olivia fire a gun, but she fired into a tree, not at Ashlynn."

"Tanya saw your daughter take out a gun and threaten to kill Ashlynn Steele in a deserted location not two hours before her body was found in that same location. We have a self-professed motive for the crime based on her antipathy toward the victim and the victim's father. We may not have the gun, but we have a bullet in the tree and a bullet in Ashlynn's head. We'll match the two, I assure you. There is no rush to judgment here, Mr. Hawk. If we've moved quickly, it's because the evidence warrants it."

"Maybe so," Chris said, "but the victim was also the daughter of one of the wealthiest and most influential men in the county."

"You think your daughter is in prison because of pressure from Florian Steele?"

"Let's say it crossed my mind."

Altman sighed and opened the center drawer of his desk. He removed a business card and slid it toward Chris with the tip of his index finger. "I haven't had to get new business cards in twenty-six years, Mr. Hawk. That's how long I've sat behind this desk. I've seen it all. Meth factories. Mayors selling city contracts for bribes. Environmental fringe groups blowing up power lines. Illegal immigrants locked in semi trailers. Right now, I've got the US attorney in Minneapolis telling me he's got hard evidence of child pornography distribution operating out of my county. Frankly, I've got too much on my plate to worry about political pressure."

"That's refreshing, Mr. Altman, but men like Florian Steele know how to get their way. If Florian is convinced that Olivia murdered his daughter, he wouldn't be shy about demanding action."

"As would you if it were your daughter."

"I'm not the CEO of Mondamin Research," Chris said.

Altman stared at Chris in silence for a long time. "I appreciate your situation, Mr. Hawk," he replied finally. "I would find it hard to imagine one of my children taking someone else's life. It's easier to believe she's being railroaded to satisfy a powerful man like Florian. Unfortunately, I live here, and you don't. I've seen too many sweet young people—people just like your daughter—who have been radicalized by this insane feud. There's a lot of misguided hatred in this county surrounding Mondamin."

"Misguided?" Chris asked. "Five teenagers in St. Croix died of leukemia."

"I realize that, but it's a tragic coincidence."

"In a town of four hundred people? That's a hell of a coincidence."

"Honestly, no, it's not. People shudder when they hear about cancer clusters, but nearly all of them are mathematical anomalies. If you flip a coin a few million times, you'll land on heads a hundred times in a row at some point. It happens. The loss of those children in St. Croix is devastating, but the families blamed Mondamin because of emotion and speculation, not facts. I'm just a lawyer, so I can't tell you anything about the science involved. That's why the judge appointed an epidemiologist as an independent special master—to analyze the scientific evidence and assess whether there's any possible causative link between Mondamin Research and the deaths of those young people in St. Croix, and none was found."

"You're a lawyer. You know a lack of evidence doesn't mean there's no link."

Altman stared at the ceiling. "Yes, I get it, Mr. Hawk, I do. People are naturally suspicious. I don't know exactly what goes on behind the walls at that company. However, one of the largest agribusinesses in the world acquired Mondamin last year, so they must be doing something right. I gather they snip at DNA strands and create new strains of seeds and pesticides. Genetically modified organisms. Nanoparticles. If you believe the hype, they're part of a revolution that will wipe out world hunger. If you believe the environmentalists, they're monsters fiddling with things they don't understand, creating mutants that will kill all of us. Take your pick. Whatever you believe, the hard truth is that the families of St. Croix lost in court. They chose not to let it end there. Ever since the judge threw out the litigation, I've had to deal with terroristic violence from teenagers in both towns. Shootings, fire bombings, animals tortured."

"Olivia wasn't involved in any of that."

"Not as far as I know, that's true. On the other hand, your daughter has been a vocal critic of Mondamin at the local high school."

"Free speech isn't a crime," Chris said.

"No, but carrying a gun without a permit is a crime. Murder is a crime. I knew Ashlynn Steele, Mr. Hawk. I used to see her at church every Sunday. Regardless of what you may think about Florian, she was a beautiful, intelligent young woman. I will see she gets justice. I would do that for any man's daughter."

"Sometimes children pay for the sins of the father," Chris said.

"Meaning what?"

"'*Destruction will rain down on all that you have created. No one will be spared.*'"

The county attorney carefully adjusted his black glasses, then steepled his fingers in front of his chin. "I see you've been reading the newspaper."

Chris nodded.

"Yes, we're investigating this man who calls himself Aquarius," Altman said, "but we don't know if he represents any actual threat."

"Whoever he is, he obviously has a bitter grudge against Florian."

"So what are you suggesting? Aquarius followed Florian's daughter and killed her?"

"I don't know. Maybe he did. Can you rule it out?"

Altman shook his head. "Mr. Hawk, I know you want to help your daughter, but you can best do that by focusing on your legal strategy, not by putting on rose-colored glasses about her innocence. Right now, a good lawyer would be thinking about ways to make a jury sympathize with what she did, not dreaming up far-fetched conspiracy theories."

"Olivia didn't do it," Chris said.

Altman spread his hands in resignation. "Fine. It's your call."

"I'd like to review everything the police have gathered so far in this case. Is that going to be a problem?"

"No, I'll make sure we get copies in your hands promptly." Altman added, "Perhaps that will open your eyes."

Chris ignored the jab. "There's a detention hearing tomorrow morning. Where do you stand on that?"

"I have to oppose, even though I'm not likely to win. Olivia doesn't have a criminal history, but there's a real threat of more violence if she's released."

"She's not going to harm anyone, Mr. Altman," Chris said. "You know that."

"Actually, I'm thinking of her own safety. You should be, too."

"What do you mean?"

Michael Altman frowned. "I mean, if she's free, she's in danger. That's the reality in this county right now, Mr. Hawk. The safest place for your daughter may be in jail."

CHRIS HAD LAST VISITED THE TOWN OF ST. CROIX FOUR YEARS EARLIER, when Hannah's mother passed away at the age of seventy-two. He thought of it as a place where kids were born, grew up, moved away, and never came back. The old-timers were the only people who stayed, living out long lives among the harsh Minnesota seasons and eventually emptying the town one by one. As the years passed, the population of the church cemetery outpaced the houses and farms.

They were dying faster in St. Croix now. Faster and younger.

He drove south on the highway out of Barron, tracking the banks of the Spirit River. Five miles later, the road turned east and followed a narrow stream for several more miles before heading south again toward Iowa. It was easy to miss St. Croix along the highway. Several miles from the split at the river, the speed limit dropped to thirty miles an hour, and he turned left into the tic-tac-toe grid of town streets. He could see the white bell tower of the Lutheran church jutting above the roofs of the houses. The wide blocks were empty. It was dusk, and the four hundred residents of St. Croix were saying grace and eating dinner.

His ex-wife's maiden name was Grohman. Hannah Grohman, daughter of Josephine and Cornelius Grohman. She'd kept the name Hawk after the divorce because she said it fit her personality better. That was true. Hannah had keen eyes for trouble, and she dove into situations fearlessly and with wicked strength. To her neighbors, though, she was Hannah Grohman, living in the house where she'd been born. She was a hero in St. Croix, because she had returned home after years away. She'd rejected the city and gone back to the country. She'd brought her daughter with her. No one did that.

Chris parked outside the Grohman home at an intersection immediately across the street from the church. He saw lights inside the two-story house and caught a glimpse of someone moving behind the curtains. He recognized her silhouette, and his heart seized. It was too early to go inside. Too early to see her.

He got out of the car and took big strides across the lawn, which was muddy from rain. Lots were large here; there was plenty of space. Trees were spread far apart, casting large pools of shade and leaving other patches for sunshine. The house itself had white wooden siding and a sprawling front porch, furnished with four Adirondack chairs. The black roof had a sharp angle above the second-floor windows. The house had stood in this place for nearly a century.

The winding branch of the Spirit River flowed immediately behind the house, so close that Olivia probably could have jumped to the water from the window in her upstairs bedroom. It felt like a river out of *Huckleberry Finn*, with evergreen trees leaning over the sides of the bank and dipping their branches in the lazy current. With no leaves on the trees yet, he could see the brown water shouldering toward a gray metal railway bridge two hundred yards away. On the other side of the stream, dormant tracts of corn fields awaited the spring thaw.

Chris stood alone on the bank, motionless, watching the quiet town of St. Croix as night fell. Above the moldy dankness of the water, he smelled the aromas from town kitchens. Roast chicken. Cookies. Two dozen types of hot dishes. A few people had left up their holiday lights to blink in white rows on the roof lines. Eventually, he heard chimes in the bell tower of the church. It was eight o'clock. When the bells tolled for the eighth time and went quiet, silence fell over the town like a shroud. He didn't see a soul.

This was what Hannah had left him for. This lonely scene stripped from a Christmas card.

He knew he was being unfair. A fifteen-year marriage didn't end in a heartbeat, and it didn't end without both of them forgetting to care for it. Back then he'd felt blindsided when his amazing, beautiful wife had turned her back on him and taken away his daughter. He'd worked for years to make a life for the three of them, to keep them safe in a world that offered little security. He'd assumed that was what she wanted, and instead she'd said: *I can't be that woman anymore.*

That woman. His wife.

It began with the death of Hannah's mother. Josephine Grohman, iron-willed like her daughter, had founded the Grohman Women's Resource Center in Barron to address what she called an appalling inattention to the health and social service needs of rural women. She'd spent decades as a lightning rod for controversy, and her death had left a gaping void in the politics of southwestern Minnesota. During her slow decline, she'd made it clear that she wanted Hannah to fill that void. To come home and continue her legacy.

Chris had never believed his wife would go; she would never leave him. He was wrong. She'd been silent for a year as she wrestled with her destiny, but then she came out of the shower, crying, took his hands, and told him she was going home. Just like that. It took him a long time to give up his bitterness. It took him two years to realize that the end of their marriage hadn't begun with Josephine's death. It had begun much earlier, as they led a slow march away from each other and watched it happen like spectators, doing nothing to stop it.

Not her fault. Not his fault. Their fault.

He thought about what Olivia had told him at the jail. *Mom's got it.* Cancer. The same disease that had claimed Josephine's life. He was devastated at the news and hurt that she had insisted on going through this alone, as if she assumed he couldn't bear it. She was probably right. He stood there, invisible among the trees, trying to gather the courage to see her. Trying to find a way not to melt at the sight of her face.

Chris headed for the house, but he stopped when a rumbling truck engine interrupted the solitude of St. Croix. Not even a quarter mile away, rubber squealed as a vehicle braked sharply and turned off the highway. He saw the twin beams of headlights, but as he watched, the headlights vanished. The pickup truck was dark. It cruised through the crisscross grid of streets, coming closer. It passed the church and came straight toward the intersection. He couldn't see faces through the dark glass.

The truck slowed in front of Hannah's house.

Then the shots began.

Chris threw himself to the wet ground as bursts of smoke and light flashed like bombs. Six loud bangs erupted in rapid succession. Glass shattered as at least one bullet smashed through a first-floor window, and he heard someone scream. He recognized the pitch of the voice. It was Hannah.

He pushed himself up and ran, shouting her name. Cheers and laughter floated from the pickup. They were young voices—teenagers—but the voices cut off in startled silence as they heard him. The truck headlights flashed on, blinding and pinning him. He ducked, conscious that he was an easy target. The pickup bolted in reverse, weaving as it retreated up the street. The headlights vanished and the car screeched into a U-turn, speeding across one of the house lawns as it veered toward the highway. He heard the engine roar. The car accelerated, racing north.

Back toward Barron.

He ran for the steps of Hannah's house and pounded on the door. He called her name again, but there was no answer. The house was quiet, and the silence fed his fear. Just as he was about to climb inside through the broken window, he saw the door slide open six inches. The pretty face of his ex-wife peered out at him.

"Chris?"

"They're gone," he said.

Hannah switched on the porch light and opened the door wider. He wanted to embrace her, but she walked past him onto the front steps. He looked over his shoulder and saw that a dozen people had already assembled near the house; they had run from their own homes to help. She waved at the street.

"I'm okay," she called. "Everything's okay."

Then to him: "Come on in, Chris." As if no time had passed.

He followed her inside. She put her hands on her hips, studying the broken glass on the dining room floor. With a sigh, she disappeared into the small kitchen and came back with a hand-broom and dustpan. She got down on her knees and began methodically sweeping up the shards of glass. That was Hannah. No panic. No drama. Get it done.

"We should call the police," he said.

Hannah stopped and looked at him. It was as if she'd realized for the first time that he was really there. They had not seen each other since she left Minneapolis and took Olivia across the state. Three years. Three years in which his only contact with the woman who had shared his life for nearly two decades was a handful of tense phone calls.

"We should," she said, "but it won't do any good."

"I couldn't see their faces or identify the car. I'm sorry."

"It was Barron boys. It doesn't really matter who."

"We should call the police anyway. They should have someone here to protect you."

Hannah finished sweeping in silence. When she was done, she stood up with a weary smile and laid the dustpan on an antique table. "No one wants to protect us. They want us to go away. Or die."

Chris heard a rapping at the front door. Hannah brushed past him, their arms touching, and opened the door. He saw a good-looking man on the porch, his own height, his own age. The man had unruly blond hair and a pale, chiseled face with a high forehead and a spattering of freckles. His blue eyes were filled with concern. He wore a white dress shirt and black slacks.

"Hannah? Are you all right?"

Chris's ex-wife put a hand on the visitor's shoulder. "Oh, yes, just more of the same. It never stops."

"Would you like me to send Johan over when he gets back from the motel? He could stay the night if you'd like."

"I appreciate it, Glenn, but that's not necessary."

The two of them hugged. Chris felt an odd pang of jealousy, watching his ex-wife embrace this man and watching his arms around her. They were obviously close. He wondered if it was anything more than that. Three years was a long time. It had foolishly never occurred to him that Hannah might be in a relationship. Olivia had never said a word.

The man detached himself awkwardly from Hannah as he noticed Chris. He reached a hand through the doorway. "I'm Glenn Magnus. I'm the minister at the church here in St. Croix."

Hannah glanced between them in embarrassment. "I'm so sorry. Glenn, this is Christopher Hawk, my ex-husband."

"How is Olivia?" the minister asked.

"As well as can be expected," Chris said.

"It's good that she has both of you here."

The minister was cordial and sincere, but Chris wanted the man to leave. He didn't want the first moments of his reunion with Hannah to be marred by the presence of anyone else. Magnus obviously leaped to the same conclusion that he was a third wheel.

"Well, I just wanted to make sure you weren't hurt," he told Hannah.

"Thank you."

"I'll speak to you tomorrow," he said. With a smile at Chris, he added, "Please let me know if I can be of any help to you or Olivia."

Chris said nothing, but he smiled back. Hannah closed the door. She turned around, leaned against it, and folded her arms over her small chest. She'd always been able to see through him, and nothing had changed.

"I'm not sleeping with him," she said. "That's what you were wondering, isn't it?"

"No," he lied.

"Glenn is a dear friend," she went on. "We've been through a lot these past three years. Life and death."

Without saying more she retreated to the kitchen, where she dumped the broken glass into a wastebasket under the sink. She reached for two chipped mugs from a cabinet over the counter and poured coffee for both of them. He sat down at an old Formica table, and she joined him. For several minutes, they did nothing but sip coffee in silence. The small kitchen had fading floral wallpaper and 1980s appliances, but it was impeccably clean. The house smelled of lilac potpourri.

Hannah was small, around five feet two, and even thinner than he remembered. Thin, but not fragile; she still looked strong. She wasn't wearing makeup, but her face was oval and perfect, like a cameo. Two crescent shadows underneath her vibrant brown eyes betrayed her fatigue. Even so, to him she didn't look older. Time hadn't passed. Only her dark hair was different. It was shorter and lacked the highlights of cherry and gold that he'd always loved.

She watched her watching him. "It's fake."

"What?"

"The hair."

Reality slapped him in the face. "Oh."

"I assume Olivia told you?"

"Yes, she did."

Hannah drank her coffee and looked away, as if seeing things in the room that weren't there.

"Why didn't you tell me?" he asked.

She laughed quietly. "What could you do, Chris? Did you cure cancer since the last time I saw you?"

"I could have provided support. I would have done anything to help."

"I know that. You're a fixer. That's who you are. But some things you can't fix."

"Maybe not, but I wish I would have heard about it from you."

"Yes, you're right," she acknowledged. "I should have told you, but I was scared. I don't know why."

His lips tightened into a thin line. "Tell me about it."

"It's ovarian cancer," she said.

"I'm so sorry."

She held up a hand, stopping him. "No pity. Please."

He searched for something to say. "What's the treatment? What do the doctors say?"

"I'm undergoing something called neoadjuvant chemotherapy. The idea is to reduce the size of the tumor before they operate. When that's done, they'll do the surgery."

"When?"

"Next month."

He ran his hand across his face. He was sweating. "What's the prognosis?"

"That depends on whether you believe me or the oncologist. I say my daughter still needs me. So do a lot of other women around here." She changed the subject, as if there were nothing more to discuss. "How is Olivia, really?"

"She's like you," he said. "Strong and stubborn."

That elicited a smile. "What did she tell you?"

"She says she didn't do it. She didn't shoot Ashlynn."

"Do you believe her?"

That was a good question. Did he believe her? Michael Altman was right that clients lied to lawyers and daughters lied to fathers. It was easier to do that than to admit you got drunk and threw away your whole life by putting a bullet in a girl's brain. He had been away from Olivia for a long time, and he didn't know how to decide if she was being honest. Even so, as a lawyer, as a father, he could only trust his gut, and his gut believed her.

"I do." He added, "Do you?"

Hannah caressed the top of the coffee mug with one finger. "I want to."

"But?"

She rubbed her moist eyes. He saw more clearly now how tired she was, all the way into her bones. "It hasn't been easy here. The two of us. Her and me."

He said nothing.

"She keeps secrets from me. She slips out at night. We're distant. I know it's been tough on her these past three years. The divorce, the move, me busy with work at the center. Now the cancer. When we got here, Glenn's daughter,

Kimberly, became her soul mate, and Olivia was inconsolable when we lost her. She did what the other teenagers did. She let all that grief and frustration become hatred."

"Did you know she had a gun?" he asked.

"Of course not. I would never have allowed it. She's still just a kid, Chris. She's got all these emotions, but she doesn't have the maturity to deal with them. That's what scares me. If she was alone with Ashlynn that night, and she had a gun with her, I worry about what she might have done."

"Hannah, I really don't think she killed her."

"I hope you're right. I feel like this is all my fault."

"Your fault? Why?"

"I was so caught up with Mondamin. It's like a chamber of horrors what they're doing there. They're cowboys. They don't have a clue about the real risks, and they don't care. I begged Rollie Swenson to file the lawsuit. I worked with the parents around here who lost kids. It wasn't about money. It was about throwing the light of day on that company, exposing what is really going on in there. The trouble is, when the litigation failed, the kids around here refused to accept it. Bad things started happening. Vandalism. Mischief."

"Was Olivia involved?"

"I don't think so, not directly, but she's a lightning rod. Like me. Kids in St. Croix listened to her talking about Mondamin and how people in Barron were profiting from the company's poison. Some of them took their anger too far. It was petty stuff, but then kids in Barron retaliated. The violence escalated. One boy in particular, a thug named Kirk Watson, became a kind of ringleader in Barron. He turned the feud into a war. We all knew it was only a matter of time before someone got killed."

"It sounds like street gangs."

"That's exactly what it is."

"In farm country?" he asked.

Hannah frowned. "This isn't Mayberry, Chris. The problems are the same as in the city, and it's even worse here because we don't have the resources to deal with it. We're all in the crossfire." She looked into the dining room where the torn curtains billowed in through the broken window. "Literally."

"Olivia is going to pay the price for this war. Michael Altman is going to come down hard on her. If she *didn't* do it, I need to figure out what really happened that night."

"I wish I knew."

"Did you see her go out on Friday?"

"No, she's become an expert at slipping out without me knowing. It's worse with the chemo. I go to bed and sleep like the dead."

It was an unfortunate turn of phrase, but Chris let it go.

"You said she's been keeping secrets. Do you have any idea what she's hiding?"

"I don't. She shuts me out. She's a deep, deep ocean, Chris. She's not a little girl anymore."

"Did she ever talk about Ashlynn Steele?"

He was surprised to see Hannah hesitate, as if the question made her uncomfortable. She took a long time to answer. "Sometimes. Ashlynn was the enemy for kids around here."

"Which kids?"

"Make a list. There are at least forty kids between the ages of thirteen and nineteen here in St. Croix. Any one of them would blame Ashlynn for who her father is. It was terribly unfair."

He couldn't help his first thought: *You're taking Ashlynn's side when our daughter is accused of killing her?* Then he realized that Hannah was right. He was being unfair, like the others. Ashlynn was dead. She was the victim.

Hannah got up abruptly, cutting off their conversation. She took their coffee mugs, put them in the sink, ran water over them, and wiped the mugs with a towel. Without looking back at Chris, she said, "I'm sorry, I know I'm not being much help. I appreciate your coming here for Olivia."

"I wouldn't have done anything else."

She turned around, and her eyes were warmer. She studied him up and down. "You're looking good, Chris. You've lost weight. Good for you."

"Thanks."

"Are you involved with someone?"

"No."

Hannah looked genuinely sad. "Still addicted, hmm?"

"What do you mean?"

"There are a lot of drugs that control people. For some it's cocaine or alcohol. For you it's adrenaline. Money. Work. Deals. It doesn't matter what you inject. It's still addiction."

He felt himself getting angry. He'd heard this before, but he tried not to fire back the way he had in the past.

"We've been down that road, Hannah," he said softly.

She stopped herself, biting her lip, as if she realized it was too tempting to fall into old habits. "Yes, you're right," she agreed. "We have."

Chris returned to the town of Barron at ten o'clock. He found his motel room wrecked.

The door hung ajar, splintered where someone had kicked it in. Inside, his clothes had been knifed into shreds and strewn like confetti around the room. The papers he'd gathered about the case had been stuffed into a garbage pail and burned. The room stank of melted plastic, and the carpet had a singed hole, revealing charred floorboards. Multi-colored spray paint made streaks around the walls and across the bed linens.

Someone had used a black marker to write on the bathroom mirror.

Fuck Olivia Hawk. Fuck St. Croix.

He tried to put himself inside the heads of teenagers who could feel such primal rage, and he couldn't. He didn't get it. All he could see was the work of animals.

The motel owner, Marco Piva, stood beside Chris. "I am so sorry, Mr. Hawk," Marco told him. "My house is a couple hundred yards behind the motel. I didn't hear anything until the fire alarm started going off. I ran down here, but the bastards were already gone."

"It's not your fault, Marco," he said.

"I've called the police."

Chris thought about Hannah's dismissive attitude toward the police and realized she was right. There was no protection. There was nothing to be done. "I'll deal with them in the morning. Right now, I just need to sleep."

"Of course, yes. I have another room for you. Do you need anything? I can get you whatever you want."

"Maybe a toothbrush and toothpaste."

"No problem." The motel owner put his hands on his fleshy hips, and his golden face screwed up in disgust. "St. Croix attacks Barron, Barron attacks St. Croix. Where does it end? A pox on both of their houses, that's what I say. I wore blue for three decades in San Jose. I saw this kind of hatred in the city, but I hoped I would never see it again."

"Whoever quits first is the loser," Chris said, "so no one quits."

"It is too bad you are in the middle of it, Mr. Hawk."

"Olivia's in the middle, and I have to get her out," Chris replied. "You said you had another room for me?"

Marco dug in his pocket for a key. "It's the last room on the corner. I was up half the night on Friday repairing the plumbing in there, so it's all new. The toilet, now it goes *whoosh*. No more floods. I'll bring you some things, all right?"

"Thank you."

Chris left the room without sifting through the remains of his luggage. He walked past the other motel rooms, where rain dripped from the roof into puddles beside him. The new room was sterile and empty, which was what he wanted. It smelled of lemon cleanser. He went to the bathroom sink, turned on the cold water, and splashed it on his face and ran his wet hands back through his hair.

He stared at himself in the mirror. He thought about Hannah.

She had said, "It doesn't matter what you inject. It's still addiction." She was right. You can be addicted to adrenaline. You can be addicted to violence.

He heard a knock on the door. It was the ever-efficient Marco, handing him a plastic bag of toiletries. He thanked the motel owner again, then closed the door and locked it. He dumped the bag on the counter of the bathroom: toothbrush, toothpaste, shampoo, mouthwash, bags of M&Ms and pretzels, microwave popcorn, a Bible, and a clean, folded pair of XXL underwear. That was life in a small town. Someone gave you their underwear if you had none.

Back inside, he took off his clothes and lay on the bed. The room was black. The mattress was a stiff board. He stared at the ceiling, but he didn't sleep. There was no way around it; he was a long way from home. He was an outsider, a foreigner, and the town of Barron was already sending him a message.

Get out while you can.

5

Kirk Watson shouldered out of the overgrown weeds near the Spirit River, bellowing "FUKYEAHHHHH" so loudly that the curse carried across the water to downtown Barron. He tossed his shoulder-length black hair out of his face. He had a long day's worth of dark stubble on his square chin. He was shirtless, and he carried a long-neck bottle of Grain Belt, which he tilted and swigged until it was dry. With his other hand, he tugged up the zipper of his jean shorts.

A teenage girl followed Kirk from the riverbank. She was as skinny as a stick, with dirty blonde hair. Her bone-white knees were smeared with mud. She wiped her mouth and shoved her grapefruit-sized breasts back inside the tight confines of her camisole. When she spotted Lenny Watson eyeing her pink nipples from the park bench, she snarled at him.

"What are you looking at?"

Lenny's face blushed beet red. He stammered an excuse, but Kirk grabbed the girl's hair and pulled until she screamed in pain.

"Hey!" Kirk warned, jabbing a finger in her face. "That's my brother there. You got that, Margie? He wants a suck, you open your hole and give him a suck."

Margie shrank as Kirk towered over her. "I'm sorry, Kirk," she whimpered.

Kirk shoved Margie toward Lenny, making her stumble in her block heels. "What about it, Leno? You want Margie here to swallow some squirt?"

Lenny squirmed on the metal bench, but he shook his head. "Nah, that's okay."

"This girl's got a tongue like a snake."

"No, thanks, man."

Kirk shrugged and grabbed a beer from the twelve-pack box beside Lenny. It was his fifth. Lenny still nursed his first. Kirk dug in his pocket and pulled out a gun and set it on the bench. He extracted a dirty roll of cash and peeled off a one-hundred-dollar bill, which he dangled in front of Margie's face.

"You want this?" he asked.

"Yeah."

"How bad?"

"Bad."

"What would you do for it?"

"I don't know. Like, anything."

"Would you lick my ass for it?"

The girl hesitated. "Yeah."

"Here, go fetch."

Kirk wadded the bill into a ball and threw it toward the riverbank. He laughed as Margie ran to retrieve it. He stretched out on his back on top of the bench, and his long hair draped behind him like a mop. His dirty bare feet dangled off the other end. He pointed his gun at the treetops and squeezed the trigger. The revolver made an empty click. He hadn't reloaded since their visit to St. Croix.

"It's like August in March," Kirk sighed. "Shit, Leno, does it get any better than this? We should be knee-deep in snow right now. Instead, we got seventy holy-shit degrees. I'd jump in the river if I thought I'd ever see my nuts again." He beat his chest with one hand like a gorilla. "FUKYEAHHHHH!!"

To Lenny Watson, his brother was a god.

He wanted to be just like Kirk, but his mother had played a mean trick on him, popping him out of the same womb like a pasty reflection of his brother. Lenny was sixteen, and Kirk was five years older. Kirk soared over Lenny by six inches and boasted an extra forty pounds of muscle. His older brother had guts, too. No one messed with Kirk. Not sluts like Margie. Not the pussy boys from St. Croix.

Not even Florian Steele.

For three years, it had been just the two of them, Kirk and Lenny, like Batman and Robin. When Lenny was six, their mother got drunk and drove her Grand Am the wrong way down an I-90 ramp into a semi. They could have buried what was left of her in a shoe box. After that, their father used Lenny as a nightly punching bag, until Kirk turned fourteen and bludgeoned the son of a bitch to death with a hammer. Kirk sawed their father's body into pieces and dropped him bit by bit into the Spirit River, which worked fine until his head rolled ashore near Redwood Falls. The police came calling for him, but Kirk only did two years in juvie. When he was out, Kirk rescued

Lenny from a foster family that didn't give a shit, and since then, they'd been a team.

Lenny would have done anything for Kirk.

"Hey, I got a new package coming," his brother told him, as he sucked down a beer on top of the bench. "Should be here in a couple of days."

"Yeah?"

"Yeah, Vietnam this time. I bet we make 10K on this one."

"Cool."

Margie returned from the river, shoving the hundred-dollar bill into the tight rear pocket of her shorts. Around them the park was dark and mostly deserted. The bare treetops loomed over their heads, but the cloudy sky wiped out the stars. It was past midnight, and only a handful of Barron teenagers hid in the shadows, making out. Lenny could hear grunts and moans and the rustle of plastic tarpaulins spread over the muddy grass.

Kirk's girl grabbed a beer as she sat down. "Ten thousand bucks? No shit? For what?"

"For keeping your mouth shut and not asking questions," Kirk snapped.

"Yeah, but can I get in on it?"

Kirk smirked. "Sure, why not. You like making movies?"

"What kind of movies?"

"Dirty ones."

"Like porno? That could be cool. How much could I make?"

Kirk stared at her. "What are you, seventeen?"

"Almost eighteen."

"Too old. You got a little sister?"

"That's sick."

His brother laughed hard. "The sickos are the ones who watch," Kirk said.

Kirk swung his legs on either side of Margie. He pulled the girl's shoulders so that she was leaning against his bare chest, and he shoved his big hands inside her top to play with her breasts. Lenny's palms grew sweaty as he thought about his own hands inside the girl's shirt. He imagined them as soft and squishy as overripe peaches, except for the nubs on each end.

"So what do you think, Leno?" Kirk asked. "Did I hit her?"

"Hit who, man?"

"Hannah Hawk."

Lenny shrugged. "I don't know. Maybe. You got one of the windows."

"I heard her screaming," Kirk said, "but that doesn't mean anything."

"I thought you were just trying to scare her," Margie said. "Not hit her."

"Hell, what's the point of that?" Kirk put his gun against the side of Margie's head. The cold metal went in her ear. "You don't shoot a gun unless you want to hit something."

"Stop that!" she told him.

"I thought you wanted to be a porno star."

"Don't," Margie begged.

Kirk hooked his arm around her throat and shoved the gun until it was almost breaking skin. As he tightened his grip, Margie twitched in panic. Her legs kicked spastically.

"Bang," he whispered as he pulled the trigger.

Click.

"It's empty, stupid," he chuckled.

Maggie squirmed in his arms and hyperventilated. "You bastard!"

"Don't be a crybaby."

"You scared the shit out of me!"

"Oh, quit whining. My gun wasn't loaded. You got off easy. Ashlynn got her brains blown out by that St. Croix bitch."

"Why do you care about her?"

"Ashlynn was a Barron girl. In Barron, we stick together."

"I heard she dumped you," Margie snickered.

"Shut the fuck up. You don't know anything."

"She was just dating you to piss off her father. Every rich girl likes to fuck her daddy's nightmare. Although the word at school is she never even let you between her legs."

Under Margie's shirt, Kirk crushed her nipples between his thick fingers, and the girl wailed. "Shit! Shit, stop it!" She wrenched away from him, crying. "You crazy asshole!"

"Don't talk about Ashlynn. You hear me? Don't even say her name to me."

Margie's knees knocked like a baby deer's. Tears of anger and pain rained down her face along with makeup, and strands of her blonde hair lay plastered on her cheeks. Her lower lip bulged in defiance. "Oh, yeah? Ashlynn, Ashlynn, Ashlynn. As in Ashlynn Steele would never dream of getting banged by Kirk Watson."

Kirk shot off the bench with his forearm cocked, and Margie ran. She fell down in her clumsy heels and got up, drenched in mud, but she ran through the park until she reached the footbridge that arched across the Spirit River into downtown Barron. They heard a frantic *clop-clop* as she sprinted across the bridge, arms pumping. In the middle of the bridge, under the twinkling lights, she finally looked back and realized that Kirk wasn't chasing her. She stopped, panting, and held out her hand with her middle finger raised. She shouted a curse at the top of her lungs.

Then she turned and ran until she disappeared into the town.

Kirk landed his fist on the bench so hard that the vibrations nearly pushed Lenny off the seat. It happened like that with Kirk sometimes. He boiled over like a pot of water, and you didn't want to be nearby when he did. Lenny had been hit. Burned. Choked. Kirk took an unopened beer bottle and marched toward the nearest oak tree and smashed it into jagged razors against the trunk. Beer foamed white, splashing over him. Glass cut and scratched his hand, drawing blood. Lenny heard murmurings of fright elsewhere in the park.

Kirk spun back, sucking the blood from his fingers. "We're not done. You got that? Ashlynn's dead. People gotta pay."

"I hear you, Kirk," Lenny said softly. "What's next?"

"We need to teach Tanya Swenson a lesson. The little bitch ran away and left Ashlynn there. Get her out of school tomorrow, Leno. Bring her to the football field for me. We'll make sure she gets a message to take home to her daddy."

"I don't know, man."

"Do it!" Kirk snapped. "I'll be waiting."

"Okay. Sure. Whatever you say."

"Then we deal with Olivia Hawk."

Lenny paled. "She's in prison," he protested.

"The judge will let her out."

"Yeah, but why bother with her? Everybody says she's going to be locked up for life."

"Then we'll give her something to think about while she rots," Kirk said.

Lenny's palms were sweating again. He felt himself growing aroused at the thought of Olivia. She was the only one he wanted, with her pouty lips and the brown hair that always fell over one eye. When she talked in class, she was so intense. So sure of herself. She was amazing. He wondered what it would be like to sleep with someone like that, but she barely knew who he was.

That didn't stop him from fantasizing about her.

Following her.

"Do you really think Olivia killed Ashlynn?" he murmured to his brother.

Kirk's eyes narrowed. "What are you talking about, Leno?"

"It just doesn't seem like something she would do. Not her."

"How the hell would you know?"

"I don't, man."

"She did it," Kirk insisted. "That bitch shot Ashlynn. End of story."

6

"Do I get to tell the judge that I'm not guilty?" Olivia asked.

Chris shook his head. "Not yet."

"So what do I say?"

"For now, nothing. Leave it to me."

"But people should know that I didn't do it," his daughter protested. "Why can't I tell them?"

"You will. Later. This is just a detention hearing. If it lasts five minutes, that's a long time. If the judge releases you, which I expect he will, we'll work through some paperwork, and then I'll take you home."

"Great. Jail still sucks."

"I know."

He didn't add that an overnight stay in jail was nothing compared to the prospect of twenty-five years.

"Florian Steele probably has the judge in his back pocket," Olivia said. "He won't let me out."

"Yes, he will. It'll be okay, but keep your cool in there. Don't say anything, don't do anything, and *don't* swear. Got it? If you act out, you give the judge an excuse to keep you locked up."

"Yeah, I know."

Chris added, "The county attorney thinks we should consider having you stay in jail for your own protection."

"No way. Not a chance."

"I didn't say that's what we're going to do, but he's right about keeping you safe. I'll hire someone to watch the house in St. Croix, and once we get there, you stay put."

"So what, I'm a prisoner at home, too?" Olivia asked. "I can take care of myself, Dad."

"No, you can't."

His daughter made a face at him, but she didn't argue.

"Did you tell Mom I didn't do it?" she asked.

"I did."

"What did she say? Did she believe me?"

"Of course, she did." Chris had no intention of sharing Hannah's secret doubts. Olivia didn't need to hear them.

He checked his watch. They needed to be in court in less than fifteen minutes. "Listen, I don't think you shot Ashlynn, but I also think you're *not* telling me everything you know. You can't keep things from me, Olivia. You're being charged with murder."

"I don't know what happened, Dad. Really."

"Let's start at the beginning. Who knew you were meeting Tanya out at the ghost town that night?"

"Nobody."

"Did you see other cars? Did you see or hear anything to suggest that someone else was in the town?"

"No, we didn't hear anyone. Nobody was around until Ashlynn showed up."

"Where did she come from?"

"She said she was heading back to Barron and got a flat tire."

"Did she say where she'd been?"

"No." After a pause, she added, "Ashlynn told us she'd been driving for hours."

"Hours?" Chris asked.

"That's what she said. I figured she was lying, but—" Olivia stopped, biting her lip.

"Why did you think she was lying?"

"I thought maybe she'd been in St. Croix."

"Why would she be there?"

"That's the way it's been for the past year. Raids and sneak attacks between the towns."

"Was Ashlynn part of that?"

"I don't know. She was from Barron. They'll do anything to hurt us."

Chris still wasn't convinced that his daughter was giving him the whole story. "What did you do after you dropped the gun and left Ashlynn in the park?"

"I went home and went to bed."

"Did you talk to your mother?"

"She was already sleeping. She sleeps pretty heavy because of the chemo."

"So she didn't hear you leave or come back?"

"I guess not."

"Did you tell anyone about Ashlynn? Did you send someone to help her?"

"No."

"Why not? You said she was stranded out there."

Olivia shrugged. Whenever she talked about Ashlynn, her face went cold. "I wasn't going to help her," she said.

"What time did you leave Ashlynn in the ghost town, and what time did you get home?"

"It was around twelve thirty when I left, and I got home ten or fifteen minutes later. It's not far."

Chris put the facts together in his head. Olivia left Ashlynn Steele stranded at half past midnight. She was alive, with a gun at her feet in a deserted park, miles from either Barron or St. Croix. Five hours later, before dawn, Tanya Swenson finally confessed to her father what had happened overnight, and Rollie Swenson called 9-1-1. The sheriff's department found Ashlynn in the park, dead from a single gunshot to the forehead. The revolver was missing. The girl's Mustang was parked in the main street of the ghost town, with a flat tire, exactly as she'd left it.

The initial estimate placed the time of death several hours before the body was discovered. In other words, she'd been killed shortly after Olivia left Ashlynn there.

Or before, he thought to himself.

Olivia could see it in his eyes. "You don't believe me, do you? You think I killed her."

"No, I don't think that, but a trial is about good facts and bad facts. Right now, we have a lot of bad facts. You were there. You had a gun. You threatened Ashlynn. Ashlynn is dead. What we need are facts to support your version of what happened. That you didn't pull the trigger. That someone else did."

"I don't know what to tell you, Dad. It could have been anyone."

"Tell me about Tanya," Chris said.

"What about her? It's not like she went back to the park and blew Ashlynn away."

"How do you know?"

"Tanya? No way."

"If you weren't there, you don't know that. Our job is to establish reasonable doubt that you killed Ashlynn. Tanya knew about the gun. She knew Ashlynn was stranded. She didn't tell her father or call the police for five hours."

"Yeah, but Tanya would never—"

"She's a suspect, Olivia."

His daughter frowned. "Whatever."

Chris opened his mouth to chastise her, but he held his tongue. He reminded himself that she was young. Sixteen-year-olds could do adult things; they could smoke, drink, have sex, and even kill. It didn't matter. She was still a kid who didn't realize that the rules of the game had changed, who didn't grasp that her whole life was hanging in the balance.

"It's time for the hearing," he told her. "Let's get you out of here."

After a hearing lasting no more than three minutes, the judge ruled that Olivia would not be kept in secure detention, and he released her without conditions, pending the next stages in the criminal proceedings. Chris wasn't surprised, because the presumption in any juvenile case, even murder, was to release the child. It was an easy victory, but going forward, the battle got much harder.

Outside the courtroom, while Olivia was in the bathroom, Michael Altman corralled Chris. The county attorney's face was concerned. "I heard about the incidents at your motel and at your ex-wife's house. The sheriff wants to talk to you about what happened."

"We didn't see who did it."

"Maybe not, but I don't want teenagers in either town thinking they can get away with these assaults without consequences."

"I understand." Chris added, "I assume you're planning to file a motion for a certification hearing."

The certification hearing would determine whether Olivia's case would continue in juvenile court or whether she would be tried as an adult, with adult punishments. Unfortunately, in a murder case, the presumption of the law worked against them. The only way to keep the proceedings in juvenile court was to mount an uphill argument that mitigating factors weighed in Olivia's favor. Judges rarely agreed.

"The hearing may be a moot point," Altman told him.

"Excuse me?"

"I plan to seek a grand jury indictment for first-degree murder. At that point, the certification is automatic."

Chris felt as if he'd been punched in the chest. "First-degree murder? You can't be serious."

"I am."

"Even if you believe Olivia pulled the trigger, you can't possibly believe she *intended* to kill Ashlynn."

Altman's face was grave. "Talk to your daughter."

"What the hell does that mean?"

"It means this wasn't just a depraved game played by a teenager without regard to the consequences. It was a deliberate revenge killing."

"Revenge for what? Kimberly's death?"

Altman hesitated with his hand on the oak door of the courtroom. "I'm afraid it goes deeper than that, Mr. Hawk," he said.

Without waiting for Chris to reply, the county attorney turned and disappeared inside the courtroom.

Chris stood alone in the hallway, inhaling the musty smell of the old building. He remembered what the motel owner, Marco Piva, had told him when he first arrived in town. *You will not be trusted. People will not tell you things you need to know.* That was already true. He felt as if there were a backstory playing out around him, and everyone but him knew what it was.

Talk to your daughter.

Olivia emerged from behind the frosted window of the women's bathroom. She wiped her mouth and rubbed her fingers on the denim of her jeans. She looked pale and fragile. Her chestnut hair hung straight down in long, dirty strands.

"Are you okay?" he asked.

"I threw up."

"I'm sorry."

She slid down onto a bench and laid her head against the wall. He sat down next to her and slid an arm around her back, which was so skinny he could feel her bones. The sweet, sickly smell of vomit clung to her. She folded herself into his shoulder the way she used to do as a child. Her eyes were vacant as she stared at the ceiling. They sat next to each other in silence, as if there were nothing to do but wait for a flood to carry them away.

First-degree murder.

The courtroom door opened again, and two people slipped through the doorway. Their footsteps on the hardwood floor sounded hollow under the high ceiling. Chris recognized them. He tensed, expecting a confrontation that he didn't want at all. Not now.

It was Florian Steele. The CEO of Mondamin Research was accompanied by his wife, Julia.

Chris knew Florian. They weren't friends, but they were both alumni from the University of Minnesota Law School, two years apart. They'd served together on the editorial board of the law review. They hadn't spoken in fifteen years. He remembered Florian as a law student whose interest was corporate law: public and private offerings, securities, and mergers and acquisitions. Even then Florian was all business, which made him a rarity. Most law students were either idealists, like Chris, who figured law was a way to change the world, or they were litigators who thought they would spend their careers in court. Florian saw law as a means to an end. Start a business. Acquire capital. Grow. Make money. Sell.

He'd followed his plans precisely.

Florian's eyes roved the hallway like a cautious tiger and found the two of them on the bench. Seeing Chris, he reacted the way any father would react when spotting an enemy to his family. His face darkened with anger and suspicion. He saw Olivia, too, and Olivia saw him, and Chris grabbed his daughter's shoulder as he felt her muscles harden into knots. Her teeth actually bared.

Florian wasn't a particularly handsome man, but he had the charisma that comes with wealth and success. He was as tall as Chris, with a high gloss on his balding head and prominent ears that grew sideways out of his skull like two halves of a severed heart. His black eyebrows were thick, straight smudges. His jaw was squared; his face was long. He had the gaunt look of a fanatical runner, someone who watched every milligram of salt and fat and measured his own cholesterol. Everything about him screamed of self-discipline, and Chris remembered that Florian had maintained a rigid work ethic in law school, when Wednesday beer parties were typically as important for most students as Morrison's constitutional law.

His wife, Julia, was a different story altogether. She was blonde and small, like a golden doll. From the photos he had seen of Ashlynn, Julia was an older portrait of her daughter. She looked born to money, wearing her gray silk dress like a runway model, with her hair up and her skin powdered and perfect. Black pearls wound around her neck and hugged her earlobes. She was the kind of woman who had always mystified Chris, because she was supremely unapproachable, like a museum sculpture protected behind glass. Hannah was the opposite. His ex-wife wore every emotion on her sleeve and never censored what was in her head, whether it was fury or passion. Julia Steele was beautiful, but she radiated no sexuality at all and her emotions were carefully masked. Even her grief didn't seep through her makeup.

Chris pressed down gently on Olivia's shoulder to keep her on the bench, and he stood up.

"Hello, Florian."

"Chris."

Florian didn't offer to shake hands. There was no small talk to make. They had been classmates once, and now they were adversaries and parents, one with a dead daughter, one with a daughter accused of murder.

"This is my wife, Julia," Florian added.

Chris didn't smile or pretend that they were pleased to meet each other. "I'm very sorry about Ashlynn," he told her.

The ice woman's eyes didn't melt. Her stare had the hardness of diamonds as her gaze flicked between Chris and Olivia. She said nothing at all. Olivia, on the bench, smoldered. Like her mother, she couldn't hide how she felt. Florian held his wife's hand, as if protecting her, but she didn't seem like the kind of woman who needed protection.

"I'd appreciate a few minutes of your time, Florian," Chris told him. "Maybe later today?"

"For what purpose?"

"I'd like to learn more about your daughter."

Florian took his time to formulate a reply. "You don't expect me to *help* you, do you, Chris?"

"No." He didn't bother arguing Olivia's innocence in front of two people who would never believe it. "We're lawyers. This is discovery. I'll do my best to make it as painless as I can, despite the circumstances."

Florian acquiesced with a glance at his wife. "Three o'clock at Mondamin."

"I'll be there."

Florian tugged on his wife's hand to pull her with him, but Julia Steele remained rooted in place. She and Olivia stared at each other. Her expression was inscrutable. When she spoke, her voice had a dark, sad music to it, which was the first hint of her emotions. "Is there anything you want to say to me, Olivia Hawk?" Julia asked.

Chris held up his hands immediately. "Olivia, don't say a word. Mrs. Steele, I'm sorry, but my daughter can't talk to you."

Julia didn't acknowledge him. She held Olivia's eyes like a magnet as the silence dragged out between them. He was afraid his daughter wouldn't be able to control herself and that she would blurt out whatever she was feeling or thinking, but Olivia finally pushed the hair out of her face and turned her eyes down to the floor. Florian's wife treated it like a victory, shaming Olivia into looking away. She allowed her husband to lead her toward the exit from the courthouse. Neither of them looked back.

Chris watched them go. He realized that Florian and Julia looked as out of place in the town of Barron as he did. They were like royalty, elevated above the crowd. The king with his queen. That was a title that Chris had never wanted. There were people who bowed to the king, but there were plenty of others who wanted to cut off his head.

It had to be lonely. Florian had his work to fill the void, and he wondered what Julia had for herself. Arts groups. Hospital board meetings. Fundraisers. He didn't think that was enough for a woman like her, and the answer jumped to his mind.

She'd had a daughter. A child to bring meaning to her life.

But not anymore.

7

CHRIS DROPPED OLIVIA AT HANNAH'S HOUSE IN ST. CROIX, AND HIS daughter retreated to her room to sleep. He let her go without asking more questions. She wasn't in any condition to talk, and he wanted to know more about Ashlynn and the feud before he confronted her again. Hannah promised to stay with her during the day. She also offered to make dinner for the three of them that evening. He was surprised, but he said yes. It was a tiny glimmer of what his life had been like in the old days, when they were a family in Minneapolis.

With that thought in his head, Chris drove back to Barron. He stopped at a shop on the main street to buy new clothes to replace what he had lost at the motel, and then he set out to find the local high school, which was located on a bluff above the river valley. The school drew students from the entire region, including St. Croix. The sprawling, one-story brick building was surrounded by acres of athletic fields that butted up against rutted rows of cornfields to the west and the tree-lined residential streets of Barron to the east. During the warmer months, the fields would be lush green, but the grass was brown and yellow now, flattened by snow and soggy from the early storms.

He parked in the crowded lot and went through the glass doors into the school lobby. Inside, he was surprised to find metal detectors and a uniformed security guard screening visitors. He gave his name, showed identification, and asked to see the school principal. He waited, smelling fried food in the cafeteria and hearing the thunder of basketballs in the gymnasium. Five minutes later, a middle-aged black woman walked past the rows of red school lockers to greet him.

"Mr. Hawk? I'm Maxine Valma. How can I help you?"

She was slender and tall, with graying hair cut in a short, practical bob and a dark ebony complexion to her skin. She wore a burgundy pantsuit and heels, making her look even taller than she was.

"I assume you know why I'm in town," Chris said. "I'm Olivia's father."

"Of course."

"I'd like some information about the young people around here."

Maxine's lips pursed with concern. "I'm not sure what I can tell you, Mr. Hawk. School records are private unless you get a court order, and I can't let you talk to any of the students on campus unless you have parental permission."

"I understand. I'm not asking you to violate any privacy laws. I was just hoping to find out what's going on in this town."

"I see. Well, I'll share what I can. I feel terrible, not just for Ashlynn and her family but for Olivia, too."

She gestured for him to join her, and Chris accompanied her down the school corridor. Two teenagers passed them going the opposite direction, and he saw their eyes lock on his face and heard them whispering as they passed him. He heard Olivia's name.

It was just as Marco Piva had told him: There were no secrets here.

"I didn't expect to find metal detectors," he told the principal.

Maxine nodded. "Sad, isn't it? I resisted for months, but the weapons problem was getting out of hand. We had knife fights. Students were bringing guns. I can't keep the feud out of the school, but I can try to keep them safe while they're here." She pointed at the freshly painted lockers. "We keep running to stay ahead of the graffiti. We no longer assign individual lockers, because too many were being vandalized."

"Hannah says it's like gang violence."

"She's right. Gangs give kids who have no future a sense of purpose, and that's what the feud does here. It's not about the cancer cluster or the litigation anymore. It's about hatred, which has become the defining theme for the children in both towns."

"So how do you stop it?"

"If I knew, we would have done it months ago." The principal shook her head. "I thought that Ashlynn's death would be a shock to everyone's senses. I hoped the kids would see that it's gone too far. That doesn't seem to be true. If anything, passions are even more inflamed."

She led him into the school cafeteria, which was mostly empty in advance of the lunch crowd. White-uniformed workers cooked over grills behind the counters. The smell of burnt oil was pungent. He saw another security guard near the door.

"Coffee?" Valma asked.

"Please."

The principal poured two cups from a silver urn, and they sat across from each other at one of the long cafeteria tables. Her fingers curled around the foam cup.

"Have you been principal here for long?" Chris asked.

Valma waited as steam wisped out of her coffee. She blew on it. "Two years."

"Are you a native to the area?"

"Do I look like a native?" she asked.

"Not really."

"No," she agreed. "My husband got a job here, and I came with him. I've been in education my whole career, but I never imagined my experiences in the St. Louis schools would be quite as useful as they've turned out to be."

"What does your husband do?"

The principal hesitated. "George is a research scientist at Mondamin."

"What does he research?"

"I could tell you . . ." she said with a smirk.

"But then you'd have to kill me?"

"Right." She added, "Seriously, Mr. Hawk, the employees all sign nondisclosure agreements. They don't talk to anyone."

"It sounds like the company has something to hide."

"They do. It's called intellectual property."

Like anyone with a spouse in a secretive profession, Maxine Valma had mastered the art of politely saying nothing. "Does it cause problems for you at school, having a husband who works at Mondamin?" he asked. "Students from St. Croix must see you as the enemy."

"Your daughter certainly did."

"Olivia?"

"Yes, I worked hard to convince her that I was scrupulously neutral, but I'm not sure she believed me."

"This is an odd question," he said, "but what can you tell me about Olivia? We talk a lot, but it's not the same when you don't see each other every day. She's changed. I need to get to know her all over again."

Maxine smiled with sincere warmth. "Olivia is smart. She's book smart, yes, but she's people smart, too, which is relatively rare for teenagers. She's a natural leader. Outspoken. Passionate. Sometimes reckless."

"That's her mother," he said.

"I know. Hannah and I are good friends, despite what my husband does. The women's center she runs is invaluable in this region. It's a resource for children and adults who face some truly desperate situations. She is an angel, Mr. Hawk, or at least that's how we feel about her."

Chris said nothing. Hannah was an angel, but she'd flown away from him, leaving a hole in his heart. "What else can you tell me about my daughter?"

"I'm afraid you can be smart and still be naive. Olivia is young. It's easy to take all that passion and have it misdirected."

"Meaning?"

"Meaning she's been one of the loudest voices against Barron and Mondamin. She's convinced that a grievous injustice was committed, and she refuses to remain silent. That's fine—commendable even—but Olivia doesn't always understand the effect she has on others. She can be an instigator with her words, deliberately or not. Other kids look to her. They follow her. Sometimes they go too far."

"Like who?"

"I'm not comfortable naming names, Mr. Hawk."

"Tanya Swenson?"

Maxine sipped her coffee and considered her response. "Tanya looks up to Olivia. I think she'd do just about anything for her. They're both children of divorce, although Tanya was left alone with Rollie at a young age."

"Tanya and her father live in Barron, don't they?"

"Yes, but the Barron teenagers have largely shunned her because of the lawsuit."

"Does she bear a grudge about that?" he asked.

The principal's brow knitted in annoyance. She leaned across the table and lowered her voice. "I know where you're going, Mr. Hawk. In order to create reasonable doubt that Olivia shot Ashlynn, you need to create a cloud of suspicion around Tanya. That may be an unpleasant necessity of being a lawyer, but please don't try to make me your co-conspirator."

"Olivia says she's innocent."

"I'd like to believe that's true, but it seems unlikely, doesn't it?"

"I think she's telling the truth. That means someone else killed Ashlynn."

"Tanya? I don't believe it."

"Anyone who can't be ruled *out* has to be ruled *in*."

"I've said all I can say about Tanya," Maxine replied. "I'm sorry."

"Okay. Talk to me about Ashlynn."

"What about her?"

"I'd like to know what was going on in her life."

The principal held the coffee cup near her lips, and he saw the smear of her lipstick on the rim. She stared at him without saying anything. She was obviously deciding what information she could safely share.

"Florian doesn't need to know you've told me anything," Chris added. "I realize it's awkward because of your husband's job."

"Florian doesn't scare me." She smiled. "If I were to be afraid of anyone, it's Julia."

"Oh?"

"She and Ashlynn were extremely close. If Julia thinks that Olivia is responsible for Ashlynn's death, she's likely to be a pit bull who wants to see her destroyed."

"Thank you for the warning."

"As for Ashlynn, there are certain young women who are obviously destined for great things. That was her. She was beautiful, confident, graceful, spiritual. It's a horrible tragedy to lose her."

"Was Ashlynn part of the Barron clique?"

Maxine shook her head. "No, Ashlynn was disgusted with the feud. She avoided the other students from Barron."

"Who did she hang out with?"

"She kept to herself a lot, particularly in the last few months. She seemed different, actually."

"How so?"

The principal tapped the table with her long fingernails. Like a lawyer, she picked her words carefully. "She was troubled. Upset. Her moods swung between highs and lows. That's not uncommon with teenage girls, but Ashlynn had a seriousness about life that made it more worrisome. On some level, I suppose she took the guilt for the violence onto herself, simply because of her father. That's nonsense, but try telling it to a teenage girl."

"Did she share any of her feelings with you?" Chris asked.

"No, I'm not sure she felt free to share her feelings with anyone. I felt bad, because it seemed to be getting worse."

"Worse?"

"Yes, for the last month, she was very depressed. She looked like she was carrying the entire world on her shoulders. I saw her crying several times. I asked her about it, but she shrugged it off. I was concerned. Honestly, if you'd told me she'd committed suicide, I wouldn't have been completely surprised, but I gather that's not the case."

"No, that's not what happened. You don't know what was causing any of this?"

"I'm sorry, no."

"Did you see her on Friday? The day she died?"

"No, Ashlynn was out of school for most of the week. She wasn't in classes after Tuesday."

"She'd been gone for three days? Do you know why?"

"Well, she gave me a note from her mother saying that she was volunteering on a church project in Nebraska, but to be honest—" She stopped.

"What?"

"To tell you the truth, I thought the note was forged."

"Did you talk to Florian or Julia?"

"No. In retrospect, I wish I had, but I didn't want Ashlynn to feel that I didn't trust her. For all I knew, the story was perfectly legitimate."

Ashlynn told Olivia she'd been driving for hours, and she arrived in the ghost town from the south, which was the route she would have taken back from Nebraska. So maybe it was true.

Or maybe, like Olivia, Ashlynn was keeping secrets.

"Do you know—" he began, but he couldn't finish his question.

Footsteps boomed on the cafeteria floor. A gangly teenager sprinted toward them and skidded to a stop, almost falling. He had a pile of schoolbooks under his arm, and two of them spilled to the ground. The boy struggled to catch his breath. The cafeteria guard, seeing the commotion, jogged in their direction.

Maxine Valma stood up. "David," she said to the boy. "What is it? What's wrong?"

The teenager gestured toward the rear of the school. "There's trouble outside."

About thirty students gathered in a rough circle in the mud of the football field.

As Chris and the principal neared the crowd, with two security guards beside them, he heard shouted expletives hurled between teenage boys. Pushing and shoving erupted, and several boys were thrown onto the wet ground. Others began throwing wild punches. A handful of girls watched in twos and threes from around the lawn. Some screamed encouragement, and others chewed their nails and stared nervously at the principal as she came closer.

One girl stood off by herself. She had a round face, with a mess of red curls on her head. She watched the fight from the shelter of a large oak tree, and she eyed the streets of Barron behind her, as if weighing whether she should run.

Through the tumult of bodies, they could see inside the circle, where two teenage boys confronted each other in a mess of blood and fists. The one with long hair tied in a ponytail, was a stranger to Chris, but he recognized the other. It was Johan Magnus, the son of the minister in St. Croix, the boy he'd met at the motel. Johan, whose sister, Kimberly, was part of the cancer cluster and Olivia's best friend.

He heard Maxine Valma mutter in dismay, spotting the other boy in the fight. "Kirk Watson. He's a Barron boy," she snapped. "One of the worst."

They descended on the feuding pack, and Maxine shouted at the students with a crisp air of anger and authority. "*Stop this!*"

Seeing them, several boys broke from the circle and escaped toward the school building. Many of the girls joined them. The others were still caught up in the fight, wrestling and exchanging blows. One by one, Chris and the security guards waded between the boys, shoving them aside and reestablishing a safe ground. The violence quieted, until only Kirk Watson and Johan Magnus were still entangled. Blood trickled from Johan's nose. Kirk had a burgundy welt on his cheek. Their clothes and faces were black with dirt.

Chris took Kirk, the larger of the security guards took Johan, and together they grabbed each boy by the shoulders and yanked the fighters apart. Kirk shrugged off Chris's grip and bolted toward Johan, but as he did, the other guard stepped in front of Johan and fired a blast of pepper spray toward Kirk's face. The guard's aim was bad, but even as Kirk twisted from the path of the spray, some of the fog seared his cheek and neck. He screamed and jerked backward, tumbling into Chris and taking them both to the ground.

Kirk clawed at his burning skin. His elbow landed hard on Chris's chin, dizzying him and knocking his teeth together. The older boy was heavy on top of Chris's body, and Chris fought unsuccessfully to dislodge him. Kirk's breath was sour as he gagged from the pepper spray, and he stank of cigarettes. He swung his elbow back again, hammering the side of Chris's skull and blinding him with an electric jolt of pain. As the guards closed in, Kirk spun his head to the side and blinked at Chris through tearing, bloodshot eyes.

"D'you get my message, fucker?" he hissed.

Chris knew what message Kirk meant. It had been scrawled on the wall of his motel room.

The guards laid their hands on Kirk's shoulders and dragged him off Chris, but with the strength of a bear, Kirk kicked free of the guards. Before anyone could hold him, he broke through the line-up of teenagers. No one reacted. No one chased him. He sprinted toward a black pickup parked on the border of the athletic field. When he was safely inside, the engine growled, and he sped away.

Chris stood up slowly. The ringing in his ears was as loud as a symphony. His neck and jaw felt stiff. His new dress shirt and pants were wet and torn. He felt someone put an arm around his waist and realized it was Maxine.

"Are you all right?" the principal asked.

"I've been better," Chris admitted, tasting blood in his mouth.

Maxine snapped her fingers at the minister's son, who stood on the edge of the circle with his hands in his jean pockets. Despite the smears of blood on his face and the mud in his blond hair, he looked in better shape than Chris.

"*Johan.*" Maxine ordered him, "Get over here."

The boy inched closer. He began to make excuses, but the principal silenced him.

"Quiet! Listen to me. I'm very disappointed in you. You're the one person in this school who has tried to *stop* the violence around here. And now I find you brawling with Kirk Watson? What were you thinking?"

"It's not what it looks like," Johan insisted.

"Then what is it?"

"I saw Kirk's brother, Lenny, going outside with Tanya Swenson. I didn't like it. I followed them, and I saw Kirk out here waiting for her."

Maxine took a long breath. "I see."

"Kirk and I got into it, and everyone else started piling in."

"Where is Lenny?" she asked.

"He bailed and ran when everything started."

"All right. Go back to my office, Johan. We need to share this with the police." Her soft voice turned sharp again. "The rest of you, I want you in the gymnasium with the guards. Right now. No talking. No fighting. You sit there and stare at your feet, is that understood? We're all going to have a chat with you *and* your parents."

The crowd of teenagers shuffled toward the school building. Chris remembered the girl who had stood off by herself near the trees, and he realized she wasn't part of the group returning to the school. When he looked in the direction where he'd first seen her, he saw the girl running toward the residential neighborhood.

"Who is that?" he asked Maxine.

The principal frowned. "It's Tanya Swenson." She shouted after the girl. "Tanya! Come back!"

Tanya stopped long enough to look back over her shoulder, but then she turned and ran even faster, losing herself among the streets of Barron.

8

CHRIS FOUND TANYA ON A SIDE STREET TWELVE BLOCKS FROM THE SCHOOL. She sat on the top step of a boxlike yellow house, with her fleshy forearms wrapped around her knees and iPod earphones shoved in her ears. When she saw his car stop, she scrambled to her feet with her red curls bouncing and he was afraid she would run. He got out quickly and held up his hands.

"Tanya, it's okay. I want to help."

The girl regarded him suspiciously. She unplugged the headphones and shoved them in her pocket.

"I'm Olivia's father," he added.

"I know who you are."

Chris studied the street in both directions. They were alone. The mature trees hung their bare branches over the neighborhood. It was a gray day. "Ms. Valma was concerned about you," he said. "Johan told us what happened."

"He shouldn't have done that."

"You're lucky he was around," Chris said.

"Yeah. I know. I just don't want to make this into a big thing."

"Are you okay? Are you hurt?"

"I'm fine."

He walked up the sidewalk to join her. The house where Tanya sat was old and small, a relic from the 1950s. The curtains on the windows were drawn. The driveway was empty. "Do you live here?" he asked her.

"No."

"Whose house is it?"

"I don't know. I was tired of running."

Chris gestured at the steps. "Mind if I sit down?"

"Whatever."

He sat three steps below her and rubbed his jaw, which moved stiffly as if he were the Tin Man in need of an oilcan. Even without rain, the painted step felt damp. The porch smelled of wood rot and of the cloud of Tanya's sugar-

74

sweet perfume. He smiled at her, and they sat in silence. She was a pretty girl, with a fresh, pink face. Her voice had a sweet lilt, but she spoke softly. She was like a timid cat. He imagined her with Olivia, and the contrast was striking. His daughter was outspoken; Tanya was a wallflower.

He thought about what he knew of this girl. Like Olivia, she'd lost a parent to divorce and a friend to cancer. She'd been rejected by her friends in Barron. Now she was the center of attention from police and attorneys in a murder investigation, and she'd been pulled into the violence between the towns. It looked like the last place she wanted to be.

"So what's up with Kirk Watson?" he asked her.

Tanya's face scrunched into a scowl. "He's a beast."

"What did Kirk want with you?"

"I don't know. I guess he blames me for what happened to Ashlynn." She added under her breath, "It's partly my fault. I left her there."

"What does Ashlynn's death have to do with Kirk?"

Tanya rolled her eyes. "It's the feud. It makes him feel important. He's always bragging about rescuing Barron from the people of St. Croix. It's like he thinks he's a general trying to win a war."

"Is that how the other kids in Barron feel?" he asked.

"Mostly they're just afraid of him. He messes with the girls. He always has money, and nobody knows where he gets it. It's like he's got the whole town under his thumb."

"What about Ashlynn?" Chris asked. "Did Kirk mess with her?"

"They dated for a while."

"From what I've heard about Ashlynn, Kirk Watson doesn't seem like her type."

Tanya shrugged. "Kirk's a jerk, but he's pretty hot. Girls want to be with him, no matter what he does. Ashlynn dumped him, though. I don't know, maybe he hit her or something."

"But now he's trying to be an avenging angel when she's dead?"

"She was a Barron girl. She was Florian Steele's daughter." Tanya added, "I'm really sorry about Livvy, you know. I feel like I betrayed her by talking to the police."

"She doesn't blame you."

"Yeah, well, we were both stupid. I can't believe what happened."

Chris tried to read her eyes. He saw a scared teenager, in over her head. She wasn't a compelling suspect to dangle in front of a jury. No one was likely to believe that she was a murderer. Even if she was.

"What *did* happen that night?" he asked.

Tanya blinked, as if she'd remembered who he was. "I don't know if I should be talking to you."

"That's okay. If you want, I'll drive you home right now, and you don't have to say a word. I'm just trying to help Olivia." He waited a beat and then added, "She says she didn't do this, Tanya. She didn't shoot Ashlynn."

"Yeah, I know."

"Do you believe her?"

"I don't know. Livvy was crazy that night. She had the gun, she was screaming at Ashlynn. That's why I got the hell out of there. I called her later and she said nothing happened, but then I found out that Ashlynn was dead. I mean, who else could have done it, right?"

"You *called* Olivia? When?"

"It was an hour or so after I got home. I couldn't sleep. I was watching TV in the living room, but I kept thinking about Ashlynn. So I called Livvy to make sure everything was okay."

"Did you tell the police?"

Tanya's eyes fluttered, as if she'd made a mistake. "I—I don't think I did."

"It's okay. Tell me about the call."

"I called Livvy's cell. She answered right away."

"Did she say where she was?"

"She said she was home. I asked if Ashlynn was okay, and she said yeah, she was fine. She told me she dropped the gun and left Ashlynn there."

That was exactly what Olivia had told him, too. An hour after the crime, and four days after the crime, she was telling the same story. That was a good thing.

"How did Olivia sound?" he asked.

"I don't know, she was pretty down. Like she'd been crying."

"Just to be clear, Olivia specifically told you that Ashlynn was fine."

"Yeah, that's what she said."

"What else did you two talk about?"

"I said, 'Should we call somebody? You know, Ashlynn was stranded, shouldn't we do something about it?' I was pretty upset."

"Okay."

"Olivia said no. I figured she wanted to teach Ashlynn a lesson."

"Then what?"

"That was it. I hung up. I went to bed, but I woke up around five o'clock, and I kept thinking about Ashlynn out there by herself. I felt really guilty that we didn't help her. She didn't deserve that. So I woke up my dad and told him the whole story, and he called the police."

Chris was nervous about his next question; he didn't want to inflame the girl's suspicions. "Did you think about going back there yourself? I mean, after you hung up with Olivia. Did you think about driving back there and helping Ashlynn?"

"Yeah, sure," Tanya admitted.

He watched her face. "But you didn't?"

"No. I should have, but I didn't want to be out there by myself."

If she was lying, she was good at it. She met his eyes dead on, as if she were daring him not to believe her.

"I really appreciate your help, Tanya," he told her. "Do you want me to drive you back to school?"

Tanya shook her head. "I want to see my dad."

"Does he have an office downtown?"

She nodded.

"I'll drive you down there." Chris pushed himself off the wet step, and as he headed down the sidewalk toward his car, Tanya caught up with him. She stopped him with a hand on his arm.

"Mr. Hawk? I didn't tell anyone about this, and I don't know if you want to hear it or not."

"What is it?"

"Well, there was something else going on between Ashlynn and Olivia."

"What do you mean?"

"I don't know exactly what it was," Tanya said, shaking her head. "Olivia keeps a lot of stuff to herself, you know? I'd get upset with her sometimes because she was keeping secrets from me. But this thing with Ashlynn, it wasn't just about Mondamin. I could tell. It was something personal."

9

THE SQUAT BUILDING THAT HOUSED ROLLIE SWENSON'S OFFICE WAS LOCATED behind a parking lot on a side street between downtown Barron and the Spirit River, with a view across the water toward the city park. It was built of tan stucco, dirty and cracked, and the sign on the outside window said simply: Law Office.

When Chris arrived with Tanya, Rollie hugged his daughter ferociously, then read her the riot act for leaving school without calling him. Maxine Valma had obviously filled him in about the fight. As he listened to the parental lecture, Chris remembered what it was like to have a child in his life every day, balancing love and discipline, security and independence. He missed it.

Seeing Rollie Swenson was like seeing an alternative version of his own life. Rollie didn't wear business suits. He wore a blue polo shirt, tan dress slacks, and a comfortable pair of loafers. The slacks sported a coffee stain near the pocket. He was tall and stocky, with a bulging stomach that sagged over the top of his belt. He was in his late thirties, and he had messy black hair and a dark beard line. A yellow highlight marker had been shoved above his ear and forgotten.

Rollie looked like a lawyer who scraped for business with ads in the yellow pages. Generic brochures on personal injury, bankruptcy, divorce, and foreclosure published by the Bar Association were stacked on the counter. His law degree was in a drugstore photo frame on the wall. An empty air freshener sat on the lobby table among copies of farm and sports magazines. The waiting room smelled of grease. Inside Rollie's office, behind the counter, Chris saw an open white foam box on his desk with a half-eaten cheeseburger and fries. Rollie's lunch sat among a mountain of legal files.

"Not exactly Faegre & Benson, is it?" Rollie asked with an ironic smile. Faegre was the state's largest corporate law firm, with a blue-chip roster of Fortune 500 clients.

"I wish I charged their hourly rates," Chris said.

"Oh, I bet you do okay." Rollie patted Tanya on the back and pointed her toward a spare office with a sofa, television, and conference table. "You hang out with your iPod for a while, okay, baby? I want to talk to Mr. Hawk."

"Sure." Tanya gave Chris a nervous glance as she retreated into the office. Rollie's eyes lingered on his girl as he pulled the door shut, and it was obvious that his daughter was the center of his world. Not his work. Not his clients. Chris wished he'd learned that lesson years ago.

"Come on back, Mr. Hawk," Rollie told him. "Sorry, I'm just finishing lunch."

"Call me Chris."

"You like fries, Chris?"

"Love 'em, but not anymore."

"I hear you." Rollie led him into his office, took four fries in his hand, and munched them together. "I admire your willpower. Me, I can't say no." He picked up the burger, took a large bite, and washed it down with Coke. "Poor Tanya, she got my genes. My ex-wife is a beanpole."

"So's mine. Olivia was lucky."

Rollie sat down and leaned back in his chair. "Thank you for bringing Tanya here. I appreciate it."

"Of course."

"You look like hell," Rollie said.

"Other than a splitting headache, I'm fine."

"You want some Advil?"

"Actually, that would be great."

Rollie dug inside the top drawer of his desk and found an old plastic bottle that looked as if it had been used and reused dozens of times. He unscrewed the top and poured three red tablets into his hand. The pills looked fresher than the container in which he stored them. He passed them to Chris, who swallowed them down.

"Tanya thinks Kirk Watson was trying to abduct her," Chris warned him.

Rollie's chest swelled with a long, fierce breath. "Kirk."

"You know him?"

"I've known him for years. Actually, I defended him when he killed his father."

"Kirk *killed* his father?" Chris asked.

"About seven years ago. He beat him to death with a hammer and then cut up the body."

"Jesus."

"Yeah. Kirk's dad beat the crap out of the younger boy, Lenny, whenever he could. With the evidence of abuse, I got the whole thing handled with a juvie sentence."

"I'm surprised Kirk would harm Tanya after you got him a slap on the wrist for murder."

"Kirk thought he should have walked."

"Tanya says the police around here won't touch him," Chris said. "Is that true?"

"Yeah, Kirk always seems to have an alibi when things happen. Or witnesses get cold feet and decide not to testify. It's ugly."

"Do you still represent him?"

"Hell no. Not anymore. Even ambulance chasers like me have some standards. I'm not in it for the money. Good thing, because I don't make much. A lot less since the Mondamin lawsuit."

"Oh?"

"People in Barron think I'm a traitor. They didn't like me representing the families in St. Croix. Fortunately, there are still enough people who want to dump their spouses or get DUIs doing 105 miles an hour on Highway 7 to keep me in business. I'm about the only game in town, and my rates are cheap."

"Did you grow up around here?"

Rollie took another bite of his cheeseburger. "In other words, why would I be practicing law in a town of five thousand people if I'm not a native? Yeah, I still live on the family farm a few miles south of town. It's all weeds now. My mom was pretty upset when I chose law over farming, but I could read the writing on the wall. Farming was a dead end. Plus, these hands weren't meant for manual labor."

"It's just you and Tanya?"

Hearing his daughter's name made Rollie smile. "Yeah, it's her and me. I met her mother when I was in law school at Billy Mitchell in the Cities. It was one of those relationships that should have fizzled after a couple months, but she got pregnant, and we got married. It didn't take her long to figure out that she hated small towns, hated being a mother, and hated me, not necessarily in that order. Tanya was only two, and I wanted custody. Sarah didn't put up a fight."

"Are you still in contact with her?"

"I don't have a clue where she is, and that's fine. Tanya does okay with me as a dad and mom rolled into one."

Chris wondered if that was true. He thought about Olivia growing up without him for the last three years. Rollie Swenson didn't have any trouble reading his mind.

"What's the deal with you and Hannah?" Rollie asked. "If you don't mind a personal question."

"Hannah's roots are here. When her mom died, she wanted to come back and make a difference."

"She's done that. There aren't many people in this region without an opinion about your ex-wife. They love her or hate her."

"What about you?" Chris asked.

"Me?" Rollie took another french fry and chewed it bite by bite. "I wish I had her passion. Somehow she held onto her idealism about this part of the world, and I lost mine a long time ago."

"You took the case against Mondamin," Chris pointed out. "That's pretty idealistic."

Rollie smiled. "Hannah was relentless. She had Glenn Magnus and the other parents who had lost kids sitting here in my office. I told them the suit was a loser, but she said they didn't care about money. They wanted discovery. They wanted to get past summary judgment, tear open the company's records, and start interviewing their scientists. She was pretty sure that we'd find plenty of dirt once we started looking."

"What kind of dirt?"

"Environmental violations. Questionable science. Bad actors. There was one scientist in particular they had suspicions about, a whack job named Vernon Clay who lived near St. Croix. He disappeared, and we tried to find him. No luck."

"The whole thing sounds like an uphill climb from a litigation standpoint."

"Well, I was hoping we could prompt a settlement offer to make us go away," Rollie admitted. "Florian was in negotiations to sell the company, and I figured he didn't want bad publicity to screw the deal. But he's a hard-ass. I got out-lawyered and out-resourced. The Bible may say different, but most of the time, when David goes up against Goliath, David gets his ass kicked."

"Causation is almost impossible to prove in these cases. That's not your fault."

Rollie shrugged. "In my line of work, I don't have too many opportunities to be on the side of the good guys. I really wanted to come through for those people, but I let them down."

The younger attorney finished his burger and dumped the empty foam container into a wastebasket under his desk. He sucked up his Coke through a straw until there was nothing left but an empty slurp, and then he threw the cup away, too. He sat silently in his office chair and studied Chris with a thoughtful expression.

"So," Rollie said finally. "Now that we know each other, should we talk about why you're really here, Chris?"

"Okay, sure. I'd like some information about the night Ashlynn Steele was killed."

Rollie rolled around the mouse on his desk, and the twenty-four-inch flat-screen monitor for his computer awakened. He typed in a password to access his files. Chris counted at least fourteen keystrokes.

"That's a pretty long password," Chris commented.

"Yeah, I learned about security during the Mondamin litigation."

"How so?"

"My office was broken into twice. I could never prove it, but I think Florian hired somebody to see what data we'd uncovered."

Rollie accessed his recent documents and sent two files to a printer in the open closet behind him. He grabbed the sheets and handed them to Chris. "Those are copies of our statements to the police. Mine and Tanya's."

"Thank you."

"I'm sure you'll get them from the sheriff soon enough, but this way, you don't have to wait."

"I have some more questions for Tanya, too, if you don't mind."

Rollie eyed him across the desk. "Here's my problem, Chris. This is the point where our legal interests don't coincide. I'm sure you understand. I'm fond of Olivia, but my only concern in this case is the welfare of my daughter. As a lawyer, I know what you have to do. I don't blame you for it, but I won't let you make Tanya into a suspect."

"Tanya may know things that will help me prove that Olivia wasn't involved in Ashlynn's death."

The other attorney didn't hide his surprise. "You're planning to argue that Olivia is innocent? You're not using emotional distress?"

"I'm not arguing anything yet."

"Maybe so, but that makes me even more nervous about letting you talk to Tanya."

"Tanya can help me corroborate Olivia's story. She already told me that she talked to Olivia after she got home. Olivia told her that she left Ashlynn in the ghost town. Alive. That's important."

Rollie frowned. "You *interrogated* Tanya?"

Chris knew he'd made a mistake. He tried to backtrack, but it was already too late. "I asked her a couple questions. I told her she didn't have to tell me anything."

"Don't play dumb with me, Chris. Did you ask Tanya whether she went back to the ghost town that night?"

"Yes, I did," he admitted.

"In other words, you tried to get her to incriminate herself."

Chris said nothing, and Rollie stood up. His demeanor made it clear that the meeting was over. "You have our statements," he announced. "For now, that's all you get. Let me be clear about something else, too, Chris."

"What's that?"

"If you want to talk to Tanya again," Rollie told him, "you talk to me first."

10

THE GUARDS AT MONDAMIN RESEARCH DIDN'T WANT TO LET CHRIS INSIDE the gate. It took ten minutes of phone calls back and forth to the administration building before they confirmed that he had an appointment with Florian Steele. One of the guards, whose tattoo suggested he was a retired Marine, climbed into the passenger seat of Chris's Lexus without being asked.

"I'll show you where to park," he told Chris, pointing at a road leading around the rear of the facility.

The main building was approximately two football fields in length. It was clean and pristine, as if the white paint were touched up daily. There were no windows along the walls of the building, but he could see extensive environmental duct work on the roof. As he drove, he saw that the larger section of the campus was connected to a smaller administrative building by a glass-enclosed walkway. He could see two employees in white coats walking behind the glass.

When he reached the opposite side of the smaller building, which overlooked the river, he saw a small parking area. The guard gestured.

"Park there."

Chris spotted several empty visitor parking places near the front door. At the far end of the first row of cars, he also saw a bright orange Mustang convertible. He didn't think there were two vehicles like that in Barron, Minnesota. This was Ashlynn's car.

He ignored the guard's instructions and drove past the building entrance. He stopped in an empty parking spot forty yards down, immediately next to the Mustang. The man next to him protested.

"Not here!" he instructed Chris. "Back up!"

Chris turned off the Lexus and hopped out. "You going to shoot me?" he asked.

While the guard climbed out of his car, Chris made a careful examination of the exterior of the Mustang. He wasn't sure what he expected to find. The flat tire that had stranded Ashlynn in the ghost town hadn't been replaced; he assumed the vehicle had been towed here. He bent and studied the tire and didn't see any obvious damage. It was most likely a puncture wound deep in the tread. The rest of the chassis was in perfect condition, without dents or scratches. If there had been dirt or dust on the frame, the rain had washed it away.

"Let's go, Mr. Hawk," the guard warned him in a growling voice.

Chris paid no attention. He tried to drown out the low machinery hum from the buildings, the murmur of the river fifty yards away, and the guard's voice. Instead, he put himself inside Ashlynn's mind that night. She was sitting in the Mustang, near midnight, stranded in a town full of dead buildings. She'd driven this car. This was the last place she'd been before she died. He cupped his hands and peered through the windows at the white leather seats inside. The interior was immaculate, not a scrap of paper, not a coffee mug in the cup holder, not a pen shoved into the visor. He assumed that anything inside had been bagged and tagged by the police. Or maybe Ashlynn simply kept a clean car. It was impeccable, except for the remnants of powder where the police had dusted for fingerprints and messy splotches of dried mud on the driver's seat and floor mat from the recent rains.

There was nothing to see. Even so, something about the Mustang bothered him.

"I didn't invite you here so you could conduct a search of my daughter's car, Chris," Florian Steele snapped.

Chris looked up from the Mustang's windows. Florian stood on the sidewalk in front of the building, ten feet away. His arms were folded across his chest. The guard began to apologize, but Florian waved him to silence.

"Shall we go inside?" Florian asked. "Or do you want to poke around the trunk and the glove compartment, too?"

"That's not necessary," Chris said.

Florian gestured toward the glass entrance to the building, and they walked side by side in silence. At the main doors, Florian swiped a magnetic card, and the doors slid aside to let them enter. They passed into a vestibule, and inside was another door that operated on the basis of a biometric fingerprint ID pad. Florian placed his right index finger on the pad and the next door opened, leading them into the company lobby. He pointed at the receptionist's desk.

"You'll need to register, have your picture taken, and get your fingerprint digitized. Then we'll issue you a personalized visitor's pass."

"Do you need a urine sample, too?" Chris asked.

Florian didn't smile.

He followed instructions and was rewarded with a white magnetic card that he clipped to his belt. Florian pointed at a floor-to-ceiling revolving door that required them to pass individually. The CEO went first, and then Chris followed, using the ID card and his fingerprint to gain access. On the other side of the door, he found himself in a windowless corridor, as bone white as the exterior of the facility. It smelled of disinfectant, and white noise hummed through hidden speakers.

"You're serious about security," Chris said.

Florian nodded as he led them down the corridor. "We have to be. It's partly for intellectual property protection, although most of those threats are more sophisticated. Electronic hacking. Moles. Attempts to bribe and blackmail employees. The physical dangers to the facility are primarily from environmental extremists."

"Are fringe groups like that a serious threat?" Chris asked.

"Absolutely," Florian replied. "Many are violent and fanatical. They're anarchists. If they could blow up or disable our facility, they would. We've had two incidents in the past ten years where individuals were caught with wire-cutters and explosive materials outside the fence."

Florian led Chris into his sprawling office, which had a wall of windows overlooking the Spirit River. It was a modern, elegant space that could have fit into any of the upscale downtown towers in Minneapolis. His desk was glass, with no drawers. He had high-definition videoconference equipment on one wall. His artwork was sterile and modern, mostly nonrepresentational bronze designs. The only traditional painting in the office was an oil rendering of Julia and Ashlynn. His wife's arm was slung around Ashlynn's shoulder in a firm, protective grip.

Florian didn't sit behind his desk but rather took a chair at a round glass conference table near the windows. Chris sat opposite him, where he could see the flow of the water meandering south from the dam. Florian rubbed the balding surface of his skull. He tugged at his shirtsleeves, balancing the amount of white fabric visible under his suit coat. He looked impatient for the interview to begin and end.

"You've done well, Florian," Chris said. "You always had a better business mind than most lawyers."

Florian shrugged. "Your own legal practice seems very successful."

"It is, but I don't really create anything. I just do deals."

"Back in law school, you were more concerned with social justice. I'm surprised you became another hired gun paid by the hour."

Chris recalled his debates with Florian in the editorial offices of the law review. Even then, Florian had been particularly skilled at finding pressure points and applying his thumb. He hadn't lost his touch. "I had a family to support," Chris replied. "I still do a lot of pro bono work."

"Good for you, but I always thought pro bono work was a worthless sop to ease the conscience of rich lawyers."

Zing.

"If you really want to help people," Florian went on, "start a business. Create jobs. That's my philosophy."

"How many people do you employ here?" Chris asked.

"More than two hundred and fifty. We're one of the largest employers in the region."

"To be honest, Florian, I'm not entirely sure what you *do* at Mondamin. No one seems to know, or they won't talk about it."

"It's not a secret. We're one of the leading research facilities in the country on applications of biotechnology and nanotechnology to the agricultural industry."

"What does that mean in practical terms?"

"It means we use the most sophisticated technological tools available to feed the world."

"That sounds noble."

"Our research is a major factor in the development of corn and soybean crops with dramatically improved yield. We develop seeds that embody a genetic resistance to various insects and fungi, in order to reduce the application of toxic pesticides. We do research that minimizes water usage, reduces the spread of disease, and improves the potential of agricultural alternatives to fossil fuels."

"So why does Mondamin attract so much controversy?" Chris asked.

"Because we represent change, and change is scary," Florian said. He may as well have been speaking to an investor group or giving an interview to the *Wall Street Journal*. "People hear about genetically modified organisms and nanosilvers, and some of them respond with irrational fears. They think making modifications to plant DNA is something unnatural, when in fact humans have been genetically modifying crops for millennia. It's merely that our process is new and efficient."

"Five children died of leukemia in a town of a few hundred people," Chris pointed out. "St. Croix is barely ten miles from here. You can understand their suspicions."

Florian folded his hands neatly on the table. He didn't take the bait or grow agitated. "I have the deepest sympathy for the parents who lost their children. I've lost a child myself now, so I know the pain it causes. You want to lash out. You want to punish someone. When disease strikes in a small town, people assume there must be a tangible cause. They don't want to believe it's just bad luck."

"Do you really think that's all it was?"

"I do. The county and state epidemiologists all told the people of St. Croix that there was no cancer cluster. When they went ahead with a lawsuit, we bent over backward to be fair. We made no objections when the judge wanted to appoint an independent special master to conduct an analysis prior to ruling on summary judgment. It was intrusive and inconvenient, but we agreed. This wasn't a biased expert hired by one side or another. Our counsel agreed with the selection, and so did Rollie Swenson. The expert analyzed groundwater, soil, and air samples; she reviewed blood samples from the victims; we invited her inside Mondamin to do a nearly limitless review of our records and lab findings. Her conclusion was that causation could not be proved and almost certainly *did not exist*. I'm truly sorry that the people of St. Croix couldn't accept that simple reality and have instead pursued a violent vendetta against me, this company, and the town of Barron."

Before Chris could reply, Florian's face reddened, and he added, "On a personal level, I also have to tell you that I am furious that your ex-wife has made me into a monster in the eyes of the public. She fanned the flames around here. In my mind, Hannah is as guilty of Ashlynn's murder as Olivia. If I could, I would ask Michael Altman to charge them both."

Chris knew he was on sensitive ground. Florian and Ashlynn. Rollie and Tanya. Himself and Olivia. They were all fathers trying to protect their daughters. For Florian, it was too late. He'd failed. Underneath the hardness of the man's exterior, the loss was eating him up.

"I do understand," Chris said.

Florian looked toward the river, obviously frustrated with himself for letting his temper sneak through his shell. "Yes, well, there I go, doing the same thing that the people of St. Croix did. Seeking revenge for my loss."

"Can you tell me about Ashlynn?" he asked.

Florian smiled for the first time. "She was a jewel."

"She was a beautiful girl," Chris agreed, admiring the painting.

"Yes, she was. Athletic. Beautiful. She had a marvelous heart. I was proud of her values. She was planning to apply to some of the top colleges in the fall. East coast, west coast. She was going to take a trip with Julia to visit them this summer."

"I imagine it was hard for her sometimes," Chris said.

"How so?"

"Having money in a small town."

"Not really. Ashlynn never flaunted her wealth, and honestly, she didn't have much money of her own. We didn't give her a blank check. The Mustang for her sixteenth birthday, that was about the only grand gesture I ever made."

"How did Ashlynn feel about the feud between the towns?"

"She hated it," Florian replied. "I'm sure she was angry that so much of the venom was directed at me, but on a religious level, she was simply distressed by the violence."

"Wasn't she dating one of the boys who was behind the feud?" he asked.

"Who?"

"Kirk Watson."

Florian's face darkened. "Nonsense. Ashlynn never dated Kirk. I would never have allowed it."

Chris felt as if he had tiptoed onto an unexploded mine. "Is it possible she didn't tell you? Parents are sometimes the last to know."

"It never happened," Florian insisted.

"Okay. I'm sorry. I got some bad information." Chris made a mental note to find out what was really going on between Ashlynn and Kirk.

"Do you know who she *was* dating?" Chris continued.

"I don't believe she was serious about anyone."

"What about friends?"

Florian hesitated. "Ashlynn could be a bit of a loner. I felt bad about that."

Chris didn't push Florian. It was obvious that the man didn't really know his daughter well at all. Like a lot of busy fathers, he couldn't say what was going on in Ashlynn's head or her heart or her life. Chris felt the same way about Olivia. He wondered if Florian's wife, Julia, had greater insights into their daughter.

"Can you think of anyone who had a grudge against Ashlynn?" he asked.

"No, of course not."

"You mentioned environmental extremists."

"So?"

"I was wondering if you had received any threats from those groups against your family."

"No, nothing like that. I'm a target. Mondamin is a target. No one has ever come after Ashlynn or Julia."

"What about this person who calls himself Aquarius?"

"What about him?"

"I was wondering if you had any idea who he is or why he's making threats against you."

Florian shook his head. "None at all."

"Did Ashlynn ever talk to you or your wife about anyone who was making her uncomfortable? Anyone who was following her?"

"No, of course not. I see where you're going with this, Chris. You want to use this mystery man—this Aquarius—as an alternate suspect. He killed my daughter to get back at me."

"It's not impossible."

"It's a desperate lawyer's trick. No one will believe it."

"I realize you don't want to hear this, Florian, but I don't believe Olivia killed Ashlynn. Not by accident. Not on purpose. She didn't do it. I also don't believe someone stumbled onto your daughter in that ghost town. Either they knew she was there, or they followed her."

"You can make up stories for a jury," Florian snapped, "but don't do it with me."

"Where was Ashlynn coming from on Friday night?"

"What?"

"If someone followed her, they had to know where she was. She told Olivia and Tanya she'd been driving all day. The principal at her school said she'd been gone from school for three days. Where was she? What was she doing?"

Florian was silent. Chris tried to decipher in the man's face whether he didn't know, or whether he didn't want to say where his daughter had spent those days. Either way, he wasn't going to answer. Florian stood up, his face was flushed and angry.

"No one followed Ashlynn," he told Chris. "Not Aquarius. Not anyone. She was alone that night. Then your daughter found her and killed her. That's the whole story. You can pretend all you want, but that's what happened."

11

CHRIS SAT IN ONE OF THE ADIRONDACK CHAIRS ON THE PORCH OUTSIDE
Hannah's house. It was dark, but the twin post lights on either side of the
front steps cast shadows onto the lawn. He sipped a glass of cheap red wine.
On the quiet street, he saw a glint of a match inside a light-blue Thunderbird,
and smoke blew out from the driver's window. The man inside was a retired
cop in his mid-fifties from Granite Falls, which was another of the nearby
towns built on the banks of the Spirit River. Chris had hired him to do
overnight security.

The porch door banged as Hannah joined him. She studied the car, too,
with her hands on her hips and a frown on her face.

"I don't really like being watched, even by someone trying to protect me,"
she told him.

Chris didn't argue. Hannah knew it was the right thing to do, but
her world was black and white. If it offended her values, she railed
against it.

"He'll circle the house three or four times an hour," Chris said. "Other
than that, he'll be in his car. You won't know he's there."

"Does he have a gun?"

"Yes."

"I hate guns," Hannah said.

His ex-wife sat down beside him. She kicked off her flip-flops, leaving
her tiny feet bare. She wore cargo shorts and a loose-fitting T-shirt over her
skinny chest. With the sun down, it was cooler outside, but she didn't act
cold. He saw the dust of rice flour on her arms; she'd been baking bread. He
could smell it in the oven through the open front door. Rain drizzled off the
porch roof, splattering on the wooden steps.

He took another drink of wine. Hannah had sparkling grape juice in a
plastic champagne glass. Her eyes were focused beyond the reach of the porch
lights, into the darkness of the trees hugging the river.

"I love a warm spring," she murmured. "No bugs yet. I'm always swatting mosquitoes when I'm out here in the summer."

"It's a beautiful spot."

"It must drive you crazy," she said.

"Why?"

"No hustle-bustle. No Starbucks. No deals closing on Christmas Eve."

"Once, Hannah. That happened once."

"Once was too many, Chris."

He didn't want to debate their lives again. "You're right. I made mistakes." She looked surprised. "So did I."

"You're a local hero," he said, changing the subject. "Good for you. People love you here."

"Some do, and some hate me. We got picketed when we started handing out condoms last year."

"How are your finances holding up at the center?"

"We pay the bills month to month and pray we get a check from the state or a grant when we need it. It's touch and go."

"I tried to help," he said. "You sent the checks back."

"I don't want your money, Chris."

"It was just money. No strings attached."

"There's no such thing."

He wondered why she was afraid of his help. "I wasn't trying to buy my way back into your life," he told her, but he knew he was lying to both of them. "Oh, hell, maybe I was."

Hannah was quiet. "The truth?"

"Sure."

"I was a little scared of letting you back in."

He thought that he might as well say it. It was as good a time as any. "You cut my heart out when you left, Hannah. I've been dead ever since."

His ex-wife closed her eyes. She started to speak, and then she stopped. When she opened her eyes again, she brushed away tears. "I know," she said. "I'm sorry."

"It's been three years, but it still hurts to think that you stopped loving me."

Hannah looked genuinely upset to hear him say those words. "Chris, that is not true. That was never true."

"Then why?"

She put down her glass and swung sideways in the chair. She leaned forward, her hands lightly on his thigh. "I wanted something else out of life. I wanted this."

"What is this?" he asked, because he really didn't know.

"This is a place where I matter."

"You mattered to me."

"I know you think so, but I'd become an afterthought to you. Olivia, too. You thought you were working for us, but you were working for yourself. It's not sports or sex for men like you. It's the code. Accomplishment. Success. Duty."

"Those are bad things?"

"If you forget why you're doing it, yes." She went to the edge of the porch, where she gripped the railing. The town of St. Croix was framed behind her in the dotted lights of the houses. "Do you know why I love being here? It's not because it's an easier way of life. It's harder. It takes more self-reliance. There's no safety net. But you know what, Chris? We've got our priorities straight. Relationships matter here. God matters. Time matters. I'm not just a mouse running in a Habitrail."

"Is that how you felt with me?" he asked. "Really?"

She didn't look at him. "Sometimes."

"You know that's the last thing I ever wanted."

Hannah turned around. He realized they were both older; they'd both walked through fire and learned that burn marks don't go away. They just toughen into scars, like permanent reminders. "I don't blame you, Chris. If anything, I blame myself for what happened between us. Here I am, talking about relationships, and I walked away from the one that meant the most to me. I'm not proud of that. I've obviously screwed up with Olivia, too."

"Not true."

"I can't get her to open up to me. I've watched her drift farther and farther away. Now look where she is. She's sixteen, and her life may be over."

She was giving him a chance to move to safer ground, and he took it. It was easier to talk about Olivia than to reopen the locked room where they kept their pasts. "Her life isn't over, but I can't help her unless I know what she's hiding."

"You're looking at the wrong woman. I'm the last person she'd tell if she had secrets."

"Then who?"

Hannah shook her head sadly. "I don't know. She's a closed book."

"Tanya Swenson said there was something personal going on between Ashlynn and Olivia. Do you know what it could be?"

"I don't."

"Did Olivia ever talk about Ashlynn?"

"Not in front of me. Not unless it was about Mondamin."

Chris was frustrated. "Something strange was going on with Ashlynn, too," he said. "She was missing for three days before Friday. Either Florian didn't know why, or he was covering for her."

Hannah turned away.

"What is it?" Chris asked.

"Nothing."

Chris pushed himself out of the chair. On the street, he saw the retired policeman climb out of his Thunderbird. The man checked the gun in his shoulder holster and wandered onto the lawn to patrol the perimeter of the house. He was built like the trunk of an oak tree, weathered and tough. Chris nodded at him, and he waited silently while the ex-cop disappeared between the rear of the house and the bank of the river.

"What's going on, Hannah?" he repeated. "I don't need you keeping secrets from me, too."

"Please, Chris, I can't talk about this."

"Do you not understand what's happening here? Olivia is facing first-degree murder charges."

"Believe me, I understand."

"Then talk to me."

"I'm telling you, I have no idea what Tanya meant. As far as I know, Olivia thought Ashlynn was the enemy. There was no relationship between them."

"You know something," Chris persisted. "What secret could possibly be so important when Olivia's life is at stake?"

Hannah folded her arms together and breathed heavily. She looked to be in physical pain, and maybe she was. Maybe it was the cancer. He softened and put a hand on her shoulder. "Are you all right?"

She spoke so quietly that he could barely hear her. "When a girl comes to me, I take an oath to uphold her privacy."

"When a girl comes to you? What are you talking about?" Then he understood. "Oh, son of a bitch. Ashlynn."

Hannah said nothing.

"Ashlynn came to you at the center, didn't she? What was happening to her?"

"I can't say anything."

"Hannah, please," Chris pressed her. "Whatever was going on in her life, it could be the reason she was killed."

"I won't betray her trust."

"You're betraying her trust by staying silent," Chris insisted. "Ashlynn has no privacy anymore. She's dead. Someone shot her in the head. She's been cut up by a pathologist. They put her on a slab for an autopsy. She has no secrets."

"An autopsy?"

"Of course."

Hannah cupped her hands in front of her mouth. "They know."

"Know what?"

He waited for her to answer, but as the question hung in the air, he realized he already knew the truth. Three days. She'd been gone for three days. Alone. Depressed. He thought about what Maxine Valma had said. *I saw her crying. If you told me she committed suicide, I wouldn't have been surprised.* He knew why a seventeen-year-old girl would go to see Hannah—why Hannah would do almost anything to protect the girl's confidences.

Because she was pregnant. And because she'd made the decision not to be pregnant anymore.

"Where did you send her?" he asked softly.

Hannah stared at him, stricken. He saw in her face what it was like to be in her office every day. To hear the stories. To feel the pain. "There's a doctor I know in Nebraska," she said. "She's discreet and professional. Ashlynn didn't want her parents to know about it. She didn't want to go to court to get permission."

"Who's the doctor?"

She shook her head. "I can't say. She's operating outside the law, ignoring parental notifications. She could be in mortal danger if people knew what she was doing. If they make her stop, some desperate girls will have no options. I won't allow it."

"Who else knew?" he asked.

"As far as I know, nobody. Me and Ashlynn. That's all."

"Olivia?"

"I don't see how."

"Who was the father?"

"Ashlynn didn't say. I don't think he knew."

"Did she say if it was consensual?"

"She didn't mention rape. I didn't pursue the circumstances, but I don't think that's what happened."

"Olivia knows more than she's telling us," Chris said. "I don't know if it's about the pregnancy or the abortion, but something else is going on here, and I want to know what it is."

"She won't open up to me."

"Maybe she'll open up to both of us."

"I wish that were true," Hannah said, "but you're better off talking to her alone."

"You can read her better than me," he said. "She's just like you. Come with me."

Instinctively, he did what he'd always done in the past. He reached out to take Hannah's hand.

That had been a ritual of their marriage. At their old house, they would sit on the porch overlooking the lake. Talk. Laugh. Cry sometimes. When it was time to go inside, he would hold out his palm, she would take it, and they would head upstairs hand in hand. There was a sacredness about the gesture that they both recognized. To hold hands was to be in love.

She flinched, and he pulled his hand back like touching a hot stove. He knew he'd made a mistake. You didn't intrude on certain memories. You left them the way they were.

"I'm sorry," he said.

Hannah said nothing, but she came with him into the house.

The uncarpeted stairs to the second floor were on his left. He let Hannah go first, and he followed. Upstairs, the hallway was dark. He recognized the lingering aroma of Hannah's perfume. Everything here smelled like her, and it was disorienting, as if they were back in the past. She knocked on the first closed door on their left.

"Olivia?"

There was silence from their daughter's bedroom. Hannah knocked again, but there was no answer. She put her ear to the door, listening for Olivia's voice on the phone or the noise of the television. They heard nothing.

"Olivia," she repeated, her voice sharper.

She turned the knob to go inside, uninvited. The door was unlocked. The two of them entered Olivia's room, and Chris felt as if he were trespassing. With a sweep of his eyes, he recognized souvenirs from her childhood—the stuffed Gund bears on her dresser, a stone Aztec calendar on the wall from a family vacation to Acapulco—but most of the bits and pieces in the messy room revealed a girl he didn't know.

The window overlooking the river, above the muddy rear yard, was open.

Olivia was gone.

12

WHEN THE EX-COP PATROLLING THEIR HOUSE DISAPPEARED AROUND THE corner, Olivia opened her window and squeezed her body through the frame. She lowered herself slowly, clinging to the peeled paint of the window ledge with her fingers. The drop from the soles of her sneakers to the wet ground was only eight feet. She let go and landed with a hard, heavy splash. She waited, making sure that no one had heard her, before she headed for the river.

She ducked under the spindly branches of the oak trees behind the house and pushed through the dead brush. Foliage above the water was dense, but the weeds on the riverbank had long since been beaten down into a path. She picked her way through black puddles that had gathered in the craters of the dirt. Wild brown grasses tipped with fur brushed against her skin on either side of the trail. Below her, no more than ten feet down the slope of the bank, she could hear the noisy slurp of the river.

Through the trees, she saw lights glowing in the houses of St. Croix. She recognized the voices of neighbors through open windows. She moved as silently as she could, like a deer, to avoid arousing suspicion. It was a small town. Everyone knew everyone else, and everyone knew everyone's business. Keeping secrets meant not being seen, and she'd had plenty of practice slipping away.

Two hundred yards down the riverbank, she reached the railroad tracks that paralleled the highway. Trains rarely passed there in that season. She stepped over the rail and stood on the crushed gravel in the center of the tracks. In the early days, when she'd first arrived in St. Croix, she'd wandered down here and thought about jumping onto a slow-moving train as it rattled south. She'd imagined lying on top of the cool steel of the freight car, watching the clouds and stars above her, feeling the jolts and vibrations and screech of the train wheels. She'd wanted to travel far away until home was a memory.

Back then, it had been Kimberly who talked her into staying. Running away was for cowards, she said.

Olivia followed the railroad tracks onto the bridge over the river. The crisscross beams of gray steel made giant Xs on either side of her. Halfway between the banks, she stepped off the tracks and climbed onto the rigid frame above the water. She leaned against one of the diagonal steel beams. The deep water had a wormy smell, dank and dead.

She heard footsteps. He'd heard her coming. She saw a silhouette, and even without lights, she knew it was him. She felt a rush of joy that made her forget everything else. She climbed down and ran. He was twenty yards away, but she felt as if she covered the distance in two steps. She threw her arms around his neck and held on. She remembered how her face felt against his and how his skin smelled. It had been months since she'd touched him.

"*Johan.*"

He stood stiffly as she embraced him. He didn't kiss her. He didn't look into her eyes. He studied the darkness on the riverbanks as if it held threats.

"We shouldn't be here," he murmured.

"I know, but I had to see you."

"What do you want, Olivia?"

"What do I want?" she asked, mystified. "How can you say that? We need to talk."

Johan turned toward the far bank of the river. She walked beside him, feeling his distance. She brushed his fingers, expecting him to hold her hand. When he didn't, she felt rejected and shoved her thumbs in her pockets. Her mother always said you could tell a man's love by how he holds your hand like he never wants to let go.

They crossed the bridge to a wide-open expanse of fields that would be thick with corn in another few weeks. In the warm summers, you could get lost in the head-high stalks as in a maze. This was their place. They'd played hide-and-seek here like children. They'd cried over Kimberly. They'd kissed. Later, during a hot August, she'd let him be the first and only boy to make love to her.

Now he was far away. Remote. Angry.

"No one knows what really happened," she said. "Not my dad, not anybody. I didn't say a word. Honestly. You're safe."

"What are you talking about?"

"I still love you, no matter what you've done."

"What *I've* done? Olivia, are you crazy?"

He kicked angrily at the dried, broken remnants of last year's crop. Forgotten ears lay rotting in the rows. She wondered if he was remembering the previous summer. When they were in love. Before Ashlynn. Instead, his words dashed her heart.

"Don't you understand what she meant to me?" Johan asked. "I loved her."

Olivia felt bitter. She felt the way she had in the ghost town, seeing Ashlynn up close, realizing that this girl had taken everything from her. "Last year, you said you loved me," she reminded him. "You said I was everything to you. I guess you only wanted one thing."

"That's not true."

"As soon as you had a chance, you dumped me for her."

Johan grimaced. "You're being unfair, Olivia. It wasn't like that. You don't understand."

"You're right. I never understood how you could be with Ashlynn, of all people. What would Kimberly say? Did you ever think about that?"

"You're wrong about Ashlynn."

"Johan, she told me she stopped seeing you a month ago. You two were over. Why didn't you let me help you? If you were hurting, you should have come to me. You know that. I swore I would never stop loving you, and I never have."

She stroked his face. His skin was smooth, and his jaw was angled. Instinctively, she ran her fingers into his thick blond hair and leaned in to kiss him. Their lips touched; his mouth felt dry. She expected him to respond, to wrap his arms around her skinny back and pull her into him. Instead, he jerked away and pushed her arms down.

"How could you let me see her like that?" he asked. His voice cracked. "How could you let me find her that way? *Dead*. In the dirt."

Olivia felt as if she'd been slapped. "Are you kidding? Is that a joke?"

"Did she want to get back together with me? Is that what she told you?" He took hold of her shoulders and demanded, "Tell me the truth, Olivia. Is that why you killed her?"

She wanted to speak, but her chest was empty of air. She could hear the words, but she couldn't say them. *You think I'm guilty? You?* If there was one person in the world who knew that she was innocent, it was Johan. She'd been willing to go to jail to protect him. To keep his secret.

"I can't believe you'd do this to me," he went on. "Tell me it was an accident. Tell me you didn't do this deliberately. I was a jerk to hurt you like I did, but I never dreamed you'd go so far."

Olivia said nothing, because there was nothing she could say. She was furious with herself, and she felt like a fool for trusting him. She spun on her heels and marched toward the bridge. She didn't want more lies. She wanted to go home and wallow in her grief. She felt as she had six months ago, without Kimberly in her life, when Johan threw her over for a girl who symbolized everything that Olivia detested. The betrayal had almost killed her.

When she heard him behind her, following her, she started to run.

"Olivia," he hissed, "come back!"

"GO AWAY!" she shouted, not caring who heard.

Drizzle made the ground slippery, but she didn't slow down. Her long hair flew behind her. The water passed under her feet. She cleared the end of the old bridge, and as she passed through the gap where the tracks cut through the trees on the riverbank, they came for her.

Six of them. At least six.

They were dressed in black, hidden behind masks. They burst from the brush on both sides like commandos, and before she could scream, she was caught up in the vise of their arms. She opened her mouth, and a wet towel choked her as someone pushed it between her teeth. She felt her neck squeezed in the crook of someone's arm. A pillowcase was thrown over her head; she was blind, and as they pulled it tight, she could barely breathe.

Behind her, she heard Johan shout as he tried to rescue her, but the shout was cut off in his throat. They descended on him, too, and she could hear the pummeling of blows as they fought him to the ground. He struggled in defiance, and several of the boys groaned in pain as he broke free and retaliated. It wasn't enough. He screamed the O in her name, but that was all, and they had him again. The beating was vicious. Relentless. When he gagged, she heard a gurgling mix of air and blood. Even when he was silent, they didn't stop; the blows rained down, boots landing on flesh. *Don't kill him*, she prayed. *Oh my God, please don't kill him.*

She heard a muffled voice. One word, "Go!"

She flailed with her arms, and her fingernail scored one of the boy's faces, drawing blood. He screamed, but his cry was cut off by one of the others. Wounding him was a hollow, temporary victory for her. Four or more strong arms pinned her with iron grips. She felt herself swept off her feet and carried over their heads in triumph, like a roast pig dug up from the ground. When she tried to kick free with her long legs, they grabbed those, too, and she was frozen in place. She was a prisoner. A sacrifice.

Her senses blurred into terror and chaos. She smelled sweat and heard the rasp of their breaths. She felt their fingers clutching her and knew her skin would be purple where they held her. She heard car doors. Running footsteps. Murmurs of laughter and anger. She was thrown inside, surrounded by invisible bodies, and they crushed her down below the seats as they fired the engines. Their shoes were on her head. Her neck. Their hands mauled her.

It wouldn't happen here, she realized. *It would happen somewhere else. It would begin, and it would never end.*

13

THEY SPLIT UP TO SEARCH THE TOWN.

Hannah stayed at home, calling her neighbors. Chris and the ex-cop he'd hired went in different directions to hunt through the streets of St. Croix. The town was confined to a few blocks surrounded by miles of open rural land. There were only so many places to go on foot.

He saw lights inside the Lutheran church, making the arched stained-glass windows glow in multiple colors. The church was the largest building in town. It felt like a church that immigrant farmers would build, with an understated beauty, rather than showy ornateness. The walls were lined with white wooden siding, and the panels were in need of fresh paint. The most prominent feature of the church was its steeple and bell tower, rising over the peaked roof, tall enough to oversee the entire community.

The glass doors were unlocked. Chris went inside. The lobby was cool and smelled of oiled wood. On his right, narrow steps led upward toward the tower. On the opposite wall, near the stairs leading to the basement, he saw a large cork bulletin board lined with notices of fundraisers, farm equipment for sale, free kittens, and chili dinners. It was like a local, handwritten Internet to connect neighbors to the goings-on of the town. There were five eight-by-ten color photographs of teenagers thumbtacked to the board, too, and he had no trouble guessing their identities. He could see the disease in their faces, despite their youth and bright white smiles. These were the five who had died.

He opened the door into the sanctuary. The ceiling angled sharply over his head. It had the silence of sacred places, magnifying the echo of his shoes. Empty, varnished pews, stocked with black Bibles, lined the main aisle. The chancel was illuminated, and he saw Glenn Magnus at the lectern, head down, as if he were praying for an invisible congregation. Beside him was an elaborate wooden altar, draped in green silk, highlighted by a brass cross that glinted under the hanging lights. Jesus stood behind the altar on a carving that dominated the wall, his arms spread wide.

The minister looked up as he heard footsteps. Chris approached apologetically. "I'm sorry to intrude."

Magnus stepped down from the pulpit and met Chris at the front of the church. "You're not intruding. What can I do for you, Chris?"

"Olivia sneaked out of her bedroom. She's not answering her cell phone."

"I haven't seen her, but let me look downstairs. Johan's bedroom is in the basement. Maybe she came to see him."

The minister marched past him. Chris followed, but he stopped halfway, imagining the church filled with devout worshippers on Sunday, dressed for God, with chins shaved and fingernails cleaned. Like him, Olivia had never been particularly religious. Hannah was another story. His ex-wife hadn't tried to impose her values on Chris, but she had always been passionate about her religious roots. She was equally passionate about a woman's right to control her body, and he wondered if that belief caused problems for her in a conservative small town.

He left the sanctuary, and the door closed softly behind him. In the lobby, Glenn Magnus was at the top of the basement stairs. He'd grabbed a flashlight from the lower level.

"She's not there." He added, "Neither is Johan."

"Was he here earlier?"

"Yes, he got back from the motel two hours ago. He was downstairs doing homework." The minister took a cell phone from his pocket and dialed. After listening for several rings, he hung up. "No answer. Maybe I'd better join you in your search. It's not safe for them outside these days."

The two men returned to the streets. The minister walked at a brisk pace, swinging the beam of the flashlight in front of them. They walked past houses to the highway leading toward Barron, but they found no sign of the teenagers. Magnus put his hands on his hips and examined the dark town. "Let's follow the river trail behind Hannah's house. Perhaps they went that way. Sometimes the teenagers hang out in the fields on the other side of the railway bridge."

"Okay."

They marched side by side. The drizzle flattened their hair and gave a sheen to their skin when they passed near house lights. The sidewalks glistened with pools of standing water.

"I told Olivia to stay in the house, but she didn't listen," Chris said.

"Teenagers rarely listen."

"Are she and Johan good friends?"

Magnus was slow to reply. "They were extremely close, but not anymore. They comforted each other after Kimberly died, but I'm afraid they won't have anything to do with each other now."

"Why? Because of the feud?"

"In part. Johan knows violence won't bring Kimberly back. Olivia hung on to the hatred. She's not alone. It's a disease around here." Magnus stopped and put a hand on Chris's shoulder. "Hannah persuaded me that we owed it to the children to find out what really happened. We tried, and we failed. Honestly, if I'd known what would happen in the aftermath, I would have stopped the lawsuit before it started. The price is too high."

They continued walking. Where the town ended at the river, they plunged into the trees at the riverbank. Even with the flashlight illuminating the ground, Chris found it nearly impossible to see, but Magnus walked with confidence, leading them toward the trail by the water. The minister was a tall silhouette. All Chris heard was the man's voice, which was deep but gentle.

"It must be hard," Magnus said, "coming back into Hannah and Olivia's lives this way."

"I don't think Hannah wanted me to come at all," Chris said.

"No, she's relieved. She told me so. She probably found it hard to ask, but she's glad you came."

"She keeps me at a distance. She didn't even tell me about the cancer. I had to find out about it from Olivia."

"I imagine she was more afraid of telling you than anyone else."

"Why?"

The minister considered his reply. Everyone around here made calculations before they spoke. The flashlight filled his face with shadows, which made him look sorrowful.

"I lost my own wife nine years ago," Magnus told him. "It was very sudden. I've been alone since then. When Hannah moved to town, the two of us clicked. To be honest, I fell in love with her."

Chris didn't want to be having this conversation. "I could tell you two were close."

"Close, yes. Dear friends, yes. Romantic, no. That door was firmly closed, with a No Trespassing sign hung outside. The sign has your picture on it, Chris."

"What are you saying? That she closed herself off emotionally because of the divorce?"

The minister shook his head. "I'm not saying anything. That's for you and Hannah to talk about, not me."

Magnus turned back to the trail. He circled the area with the flashlight, catching the brown water of the river and the winter brush in its glow. They were still alone.

"If Olivia and Johan don't talk to each other anymore," Chris asked, "why would she sneak out of her room to meet him as soon as she got home?"

Magnus hesitated. "I couldn't say."

"It must have something to do with Ashlynn."

"When we find them, we'll ask them."

Chris could hear in the minister's voice that he was hiding something. "I'm getting tired of people in this town keeping the truth from me, Glenn."

"I can't divulge anything," he replied. "You know that. I'm bound by the same ethics that bind you."

Chris let the man walk away, and then he called after him. It was a shot in the dark. "Did you know about Ashlynn's abortion?"

Magnus stopped. The news hit him like a physical blow. His knees sagged, as if he were thunderstruck. "Abortion?"

"Ashlynn went to Nebraska to get an abortion. Hannah told me. That's where she'd been when she was driving home on Friday."

"Oh, dear Lord, that poor girl."

"Did you know?"

"No."

"Did you know she was pregnant?"

"I didn't. I had no idea."

"Talk to me, Glenn. Were Johan and Ashlynn involved? Is that what you're not telling me?"

Magnus was silent, but Chris knew what his silence meant. *Yes.*

A secret affair. Johan and Ashlynn. A St. Croix boy and a Barron girl, like Romeo and Juliet caught between warring clans. It was a dangerous place for both of them to be.

"How does Olivia fit into this?" he asked.

"Chris, please—"

"Is Olivia protecting Johan? Why?"

"You need to talk to them, not me. There's nothing I can say."

Chris thought about Tanya, who had said there was something else going on between Ashlynn and Olivia. Not just the feud. Something personal.

Johan.

Standing on the river trail with Glenn Magnus, Chris heard the crash of breaking branches in the trees. The minister swung the flashlight in front of them. He expected to see Olivia on her secret route home, but his relief evaporated as the beam illuminated a face out of a Halloween nightmare.

It was Johan, pale and beaten. The boy held himself up by clinging to the tree trunks on either side of the trail. One eye was swollen shut. Twin trails of blood streaked from his nose.

"Johan, oh my God," Magnus called. He ran to his son, who staggered forward into his arms. His knees sank down to the mud.

Chris was already dialing 9-1-1 when Johan spoke through fat lips: "Olivia."

"What about her?" Chris asked urgently. He could hardly breathe. "Where is Olivia? Tell me."

"They have her," he whispered.

"Who?"

"Barron boys."

14

LENNY WATSON SLID DOWN ONTO THE WET GROUND IN THE DILAPIDATED shell of an old Milwaukee Road railway car. Water dripped through the rusted holes in the steel roof and landed in splatters around him. The dirt of the railroad boneyard was littered with twisted sheet metal. He had a book of matches in his hand, and he lit one, letting it burn down, watching the painted graffiti dance on the walls inside the train car. When the flame grew hot on his fingers, he tossed the match into the mud, where it fizzled with a gray trail of smoke.

He touched his face and winced. The deep cut stung where Olivia had scratched him. It oozed blood again as he felt it. His fingers came away sticky, and he sucked them clean like a vampire. He was bare-chested and cold in the darkness. He hugged his knees to keep them from trembling.

Awful noises assaulted his ears as the boys dragged Olivia toward the abandoned freight car that sat on dead-end tracks thirty yards away. He'd been inside many times with Kirk. It was windowless and pitch black. There was nothing but a square hole on one end where you could squeeze in and out. When they'd explored it for the first time last summer, there had been a homeless man living there among the rats and roaches. Kirk had beaten the shit out of him, and he never came back.

Olivia couldn't scream; they'd gagged her. Her cries escaped from her throat in wild, muffled lilts of rage and panic. He thought about shouting. Or singing. *La la la la la la la la.* Anything so he couldn't hear her.

A huge shadow loomed near him, and he heard breathing. He lit another match, and Kirk's dirty, rain-slick skin flickered in the light. The bent triangles of steel on the corroded end of the train car shell looked like teeth in a shark's mouth, ready to bite his brother in half. "Last chance, Leno," Kirk said.

"No."

"I told the others you wanted her first. You're making me look bad."

"I can't."

Kirk spat in a puddle. "What, are you scared?"

"I just don't want to."

"You're a pussy, Leno. Sit here and jerk off for all I care."

Lenny listened to the angry crunch of his brother's footsteps as Kirk stalked toward the train car. He forgot about the match in his hand, and it sizzled down to the nub and scorched his thumb. He cursed.

"Get the bitch inside," he heard Kirk call.

Guilt ate a hole in Lenny's stomach. His body ached to go with the others. He wanted her so badly, but his brain screamed at him, *Stop this! Save her!* He dreamed of clawing the other boys away from her and rescuing her like a hero. It was a stupid dream. Lenny was no hero. He sat and did nothing. He squeezed his eyes shut and tightened his hands into fists. He wanted it to be over and done. He wanted it to end.

He had Olivia's cell phone in his hand. It vibrated and rang in his palm, playing a song by Lady Gaga. "Bad Romance." Her father was calling, hunting for his daughter. He let the call go to voice mail. He flipped open the phone and stared at a photo of Olivia on the screen saver. It was a serious photo; she was in profile to the camera, hair blowing across her face, eyes closed. He flicked his thumb to look at her other photos and recognized most of the faces. Kimberly Magnus, laughing for the camera, even though she was bony and bald. Tanya Swenson, up to her neck in the Spirit River. Picture after picture of Johan Magnus, as if he were a *GQ* model. Johan in a black leather jacket in the corn fields. Johan posed on the railway bridge in St. Croix. Johan near the slats of the church bell tower, with divided sunlight making stripes on his face.

And then, Olivia herself. Naked. She was in her bedroom; Lenny recognized it. She must have used a tripod. She stood near the window overlooking the river, with darkness behind her. She was skinny, and her skin was china white. She had small rose nipples on the tips of her breasts. Her mound was curly and light brown. She stared into the camera with her mouth slightly open in a clumsy attempt at seduction. Her eyes had a fragile innocence. He didn't know what boy had received the photo, but he could guess. It was Johan. He wondered if Olivia was still a virgin or if she had let the minister's son make love to her.

Seeing her nude felt private and intimate, but he couldn't enjoy it—not when she was so close to him, in the old train car. Crying. Resisting. Fighting back against the boys intent on mauling and punishing her. He knew she couldn't see. She could only feel them holding her down. It was seven against one, but she struggled like a warrior. Still fighting. Not giving in. The battle was so ferocious that Lenny could hear the thump of her body slamming on the steel floor of the car.

She was being destroyed.

Stop this!

His thumb hovered over the phone. He caressed it, leaving sweat on the keys. He squeezed the green telephone button with his thumb, and the most recent call on the caller ID, which was simply labeled "Dad" popped up. He hesitated. If Kirk found out, his brother would beat him senseless. Lenny was terrified of Kirk's explosive temper. When Ashlynn dumped him, Kirk had given Lenny three broken ribs and a dislocated jaw.

He listened. Olivia still fought the boys, but soon there would be no more struggle, no more resistance. There would only be silence and surrender. He couldn't bear to hear it. Not from her.

Lenny pushed the call button.

Christopher Hawk answered on the first ring. "*Olivia?*"

"She's in the railroad boneyard south of Barron," he whispered, disguising his voice. "Hurry."

Chris heard the police sirens wailing, getting closer and louder as they converged on the hideaway where Olivia was being held. He turned off the northbound highway, but as he bumped across an unsigned railway crossing, two trucks ran him off the dirt road. Their high beams blinded him, and mud splashed across his windshield. He could have turned and chased them, but he had to make a life-or-death bet, and he bet that these boys would have left Olivia behind in a race to save their own necks.

He let them escape.

He sped into the abandoned rail yard, which sprawled over several hundred yards of parallel tracks. His headlights lit up decaying shells of freight cars, painted with stripes of orange and red. They'd been gutted; some were overturned. Other train cars lingered on weed-covered tracks, as if they had been dropped there and forgotten. Swirls of spray paint marked the metal walls. The ground was strewn with railway ties and broken glass. The railroad had moved elsewhere and left its detritus to rot.

He drove into the heart of the ruins. The land around him was flat and huge. He was surrounded by dozens of train cars, like a cemetery for giants. He got out and took Glenn Magnus's flashlight with him.

"Olivia!" he shouted. He listened for any sound, any clue, to where she was. He shouted her name again. "Olivia!"

Chris followed the nearest tracks, swinging the flashlight ahead of him. He wiped rain from his eyes. At each train car, he pointed the light inside the hollowed-out windows, illuminating garbage and rats. He looked for tire tracks from the trucks, but the gravel was so rutted and uneven that nothing looked fresh. He called again, but Olivia didn't answer.

Distantly, above the growing scream of the sirens, he heard music. What the hell was it? It stopped, and then it started again, and then it stopped. He realized the music was a ringtone for a cell phone, but it went silent before he could pinpoint its location. He stepped across more tracks, cutting between hulking slabs of corrugated metal. He thought to himself, *Whoever called me used Olivia's phone.* He yanked out his own phone and dialed his daughter's number. He held his breath, waiting.

The music began again, not even thirty yards away, an annoying staccato beat. He shifted the flashlight in that direction like a spotlight and ran. The music got louder, and he saw the phone, dropped in the gravel, glinting in hot pink as the beam found it. He stood directly over the phone and spun in a circle, lighting up the ground, looking for her.

"Olivia!"

The sirens became a deafening roar as half a dozen squad cars rumbled off the dirt road. Headlights crisscrossed the boneyard. He was happy to have the police here, but he wanted silence to hear his daughter answer his cries. If she was conscious. If she could call to him. He checked inside two passenger cars, shining his light through dirty, cracked windows. A police searchlight caught him in its glare like an escaping prisoner, and two voices shouted at him. He squinted into the beam and waved them closer. "Here! Over here!"

Chris saw another freight car set apart from the others at the end of a track circle. It was untouched by the elements, with riveted steel walls. The only access was a small rectangular hole at the rear of the car. In the glow of the flashlight, something on the ground near the tracks caught his eye. It was a Nike shoe. Pink, like the phone.

Olivia's shoe.

He sprinted. At the freight car, he used the metal handrail to pull himself onto the bumper near the access hole. He cast the light into the dark interior. Blankets lined the floor. He saw bottles of beer and porn magazines. With his head and shoulders thrust inside, he smelled a powerful sweet aroma of marijuana, concentrated in the closed space. He swung the light, seeing torn clothes strewn around the interior. Fragments of a T-shirt. Jeans. Socks. Panties ripped in half.

He heard a low moan, and he snapped the light toward it. There she was. His baby girl.

Chris reared backward from the car. He was bathed in the tunnels of numerous searchlights, and when he shielded his eyes, he saw half a dozen shadows racing toward him. He waved both hands frantically.

"Over here! She's in here!"

He threw himself inside the freight car. The metal floor rumbled and boomed as he crawled toward Olivia, who was on her back, ten feet away. Her eyes were closed. Her long brown hair covered most of her face. Her body was badly bruised and scratched, but he saw no blood on her skin. When he touched her shoulder, she kicked spastically, her fists beat against his chest. She was too weak to hurt him.

Chris wrapped her up gently in his arms. He pulled a blanket over her skin to warm her. "Shhh," he whispered as he held her. "I'm here, it's all right."

She struggled, but she had little fight left. He hung on, hearing voices, seeing the beams of light invade the freight car. He stroked Olivia's hair and continued to whisper to her softly, reassuring her. Help was coming. Help was close. She was safe. It was over.

He didn't tell her what was really in his heart. The raw intensity of the emotion churning in his body scared him and tasted like acid in his mouth. It was hatred. He wanted nothing but revenge against the boys who had done this to his child. He wanted their throats in his hands. He wanted them dead.

Hatred.

That was the real disease spreading through this town, and he'd caught it. He wasn't an outsider anymore. He was part of the war.

15

It was four in the morning.

Hannah had drifted to sleep, but Chris stared into space, unable to close his eyes. The hospital was dark and hushed around them. Nurses talked in the hallway in low voices while the patients slept. He sipped bad coffee from a foam cup and listened to the ticking of the wall clock. His body hurt, and he needed a shower.

Outside the visitor's lounge, the elevator dinged. When the doors slid open, Michael Altman stepped out, looking neat and alert despite the late hour. The county attorney had his raincoat slung over his arm, and he carried a large cardboard box. His fedora was low on his forehead. He spotted Chris on the sofa and nodded to him.

Chris detached himself from Hannah, who had slouched against his shoulder. He met Altman in the hallway and pulled the lounge door shut behind him.

Altman spoke in a low voice. "How is Olivia?"

"Stable. She's sleeping now."

"What's the extent of her injuries?"

Chris took a slow breath to calm himself. "She's in better shape than I feared. She's pretty beaten up, but there are no broken bones and no concussion or head injury."

"I hate to ask, but—"

"If they were planning to rape her, they didn't get that far."

"I'm relieved to hear it," Altman told him, "and I'm very sorry about all of this. What about Johan Magnus?"

"He has a couple bruised ribs, and he's got a black eye. He'll need dental work; two molars are loose. He's a tough kid, though. He wanted to go home, but the doctors insisted he stay. They're running tests to make sure there are no internal injuries."

Altman shook his head. "This is infuriating. This violence has to stop."

Chris said nothing, and the county attorney read his expression with sharp eyes. "I hope you know better than to get involved in this yourself, Mr. Hawk. I don't need any more vigilantes."

"This didn't happen to your daughter," Chris said.

"I understand, but you need to let me and the police do our jobs."

Chris was too tired to hide his sarcasm. "How's that been working out for you lately?"

"We will catch them, Mr. Hawk," Altman insisted. "The train car is a trove of evidence. The boys left in a hurry. We'll get DNA and fingerprints."

"Start with Kirk Watson."

Altman looked uncomfortable. "We did."

"And?"

"Kirk and his brother have a house on the river south of town. It's not far from the railway yard. He says he was home all evening, and three girls vouched for his whereabouts."

"They're lying."

"Very likely. We'll try to break his alibi. If we can identify any of the other boys who were involved, we can turn them on each other. It will happen, but it will take time."

Time meant days. Weeks. Months. Chris was already cynical about law enforcement in Barron. He rubbed his hands over his face, feeling his exhaustion.

"You need sleep," Altman told him.

"Someday." He eyed the box that Altman was carrying. "What's that?"

The county attorney bent at the knees and laid the box on the floor. "I promised you copies of the documentation we've gathered in the investigation so far."

"You're efficient."

"I told you, I don't play games. We can arrange for you to review the physical evidence, too." He added, "As painful as it is, I hope you realize this incident doesn't change Olivia's legal situation. I'll still be proceeding to a grand jury indictment."

"I assumed you would."

"It may take more time, however."

"I appreciate it."

Chris thought about asking Altman about the autopsy results. The abortion. The triangle involving Olivia, Johan, and Ashlynn. He assumed Altman knew about all of those things, but he didn't want to risk opening a window that was closed to the opposition.

"Tanya Swenson told me that Ashlynn dated Kirk last year," Chris said. "Florian denied it. Do you know if it's true?"

"I don't, but what difference does that make?"

"Kirk's a bad actor. If Ashlynn dumped him, he had a motive to kill her."

"There's no evidence he was at the scene."

"Not yet," Chris said. "Did you review the evidence gathered from Ashlynn's Mustang?"

Altman nodded. "Of course."

"I saw the car when I went to see Florian at Mondamin. Something bothered me when I looked inside. I figured out what it was."

"What?"

"Mud," Chris said.

"Excuse me?"

"There was mud on the driver's seat."

"So? It's been raining around here for weeks."

"Yes, but Tanya says that Olivia pushed Ashlynn in the park that night. Ashlynn fell. She got mud on her clothes."

"I'm not following you."

"Maybe Ashlynn tracked that mud back to her car. If Olivia left Ashlynn in the ghost town—alive—what would Ashlynn do? She'd go back to her car and wait. Then someone else arrived. Someone who killed her."

"That's an interesting theory, Mr. Hawk, but Ashlynn's body was found in the park, exactly where Olivia confronted her. If she went back to her car, why wasn't she killed there? The more likely explanation is that the dirt on the seat of the Mustang was days old."

Chris frowned. Altman was right. He couldn't explain why Ashlynn would have gone back to the park. Even so, the mud in the car raised a doubt, and doubt to a lawyer was like a dripping faucet. Eventually, drip by drip, it made a flood.

Altman put a hand on Chris's shoulder. "Get some sleep, Mr. Hawk."

"I'll try."

"I meant what I said. I'm sorry about Olivia, and I will do everything I can to catch the boys who did this."

"Thank you."

"I also meant the part about staying out of it. Revenge doesn't give you a free pass for violence."

"Message received," Chris said.

Altman returned to the elevator, leaving Chris alone in the hospital hallway. He watched the doors close. With Altman gone, he left the evidence box on the floor and wandered toward the first patient room beyond the nurse's station. From the doorway, he watched Olivia in bed, asleep, at peace. Her face was angelic. She bore no scars on the outside. It was her head and heart that worried him.

He needed fresh air. He returned to the hallway and hoisted the evidence box on his shoulder. Inside the elevator, he sagged against the rear wall and closed his eyes, and for a second or two, he slept. The opening of the doors on the first floor jarred him. He shook himself and exited into the hospital lobby. Outside, the night was cool and the rain had stopped, but the air was damp. His Lexus was parked at the back of the lot, facing a grassy field. He carried the box to his car, popped the trunk, and deposited it inside. Tomorrow, he would review what the police had found, looking for more evidence. More doubt. Drip by drip.

Chris slammed the trunk. He saw no cars on the streets, and there were no lights in the nearby houses. The town of Barron was quiet. Even so, he felt as if a voyeur were watching him. It was a strange, uncomfortable sensation. He studied the parked cars in the hospital lot, but he was alone. He looked across the street to the dark field, which was buried in shadows. If anyone was there, he was invisible.

He was about to return to the hospital when he noticed something under the windshield wiper of his car. It hadn't been there when he parked. He assumed it was the kind of annoying advertisement that sandwich shops placed on cars on the Minneapolis streets, but when he plucked it from the windshield, he saw that it was an envelope. Nothing was written on the outside. It wasn't sealed.

Chris slid a single sheet of paper from the interior, and when he unfolded it, he looked up sharply, staring into the empty darkness around him. He hadn't been wrong. He wasn't alone.

He read the black printed letters on the page.

TO THE ATTENTION OF

MR. CHRISTOPHER HAWK

YOU HAVE SUFFERED TONIGHT

YOU ARE IN A WORLD

WHOSE EVIL IS BEYOND SALVATION

YOU ARE IN A WORLD

THAT WILL SOON BE DESTROYED

LET THIS BE YOUR WARNING

THERE WILL BE NO ESCAPE

IF YOU STAY YOU WILL DIE

MY NAME IS

AQUARIUS

PART TWO
THE DEAD LAND

IN THE EARLY MORNING HOURS, CHRIS FOUND THE MINISTER'S SON, Johan, awake and alone in his hospital room. The teenager sat up in bed, staring out the window at the pre-dawn darkness and using an incentive spirometer for deep breathing. It was obviously painful, and he winced as he inhaled. Seeing Chris, Johan put the device aside. His face bore the welts and bruises of the beating he'd taken, but the wary demeanor that Chris had observed when he first met Johan at the motel had softened.

"Mr. Hawk, I'm really sorry," Johan told him.

Chris pulled a chair next to the bed. "Why are you sorry?"

"It's my fault. I couldn't stop them."

"There was one of you against half a dozen or more of them," he told the boy. "Don't blame yourself."

Johan rolled his head back. His fingers curled together into fists. "Those bastards."

Chris saw in the boy what he'd felt in himself the previous night. It was so easy, so tempting, to be consumed by hatred in this town. Marco Piva at the motel had said the same thing. Everyone wants revenge.

"I'd like to ask you some questions, Johan, if you're up to it."

"Okay."

"It's about you and Ashlynn," he said.

The teenager didn't look surprised. "I figured people were going to find out sooner or later."

"You were involved with Ashlynn, weren't you?" Chris asked.

"Yeah."

"Was it serious?"

"Yeah. Very."

"Who knew about it?"

"Almost nobody. It wasn't safe, you know? My Dad knew. Ashlynn told her mom. That was it. We didn't tell anybody else."

"What about Olivia?"

Johan hesitated. "Yeah, she found out," he admitted. "She saw us together. She was really upset."

"Why? Because of Kimberly?"

"Not just that." The boy hooded his eyes. "She was—well, she was really jealous."

Chris was confused, and then he realized he'd missed the answer that was staring him in the face. *Something personal.* A teenage triangle. Boy, girl, girl. That was why Olivia hated Ashlynn so much. Olivia loved Johan.

"Did you and Olivia have a relationship, too?" he asked.

"Yeah. Last summer."

"Did you break up with her because of Ashlynn?"

"Look, Mr. Hawk, I never meant—"

Chris held up his hands to stop him. "I'm not playing the outraged father here. I just want the truth."

He saw genuine conflict in Johan's face. "Olivia thought so, but that's not how it happened. I really care for Olivia a lot, but we're so different. She thinks religion is a waste of time, and me, well, it's a big part of my life. There were lots of things like that, where we just didn't see life the same way. The more we dated, the more I began to realize we didn't have that much in common. The one thing we did have was Kimberly, but you can't build a relationship around losing someone, right?"

"That's true."

"I tried to tell her that, but she said she loved me. She was really hurt."

"What about you and Ashlynn? How did that happen? You two were on opposite sides of a pretty big divide."

Johan looked uncomfortable, as if he was reluctant to share the secret even though Ashlynn was dead. "We met at church."

"In St. Croix?" Chris was surprised.

"Yeah. Ashlynn started coming to see my dad."

"Ashlynn was visiting *Glenn*?"

Johan nodded.

"When was this?"

"About six months ago."

"Why?"

Johan swung his legs over the side of the bed. Gingerly, he got up. He walked with a slight limp, but he was a fit teenager and was already bouncing back from his injuries. He crossed the hospital room and closed the door. "It was very secret. She didn't want anyone to know."

"I'm sure."

"The thing is, Ashlynn hated what the feud was doing to this area. She was heartbroken about the kids who died, too. She felt guilty, because of who she was. She wanted to reach out, so she began to visit my dad. At first, she just wanted to tell him how sorry she was about Kimberly and how bad she felt. Then she started getting religious counseling, too."

"How did your relationship with her develop?"

"I'd help her get to and from the church, because she didn't want anyone seeing her car in St. Croix. We talked for hours. Sometimes all night. She visited me at the motel, too, when I was working. I realized how amazing she was. Not just pretty—she was also this incredible person. I knew things weren't working out with Olivia, and after we broke up, Ashlynn and I started talking about how we felt about each other. It was serious."

"How serious?" Chris asked.

"We were in love."

"Were you having sex?"

"Does that matter?" Johan asked.

"Actually, it does. I'm sorry."

Johan looked at the floor. "Ashlynn was a virgin. She didn't like the idea of sex before marriage. I'd had sex before. I mean, Olivia and I—that is, we had—"

"I get it," Chris said. "Did you and Ashlynn eventually have sex?"

The teenager nodded. "After a few months, we decided we were ready for it. We'd already been talking about getting married after school. It felt right."

Chris heard regret in Johan's voice. "Was it a mistake?"

"I guess."

"What do you mean?"

"Ashlynn got really distant after we did it. I could tell it was bothering her. I apologized, but she didn't want to talk. Then, like a month ago, she texted me that we should stop seeing each other. I couldn't believe it. I thought she loved me."

"Did she say why she wanted to break it off?"

"She said things were moving too fast. That's it."

"Nothing else?"

"No."

Chris waited for Johan to talk about the pregnancy. The abortion. He studied the teenager's face and saw nothing but confusion. Johan was telling the truth about being in the dark. He didn't know what was really happening to Ashlynn. For whatever reason, Ashlynn had chosen to go through this on her own. She had turned to Hannah for guidance. Not Johan. Not Glenn Magnus. Not her own parents.

"Tanya told me Ashlynn dated Kirk Watson last year," Chris said. "Is that true?"

"Kirk," Johan snapped, his lip curling. "That vicious son of a bitch. He did this to Olivia. It was him."

"Do you know that for a fact?"

"No, but none of the Barron boys do anything without his say-so."

"What about Kirk and Ashlynn?" Chris asked again.

"There was nothing between them. They went out a few times. That was it. She cut him off at the knees when he wanted more."

"He doesn't seem like her type," Chris said.

"He wasn't."

"So why did she go out with him at all?"

"I don't know. She didn't want to talk about it."

"Is it possible something happened between them?"

Johan's eyes narrowed. "What do you mean?"

"Could Kirk have assaulted her?"

"He's capable of anything, but I think she would have told me if he did."

"Did Kirk know you and Ashlynn were involved?"

"I don't think so. If he knew, he would have done something."

"Maybe he did," Chris said. "Maybe he killed her."

Johan said nothing. Chris could see in his face that the boy had already leaped to a totally different conclusion about Ashlynn's death. Like everyone else, he assumed Olivia was guilty.

"How did Olivia find out about you and Ashlynn?" Chris asked.

"She saw us parked near the town. We were—we were kissing. She confronted me about it."

"What did she say?"

"She accused me of cheating on her. I told her that Ashlynn and I didn't start seeing each other until after I broke up with her. She didn't believe me. She called Ashlynn some terrible things. It was ugly."

"When did this happen?" he asked.

"Right before Christmas."

"And since then?"

"She hasn't really talked to me."

"So what happened the night of Ashlynn's murder?"

Johan paled. "What do you mean?"

"I mean, Olivia was arrested for shooting Ashlynn, and the first thing she did when she was released was go to see you. Even though she hadn't talked to you in months. Why?"

The teenager glanced at the closed door. "I don't think you want to ask me about this, Mr. Hawk. I don't want to make it worse for Olivia."

"It's already bad." He added, "Where were you on Friday night?"

"There was a big plumbing problem in one of the motel rooms. Water everywhere. I was helping Marco until after midnight. He finally called a plumber. They didn't need me sticking around, so I left."

"You went home?"

"Yeah."

"Did Olivia come to see you?"

Johan nodded reluctantly. "Yeah, she did."

"When?"

"Late. After one. She came to my window."

"What did she tell you?"

"She told me what happened in the ghost town. About finding Ashlynn there. About—the gun. She said Ashlynn told her that we had broken up, and she wanted to know why I hadn't said anything. She wanted to get back together."

"What did you say?" Chris asked.

"It didn't go well. I was furious with Olivia for treating Ashlynn like that. I couldn't believe she left her stranded there. Olivia got upset, and she stormed off."

"What did you do?" Chris asked, but there was only one thing that a boy like Johan would do. He went out there. He went to rescue Ashlynn.

"I drove to the ghost town," he said.

Chris waited.

"She was dead," Johan murmured, his face contorting in pain as heavy breaths squeezed his chest. "All I could think was: Olivia killed her. She left her there in the mud for me to find. I hated her for it. I didn't know what to do."

"What time was this?" Chris asked, dodging the boy's emotions.

"Between one-thirty and two, I guess."

"Did you see anyone else around?"

"No."

"Did you touch anything on the scene? Did you move the body? Did you touch her car?"

"No, no, nothing like that."

"What did you do?"

"I left." He added, "As bad as it was, I didn't want to tell anyone, Mr. Hawk. I didn't want to do that to Olivia. I'd already hurt her enough. I couldn't believe she would do something so horrible, but I was willing to keep it a secret. I still am. I won't tell a soul."

"It's too late for that," Chris said.

He didn't tell Johan the truth, because the truth was cruel. Keeping silent until now was the best thing the boy could have done to help Olivia. Keeping silent was what guilty people did. Lying to the police was what guilty people did. When Johan told his story now, he established for the whole world that there was someone else who had been in the park with Ashlynn *after* Olivia. Someone who knew her, who had been involved with her, whose heart she had broken. Someone of deep faith whose child she had terminated in her womb. Someone who hadn't been tested for gunshot residue that night.

Another suspect.

Johan.

CHRIS WAS DROWNING.

He felt himself carried on the shoulders of turbulent waters in his dream, surrounded by debris, caught in an undertow that sucked him down like a whirlpool. Each time he broke through the surface, gasping for breath, he spun in circles. He wasn't alone. Hannah was with him in the water, reaching for him with her hand in the gesture that had always said *I love you*. They were sinking together, dragged down by the sheer muscle of the rapids. The river carried them toward a bridge, where Chris flailed for the steel I beam over his head like a lifeline. He held on, and Hannah held onto him, but the water wrenched his fingers away and washed them downstream. As the bridge vanished behind them, he saw the silhouette of a man on the span, watching the flood overpower them. His voice boomed like the voice of God.

"*My name is Aquarius.*"

Chris bolted upright in the motel bed. He checked the clock on the nightstand and saw that he had slept for two hours. It was nearly ten in the morning. Sunshine streamed through a crack in the curtains, and dust floated in the light. He blinked, shaking off his dream. He got up and turned on the shower. The hot water revived him. When he was dressed, he stepped outside into the motel parking lot and found a beautiful day. The rain and clouds had moved east, and the temperature was still unseasonably warm. It made the previous night seem almost unreal.

He stopped at the motel office to pour a cup of weak coffee from a silver thermos and grab a powdered doughnut from an open Little Debbie's box. That was Marco's idea of a continental breakfast. He ate two doughnuts and wiped the white sugar from his mouth. He spotted the local newspaper on the motel counter, and he picked it up to read the Barron headlines. To his dismay, he and Olivia were on the front page. A reporter had snapped their photo coming out of the courthouse after the detention hearing. They both looked wet and guilty. In contrast, Ashlynn Steele's yearbook picture, which the paper printed next to the courthouse photo, was perfect and pretty. The accompanying article speculated on the likelihood that Olivia would be tried as an adult for Ashlynn's murder. It was more poison for the jury pool.

Michael Altman was on the front page, too, but he was talking about a different investigation. The county attorney offered details of a recent arrest in the Twin Cities suburb of Hugo, in which a police search related to embezzlement by a city worker had unearthed a trove of child pornography. The stash included a flash drive of videos mailed with a postmark from the Minnesota town of Ortonville, which was an hour northwest of Barron. Altman sought the public's help in identifying those involved in trafficking child porn in Spirit County.

Chris thought about what Hannah had said: *This isn't Mayberry.* No, it wasn't. The idyll of small-town life was an illusion.

"Mr. Hawk."

Chris put down the newspaper. Marco Piva stood behind the counter, his fleshy Italian face grim. "Mr. Hawk, there are no words."

"Thank you, Marco."

"How is your daughter?"

"She'll be okay. I'm going back to the hospital to see her now."

"When I heard the news, I fell on my knees and prayed for both of you," Marco said.

"I appreciate that."

"Do the police know who did this terrible thing?"

"They're investigating. Sometimes you know who did it, but you can't prove it. I'm worried this could be one of those times."

Marco studied Chris long and hard across the counter. His black mustache twitched as he frowned. "I see something in your face, Mr. Hawk."

"What's that?"

"Anger. It is a dangerous thing."

"I'm just tired."

"No, no, that's not it. I understand, my friend. I know anger. I'm still angry about losing my wife, but for you, it's your child, your own flesh and blood. Something has been taken from you, and you don't know how to get it back. You want to rage against the world."

"Banging my head against a wall gives me a headache," Chris said.

"I know, but we're men. We bang our heads anyway."

He managed a smile. "You're a wise man, Marco."

"Wise men can be the most foolish. We ask, is it better to do nothing in the face of injustice or do the wrong thing?"

"I don't like doing nothing," Chris said.

"That's what worries me. I like you, Mr. Hawk. You seem like a solid man, and that's the highest praise I can offer. Doing nothing is like surrendering for men like us. However, it's one thing if you're alone in this world like me. You—you have a daughter. Remember that."

"I do."

"You remind me of a friend in San Jose," Marco told him. "He had a daughter, like you. Married. Two kids. Beautiful girl. Unfortunately, her job took her to one of those Indian casinos in the desert. Those gaming places, they prey on people. This girl started gambling, and it took over her life. She lost her job. Her house. It broke up her marriage. Terrible."

"I'm so sorry," Chris said.

Marco wagged a finger at him. "My friend banged his head against the wall until it was bloody. He wanted justice."

"I'm not sure I want to know," Chris said, "but what did he do?"

"He drove out to the desert, and he waited in the parking lot for two of the tribal leaders to come out. Then he shot them both in the head."

"That was a bad choice," Chris said.

"Yes, it was. He's in jail, and he'll never get out. But I think when he sleeps, he still sees those bodies on the ground, and I bet you he smiles about it."

"You sound like you're defending him."

The motel owner shook his head. "Oh, no, no, don't think that at all. I'm saying I understand him. I know what he went through. I know what you're going through, too, Mr. Hawk. Sometimes choices are easy. Sometimes they are hard."

Marco slid open the top drawer of the desk behind the counter. Inside was a revolver with a wooden grip and a two-inch barrel. He removed the gun from the drawer and laid it on the counter next to a scattering of reservation forms and a glass jar stocked with spiky white candies. "We all have to be careful these days, don't we?" he asked.

"Yes, we do."

Marco took a handkerchief from the pocket of his pants and carefully wiped the surfaces of the gun, rubbing them clean with firm buffing of the cloth. The butt. The barrel. The hammer. The revolver was fully loaded, and he opened the cylinder and wiped each cartridge, too, before replacing them. "I keep a gun for safety," he said. "People don't often get robbed here, but you never know. There are vagrants everywhere who make a point of seeking out deserted motels like this. A loaded revolver gives me peace of mind."

Chris said nothing.

Marco opened the drawer again, placed the gun inside, and replaced the handkerchief in his pocket. "Of course, guns have been known to be stolen. Who knows, a guest sees what I keep in my drawer, and I turn my back, and it's gone. Things like that happen. What can I do?"

He slid the drawer shut. His eyes were dark and meaningful.

"I will keep praying for you, Mr. Hawk," Marco told him. "When you see your daughter, you hug her to your chest, okay? Keep her safe, and make sure she always has her father to look after her."

Marco disappeared into the living room behind the office and shut the door, leaving Chris alone. The only noise was the hum of the old house fan, rattling as its blades turned.

Do nothing or do the wrong thing.

Chris was shocked by how quickly he made the decision. Some choices are hard, some are easy. He leaned his chest across the counter, opened the drawer with his long arm, and took Marco's gun.

18

"I DON'T REMEMBER BEING IN THE TRAIN CAR," OLIVIA TOLD HIM. "I was in the back of a truck, and they were holding me down. Then it's like the film stops, you know? I woke up here."

Chris sat beside the hospital bed and stroked her hair with the back of his fingers. He remembered caressing her that way when she was a child, as she sat on his lap and he read to her from Curious George books until she fell asleep on his chest. "It happens that way sometimes," he said.

She stared at him, and her eyes were dead serious. "So what am I blocking out?"

"An assault you didn't deserve," he said.

"The doctor said I wasn't raped. Is that a lie? I don't want anybody protecting me like I'm a kid."

"Doctors don't lie about that kind of thing."

"I want to remember what happened," she said.

"Why?"

"I don't like my brain hiding stuff."

"Well, when your brain figures it's safe to remember, you'll remember. Until then, focus on getting your strength back."

Olivia nodded. "Sorry," she added.

"For what?"

"For sneaking out. Mom must be pissed."

Chris took her hand. Her grip was firm, but her skin was clammy. The hospital room was uncomfortably warm. "The only thing we care about is that you're safe."

"Can I get out of here now? I'm sick of being poked and prodded."

"Maybe tomorrow. The doctors want to keep you around for a little while." Chris added, "Your mother called a friend of hers in Mankato. A counselor. She's going to drive up here and talk to you this afternoon."

"I don't want to see a shrink."

"Give her a chance."

"I already said I don't remember."

"Just talk to her, okay?"

Olivia shrugged. "Okay. If you say so."

Chris wondered how much of her bravery was real and how much was an act. "After you get out, how would you like to go see my sister? Aunt Jennie has that great place outside Little Rock. You and she could hang out for a couple of months and have some girl time."

"What about the murder trial?" Olivia asked.

"There's a lot of legal stuff that has to be done first. Given what happened, I can get the court's permission for you to stay with her."

Olivia shook her head. "No. I won't run away."

"That's not what I'm talking about," Chris said.

"Sure it is, and I won't do it. I'm not going anywhere."

Chris didn't fight her. He would have preferred that Olivia stay far away from Barron, but he was learning what Hannah had discovered years earlier. His daughter was every bit as stubborn as her mother.

Olivia played with the steel railing of the bed, tapping on it with her chipped nails. "I suppose you know, huh?"

"Know what?"

"About me and Johan."

"I talked to him," Chris admitted. "He told me about you two. And about Ashlynn."

"How is he? Is he okay?"

"He'll be fine."

"Can I see him? Where is he?"

"Olivia, it would be better if you didn't talk to him for a while, until we get your legal situation straightened out."

"What does that mean?"

"It means you're both witnesses in a murder investigation, and witnesses shouldn't talk to each other."

Olivia's lower lip bulged unhappily. "You think he was the one who killed her, don't you?"

"What do you think?"

"Johan wouldn't do that."

"If that's true, why were you protecting him?" Chris said. "You didn't tell me that you talked to him that night. That sounds to me like you think he did it."

"All I know is Ashlynn was alive when I left her," Olivia said. "When I heard she was dead, I thought—well, I knew Johan would go out to the ghost town to rescue her."

Chris nodded. "Yes, he did. He said she was dead when he got there."

"You don't believe him?"

"I don't know, but it sounds like Ashlynn broke his heart. I think people, even good people, can do things they regret in the heat of the moment." He paused. "You had a motive, too, Olivia. You should have told me about it. The police will think you hated Ashlynn because she took away your boyfriend, and that's why you shot her."

Olivia sighed. "She did steal Johan from me. I'm not going to pretend I wasn't angry."

He didn't like to hear her confessing emotions that made her look guilty, but he also knew that she was finally being honest with him. He needed more details. He needed the whole story. "Do you feel strong enough to talk?" he asked.

"Yeah. I'm okay."

"Tell me the truth," he said. "What really happened between you and Ashlynn that night?"

Olivia lay back in bed. She didn't flinch. Her eyes drifted to the ceiling, and he could see her mind retreating. Remembering. She was standing in the mud of the park, alone in the ghost town with Ashlynn. Her anger was raging. The gun was in her hand.

One.
Two.
Three.

The count went on in Olivia's head—four, five, six, seven—but she couldn't pull the trigger. It was like jumping from a bridge; there was no going back once your feet left the ground. She couldn't do it. She couldn't go that far. She cursed under her breath and took a step backward. The gun felt like a foreign thing, ugly, heavy, and unwanted. She spread her fingers and let it drop to the wet ground.

Ashlynn opened her eyes. Fear became confusion, then relief. "Thank you," *she murmured.*

Olivia didn't want to look at Ashlynn. Seeing her perfect face brought back all of the envy, all of the loss. It was no mystery why Johan had chosen her. Who wouldn't? The blonde cheerleader over the nerdy brunette. The full, ripe breasts over the little-boy chest. The curves instead of skin and bones.

"You were with him tonight, weren't you?" Olivia asked. "Don't lie to me."

"No, I wasn't. Honestly."

Olivia didn't know whether to believe her, but it didn't matter. It didn't change anything.

"I know you think I took him away from you," Ashlynn went on, "but I didn't. Really. I would never have let anything happen between us while the two of you were involved."

"You think that helps?"

"I guess not."

"I hate you both," Olivia snapped.

"I'm sorry you feel that way, Olivia. I know I can't change it, but I'm sorry."

"I don't want your sympathy. I lost Kimberly, and I lost Johan. You don't know what it feels like."

"I've lost something even worse."

"Like what?"

"It doesn't matter. It's my problem, not yours."

"I'm leaving," Olivia said.

"Please, wait. At least give me a ride home, okay? We don't have to talk. Just drop me off."

It was the right thing to do. Olivia knew that. She thought about saying yes, but some favors went too far. Taking Ashlynn in her car. Chauffeuring her to the house where her father lived. Pretending her own hurt meant nothing.

"No," she said.

Ashlynn's voice cracked with despair. "Olivia, please, I need help tonight. It's hard to explain, but I really need your help."

"I can't do it," she said.

She turned on her heels and walked away, then stopped in frustration. She knew she was being mean to leave her alone. "I'll tell Johan you're here. He'll come get you."

"No! Don't do that!"

"Why not?"

"I can't see him." Ashlynn took a step toward Olivia, then grimaced and sat down on the swing. "I broke up with Johan a month ago. I told him I couldn't see him anymore."

"I don't believe you. He never said a word."

"It's true."

"Why did you do that?"

"It's complicated," she said. "Please."

Olivia wanted to believe her, but it was too easy to read the truth in her face. Ashlynn couldn't hide how she felt.

"You're a liar," she said. "You still love him."

Olivia stalked away without looking back. When she reached the street, she ran for her car, which was parked in a cornfield south of town. She left the gun where she had dropped it. She left Ashlynn alone.

"We all make choices we'd like to take back, Olivia," Chris murmured.

"I know. I was drunk, I was mad at her, I was mad at myself. If I'd just driven her home, she'd be alive."

He had nothing to say, because he couldn't make this better for her. When she was younger, he'd been able to fix the things that were broken in her life. Not now. Not anymore.

"What happened next?" he asked.

"I went home."

"Did you go see Johan?"

Olivia shook her head. Her hair fell across her face. "Not right away. I went to bed, but I was too upset to sleep. I thought about driving back there to get her, but I couldn't bring myself to do it."

Chris waited.

"Tanya called me," she went on. "She was all freaked out, shouting at me, wanting to know what happened. I told her that Ashlynn was fine. She went on and on, shouldn't we tell someone, shouldn't we go back and help her. So I got dressed and went to the church, and I told Johan what happened."

"What did he say?"

"He was angry with me for leaving her there."

"Did you ask him about the breakup?"

"Sure."

"Did he say it was true? Did he say Ashlynn ended their relationship?"

"Yeah, but I could see it in his face, just like hers. They still loved each other."

"Why did Ashlynn break it off?"

"He didn't know. He looked crushed."

"Do you think he could have killed her?"

"He loved her," she said with teary eyes. "More than he ever loved me. I can't imagine him killing her. It makes no sense."

"What if she did something he could never forgive?" Chris asked.

"Like what? I don't get it."

Chris watched her face, but she was genuinely at a loss. She didn't know. "Ashlynn was coming home from having an abortion," he told her. "I think the baby was Johan's."

Olivia turned ghostly pale. Her lower lip trembled, and her eyes grew huge. "I can't believe Ashlynn would do that. She was super-religious."

"She came to your mother," Chris said. "She didn't want her parents to know. She didn't want Johan to know, either."

"Oh, my God, I left her there. I just left her there. What did I do, Dad?"

"You had no way of knowing."

"She needed help, and I walked away."

"*Olivia.*" Chris grabbed her hand and cupped her chin with his other palm. "Listen to me. This is not your fault. You didn't do this."

He wished he could lift the guilt from her shoulders. He wished he could change the past. Some mistakes couldn't be corrected; they could only be endured.

"I need to know something," he went on. "Did Johan give you any indication at all that he knew Ashlynn was pregnant?"

She shook her head mutely.

"What would he have done if she told him, Olivia? What if he knew she'd ended it? Could he have been desperate enough to kill her?"

Olivia closed her eyes, as if she couldn't bear to answer, but she nodded her agreement. "It would have destroyed him," she whispered.

19

CHRIS BOUGHT A SANDWICH AND STROLLED ONTO THE FOOTBRIDGE ACROSS the Spirit River that connected downtown Barron with the park on the opposite shore. He stopped in the middle of the bridge and watched the brown water pushing south from the dam. He loosened the knot of his tie and undid the top button of his shirt. After two bites of a turkey sandwich, he decided that he wasn't hungry and rewrapped his lunch for later.

He heard footsteps on the bridge. A teenage boy shuffled from the town park with his head down and his hands in the pockets of beige corduroys. The boy was small, no more than five feet seven, and wiry. He wore an oversize Lil Wayne T-shirt that was badly tucked in at his waist. His brown hair was unruly and hung below his ears. His face was long with a pointy chin and dots of acne. On his right cheek, Chris saw two bandages taped together to cover all but the top and bottom edges of a long cut, which was still red and fresh.

The boy didn't notice Chris until they were practically on top of each other, and when he finally looked up, his eyes widened and he froze, like an animal sensing danger. Before Chris could say a word, the boy turned and fled, sprinting toward the opposite side of the river.

"Hey!" Chris shouted.

He charged in pursuit. His dress shoes slowed him down, and the kid was young and fast. The distance between them widened, but the teenager slipped as his sneakers hit a slick patch of grass. He flew into a somersault, feet over head, and landed on his back, splashing into the mud. As the kid scrambled to get up, Chris stopped him with a foot on his chest. He collared him and marched him to a weathered picnic bench.

"What the hell do you want?" the boy complained. "I didn't do anything. Let me go."

"Why did you run?"

"Because I know who you are, man."

"So?"

"So I've got nothing to say to you."

Chris sat down next to the teenager on the bench. "What's your name?"

"Lenny."

"Lenny who?"

"Lenny Watson."

Chris made the connection. "Kirk is your brother."

"Yeah, and if you lay a hand on me, he'll beat the shit out of you, man."

"I'm not going to hurt you, Lenny."

"Damn right you're not." The kid got up from the bench, but Chris yanked him down by his shoulder.

"Hang on," he said. "Let's talk."

"About what?"

"First of all, about that cut on your face. Where did you get it?"

"Broken glass."

"Yeah? How'd that happen?"

"I tripped," Lenny said.

"You're lucky you didn't lose an eye."

"Whatever. It hurts like hell."

Chris leaned forward and whispered, "You know what hurts worse than a scratch like that, Lenny? Being kidnapped and assaulted by a bunch of thugs. That hurts. That's something you carry with you your whole life." He didn't add, *If I find out you were one of them, I will kill you. First your brother, then you.*

Lenny paled. His face constricted. "Look, man, I know about Olivia. That was real awful what happened to her. I—I like her."

"If you like her, you'll help me catch the boys who did this," Chris told him.

Lenny twitched. "I don't know nothing, man."

"What about your brother? Were you with him last night?"

"Uh, yeah."

"Where?"

"Home, man."

"Where's home?"

"Kirk and me got a house right on the river off 120th."

"Who else was with you?"

"I don't know. Kirk had some girls over. He usually does."

Chris nodded. "The two of you live there by yourselves?"

"Yeah."

"So you weren't in that train yard last night?"

"No, man, no!"

He listened to the pitch of the teenager's voice and tried to remember the call from Olivia's cell phone the previous night. The voices were similar. That was all he could say.

"Someone called me last night," Chris said, "and told me where to find Olivia. Whoever did that probably saved her life. That's what a real man does. It's not someone who beats the hell out of defenseless girls."

"I told you, I hope she's okay."

"How well do you know her?" Chris asked.

"I see her around, that's all."

"Everybody around here thinks she killed Ashlynn," Chris said, "but I don't think she did."

Lenny shrugged. "Yeah, well, hope you're right."

"Do you have any idea who *did* kill Ashlynn?"

"Beats me."

"Someone told me your brother was dating Ashlynn, and she dumped him. Is that true?"

"What about it?"

"He must have been angry."

"Yeah, so what? If you think he killed her, you're wrong. He wouldn't touch her. Kirk would never do anything to Florian's daughter."

"Florian?" Chris asked. "What does Kirk have to do with Florian?"

Lenny looked as if he wanted to bite off his tongue. "Kirk works for him sometimes."

"What kind of work?"

"Security. Shit like that."

"What exactly does Kirk do? Kick the crap out of environmental protesters who get too close to the facility?"

Lenny fidgeted. He knew he'd said too much. "I don't know what he does, man."

Chris drew a dotted line in his head between Florian Steele and Kirk Watson, and he didn't like it. It made him wonder if Florian was more closely involved in the feud than he let on. It also made him wonder if Florian had some special interest in hiding the truth about what had happened to his daughter.

"Did Kirk mention anybody who was causing trouble for Florian? Anyone threatening him or his family?"

Lenny shook his head. "No."

"What about this guy Aquarius? Any idea who he is?"

"I don't have a clue." The boy fidgeted. "Man, I really have to get out of here. If anyone sees me talking to you, it's not good, okay?"

Chris nodded. "Okay, Lenny."

Lenny got up, and Chris didn't stop him. The teenager cast a suspicious eye around the park to make sure they were alone. He tugged at his wet clothes and headed for the Barron bridge, but Chris called after him.

"Hey, do me a favor, Lenny."

The boy stopped and looked back nervously. "What?"

"You say you like Olivia. If you hear about any trouble involving her, you do the right thing, okay?"

Lenny didn't respond, but he stared at his feet and gave the barest nod. Chris let him shuffle away. Somewhere inside Lenny was a decent kid, but he would always be doing the wrong thing to impress the wrong person. It was the way of the world. Chris thought about Olivia and realized that even sweet kids with parents who love them can make terrible mistakes.

Chris had made his own share of mistakes in life. Deep down, in the privacy of his conscience, he was thinking about making another one. He was conscious of the heaviness of Marco Piva's gun on the small of his back, where he had it tucked inside his belt.

He knew how to use it, and, thanks to Lenny, he knew where Kirk Watson lived.

20

KIRK WATSON SAT IN HIS PICKUP TRUCK THREE BLOCKS FROM THE POST office building in Madison, which was a fly-speck town twenty miles from Barron. He had the window rolled down, and he dangled a cigarette between his fingers. Toby Keith played on the radio. With his other hand, he used binoculars to watch the cars coming and going from the parking lot. People in, people out, nothing to worry about. Even so, he took his time and kept an eye on the traffic in the mirrors.

You couldn't be too careful.

That stupid son of a bitch in Hugo had gotten himself arrested on embezzlement charges, and then they'd found the stash of porn on his computer. The asshole wasn't even smart enough to destroy the envelope in which he'd received his last delivery. Thanks to him, feds were watching the post office in Ortonville now. Kirk had driven by the building earlier in the day, and there they were, in their sedan, in their suits, as obvious as Vegas hookers. That was why he stuck to the rules he'd made for himself. Always wear gloves. Never lick a stamp. Never use the same mailbox twice. Never buy materials in the same store. Use a prepaid phone, and keep it turned off between calls. Keep the house clean, because you never know when a cop will show up with a warrant.

When he was satisfied no one was watching, he drove down the rural street to the parking lot and got out of the truck. The town's co-op corn elevator towered in gleaming silver behind the post office. He leaned on his door, finishing his cigarette as he took a last, hawk-eyed look around the street. He crushed the butt on the asphalt, pulled his baseball cap low on his forehead, and went inside the red-brick building, avoiding the ceiling-mounted cameras. Damn government employees, snooping on everybody. Like terrorists would want to blow up the Lutefisk Capital of the USA.

He squatted at his PO box. There was junk mail inside, but stuffed among the coupons was the package he'd been expecting. It was the size of a greeting card and just slightly thicker where the flash drive was secreted inside. The foreign stamps showed paintings of purple flowers. On the back of the envelope, someone had written "Happy Bithday" in an awkward hand. Sometimes it read "Mery Christmass" or "I Love U." Stupid sentiments always deflected suspicion for anyone inclined to take a closer look.

He shoved the card in his back pocket and left the post office. He'd been inside less than thirty seconds. He headed south on Highway 75 into the desolate rural lands. He picked a dirt county road at random, turned east, and stopped on the shoulder. He got out of the truck, opened the envelope, and slid out the slim black USB flash drive from inside the greeting card. He flicked his cigarette lighter and incinerated the card and the envelope, letting them burn to ashes at his feet. After the fire was out, he scattered the ash with the sole of his boot.

That's what you do with deliveries, fucking Hugo man.

Kirk drove on the county road until he reconnected with the Barron highway. A mile from downtown, he reached the dirt road that led south toward the ghost town where Ashlynn had been killed. He didn't go as far as the deserted town. Instead, he turned at a driveway with a battered U-Stor sign. The driveway led to two rows of self-storage units in the middle of an old field.

His own unit was at the far end of the first row. He parked and snapped on gloves, then undid the heavy padlock on the metal door and threw the door upward on its track with a clang. Inside, he lowered the door again. When he was alone inside the windowless space, he pulled the string that lit up a single bare bulb.

This was his man cave. His business headquarters. His armory. Only Lenny knew about it, and he'd made it clear to his brother that he would bury a pick-ax in the kid's brain if he told anyone. The guy who owned the U-Stor lived in Marshall, which was an hour away. He didn't ask for identification, as long as he got his fee in cash. When you ran a storage business, you knew that people stored things behind those garage doors that they didn't want anyone else to find, and if you were smart, you didn't ask questions.

Kirk kept his guns there: almost a dozen pistols, mostly Rugers and Glocks bought from online dealers. A smaller number of revolvers. Two shotguns. Three hunting rifles. Ammunition in several dozen boxes on metal shelves. Solvents, oils, brushes, and rags. There was an abandoned farm near Hazel

Run where he practiced every month, and he was careful to collect his spent casings and dig his bullets out of the barn wall where he hung his targets. Whenever he needed a gun, he wanted it to be a virgin. Untraceable.

The revolver he'd used in St. Croix, shooting up Hannah Hawk's house, was already at the bottom of the lake behind the Spirit Dam.

He sat down behind a garage-sale desk and booted up his computer. He played with a burnt hole in the leather of the old chair through the finger of his glove. There wasn't a fingerprint to be found anywhere in the storage unit. He kept his long hair tucked under his cap to avoid leaving DNA samples. He always told Lenny, "*You don't even blow your nose in here, okay? Snort up your snot, and keep it there.*"

His own name and address couldn't be found anywhere inside the unit. Not on the computer. Not on an envelope or piece of paper. If the feds found this place, they couldn't tie it back to him. He was a ghost.

Kirk had to be careful. Prosecutors and judges played hardball with child porn, because it made great get-tough shit for the voters at reelection time. Get caught, and expect to give up twenty-five years, maybe more. This wasn't juvie time.

He removed the Vietnamese flash drive from his pocket and shoved it into one of the USB ports on the front of his computer. The drive contained four gigabytes of material, including hundreds of photos and videos. It was top-quality shit, hi-res, good close-ups. Everybody wanted the eyes; you had to see the eyes. He sifted through the photos and shook his head in disgust. This kind of sick shit did nothing for him; he was normal, not a fucking pervert. To him, it was about money, end of story. If he could have put a bullet in the head of every one of his customers, he would have done it. Once, with a problem customer in Mankato, he'd had to do just that. The guy had come down with a fit of conscience and threatened to call the cops. Most of the ones with conscience were fakers. They were like chain smokers, always taking one last cigarette and promising to quit. This one was different. Every now and then, you got a real reformed sinner.

The guy was a threat, but he didn't realize that Kirk knew who he was. That was his big mistake, thinking you could be a buyer of this shit and keep your secrets to yourself. Kirk had photos and video of all of his customers as a sort of insurance policy. It was leverage against bad things happening. He'd scouted every house, every office, every PO box, where he'd made a shipment, and he'd identified every buyer. They belonged to him. The guy in Mankato thought he could vanish and make an anonymous confession to the feds, but Kirk got to him first. Shot him in the head. Sanitized his apartment. Dumped his body near a crack house in south Minneapolis.

He'd sent a newspaper clipping about the murder to all of his other customers. It was an object lesson in keeping your mouth shut.

Kirk reviewed the flash drive, looking for a special folder. It was a custom order, like buying tiles for your kitchen floor or commissioning an artist to do a portrait of your wife. This was a service biz like anything else. You gave the customers what they wanted. If someone had a special request, they could have it. For a price. He found the folder and examined the files to make sure they met the specifications: the layout of the bedroom, the angle of the photos, the specific positions in the video. The devil was in the details. He didn't ask why the jerk-off wanted it this way, and he didn't care. He took the specs, and he delivered.

Kirk turned on his prepaid phone in order to make the call. He plugged in his voice changer to disguise his voice. There were four settings. You could sound like a robot, or an alien, or a sexy woman, but he always picked door number four. The little child's voice. He loved the joke. He loved twisting the knife.

The son of a bitch didn't know that Kirk was the dealer behind the business. Their relationship was a one-way street. All the sick fuck knew was that a little boy called him every few months to arrange the cash drop, and then his latest precious package arrived in the mail the following day.

All secret. All anonymous.

He didn't know that Kirk was the man who controlled his life. Who knew his most horrible secret. Who could destroy him on a whim.

But I know who you are, Kirk thought as he dialed, and his mouth folded into a grin. *Oh, yeah, I know you, Daddy.*

His phone rang.

It was the special phone, the unlocked, pay-as-you-go Samsung flip phone that he kept in the locked drawer. It was the phone that separated his angels from his demons. It was the phone that enabled his disease. Buy an access card for cash in any drugstore, and you were good to go. Make calls or get calls, and no one knew who you were.

He hated the phone. He dreamed of destroying it. More times than he could remember, he had taken it to the river to throw it into the rapids. He had held a hammer over it to smash it into bits. He had stared at the fireplace and tried to throw it into the flames. Every time, he bowed to reality. He couldn't give it up. If he did, time would pass, the urge would come back, and he would start again. He'd been a slave to the cycle of depravity his entire life.

There was another choice. The permanent choice. You kill yourself, and you kill the disease. He'd bought a gun to do it. The gun was in the locked drawer next to the phone. Loaded. There were always two choices for him. The gun or the phone.

He unlocked the drawer, opened it, and saw both of them. Reaching in, he stroked the butt of the gun with his fingers. He told himself for the millionth time, *Do it*. In a millisecond of light and pain, he would be free. The black hood would be lifted. He wouldn't endure the guilt that kept him in a vise. He wouldn't have to do terrible things to protect himself. He could finally kill the thing inside him once and for all.

Ring ring ring ring ring went the phone. Laughing at him. As if it knew exactly what he would do.

He answered the phone, clutching it as if he could crush it with his hand. Tears pushed out of his eyes. He cringed, awaiting the hideous voice. It was always the same.

"Hello, Daddy," the strange, hollow, false child said to him.

He wanted to scream. "*Stop that*," he hissed. "Don't use that voice."

"Are you mad at me, Daddy?"

He beat his fist against his skull and wished again that he were dead. *Hang up. Pick up the gun.* It was so easy, but he couldn't do it.

"Your latest order is in. It will make you very happy, Daddy."

"I don't want it. Stop calling me that."

"You owe me money, Daddy, and you need to pay."

"Fine, I'll pay, but forget the delivery."

"It doesn't work like that, Daddy."

He heard childish laughter. It sounded wicked, coming from this stranger's mouth.

"Tomorrow morning. Seven a.m. You know where. Throw the red backpack with the cash into the field. Turn around and go back the way you came. Your package will be waiting in your box." The child laughed again. "Don't be late, Daddy."

"This is the last time."

A childish giggle. "Oh, you always say that, Daddy."

That was true. He swore every time that he was done, but it was a hollow boast. They both knew it. The man on the other end of the line knew he would make the drop and pick up the package. He couldn't walk away.

"I know what you did to me," he whispered into the phone. "Why? For God's sake, why?"

This time, the child's voice was silent, which was almost worse than his taunting. He wished he knew who the caller really was. He wished he could find him and kill him. Maybe that would end this torment.

"*Why?*" he repeated, hating the crack in his voice. "Why did you have to destroy me?"

"Why not, Daddy?" the child replied.

The line went dead.

21

THE BOX OF POLICE EVIDENCE SUPPLIED BY MICHAEL ALTMAN TOOK CHRIS back to the early hours of Saturday morning.

The first responder was a Spirit County sheriff's deputy, whose emotionless report from the crime scene belied the horrifying reality of what he'd found. It was strange that an act like murder, which was bound up in so much emotion, could be distilled to bloodless facts.

> I responded to a referral from a 9-1-1 emergency operator that a teenage girl, identified as Ashlynn Steele, seventeen years old, of Barron, was potentially stranded in the ruins of the unincorporated town of Bell Valley. I arrived in the town at 5:43 a.m. and discovered an orange Mustang convertible, license plates 489 BAW. The vehicle was unoccupied, and the driver's side rear tire was flat. Registration of the vehicle was to Florian Steele of Barron. I made several verbal announcements of my presence in an attempt to locate the missing girl. When I received no response, I began a search of the area, including the unoccupied buildings. Seven minutes later, I observed the body of a woman in a park approximately one hundred yards from the vehicle. I determined that the woman was deceased and noted a gunshot entry wound in the center of her forehead. Her face matched the driver's license photograph of Ashlynn Steele. I saw no sign of a weapon at the scene of the crime. At that time, I reported the incident and remained on-site to secure the scene pending the arrival of investigative and medical personnel.

That was all it took to mark the end of a young life and begin the ripples that threatened to destroy many more.

Chris removed the police material page by page and organized the documents into piles on the table in the hospital lounge. Olivia was talking with the counselor Hannah had hired, and Chris passed the time by reviewing the chain of events that had led from Rollie Swenson's 9-1-1 call after Tanya awakened her father on Saturday morning, to the arrest of Olivia two days later.

He laid out witness statements and interview reports. Diagrams and crime scene photos. Early test results. Warrants. Records pulled from Ashlynn's life. Records pulled from Olivia's life. Reading between the lines, he could see an overarching theme emerging from the first minutes of the investigation.

This was an open-and-shut case.

The police knew who did it. They had Tanya's statement about Olivia and Ashlynn. If you already had a theory of the crime, you looked for evidence to support your theory and you tended to play down evidence that pointed in other directions. Rather than widen the search, the police focused on making sure that the evidence gathered against Olivia would hold up in court. No screw-ups in the chain of custody. No procedural errors. No technicalities. Not with the daughter of Florian Steele as a victim.

Chris looked at the evidence from a different perspective—a perspective where Olivia was innocent, not presumed guilty. A perspective in which Ashlynn was alive when Olivia left her in the ghost town.

In the early hours of the police investigation, there was no suspicion that Ashlynn's personal life was a contributing factor in her death. She was simply in the wrong place at the wrong time, with a St. Croix girl who was obsessed with the blood feud against Mondamin. The initial interviews with Florian and Julia revealed nothing about Ashlynn's relationships or her pregnancy. Either her parents didn't know or they didn't divulge it. No one mentioned Johan.

That changed after the autopsy. The follow-up interview with Julia reflected shock and horror that Ashlynn had been pregnant and that her daughter had made the decision to terminate the fetus. According to the interview notes, Ashlynn's mother had flatly refused to believe the coroner's findings. She told police that her daughter would never make such a godless choice, no matter what the physical evidence showed about her body. However, faced with the reality of Ashlynn's pregnancy, Julia did confess something she had not shared with her husband—that Ashlynn had secretly been dating Johan Magnus for months. After that revelation, it didn't take long for the dominoes to fall. The police discovered that Olivia had dated Johan, too, and that he had dumped her to be with Ashlynn.

Olivia knew about their affair. She had a whole new motive for murder.

Chris wasn't surprised that the physical and personal evidence had cemented suspicions among the police and the county attorney about Olivia's guilt. If he'd been in their shoes, he would have believed it, too. Even so, there were holes in the case. Johan had covered up his own visit to the ghost town when the police questioned him. There was nothing about Mondamin and the company's struggles with environmental activists. No one had asked about threats against Florian's family. No one mentioned Aquarius.

When he checked the inventory of Ashlynn's personal effects compiled from her wallet, her Mustang, and her bedroom at Florian's home in Barron, he also discovered a surprising omission. Something that should have been there wasn't on the list, and he checked it three times to be sure he hadn't missed it. It was possible that the police had failed to note it in their catalog, but that seemed unlikely. Ashlynn had packed a small suitcase for her trip, and the police had found the case in the trunk of the Mustang. It included the usual personal items, such as clothes and toiletries, but nothing else. No books. No homework.

No laptop.

There was no computer in her car. There was no computer in her bedroom, either, according to the inventory and photographs. To Chris, that was inconceivable. The daughter of Florian Steele owned a laptop. Where was it?

It was missing. Why?

He dug in the box for the girl's cell phone records and found a copy of an online statement showing activity for the preceding month. If the police had already done the legwork of tracing each number, they had opted not to make it easy for Chris by writing the results down on the copy they had given him. Instead, as he reviewed the list of calls that Ashlynn had made and received, he booted up his own laptop and went to a reverse directory website to identify the numbers.

He was surprised at how few calls he found to other teenagers in Barron, and he remembered Maxine Valma mentioning that Ashlynn had withdrawn from the Barron clique because of the feud. Based on Ashlynn's phone records, he knew she hadn't replaced them with a different group of friends. Her life looked lonely.

He saw numerous calls from the same phone number early in the month, and he tracked the number to Johan Magnus. Most of the calls were no more than a minute in length. Ashlynn had ended their relationship a month before her death, and in the days following the split, he had obviously tried repeatedly to get in touch with her. Either she had let the calls go to voice mail, or she had hung up after answering. Eventually, he'd quit trying to change her mind. There were no more calls between them.

Instead, he saw calls back and forth between Ashlynn and the very clinic in which he was sitting. The Barron hospital. He wondered if that was when she discovered she was pregnant. He'd assumed that her pregnancy had prompted the breakup with Johan, but maybe he was wrong. Regardless of the timing, the day after the last call she received from the clinic she'd dialed a new phone number. He recognized the number without having to feed it to the reverse directory. It was the number for the Grohman Women's Resource Center.

Ashlynn had made her choice.

There was an ominous silence in her phone records in the succeeding days, as if she were wrestling with her demons alone. She made no calls for nearly a week. None. To anyone. She received no calls either. Then he saw an out-of-state number on an outgoing call, and he traced it to the switchboard at Stanford University. He remembered Florian's comment that Ashlynn was looking at her options for college applications. Shortly after the call to Stanford, he spotted another local call, this time to Maxine Valma, and he wondered if Ashlynn was asking the principal to write a college reference letter. Maybe she'd begun to make peace with her decision about the baby and had started to turn her eyes back to her future. Or maybe she was just trying to think about anything other than the reality she faced.

Days later, she left for Nebraska.

During that awful period, he saw one call to her home number. It made him wonder whether Julia Steele had lied about knowing what her daughter was doing in those days away from home. Or maybe Ashlynn had lied to her mother and covered up her pain and grief and told her that everything was fine. *The church project is great, Mom. Don't worry, I'll be home on Friday.*

There was another call, too. He noted one outgoing call from Ashlynn's phone, lasting five minutes, on the day before she made the long drive back to Barron. The day before her death. She must have been in Nebraska at the time, recovering from the abortion procedure. Chris ran the number through the reverse directory, and when he did, he rocked back in his chair in surprise. It was about the last thing he expected to see on the girl's phone records.

There she was, alone, miles from home, experiencing the worst event of her young life. She made only one call that night, like a prisoner calling for help, and it was the last call she ever made.

Ashlynn called Tanya Swenson.

22

Hannah buzzed Chris through the street door into the Women's Resource Center. He waited until the door closed behind him with a solid click before he went upstairs. The steps were old and steep, worn low in the middle by decades of foot traffic, and the narrow hallway was claustrophobic. He smelled pizza from the ovens of the Italian restaurant next door. At the top of the steps, he opened another door and found himself in the small lobby of the center. It was gloomy, lit by a few table lamps. The aluminum mini-blinds on the windows were down. There was no receptionist, just a handful of chairs on the beige shag carpet, a water dispenser with packets to make tea or coffee, and a brochure rack sitting on a square oak table. The room was warm.

He wasn't alone. A woman in her twenties sat in a straight-backed chair, with a copy of *Redbook* in her lap. She had strawberry-blonde hair, and her closed eyes snapped open at the sound of the door. Her eyes were a pretty shade of pale blue, but they were alert and fearful. Her entire body flinched when she saw him, like a cat alarmed by the smallest sound. He was reminded of where he was, in a place that was often the last stop on a brutal road, where it took courage even to walk through the door.

He took a seat as far away from her as he could, near the window overlooking the street. He separated two of the blinds to peer outside and noticed a round hole in the glass, large enough to poke his finger through. When he eyed the opposite wall of the lobby, he spotted a matching hole near the ceiling, where the bullet fired from the street had buried itself in the plaster.

Abortion protester. Enraged husband. Barron boy. Take your pick.

The door to the inner office opened. It was Hannah. Seeing her, the young woman in the lobby bounded to her feet and threw her arms around Hannah's neck. Her nervous face blossomed with relief, as if she'd found a life preserver in a big ocean. Hannah hugged her back, then whispered in the woman's ear.

The visitor nodded shyly and disappeared into the open office with a final, furtive look at Chris.

Hannah gave him a smile that was unusually warm. "I'll only be a minute," she said. "Do you mind?"

"Take your time."

She closed the door, leaving him alone. He found himself daydreaming about the past, remembering Hannah. The woman in the doorway was the same woman he had met in college. Time didn't matter; she was still the girl in the tie-dye shirt and sweatpants who nursed abused dogs at the Humane Society, who screamed at politicians at the state fair, who drove four hours to swing sandbags at the Red River, who made love until sweat covered their bodies. He was the one who had changed, not her. In the early years, he'd been an idealist, like her. Young. Naive. The crappy apartment in Uptown was fine. Mac and cheese was the best dinner on earth. They both worked in a South Minneapolis urban center, the lawyer and the psychologist, out to rescue their corner of the world. They laughed, they fought, they made up. They were happy.

Olivia changed everything. He held that fragile baby in his arms, and he got scared. He grew up; he got older. Barely getting by wasn't enough anymore. Other people, other causes, didn't matter; only that little girl mattered to him. He made a bargain with Hannah, and neither of them realized at the time that it was a devil's bargain. She stayed home with their daughter, and he went to work. Real work. Lawyer's work. He made money and played the game. He moved them out of Uptown and west to the exclusive lakeshore suburbs. In the early years, he thought he was building a fortress, but it was really a maze. Eventually, he lost Hannah in it.

The door opened again. She stood there, waiting for him. Behind her, the office was empty. There was a rear entrance that she used to make it easier for women to come and go in secret, and the woman from the waiting room had slipped away. It was just the two of them. Hannah stared at him in silence, and he stared back. It felt to Chris as if she could read his mind and see that he had been reliving their years together, the highs and the lows. Her face had a sweet sadness. He stood up, and she came to him and quietly put her arms around his chest.

"Thank you, Chris," she said.

"For what?"

"For being here. For saving her. I married a good man."

He said nothing. It felt like the first scar over a wound, and he didn't want to risk breaking it open by saying the wrong thing.

They stayed in the waiting room in the dim, dusty light. She sat down next to him and played nervously with the shade of an old lamp. Her hand trembled with little involuntary spasms. He saw weakness and fatigue in her pale face. Even Hannah had her limits. Fighting Mondamin. Fighting cancer. Fighting the violence that had swept up Olivia in its currents. There was a point at which you simply wanted to throw yourself into the wave and get carried away.

"I never wanted to kill anyone before last night," she said. "If I'd had a gun, I would have shot every one of those bastards."

He thought, *I have a gun.* In a few hours it would be dark, and he would have to make a choice.

"We'll get them," he said.

"Does it matter?" she asked. "We can't un-ring the bell for Olivia."

"No, but we can get justice."

Hannah grimaced and sucked in her breath. Her eyes closed. Chris put a hand on her shoulder and leaned closer. "Are you okay?"

"There are good days and bad days. This is a bad day."

"I'm sorry. If there's anything I can—"

Hannah stopped him with a finger on his lips. The smallest touch of her skin was sensual. "Please don't. Don't say it. You're already worried about Olivia. You don't have to worry about me, too."

"I do anyway."

"I didn't ask you here to take care of me."

"That doesn't mean I can't," he said.

Hannah offered a small smile of surrender. "I know. Thank you."

"Do you mind if I ask you something? You don't have to tell me, but I'm curious."

"What is it?"

"Glenn Magnus told me he was interested in you, and you turned him down. Why?"

"Glenn shouldn't have told you that," she replied, frowning.

"Maybe not, but why? You obviously care for him."

"I wasn't ready."

Chris was surprised to see her look away and cover her face. In trying to be tender, he felt as if he had said the most hurtful thing imaginable. His temptation was to reach for her, but he resisted it. Instead, he got up and took a box of tissues from the coffee table and handed it to her.

"I guess we should avoid certain topics," he said.

Hannah sniffled and nodded. "I guess."

"You heard about Johan and Ashlynn?" he asked.

She nodded again.

"You didn't know?" he asked. "Olivia never told you?"

"She tells me very little."

"He was in the ghost town the night of the murder. He may have killed her."

Hannah shook her head. "I know the boy, Chris. He hates violence as much as Glenn does. It's hard to believe he would do something like that."

"I can't look the other way, even though he's Glenn's son. There are certain realities of defending a murder charge, Hannah. Evidence pointing to someone else helps Olivia. She's our priority."

She opened her mouth as if to protest, but she closed it without saying anything. She squared her shoulders, reclaiming her strength. "You're right. I'm sorry."

"I need to know more about Ashlynn," he said.

"What do you want to know?"

"Ashlynn called Tanya Swenson from Nebraska the day before she was killed. Do you have any idea why she would do that?"

"No, I don't."

"Were they friends?"

"I have no idea."

He frowned, wondering if she was hiding things again.

"Chris, it's true," Hannah went on. "You have to understand, I barely knew Ashlynn. She called me two weeks ago. She was in trouble, and I helped her as best I could. That's the only communication I had with her."

"There are too many missing pieces about this girl," he said.

"Like what?"

"Like the abortion."

"Christopher, put yourself in her shoes. She was scared and alone."

"I realize that, but everyone tells me she was close to her mother. Why didn't she go to Julia?"

"Even good girls are afraid to admit their mistakes. Particularly when they face the awful choice that Ashlynn did."

"She was a teenager, Hannah."

"Do you think she did this lightly? Do you think having a baby was a trifling inconvenience to her?"

"I don't know. Tell me."

"I *saw* her, Chris. That girl was in despair. She was inconsolable. The idea of terminating her pregnancy was horrifying to her. It went against every spiritual value she held."

"Then why do it? You said you didn't think she'd been raped."

"I don't believe she was."

"Did she tell you who the father was?"

"I told you, no. I assume now it was Johan, but she didn't say."

"Maybe she was seeing someone else. Johan said she broke up with him a month ago, but her phone records show that she exchanged calls with the clinic shortly before she called you. That was only a couple of weeks ago. If she just found out she was pregnant—"

Hannah held up your hands. "Chris, no, you're wrong."

"How do you know?"

"Because Ashlynn was already in her second trimester when she came to me. She was slow to realize she was pregnant. She'd been struggling with how to deal with it, but she'd made the decision to tell her parents. She was planning to *have* the baby. She was going through with it."

"So what changed?" Chris asked.

Hannah hesitated. "I don't know what difference it makes to tell the world what this poor girl was going through."

"I still need to know," he told her softly.

"The calls from the clinic were about her ultrasound," Hannah said. "Ashlynn was obsessed with the health of the child. She told me she'd been having premonitions that she'd lose the baby. It was taking over her life. I don't know how, but somehow she knew that something was terribly wrong."

He thought about Ashlynn's phone records. She hadn't told Johan. She hadn't told her parents. She'd gone through it all alone. It must have been excruciating.

"What did the ultrasound show?" he asked.

"Anencephaly."

Chris bowed his head. "Oh no."

"That's the only reason she chose the abortion, Chris. It's not because she wanted to give up her child. She had to. Her baby was going to die."

23

THE CHURCHYARD IN ST. CROIX WAS DESERTED.

It was late afternoon. The sun was low and feeble. Chris saw no one in the neighborhood streets or in the neat rows of the small Lutheran cemetery. He knocked on the door of the attached house where Glenn Magnus lived, but the minister didn't answer. He assumed Magnus was with his son at the hospital. The door to the church itself was unlocked, for anyone who wanted to pray.

Chris went inside.

The silence was unnerving. He shoved his hands in his pockets and stood motionless in the foyer. On his right, above the winding steps to the steeple, he heard the whistle of wind sucked from the tower and the tinny vibration of the church bells. He checked the sanctuary, but the long wooden pews were empty. He was alone.

He took the steps down to the church basement. It smelled moldy, as if moisture had seeped behind the walls. Through an open door, he saw a large meeting room with a speckled linoleum floor. Folded utility tables and chairs were stacked against the wall. One table was open, and he saw a messy stack of children's Bible books and boxes of crayons. The only natural light sneaked through small window squares at ground level. He clicked on the harsh fluorescents, illuminating the room. Winter was past, but no one had taken down the Christmas posters, made with multicolored construction paper and stuck with yellowing tape.

He wandered around the perimeter of the room, studying the posters on the walls. He saw stick figures of the baby Jesus in a crèche. Sheep that looked like cotton balls. Pointy boughs of holly like barbed wire. Three wise men with long white beards. One poster featured a slogan with each letter in a different color: Love Thy Neighbor. When he peered closer, he saw that someone had written underneath, in tiny script: Except Barron.

Chris switched off the lights as he left the room. In the basement hallway, he called, "Anyone here?" His voice sounded hollow. There was no response.

He saw a closed door. A large wooden cross was hung on a nail, and photographs were thumbtacked to the door. Johan was in all of them, mostly with his arms around young children. The boy's handsome face had a broad smile. Some of the photos were taken at sports games, some at church retreats. Conspicuously, he didn't see Olivia or Ashlynn in any of the pictures. Everyone kept their real lives under wraps here.

Chris knocked sharply and heard nothing. He glanced behind him at the empty hallway and turned the knob. The door was unlocked. He went inside, leaving the door ajar. He switched on the overhead light.

Johan's bedroom was unusually neat for a teenager. His bed was made with creased corners. His schoolbooks—*Precalculus*, *Human Biology*, *The Civil War*, *Economics*, and *Moby-Dick*—were stacked neatly on a corner of his wooden desk. A green light glowed on his computer monitor, but the screen was black. The keyboard was tucked inside a drawer. He saw manila folders and school notes, taken in precise handwriting. His pens were organized in an ELCA mug with the points downward.

Above Johan's bed, Chris saw a rectangular window fronting the street. He imagined Olivia crouching there, tapping on it at one in the morning. *Johan, wake up, we need to talk.*

He booted up Johan's computer. He clicked the Start button on the screen and ran a search of the documents on the hard drive, using the keyword Ashlynn. He hoped to find e-mail drafts or letters, but if there were written communications between the two of them, they'd been done through mobile texts or web-based e-mails. Instead, he found a photo file with Ashlynn's name. He opened it and saw an achingly beautiful picture of Ashlynn Steele, taken in winter with snow up to her calves. She wore a down vest, her blonde hair was loose and windswept, her cheeks pink from cold. Her mouth was composed in a beaming, carefree smile.

From everything he had learned, Chris didn't think Ashlynn had enjoyed many moments of that kind of happiness in her final months. He was pleased to see a glimmer of joy in her face and heartbroken to think of the tragedy that had consumed her. This case had become about more to him than just saving Olivia. He wanted to know what had happened to destroy this girl's peace and cut short her life.

Chris studied the rest of Johan's room. He opened the teenager's dresser drawers and found stacks of folded clothes. He opened the closet door and saw two laundry baskets on the floor, brimming with whites and darks. The shut-in space had an aroma of sweat. He squatted and removed the darks piece by piece, examining each one and depositing them on the closet floor. Near the bottom of the basket, he found a pair of stonewashed blue jeans. Mud soiled the knees, and dirt and brown grass clung to the cuffs.

He recognized a reddish-brown stain stretching down the pant leg, long and spidery. It was blood. He put the jeans aside and sifted quickly through the whites and found a baseball jersey with similar stains soaked into the sleeves.

More blood. Lots of it.

"Hello, Chris."

He spun around, startled at the voice behind him. He'd been caught, and he had no excuses. Glenn Magnus stood in the doorway of Johan's room. His face was expressionless.

Chris sank back against the frame of the closet door. "Glenn."

"You could have asked," the minister said.

"You're right."

"I suppose you figured I would have cleaned up first."

"You're a father," Chris said. "I know how fathers think."

"That's true."

Chris held up the jersey. "He was there, Glenn."

"I know. He told me."

"Did he kill her?"

"Johan isn't capable of that kind of violence."

"Anyone can lose control," Chris said. "This is blood. Johan told me he didn't touch anything at the scene, but that was a lie. He lied to the police about being there at all."

The minister's brow wrinkled in anger. "Johan lied to protect Olivia. It was foolish, but it was noble. As for the blood, what do you think he did when he saw the girl he was hopelessly in love with lying dead in the park? He knelt at her side. He embraced her. He grieved for her."

"That's possible."

"It's what happened."

"I'm not saying you're wrong, Glenn, but it doesn't change what I have to do."

"I'm aware of that. Take the clothes. Talk to the police. If false accusations help Olivia, so be it."

"She's innocent."

"So is Johan."

The minister walked into his son's room and sat down on the twin bed. He ran his hand along the folded lines of the comforter. He was at sea. Chris wondered if he truly believed that Johan didn't kill Ashlynn or if he worried that his son had been overrun by passion and grief. Even men of faith couldn't run from doubt forever.

"Johan is devastated about the assault on Olivia," Magnus went on. "He really cares for her, you know. I was strict with Johan when he told me he was planning to break up with her. I didn't want him to be unkind. I didn't want him breaking her heart."

"It broke anyway," Chris said.

"Even so, I don't want you thinking Johan is cavalier with girls. He's a handsome boy, and girls develop crushes pretty easily at this age, but I've drummed into his head that he needs to treat them with respect."

"He and Olivia were having sex," Chris said.

The minister frowned. "Yes, I know. I wasn't happy about it. I think Johan and Olivia both thought they were in love for a while, but things obviously went too far."

"Were there other girls?"

"Not that I know of. Not until Ashlynn."

"What about girls who were in love with him? Even if he didn't feel the same way."

"A few, I'm sure."

"Tanya Swenson?"

Magnus raised an eyebrow. "Tanya? I have no idea. She spent a lot of time with him, but Johan never mentioned her having feelings for him. Why?"

"Ashlynn called Tanya the day before her death. I just wondered if there could have been another love triangle at work. An unrequited one."

"If there was, I never heard about it."

"Johan told me that he met Ashlynn because of you," Chris said. "She was visiting you here at the church."

"Yes, she reached out to me as a religious adviser. She was looking for ways to build bridges between the towns. We became very close. Ashlynn was one of the loveliest, most spiritual girls I have ever met. It's devastating how it all turned out. I miss her."

"How did she hope to reconcile the towns?" Chris asked.

"She was seventeen. Seventeen-year-old girls believe they can do anything. She wanted to heal the wound caused by the deaths of our children here in St. Croix. I told her she was taking too much onto her shoulders, but she didn't listen. She had such a sense of purpose and mission. One time, she even insisted I come with her to pray at the Continental Divide. She said it was very symbolic."

"The Continental Divide?"

"Yes, the glacial ridges meet near Browns Valley north of Ortonville. On one side of the divide, the rivers flow north to Hudson Bay. On the other, water travels south to the Gulf of Mexico. For Ashlynn, that was the problem between Barron and St. Croix. We were neighbors living next door to each other but flowing in opposite directions."

"She sounds like a remarkable girl."

"She was. Johan was very serious about her. I truly thought they would get married."

"And yet Ashlynn broke up with him."

"I didn't understand it at the time, but now I know why," Magnus said. "I suppose Ashlynn felt she couldn't talk to either of us about her pregnancy. As spiritual as she was, she was a young girl. She was unprepared. Still, I just can't imagine that she would have had an abortion. Not Ashlynn. It must be a mistake."

Chris shook his head. "It's not a mistake, and it's not what you think. The baby was anencephalic."

"I'm sorry, what does that mean?"

"It's a severe birth defect, invariably fatal. If the baby survives to term, it dies within days or hours. Essentially, the fetus develops without a brain."

Magnus shook his head, mute with horror.

"You should tell Johan," Chris said. "If the police don't already know, they'll find out soon. It'll be better coming from you."

"Yes, yes, of course."

"You're sure Ashlynn didn't tell him about the baby?" he asked quietly.

"Johan? Never. He couldn't have remained silent about this." Magnus stared at the ceiling, his face wretched, as if he were questioning the mercy of God. "How that girl must have suffered. I can't imagine it. She must have believed she was being punished."

"Punished? For what?"

"For the cancer cluster. I'm sure she believed God was taking her baby, the way he took Kimberly and the others."

"Their deaths had nothing to do with her," Chris said.

"Maybe so, but tell that to Ashlynn. That was one of the reasons she first came to me for spiritual counsel. She was convinced that the cancer cluster in St. Croix was real. She was convinced that her father's company was causing it."

24

FLORIAN STEELE STOOD ON THE SPRAWLING PORCH OF HIS CLIFF-SIDE HOME. He swirled Stags' Leap chardonnay in a bell-shaped glass. Leaning on the balcony, he watched the rocky promontory of the bluff descend below him into a nest of trees. From where he stood, he could see the town of Barron and the stark white headquarters of Mondamin. For ten years, the company had been his dream. His life. He had built it from nothing, and for the first time, a decade of labor felt utterly empty.

He heard Julia behind him. Her heels were unmistakable. His wife stood next to him at the balcony, and he stole a glance at her. She was perfectly put together, as she always was. The cross on her neck. The pinned-up blonde hair. The rose dress hanging as if it were cut to her figure, which it was. Her back stiff and proud. He had been married to her for nearly twenty years, and there were days when he didn't understand her at all.

"There's something wrong with us that we can't cry," he said.

Julia didn't look at him. "I know exactly what I've lost. I don't need tears to grieve for her."

"I do."

His wife brushed a stray hair from her eyes. She was impatient with him. "Maybe you can't cry because you feel guilty. Did you think about that?"

"Olivia Hawk is guilty. Not me."

"Maybe Olivia is simply the instrument with which God chose to punish us."

Florian scowled. "I don't need a Bible lecture from you, Julia. Ashlynn's death is not my fault."

He slugged down the rest of his wine. He didn't want to have this argument with her. He was tired of feeling angry when he should have been crying his eyes out. What made it worse was that Julia was right. He felt guilty. He had let Ashlynn drift out of his life without fighting to get her back. His precious little girl had begun to treat him like an enemy.

He left the porch. Inside the patio doors was the family room, rustic and huge, with a vaulted ceiling and a fieldstone fireplace. It was his room. His space. Everything else had been designed and selected by Julia, even the décor of his Mondamin office. He'd insisted on one place for himself. Dead animal heads—deer and moose, even a bear he'd shot near Grand Marais—adorned the wall. If you were a Minnesota CEO in farm country, you had to hunt. It was part of the job description. Florian had never hunted as a child, but like his other endeavors, he had researched it, practiced it, and become expert at it. Ashlynn had joined him once when she was ten. She was a natural with a perfect eye. After her first kill, though, she'd cried for hours and never hunted with him again.

Ashlynn. His little girl. Gone. There were still no tears to squeeze from his eyes. He was a void.

Florian sat on the stone hearth. Julia walked inside and adjusted the angle of the paintings on the wall like a slave to her obsessive-compulsive ways. He resented her presence, and he hated himself for it. They'd turned on each other since Ashlynn's death. She blamed him, and he blamed her. He felt as if his wife had been a co-conspirator in turning his daughter against him. It was ironic. In the early years, he'd been the one to put Ashlynn to bed and sing lullabies to her. He wondered if his daughter even remembered those days. As she got older, though, things changed. He ran out of time as the business demanded more and more of his attention. Ashlynn became Julia's child, molded in his wife's image, graceful and beautiful.

"Why did you lie to me?" he asked his wife.

Julia stopped with her hand on the frame of a watercolor of the Spirit River. "About what?"

"You knew Ashlynn was seeing Johan Magnus."

"She asked me not to tell you about it, and I didn't. That's not a lie."

"I wanted to know if she was seeing anyone."

"You wanted to know if she was seeing *Kirk*," Julia said. "I told you no."

"George Valma told me that Maxine saw Ashlynn and Kirk together near the school. I was concerned."

"You mean you were concerned what Kirk might tell her."

"Damn it, Julia!" Florian shouted, his face flushing. He rose unsteadily, feeling the effects of two-thirds of a bottle of wine. "I don't want to talk about Kirk!"

Julia's pointed look made him feel like an insect. Everyone thought of him as a tower of strength at Mondamin. If only they knew the truth. Julia ruled the house. Julia ruled him.

"You're still paying him, aren't you?" she asked.

He didn't say anything. That was enough to give her an answer.

"Forget Kirk," he said. "This is about Ashlynn and Johan. You didn't see any problem with her dating him?"

"No, I didn't."

"You should have known that he and his father would brainwash her. They'd turn her against me."

"Ashlynn didn't need Johan for that, Florian. Her relationship with him had nothing to do with you. He's a handsome, decent boy. Ashlynn was in love with him, and from everything I saw, he loved her, too. I was not going to let you come between them. She was perfectly capable of making up her own mind."

"You should have told me," he repeated.

"What would you have done? Would you have had Kirk pay him a visit? Isn't that how you solve your problems?"

"Shut up, Julia."

"I heard about the assault on Olivia Hawk. Was your hand in that?"

"No! How can you say that? How can you think I would be part of something like that?"

"I think you sold your soul a long time ago, Florian. It's a little late to start talking about morality."

"I had nothing to do with it," he insisted. "I want to see Olivia Hawk in jail. That's all."

"If she killed our girl, God will punish her."

"If? What do you mean by that?"

Julia ran a fingernail slowly along the line of her chin. "We don't know exactly what happened."

"Maybe you don't, but I do."

"I'm having doubts."

"Don't be ridiculous. Why?"

"Because I thought I knew everything about Ashlynn, and now I realize I was wrong. She shut me out of the most intimate part of her life."

"Are you saying you really didn't know she was pregnant? She didn't tell you?"

"No, she didn't. I knew something was wrong. She was different. I should have been more attuned."

"I assumed you were simply keeping it from me."

"I'm not saying I would have told you if I knew."

"Naturally."

"I don't know what to believe anymore," Julia said. "Ashlynn didn't trust me with the most difficult decision she'd ever faced. She went and did something she knew I would find abhorrent."

"Maybe that's why she didn't tell you," he said. "She knew what you'd say. Or maybe she figured it was none of your business. You said it yourself. She was perfectly capable of making up her own mind."

"Not about this."

"You can't have it both ways, Julia."

His wife looked as if she would fire back at him, but she didn't. Her icy face bled into sorrow, and he thought the religious calm she affected would finally break into tears. It didn't. She held herself in check, stiffening her resolve. With Julia, it was as if God was holding back a dam. With him, it was as if he were alone in a giant dark space.

Julia poured herself a glass of wine. That told him how upset she was, in the places where she didn't invite him. She rarely drank. She took a sip, twisted her mouth at the sharpness, and came and sat next to him.

"There are days when I hate what we've become," she murmured.

"Don't you think I feel that way, too?"

"I don't know what you feel anymore."

"I loved her," Florian said. "I loved her more than anything else in my life. Except maybe you."

Julia didn't melt at the compliment. "Thank you for saying that, but Ashlynn and I have always been fourth on your list. There's Mondamin, money, and yourself. Then us."

"That's not true. It's never been about money, and I've never done this for myself. I started Mondamin to make a difference."

"Oh, you don't think you're noble, do you? You started Mondamin to build a mountain. You wanted to be king. I don't blame you for that, Florian. I knew you were going to be rich and do great things. God had big plans for you. I wanted to be a part of them. Did I complain when you dragged me to this wasteland? Did I tell you not to work eighteen hours a day? No. Never a word."

"I know you made sacrifices," he said. "So did I."

"Sacrifices didn't bother me. I believed in you. I believed in what you were doing at Mondamin."

He could see the truth in her eyes. She didn't believe in him now. "What changed?"

Julia got up without finishing her wine. "Maybe I began to see you through Ashlynn's eyes."

He felt as if she'd run him through with a sword. "What does that mean?"

"It means my baby girl is dead," she replied in a rising voice, "and I'm bitter at God, and I'm bitter at you. But God isn't here right now, and you are. So you're the one I blame. I always knew there would be a price to pay, but I never dreamed it would be so high."

He shook his head. "If it helps you to lay her death at my feet, fine, but it's not my fault."

"Are you sure? The pregnancy wasn't the only thing she was keeping from us, Florian. There was more."

"What do you mean?"

"I found her in your downstairs office a couple of weeks ago."

"What was she doing there?"

"I don't know. I didn't interrupt her."

"You should have told me," he said. "Or you should have talked to her."

"She obviously didn't want us to know."

"It doesn't mean anything."

"No? Last fall, she asked me about Vernon Clay, too," Julia told him.

Florian tensed. He'd hoped never to hear that name again. He certainly never wanted to hear it on Ashlynn's lips. "What about him?"

"She wanted to know what he did for you at Mondamin. She wanted to know what happened to him."

"What did you say?"

"I said he was a scientist who used to work for you. That he left town years ago."

"Why was she asking about him?"

"Why do you think? She suspected something."

"That's impossible."

"Don't be so sure. Ashlynn was a smart girl, Florian." His wife marched toward the kitchen, but she stopped in the doorway and fingered the cross on her neck. "This man Aquarius seems to know a lot about us, too."

"Don't worry about him."

"I've been wondering. What if it's Vernon? What if he's back?"

"He's not. It's not him."

"How do you know? Vernon was insane enough to do this. The notes sound like him."

"Aquarius is not Vernon Clay. He's just another nut from the anarchist fringe and nothing more."

"This one is different," Julia said. "You know what I think? I think he plans to kill us."

"That's crazy."

"Maybe he already started. Did you think about that? Maybe he started with Ashlynn."

Florian pushed himself off the hearth and stabbed a finger at his wife. "Don't talk like that. You're giving Chris Hawk exactly what he wants. All you're doing is helping Olivia get away with murder. Aquarius had nothing to do with Ashlynn's death. Nothing."

Julia shook her head. "I'm not so sure, Florian. There's a part of me that thinks Aquarius was sent here by God on a special mission to punish us. He was sent to wash us away like we never existed."

25

THE FIELDS SURROUNDING ROLLIE SWENSON'S HOUSE HADN'T BEEN PLOWED in years. The dormant acres had been reclaimed by prairie. The red barn was a relic, its walls bowing, its roof near collapse. A tractor sat on the lawn, swallowed by mud and rust, as if it had been driven out of the corn rows one day and left to fend for itself against the elements. The long brown grass of the yard was dotted with last season's fallen leaves blown from the riverbank on the other side of the highway.

Chris parked next to a Chevy Tahoe near the house. It was dusk. Lights were on downstairs and upstairs, and the screened windows were open, letting in the evening breeze. He got out and heard barking. A white Westie terrier shot from the porch and ran around him in frantic circles. He squatted to rub its head, but the dog was too busy to stop for attention. It snorted and charged for the deck and sniffed its way along the foundation.

"He's always flushing out rabbits and mice," Rollie called from the porch. The Barron lawyer had a can of Miller Lite in his hand. "He chases planes, too, when they fly overhead. I guess he figures they might land here."

"You can't be too careful," Chris said with a smile.

"Well, we haven't had a plane land in the yard since he started going after them. That can't be a coincidence." Rollie winked and came down the steps. He wore jeans and an untucked gray turtleneck that was snug on his stocky chest. "Welcome to the Swenson family farm."

Chris heard the irony. "I take it you're not getting ready for spring planting."

"I told you, calloused hands aren't my style. I could lease the fields, but I don't want diesel motors waking me up at five in the morning."

"This was your parents' place?" he asked.

"And my grandparents' place and my great-grandparents' place. The Swenson dynasty ends with me. Hopefully, Tanya will wise up and move to the city." He held up his can of beer. "You want one?"

"No, thanks."

Rollie took a swig of beer and admired the Lexus. "Nice car, but not too practical out here. This is truck country. You want something that takes out a deer on the highway like a speed bump." He added, "How's Olivia?"

"Physically, she's better than I feared. We'll see how she does in the next few weeks."

"That's good. Tanya wanted to visit her, but I had to tell her not to do that."

"I understand."

"Be sure to let her know that Tanya is thinking about her, okay?"

"I will," Chris said.

"I heard rumors that you're looking at Johan Magnus as a suspect in Ashlynn's death."

"Where did you hear that?"

Rollie shrugged. "I know every cop in the county. Word gets around."

Chris debated how much to say. "Johan and Ashlynn were involved."

"So I hear."

"Does that surprise you?"

"What, because of the Romeo and Juliet angle? Sure, I guess. Otherwise, there's nothing surprising about two kids in a small town getting together. I don't see how it helps your case. The cops think Johan dumped Olivia to be with Ashlynn, so all you've got is another motive."

"Johan went to the ghost town that night after Olivia and Tanya left," Chris said.

Rollie digested this information like a poker player. "Is that guesswork or can you prove it?"

"He admitted being there. I found bloody clothes."

"Well, son of a bitch," Rollie said. "Did he admit to killing her?"

"No, he claims Ashlynn was already dead."

"That's still good news for Olivia. Honestly, I thought you were blowing smoke about her not pulling the trigger. I figured you were laying a foundation for a plea bargain. This gives you a chance of actually getting her off."

"Did Tanya know that Johan and Ashlynn were an item?" he asked.

"She never mentioned it to me, but I don't expect she would even if she knew."

"Is she home? I'd like to ask her a few questions."

Rollie finished his beer without replying. Chris didn't think the can of

Miller Lite was his first of the evening. It was the end of the day, and the lawyer's black hair was dirty, his beard line heavy. "You talk about Tanya, and I start to get nervous, Chris. What do you want to know?"

"Tanya and Johan are friends. I was wondering if he said anything to her about Ashlynn."

He watched the calculations in Rollie's mind. He'd spent years reading faces on the other side of a bargaining table. That was how lawyers worked, trying to guess the other lawyer's game and figure out how to outfox them. Rollie did the same.

"If Johan and Ashlynn's affair was a big secret," Rollie said, "it's hard to imagine him saying anything to Tanya."

"Maybe he told Tanya something about a new girlfriend, even if he didn't say who it was."

"Or maybe he said something that will hurt your case and blow him out of the water as a suspect. Did you think about that? I'm surprised you'd take the risk, Chris. You know the golden rule of interrogating witnesses. Don't ask a question if there's a chance you won't like the answer."

"If I don't ask her, the police will," Chris said. "I can't afford to be blindsided."

Rollie studied the Lexus again, as if the car were a witness on the stand spilling its secrets. "I'll bet you're a great dealmaker, Chris. The trouble is, I never believe a word that another lawyer tells me. The more you say you want to talk about Johan, the more I think you really want to talk about Tanya."

"I simply want to find out what she knows."

"Which means you think she knows *something*."

Chris decided that he wasn't going to finesse any information out of Rollie Swenson. The only approach was the direct approach. "Cards on the table?"

"Sure."

"How well did Tanya know Ashlynn?"

"As well as two students in the same school. She had zero motive to kill her."

"I didn't say she did."

"Yes, but you'd love to find one," Rollie retorted. "Johan is the prime suspect, but it's always nice to have a fallback, right? Tanya called Olivia that night, and then she snuck back to the ghost town to shoot Ashlynn. That's the idea. I get it. Except if you want to sell that nonsense to a jury, you need a motive. I'm curious, do you have a theory, or are you just throwing shit at the wall to see what sticks? Let me guess. Tanya and Ashlynn were having a torrid lesbian affair. Or maybe Tanya was secretly in love with Johan and wanted to get her rival out of the way. Or maybe my daughter is just a serial killer who's after rich blonde girls, Chris. Is that it? Do you think this is some kind of James Patterson novel?"

"I'm not trying to pin anything on her, but Tanya knows more than she's telling me."

"What makes you think so?"

"Ashlynn called Tanya the day before she died," Chris said.

Rollie shook his head and looked amused. "That's the big secret? I hate to burst your bubble, but I know about the call."

"Neither of you mentioned it to the police," Chris said.

"You're right. That's my fault. No offense, but we were both pretty tired and stressed on Saturday morning, okay?"

"So what was the call?" Chris asked.

"Tanya sits next to Ashlynn in a religious studies class. Ashlynn missed the class on Thursday, and she wanted to know if the teacher assigned homework for the weekend."

"That's it?"

"That's it," Rollie said. "I was sitting with her in the living room when she got the call."

"Why did Ashlynn call Tanya and not someone else?"

"Probably because they're the two best students in the class. Not that I understand why. Tanya sure doesn't get her religious savvy from me."

Chris frowned. The explanation made sense. It was simple. Logical. Unmysterious. Even so, it bothered him. "Do you know what Ashlynn was doing that day?" he asked.

"No, Tanya just said she missed class."

"She was in Nebraska having an abortion," Chris said.

Rollie looked sucker punched. He was genuinely upset. "Is that true?"

"Yes."

"Shit, I'm sorry. I didn't mean to be flip, Chris. I had no idea."

"It's hard to believe Ashlynn was worried about a homework assignment while she was losing her baby," Chris said.

"I don't know what to tell you. Tanya told me what the call was about, and I believe her."

"I'd really like to talk to her."

"Chris, she's scared, she's fragile, and she didn't do anything. I'm not putting her through more intimidation." Rollie turned as the noise of a buzzer floated through the open door of the house. "That's our dinner, too, so I'm going to say good night."

"What's on the menu?"

"Tater Tot hot dish. Tanya's favorite."

"Enjoy it," Chris said.

"Be sure to give Olivia her best wishes, okay?"

"I'll do that."

The younger lawyer climbed up the stairs and shut the door behind him. Chris stood next to his Lexus without getting inside. The phone call still bothered him. He didn't like it, and he didn't believe it was that simple, no matter what Tanya had told her father. Something else was going on between her and Ashlynn, and he wanted to find out what it was.

He opened his car door, but as he did, he saw movement rustling the curtains in an upstairs bedroom. A face quickly vanished from sight, but their eyes met across the dark space. It was Tanya Swenson. She'd been hiding near the open window as Chris talked to her father.

She'd heard everything.

26

It was nightfall. Under the barest sliver of moon, the open lands of the Spirit River valley were barely visible.

Chris pulled to a stop on the shoulder of the road where 120th Street led to the river. His engine ran. He switched his lights off. Trees hung low over the asphalt, draping their branches on the roof of the Lexus. He gripped the steering wheel, debating whether to turn. He had been agonizing all day about what he needed to do. There were certain lines in life that were indelible, and if you crossed them you couldn't go back.

The gun was on the passenger seat beside him.

His daughter was in the hospital. She'd been brutally violated. She would recover, but the stain would be with her forever, like a tattoo inked into her brain. Like graffiti scrawled on a perfect, beautiful painting. His anger was so deep it left him speechless. Something needed to be done; someone needed to pay. He thought about Marco Piva, who had become his conscience and his compass in the short time he had known him. *You want to rage against the world.* That was true, but his rage had a focus and a purpose now. Kirk Watson.

Half a mile behind him, headlights drew closer on the highway. He couldn't afford to be seen here, and he had to make a choice: stay or go. With a tap of the accelerator, he swung into the woods that lined the river road. He coasted toward the water. Acorns and branches popped and snapped under his tires. He squinted, but he was mostly blind. Lights winked through the trees, marking the handful of houses built well back inside the forest. He lowered his window, and he could smell the dankness of the river not far away. Ahead of him, where the lights vanished, the road ended at the water. He was as close as he dared go.

He did a three-point turn and pulled as far to the side of the road as he could. He didn't get out immediately; instead, he stared into nothingness. Wet leaves clung to his windshield. A crow screamed in the treetops. He took the revolver from the seat and felt its heft in the palm of his hand. He was like Hannah, he'd always hated guns. It wasn't until this moment that he felt they had a place in this world.

Chris got out silently. He kept the ignition key in his hand and held it apart from the other keys on his ring. Carefully, he laid the key ring on the front seat, so that he could sweep up the ignition key without struggling to find it in the darkness. He eased the door shut with a quiet click. The gun nestled in his hand.

He planted each step softly. His pulse thudded through his throat and made a roar in his brain. Drooping pine branches scraped his face like fingers, startling him. He stopped, listening. Something scurried in the brush, like a small animal alarmed by his presence. The river water slapped on the bank. In the still air, he heard a murmur of voices. Someone laughed.

The lights of the last house were twenty yards away. Kirk's house.

A yellow lightbulb flickered like Morse code on one corner of a detached garage. The bulb on the other corner, closest to the house, was burned out. He saw an F-Series pickup truck parked outside. The house itself was small, one story, with peeling white siding. The front porch was dark. So was the deck overlooking the river. The lights he saw and the voices he heard came from the near side of the house, beyond the garage. A square glow framed the window.

Chris approached the pickup, which was spattered with mud. Between the garage and the house, the wet ground was covered with long brown grass. The flickering light on the wall of the garage cast faint, moving shadows. He veered to the corner and used the sleeves of his shirt to turn the hot bulb until it went black. He was invisible now to anyone who looked into the woods. He crossed to the house and crept toward the rear window. It was a casement window, cranked open, with no screen. The voices got louder. He distinguished two sets of male voices. Kirk wasn't alone.

Chris peered inside the bedroom. A king-size bed with no headboard was shoved against the nearest wall, immediately under the open window. The bed was empty, and the sheets and blankets were tousled into knots. He saw a high-definition television on the other side of the room; the screen was at least fifty inches wide. An elaborate weight-training system was positioned in the corner. The walls were painted navy blue, and he saw several crushed holes in the Sheetrock, the size of an angry fist.

Kirk Watson sat in a leather recliner. His chest was bare, and he wore checkered boxers. His long hair was loose around his shoulders. His arms and legs bulged with well-defined muscles. In the doorway of the bedroom, Chris spotted Lenny Watson, smaller and younger, still with a bandage on his face. Lenny stared straight at Chris, and Chris tensed, expecting the kid to shout. Instead, Lenny kept talking to his brother, unable to see into the darkness outside the window.

"Six in the morning, man," Lenny said. "Shit, that's early."

"Well, it's not the kind of business I'm going to do at noon in front of the courthouse, Leno. Don't be stupid." Kirk reached for a bottle of beer. "You want to stay in bed, you lie there and have a wet dream. I don't need you."

"No, I want to come with you."

"Just make sure you're ready. I'm not waking you up, Leno, got that?"

"I got it."

"I want you in place by six thirty. Sun's up at seven."

"Yeah, I know."

"You remember the deal, right? I drop you at the monument site with the binocs, and you keep your eye on every car heading out of Barron toward the drop site."

"I got it, man, it's not the first time."

"All it takes is one mistake, Leno. You tell me when he's getting close; you tell me when he heads back to town. He does anything funny, you shout. You smell a cop, you give me the emergency signal, and then you keep your head down and stay put."

"I won't let you down, man."

Chris heard the eagerness in Lenny's voice. Younger brothers picked older brothers for heroes, even when they didn't deserve it. He didn't know what scam they were planning, but sooner or later, he was certain that Kirk's manipulation would lead Lenny in only one direction. Jail or worse.

Kirk stretched his arms over his head and yawned. He climbed out of the recliner. "I could use some pussy."

"Who?" Lenny asked.

"I don't know. Who do you think?"

"What about that freshman, Sammi?"

"The punk one with the nose ring? Yeah, why not? Toss me the phone."

Lenny tossed a cell phone to his brother, and Kirk dialed.

"Sammi? It's Kirk Watson. Hey, gorgeous, I'm having a party. Booze included. You want to come? Yeah, bring a friend, fuck yeah. Absolutely. I'll have Leno come get you in my truck. Twenty minutes, and dress like you want it."

Kirk switched off the phone. It was that easy, like ordering a pizza. Chris was horrified.

He also realized he was running out of time.

"Take the pickup, Leno," Kirk told his brother, "and don't get pulled over, doofus."

"I have to take a dump first."

"What, girls give you diarrhea, Leno? Sammi's going to have another girl with her, so don't go squirting inside your pants, okay? You want seconds when I'm done?"

Lenny shrugged. "Nah."

"Shit, Leno, you're not queer, are you?"

"No!"

"So why are you always saying no when I get you pussy? Oh, I forgot, the only girl you want is Olivia Hawk."

Chris's whole body went rigid. He waited like stone for what happened next. All he wanted was hard proof. Some kind of admission, some kind of confession. He wanted to hear from Kirk's lips what he had done. He wanted no doubt whatsoever that it meant justice to pull the trigger.

The words flowed out of Kirk as easily as river water. The meaning was unmistakable. "Well, you had your chance last night, Leno, and you blew it."

Chris wanted to scream. This man had just told him what he'd done to his daughter. He didn't want to use a gun; he wanted to wrap his fingers around this beast's throat. He wanted to watch his eyes bulge and his blood vessels burst and the oxygen drain from his skin. *Kill him.*

Lenny Watson said nothing in response to Kirk's taunting, but the boy's face screwed up in what looked like impotent frustration. Then his legs squirmed, and he held his breath as he let out a monster fart. He swore loudly, and he turned and ran for the bathroom.

Kirk grabbed his knees because he was laughing so hard. His laughter followed Lenny down the hallway, and Chris heard the bathroom door slam. This was his chance. Kirk was alone. It was just the two of them. He could pull the trigger and be gone, and no one would know. They would all suspect, but they would never know.

Silently, he eased the hammer back on the revolver. He slid his finger onto the trigger.

Kirk turned on the television and rolled onto the bed. He put on a DVD and groaned with satisfaction. It was girl-on-girl porn. A blonde with dangling, inflated breasts hiked her ass in the air and buried her mouth between the legs of a brunette who moaned in exaggerated pleasure.

"Shit, yeah," Kirk murmured. His hand slipped inside his boxers. A tent developed in the cotton.

Chris took a step closer to the window. It was the perfect opportunity, a frozen moment in time. Lenny was occupied. Kirk was distracted. The back of the monster's head was only inches away. All he had to do was fire one shot and watch Kirk's skull explode in a sticky mass of bone, blood, and brain. He raised the gun. Kirk had no idea what was happening behind him, no sixth sense that death was so close.

He thought about Olivia. Images of her prone body in the train car, battered and abused, popped in his head like flashbulbs. He breathed faster, so loudly and raggedly that he feared Kirk would hear him, but Kirk's mind was focused on the naked bodies intertwined in high definition on the big screen. In Chris's head, Olivia cried. She begged for help.

The gun was steady in his hand, and his arm didn't tremble. It would take almost no pressure on the trigger at all. He thought to himself, *On three.*

One.

Two.

Thr—

He tried to fire, but he couldn't. He thought about Olivia and Ashlynn in the park. Olivia holding the gun. Olivia, desperate for revenge, angry, upset, confused, hurt, alone. His daughter, on the verge of taking an innocent life.

Kirk Watson wasn't innocent. It wasn't the same, and yet it was.

Chris wanted nothing more than to kill him, but with each second, the opportunity slipped away, and he knew it was irreversible. Ticktock, ticktock.

Lenny would be done soon. Time was running out. It didn't matter. It could be a second or an hour, and he would still be standing there, unable to fire.

His arm buckled.

He removed his finger from the trigger. He disabled the revolver.

He did just what Olivia had done. He walked away, recoiling in horror at how close he'd come to joining the ranks of the evil.

27

CHRIS DIDN'T GO BACK TO THE MOTEL RIGHT AWAY, BECAUSE HE DIDN'T WANT to spend time with his conscience. He told himself that someone else had stood in the dark, holding a gun to a man's head—not him. He wasn't ready to be alone with a lie. Instead, where the northbound highway split near Barron, he followed the steep bluff toward the hilltop. He knew from the documents the county attorney had given him that Maxine Valma lived within a few blocks of the high school.

The tall black principal answered the door herself. She was still dressed for work, and her needle-thin eyebrows arched in surprise when she saw him. "Mr. Hawk."

"Ms. Valma, I'm sorry to bother you. I hope I'm not interrupting."

Her face had the awkward look of someone who was too polite to admit that his arrival was an unwanted intrusion. "George and I just got back from dinner in town. He's putting the kids to bed."

"I have a couple questions for you. It won't take long."

She shrugged. "Come in."

Maxine led him inside her house. The living room was furnished with antique furniture that had been painstakingly refinished. He saw framed concert posters on the wall from the jazz era heyday in Harlem in the 1920s. The posters looked original. Saxophone music played on the stereo, and Maxine lowered the volume as he sat down in an armchair.

"What can I do for you, Mr. Hawk?"

"Well, you can call me Chris, for starters."

"All right. Chris. I stopped by to see Olivia at the hospital. I hope you don't mind."

"Not at all. I'm glad you did."

"I don't know if she was pleased to see me. She still associates me with Mondamin because of George's work. However, I wanted to make sure she knew that all of us at the school were thinking of her."

"I appreciate that."

"You're not seeing the true heart of this town," she told him. "The true heart is good. I really believe that."

"I hope you're right."

"What is it you need, Chris?" she asked.

"Well, this is a strange question, but do you know if Ashlynn was sharing a class this term with Tanya Swenson? It's a course on religious studies that meets Tuesday and Thursdays."

"I'd like to tell you I've memorized the class schedule for every student in my school, but I'm afraid I haven't," she said.

"Is it something you can look up from here?"

She nodded reluctantly. "I suppose so. It will take me a moment. My office is upstairs."

"I really appreciate it."

Maxine left Chris alone. He heard the precise click of her heels on wooden steps, and then he heard unhappy voices above him. After a sharp silence, another, heavier set of footsteps thudded to the ground level. A large black man filled the doorway. Like his wife, George Valma's face had a strained politeness, as if Chris were interrupting them during something important. He wondered if they were in the midst of an argument.

George shook hands like a football player with a crushing grip. He had a rumbling voice that was unusually soft for such a big man. He had wiry gray hair and wore a navy silk shirt with an open collar and gray dress slacks. He was a few years older than his wife, probably in his midfifties. Despite his size, he looked fit, not heavy.

"Did Maxine offer you a glass of wine?" George asked as he sat on the sofa.

"Thanks, but I'm fine."

"It's just awful what happened to your daughter."

"Yes, it is."

"I have two girls. They're nine and twelve. If someone did anything like that to one of my babies, I think I'd tear their heads from their shoulders with my bare hands." George looked like he could make good on his threat.

"We're fathers," Chris said.

"Exactly."

"Your wife told me that you work at Mondamin."

George nodded. "That's right. I joined the company when they were acquired. Before then, I worked with the parent company in Missouri."

"It's a controversial place."

George's lips wriggled like a caterpillar as he phrased his reply. "I'm a scientist. I stay out of politics and PR."

"Was it hard to move here? Rural areas don't always welcome strangers."

"Particularly African-American strangers?" George said.

"I mean any strangers, but Barron isn't exactly St. Louis in terms of diversity."

"You hear a lot more Hank Williams than Charles Mingus in this neighborhood, no doubt about that. I feel like a zoo animal sometimes, but these are decent Christians living here. I can't say they've ever made us feel unwelcome. They've taken us into their church. I'm much happier with my girls growing up in this town than in St. Louis. I go to work with a smile on my face."

His voice rose oddly as he said this, as if he were trying to convince himself.

"What kind of work do you do?"

"I'm afraid I can't say much about it. I'm sorry."

Chris held up his hands. "I'm not trying to steal your trade secrets."

"No, but you'd be surprised at the lengths to which people will go. Some companies hire private investigators to ride elevators at trade conferences in order to eavesdrop on conversations between researchers. Others train hookers to obtain information. It's a cutthroat business."

"A lot of money must be at stake."

"Billions."

Maxine returned to the living room, but she didn't sit next to her husband. Instead, she stood in the doorway with her arms folded across her chest. Chris thought she didn't want him lingering in their house any longer than necessary. "Are you asking questions about Mondamin?" she said. "I warned you that we'd have to kill you, didn't I?"

The joke fell flat. None of them laughed. George shot his wife an uncomfortable glance.

"Anyway, the answer is yes," she went on. "Ashlynn was in a religious studies class with Tanya Swenson this term."

"Thank you for checking."

"Was there anything else you wanted?" she asked.

"What do you know about the relationship between the two girls?"

"I'd be surprised if there was much of a relationship at all, given the situation. Why?"

"Ashlynn called Tanya the day before she was killed. Tanya told her father it was about a school assignment in their religion class."

"That sounds reasonable."

"Yes, I suppose it does," Chris said. "Anyway, I'm sorry to bother you." He stood up from the armchair and then added, "Actually, I do have one more question. Ashlynn called you here at home a couple of weeks ago. Do you remember what that was about?"

The principal shook her head. "Students call here from time to time, but I don't remember a call from Ashlynn."

"Sure you do, Maxy," George reminded her. "She told you that one of the exit doors in the gym was sticking. She was concerned it was a safety hazard."

Maxine blinked, and her face softened. "Of course. That's right. I'd forgotten it was Ashlynn who told me about that."

"Did she talk about anything else?" Chris asked.

"Just the typical pleasantries."

"Nothing unusual about it?"

She smiled. "Sorry."

Chris nodded. He was hitting dead ends in every direction. "Well, I appreciate your time."

"Not at all."

He shook hands with both of them, and the principal led him to the front door. She shut it behind him as he left, and as he reached the sidewalk at the bottom of the steps, the porch light went off, leaving the front yard dark. He blindly navigated his way to his car, which was parked on the street, and climbed inside.

Chris started the engine and sat in the darkness, thinking. Before he could pull away, someone rapped on the passenger window.

George Valma was outside.

Chris switched off the car, and the bulky scientist got in next to him. George sat uncomfortably with his hands in his lap and his big lips pinched together. He was as large as a bear in the passenger seat. Chris waited. Finally, George swiveled his head and met Chris's inquiring stare.

"This conversation never happened," George said.

"Okay."

"If you tell anyone, I'll deny it."

"Understood."

"Maxine and I are careful what we say in the house. We're never sure who's listening."

"Are you saying you think your house is bugged?"

"I don't know, but it pays to be careful."

"Who would want to do that? Florian?"

"Maybe. Or maybe others. There are always people who want to listen."

"So what is it you want to tell me?" Chris asked.

George twisted his fire-hydrant neck in both directions to study the street, as if looking for strangers in the shadows or cars in the neighborhood that he didn't recognize. When he was satisfied they were alone, he rumbled, "The phone call wasn't what I said it was."

"Then what was it?"

"Ashlynn didn't call Maxine," George told him. "She called me."

George gave instructions as Chris drove. They stayed off the north-south highway and instead followed bumpy, unpaved roads through the empty rural lands. Chris quickly got lost in the maze of turns at unmarked intersections, but the scientist had a confident sense of direction. Chris peppered him with questions, but George said little during the fifteen-minute ride.

"Stop here," he said finally.

When Chris did, George climbed out and marched into an abandoned field that was a sea of mud and rocks. The black man's hands were shoved in his pockets, and his shoulders were hunched. Chris followed. They were near an old gravel driveway, but the driveway led nowhere. There were no buildings around them. Massive trees dwarfed the two men, making the lot feel secluded. With the barest moonlight, the constellations above them were easy to distinguish.

"So where are we, George?" Chris asked.

The black man was almost invisible, even though he was barely six feet away. "This land belonged to a man named Vernon Clay. Until four years ago, he was a research scientist at Mondamin. He and I share the same specialty."

"Are you going to tell me what that is?"

George hesitated. "Pesticides."

"You mean DDT, atrazine, Roundup, nasty stuff like that?"

"It's not nasty stuff when used appropriately."

"And when it is used inappropriately, you grow a tail, right?"

"That's a gross exaggeration," George huffed. "Environmental extremists make wild claims about the risks of pesticides in the food chain, but it's mostly junk science. Without pesticides to protect our crops, we don't feed the world—particularly the developing world. My research is aimed at ways to get better crop results with less chemical exposure."

"Okay, so why are we here? And what does this have to do with Ashlynn Steele?"

Chris heard George Valma's growly breath in the darkness. The man ginned up his courage to talk. "Last fall, Ashlynn pulled me aside during a party at Florian's house. She asked me what I knew about Vernon Clay's work at Mondamin."

"Did she say why?"

"She said she was doing a paper on agricultural research for her biology class. I didn't question it at the time. It seemed like a reasonable query coming from Florian's daughter."

"What did you tell her?"

"I told her what I knew about Vernon. The sanitized version, anyway. Vernon was young, but he was one of those scientists who develops a whole new paradigm for his field. It was a coup for Mondamin to land him. He was among the pioneers using nanometals in pesticides when the rest of us were still snipping up corn DNA."

"It all sounds like Frankenstein stuff to me."

"Just the opposite. Would you rather eat tomatoes from a field that had been treated with tons of chemical pesticides or from a field where the crop had developed its own structural resistance to insects?"

"I'd rather eat tomatoes my neighbor grows in his window box." Before George could protest, Chris added, "What's the unsanitized story about Vernon Clay?"

"The rumor is he was sick. He left Mondamin four years ago and dropped off the radar screen. He hasn't resurfaced."

"What do you mean, sick? Like cancer?"

"More like mental illness."

"So what does his land have to do with anything?"

"Probably nothing."

"You didn't drag me out here for nothing, George."

The scientist squatted in the field. Chris could hear him squeezing mud through his fingers. "Ashlynn's question made me curious. It's not often that someone like Vernon walks away at the peak of his career. I started asking around about him at Mondamin, and I hit a stone wall. No one wanted to talk about him. They told me to drop it. That made me more curious. I looked him up in an old phone book, and this was his address. Right here where we're standing. Only when I came out here, I found nothing left. Google Earth showed a house here five years ago."

"Okay, so where is it?"

"Gone. Torn down. The fields were plowed over, too, and sterilized. Nothing grows here. It's like a dead land. And guess who owns the property. It's not Vernon Clay anymore."

"Florian Steele," Chris said.

"That's right."

"Did you talk to anyone about this?"

"Hell, no. I didn't tell anyone. I don't want to lose my job."

"So why tell me now?"

George got to his feet, and Chris heard his knees pop. "Ashlynn called me two weeks ago. She was asking about Vernon again. She wanted to know where he was and where she could find him."

"What did you tell her?"

"I told her I didn't know."

"Did Ashlynn say why she wanted to locate him?"

"She was trying to find out whether Vernon's research could have been responsible for the cancer cluster in St. Croix. She also wondered if the pesticides he was developing could cause birth defects."

Anencephaly.

"What did you tell her?" Chris asked.

"I told her no. No way. Even if you accept that environmental factors may play a role in some cancers, it would normally take years of exposure to have an impact. Mondamin has only been around for a decade, and the first cases of leukemia developed six years ago. It would have taken a catastrophic level of exposure for there to be any connection."

"Catastrophic?"

"Yes. As in *deliberate*. Plus, the lawsuit prompted an investigation by one of the top university epidemiologists in the country. Her name is Lucia Causey. I've met her. She's thorough. If there was even the slightest possibility that the cancer cluster involved Mondamin, she would have found it. So the answer is no. There's no connection. That's what I told Ashlynn."

Chris heard the conviction in the man's voice. It was the conviction of someone who wanted to believe he was right. "Then why are we here?"

"I'm a scientist, Chris. I only believe what I can prove. I don't trust coincidences."

"You didn't answer my question."

George Valma spoke softly. His words breathed out into the night. "Do you know where we are?"

"I lost track of where we were going miles ago," Chris said. "Where are we?"

George took Chris's shoulder in an iron grip and turned him toward the dark trees bordering the field. "Beyond those trees, we're not even half a mile from the town of St. Croix," he said. "The land shares the same aquifer. Whatever you put in the ground here makes its way to their water supply."

28

CHRIS STARED AT THE DECREPIT STOREFRONTS OF THE GHOST TOWN and tried to see the world through Ashlynn Steele's eyes.

It was midnight, just as it had been when the girl limped into this town with a flat tire. She must have felt like the last person on earth, awakening to find that some cataclysm had left the land in ruins. He wondered if she was keenly aware of the irony of her location. She'd been forced to give up the life inside her, and she'd been stranded in a place that had proved unable to support life.

She must have asked herself why God had led her there.

Chris's Lexus was parked where Ashlynn's Mustang had drifted to a stop. He wandered the street, like her, listening to the empty noise of his footsteps. He was alone, but he didn't feel alone. The broken glass, the boarded-up doors, the rusted signs, made him feel as if eyes were watching him. It might have been animals, or it might have been ghosts, or it might simply have been his imagination. Ashlynn would have felt the same way, but she didn't know then that she really was being watched. Olivia and Tanya were in the shadows.

He wondered if someone else had been there, too.

Chris tried to re-create what had been happening in Ashlynn's life. Six months earlier, she had gone to George Valma with a seemingly innocent inquiry about a Mondamin research scientist named Vernon Clay. Days before her death, she'd called George Valma again with more questions about the same missing scientist. True or not, she had begun to link Vernon Clay to the cancer cluster in St. Croix and to the tragic situation with her own baby.

Had she actually discovered something? Or did she simply need someone to blame? If you knew your child was going to die, you could believe almost anything to explain it. You wanted answers. You wanted justice, just like the people in St. Croix who had watched their own children die. By the time she arrived in the ghost town that night, Ashlynn had begun to blame Mondamin. She'd begun to blame her father.

Chris saw the park where she died. Police tape still clung to the trees. The swing where Ashlynn had sat was a black silhouette. Behind the park, a minimum-maintenance road vanished into the desolate cornfields. He pricked up his ears, as if he could hear Ashlynn humming when he listened hard enough. As if he could hear the confrontation between Ashlynn and his own daughter. The gunshot, the screams, the crying. The horror of it made him close his eyes. Olivia had no way of knowing that she had arrived at the lowest pit of Ashlynn's life, a well from which there must have seemed no escape. Instead, she had taunted and tortured her for crimes that weren't hers. She had poured salt into an open wound. He wished he could have been there to stop it, to rescue them both.

He reminded himself: Olivia didn't know. She was young. She was drunk. She'd made a cruel mistake, and she'd already paid a horrible price for it. So had Ashlynn.

Chris thought about Olivia leaving Ashlynn alone. Alive. What happened in that next tragic hour? *Who did this to you? Who found you in the park, consumed by your grief, and put a bullet in your brain?* He knew that Michael Altman would say he was creating a conspiracy out of something simple. The simple explanation was the one supported by the evidence. The easy, logical answer was what everyone believed. Olivia was there. She had a gun. She pulled the trigger.

No.

She'd walked away. Sometimes it happened that way. Chris had pointed a gun at Kirk Watson's head, and he'd walked away, too.

He saw headlights approaching the ghost town from the south. He knew it was Hannah's car. He stood on the dirt shoulder until her high beams caught him in their glare, and he lifted a hand to shield his eyes. She pulled past him and parked. When she got out, the light of her flashlight splashed across the ground between them.

"Thanks for coming," he told her.

"You said it was important."

"It could be."

He had no idea if Vernon Clay was important. The simple truth was that Chris felt a need to be with Hannah. Apparently she sensed it, too. In the glow of the light, he saw that she was holding a wine bottle by the neck.

"I still have a bottle of that Cosentino Cab we bought in Napa," she said. "I thought you could use some."

"You're right."

Hannah opened the rear door of her SUV. They sat next to each other on the bumper. The cork was halfway into the bottle, and she released it with a pop. When she passed it to him, he tilted the neck and drank. There was something about drinking expensive red wine straight from the bottle that made him feel free. He passed it back to her, and Hannah drank from it, too.

He wondered if she remembered the last time they had done this, on the Saturday night of their California vacation, while Olivia slept in the motel room in Calistoga. They'd sat just like this on the rear bumper in the motel parking lot. They'd finished a bottle together, and they'd made love in the back seat like teenagers. From that moment to the divorce two years later seemed like a long way to fall.

"I was late the next month," she said softly. "Do you remember?"

"Of course."

Hannah hadn't forgotten. She'd been thinking about that same warm night. Two weeks later, she had been a day and a half overdue for her period, and they'd spent those thirty-six hours convinced that their backseat romance had given Olivia a sibling. It wasn't to be. She was simply late. He'd been stupid enough to announce his feelings before he knew what was in her heart. "I guess I'm relieved," he'd said, fully expecting her to laugh and say, "Me, too."

She hadn't said that at all. She'd cried a flood of tears, and he knew he had made the worst mistake of his life.

Such a long way to fall.

"Should you be drinking?" he asked.

"No," Hannah replied, and she tilted back the bottle and drank again.

"Are you scared?" he asked.

"Terrified."

"How bad is it, Hannah, really?"

"Pretty bad. I won't kid you. It's pretty bad."

"If I were cancer, I wouldn't mess with you," he said.

Hannah laughed, but it was a broken laugh. "Thank you."

"Does Olivia know?"

"The odds? No, I haven't told her. She doesn't need that burden." His ex-wife turned toward him. The soft glow of the flashlight on the bed of the truck between them made her skin look young. "If something happens to me, Chris, you need to be there for her."

"Don't talk like that."

"I don't dwell on it, but I don't pretend it's not one of the possible outcomes."

"I'll be there for her," he said. "You know I will."

She nodded. She was grateful to hear him say it.

"You'll beat this," he added.

"That's my plan."

He wanted to hold her, but he didn't know if she wanted or needed his comfort. He wanted to let her cry in his arms, but he was worried that she would hate being vulnerable in front of him. It was messy and awkward, not like the early days, when they'd been able to divine each other's thoughts simply by the look on their faces.

"So why are we here?" she asked.

He drank more wine. "I don't know. I'm sorry. I wanted to see where Ashlynn was killed, but I shouldn't have called you. It's late. This could have waited."

"No, I'm glad you did."

They sat in silence, with nothing but the soft voice of wind alive in the town. The wine in the bottle slowly disappeared, swallow by swallow, and went to their heads. He looked at Hannah at one point, and her face was bowed, as if she were praying. That was what you did on hallowed ground, where someone innocent had been lost.

"I almost killed someone tonight," he said, filling the void with his confession.

Hannah stared at him. "What?"

He explained about the gun and Kirk Watson and his date with the devil outside Kirk's window. It made him feel better to admit it to her. The guilt was too heavy to carry on his own.

"You would never have done it," she told him.

"I almost did."

"I know you, Christopher. You're incapable of murder, no matter who it is, no matter what he did."

"I'm not so sure."

"I am." Hannah poked him in the side. "Now if it was me, I would have blown the fucker's head off."

She grinned, and laughter bubbled out of both of them, defusing the tension. It felt easy and familiar. If things had been different, he would have pulled her into his shoulder. He would have kissed her and taken her hand and held it, sending the old silent message, *I love you.* He didn't do any of those things, but he wished he could have preserved the moment for a while longer. He wanted to be a couple again.

"Listen, I learned something else tonight," he said. "It's why I called you."

"What is it?"

"Have you ever heard of a man named Vernon Clay?"

Hannah looked unhappy to hear the name. "He was a Mondamin scientist. We tried to find him during the litigation, but we couldn't."

"Why did you want to find him?"

"Because Florian Steele obviously wanted to keep him a secret." She paused and then said, "Glenn can tell you more about him. He disappeared before I moved here, but it sounds like he was a strange character. Disturbed. Who knows what he was doing on that land of his?"

"So you know about his land near St. Croix?" Chris asked.

"The dead land? Sure. There's nothing to find now, but we were always suspicious that it was at the root of the cancer cluster. How did you find out about it?"

"George Valma," he said. "Ashlynn contacted him."

"Ashlynn did? Why?"

"She wanted to know the same thing—whether Vernon Clay's research could have been connected to the cancer in St. Croix. And, I'm guessing, to her own baby."

"That poor girl." Hannah shook her head. "Bad enough to go through what she did, but to think that your own father's company was responsible. It must have been unbearable."

"George told her there was no connection."

"Well, he would say that. He's a Mondamin guy."

"He said a top epidemiologist looked into it during the litigation and found nothing."

"I don't care. She missed something."

Chris wanted to believe her, but he wasn't convinced. "If there was really something to find, Florian would never have agreed to a special master's investigation. He's a lawyer. He knows you can't bury bad facts."

"I think Florian can bury whatever he wants," Hannah said. "If Ashlynn was talking to George, do you think she discovered something that got her killed?"

"You mean something about Mondamin?"

"That's right. She lived in Florian's house. She might have known what he was hiding. Or she found out enough to start asking questions."

"What are you suggesting, Hannah? That Florian murdered his own daughter? He may be a son of a bitch, but I simply don't believe he's that cold-blooded."

"I'm not saying it was Florian, but he's not the only one with an interest in that company," Hannah said. "You said she was talking to George, right? She was already suspicious."

"Right."

"So maybe Ashlynn talked to someone else, too."

"Like who?"

"I don't know." Hannah studied the ghost town in the darkness, and she shivered. "Maybe she talked to the wrong person."

29

He knew her.

To him, she was the essence of youth, pretty and vivacious. You couldn't see her and not smile. You couldn't be in her presence and not fall in love. Her expressions changed with the speed of coins dropping from a slot machine, always different, always inviting. She moved with confident grace, not like the other gangly teenagers who were catching up with their bodies. She was young, and yet she was already mature in ways that counted. You could hear it in her seriousness of emotion when she talked about love and loss. She wasn't a melodramatic teenager weeping over a dead kitten on the highway. She understood better than most adults that life was fragile, quickly birthed, quickly spent.

Seeing her, talking to her, laughing with her made his heart ache. She reminded him that his own youth was behind him. She made him wish he could go back and live it all over, even if he could change nothing. Then again, Ashlynn made his heart sing, too, because she had such promise. When he was caught up in the evil of the world, she showed him a glimmer of light. He imagined her growing up, learning, working, marrying, having children of her own. Someone like her couldn't help but do great things.

For that reason, he'd hoped to spare her. He would have found a way to keep her safe, even if it meant taking her to a sanctuary where she couldn't escape. He wouldn't let her become a victim of his plan.

It was not to be.

He remembered the rainy afternoon when she showed up in his doorway. He hadn't seen her in a long time, so he was surprised. Without her saying a word, he realized that she *knew*. It was in her face. She looked at him in a new way, as if she were seeing him for the first time. Her hair was wet, and the rain poured over her, but she didn't hunt for cover. She simply stared at him. He could feel her reaching out, as if the secret they shared had drawn them closer together.

Ashlynn was a smart girl. You could see it in those ocean-blue eyes, how they didn't miss anything. He wasn't really surprised that she'd learned the truth. He'd fooled everyone else, but not her.

"I know who you are," she told him. "I know what you're doing."

He didn't answer, and she didn't give him time to explain. She vanished as quickly as she'd come, as if she didn't want anyone to see her. Maybe she'd simply wanted to deliver a warning, to let him know that if she could figure it out, others would, too. She didn't tell him to stop. There was no judgment in her face.

Now it was too late to save her. She'd become another victim of the sins of Florian Steele. Her death hurt him more deeply than he'd ever imagined, but if anything, it made him more convinced that he'd chosen the only path possible.

Retribution. Destruction.

He was parked behind an old barn twenty miles west of Barron. After months of acquiring materials and weeks of overnight labor, he was nearly ready. He got out and undid the deadbolt on the tall side door, and when he was inside, he relocked the door behind him. The floor under his feet was lined with a thick rubber sheath. He couldn't risk static during the dry winter. He disabled the motion-sensor alarm by entering his security code. He switched on the fluorescent lights strung across the ceiling, making the oversize building as bright as an airport hangar.

The Ford E-350 cargo van waited in the center of a musty space that still carried a decades-old smell of farm fertilizer. The van was dark blue and windowless, except for the privacy glass installed on the windshield and front doors. He had purchased it used in December for cash from a seller in Ames who he had found on Craigslist. The maximum payload was four thousand pounds, which was more than adequate for his purposes.

He'd left bread crumbs for the police in Ames. He'd done the same here in Barron—little tracks for them to follow if they were smart. In the end, in the aftermath, he wanted everyone to know why. He wanted them to understand. He wondered if the police had begun to nibble at the crumbs. He wondered how close they were to finding him. It didn't matter. He would drive the cargo van out of the barn tonight and never return. His plan began tomorrow. He didn't expect to sleep between now and then.

He'd barely slept at all for days, as the time of execution drew near. Death had a way of focusing the mind.

It would begin in the darkness, and in the first light of dawn, it would be over.

I am the vengeance of God.

My name is Aquarius.

PART THREE

SINS OF THE FATHER

30

CHRIS DIDN'T SLEEP.

He stayed with Hannah in the ghost town until two in the morning. When they finally parted, he sensed her reluctance to go home alone. Or maybe it was pent-up desire. He thought that she wanted to ask him to come with her but couldn't find the words to say so. Something had changed between them, but neither was ready to acknowledge it. Even so, he returned to the motel and lay in bed without closing his eyes, and all he could think about was Hannah.

At six in the morning, he gave up on sleep and went back to the hospital. He wasn't alone there. Glenn Magnus lay in the visitor's lounge, his long legs stretched out on the sofa, his arms behind his head. His tired eyes were open, staring at the ceiling. His unruly blond hair hadn't been washed, and he was dressed casually, in a sweatshirt and jeans. The lights in the lounge made the room unnaturally bright.

"You couldn't sleep either?" Chris asked.

The minister nodded. The fluorescent bulbs made his pale face look almost dead. "I got here an hour ago."

"How's Johan?"

"Angry. I'm worried about him."

"Did you tell him about Ashlynn and the baby?"

"I did. There was no way to cushion the blow. I'm afraid I lit a fire with him, and I don't know what he'll do."

The minister pushed himself up on the sofa. Chris sat down next to him.

"Can I ask you something about Ashlynn?" Chris said.

"Of course."

"When did you last talk to her?"

Magnus rubbed his face with both hands to awaken himself. "Sometime in February. It was shortly before she broke up with Johan. I didn't talk to her again after that."

"How did she seem?"

"Depressed. Of course, I had no idea at the time what she was wrestling with. I wish I'd known."

"You told me that when Ashlynn first came to you, she suspected her father's company of causing the cancer cluster. Did she say why?"

"I think she simply found it hard to believe that God would be so arbitrary," Magnus said. "She refused to accept what everyone told us, that the deaths were simply a mathematical anomaly. An accident of fate."

"Do you believe that's true?" Chris asked.

The minister stared blankly at the paintings on the hospital wall. "I lost my little girl, Chris. I had to watch Kimberly suffer. I couldn't blame God, so I blamed Florian and Mondamin. They were responsible. They were guilty."

"And now?"

"Now I've run out of blame. I shouldn't have questioned God's will."

"Are you saying you no longer believe there is a connection between Mondamin and the deaths in St. Croix?"

"I'm no expert in science, but I know what the experts told us. The people at the county and state said they had no basis to run tests, given the size of the cluster. We didn't listen. A Stanford scientist studied everything during the litigation, and she told the judge there was no connection. Still we didn't listen. Who am I to say they were wrong and we were right? It's over, it's done. I've let it go."

"Ashlynn didn't."

"She was a young, idealistic girl. She wanted an explanation. God isn't in that business."

"What about Vernon Clay?" Chris asked. "Did you and Ashlynn talk about him?"

He nodded. "Yes, we did. Remember, Vernon was our principal suspect. Ashlynn fixated on Vernon when I talked about him."

"Did she know anything about his work that would have connected him to the deaths in St. Croix?"

"Not that she ever told me. Why?"

"She was still talking about him only days before her death. She seemed to blame him for what happened to her baby."

Magnus ran a big hand through his hair, leaving it a mess of cowlicks. "I never should have put the idea in her head."

"Did you know Vernon Clay?" Chris asked.

"Of course. He worked at Mondamin in the early days, and he lived near St. Croix. He came to our church, but he didn't really interact with the other parishioners. He was a loner. My wife was the only one who ever got close to him. She had a weakness for vulnerable adults."

"Vulnerable adults? What does that mean?"

"Vernon was extraordinarily intelligent, but he was unable to function in the real world. Clinically, I'd say he was borderline schizophrenic. He spouted conspiracy theories right and left, truly crazy ideas. He was deeply paranoid, always convinced that people were scheming to steal his research. And yet his mind was wired for science. He had a gift. There are more people like that than you'd believe—people who work and make a living but who are barely competent on other levels."

"But your wife got through to him?"

Magnus smiled. "Leah was persistent. She'd bring him meals, talk to him, sit by him in church. Really, she became his social lifeline. I think she was the one thread connecting him to the real world. She was probably the only person who took an interest in him for something other than his work."

"You said you lost your wife almost ten years ago," Chris said. "How did that happen?"

"It was a brain aneurysm. The doctors said she'd probably carried it all her life. One morning, she simply never woke up."

"I'm sorry."

"It was painless, and she was gone in an instant. If God was going to take her, at least he did so quickly. It was merciful, compared to what happened to Kimberly."

"How did Vernon Clay react to losing his social lifeline?" Chris asked.

Magnus shook his head. "Oh, it was very sad. He withdrew even further inside himself. His delusions became much worse. He blamed everyone in town for Leah's death. He showed up in church one day and ranted about our being murderers and the Devil coming for us and even about the Mafia and the CIA, as I recall. That was the last time he set foot in St. Croix."

"I can't believe Florian kept him on at Mondamin."

"Well, I told you, he was perfectly functional when he put on his lab coat. From what I heard, Vernon was as much a genius as ever in his own world. If anything, he was even more obsessive about it. He worked seven days a week. I think he mostly went home to sleep, and then he went back to his lab. That was the only place he felt comfortable."

"What happened to him?"

"I have no idea. About four years ago, he disappeared. Honestly, he could have been gone longer, and I'm not sure anyone outside Mondamin would have realized it. We only found out he was gone was when his house burned down."

"Was that an accident?" Chris asked.

"No, it was arson. Whoever did it was never caught. Most people suspected local kids." Magnus frowned.

"You sound like you don't believe it."

"Well, that was when the rumors started. We were in the midst of the cancer diagnoses among the children when Vernon vanished. Some people thought Florian arranged for the house to be burned to erase evidence."

"Evidence of what?"

"Evidence that Vernon had been poisoning us for years. There were those who suspected he had a delusional vendetta against us going back to my wife's death. Others said that Vernon had taken to writing his formulas on the walls of his house, and so Florian had to destroy the house to secure any trade secrets. Believe what you want."

"What about the dead land?"

"Same rumors. People suspected that Vernon had been testing experimental pesticides on the fields around his house. They said Florian wanted to erase all evidence of what had been used. Maybe it was to protect company secrets. Maybe it was toxic. When we filed the lawsuit, we were desperate to believe almost anything."

"You tried to find him."

"Yes, without success. Vernon never reentered the scientific community. He became our mystery man." He added, "I'm not sure where you're going with all of this, Chris."

"It's the timing that bothers me. All of this coming up just before Ashlynn was killed. Hannah and I wondered if she could have discovered something about Vernon that everyone else missed. Something that became a motive for her murder."

"What do you think, that she found out where he was hiding? That he came back here and killed her? I realize you're trying to help Olivia, but I don't think anyone is going to believe that."

Chris nodded. Magnus was right. He knew he was chasing ghosts, and he didn't know whether to believe in them. "I admit, it may be nothing at all. So far, I can't connect the dots."

"I suppose that leaves you back where you started," the minister said. "In other words, you're back to Johan. If Olivia is innocent, my son must be guilty."

"I didn't say that."

"You didn't have to, Chris, but you're wrong."

He knew what the minister was really thinking. "You're convinced that Olivia killed her, aren't you? That's what you've believed all along."

"I hope that's not true. Truly, I do. I only know that Johan didn't kill her."

"He went to the ghost town," Chris reminded him. "Her blood is on his clothes. You can't run away from that, Glenn."

"Olivia was there, too, and she had the gun in her hand. She was pointing it at Ashlynn's head. I'm sorry, Chris. Can you really not accept the possibility that she made a youthful, impulsive mistake? That she pulled the trigger and can't bear to admit it?"

The minister's voice was calm, and his composure was infuriating because everything he said was logical. Chris was alone in defending Olivia. Everyone else assumed she was guilty. Even Hannah had doubts. Maybe he was the outlier who couldn't face the truth.

He also heard another undercurrent in what Magnus was saying. The minister knew Olivia better than he did. Olivia had grown up without him. He'd been missing in action, far away from the turmoil of her life. Did he really know whether his daughter was capable of murder?

"That's not what happened," Chris insisted.

"Fair enough. We both have faith. I hope we're both right."

Chris realized how far they were divided by their beliefs in their children. He glanced up as he saw a nurse hovering in the doorway of the lounge. She was obviously reluctant to interrupt them, but her eyes flicked around the room with concern. She backed out without saying anything, but Chris got up to stop her.

"Is something wrong?" he asked.

The nurse looked at Glenn Magnus nervously. "I was hoping your son was in here with you."

Magnus stood up, too. "Johan's not in his room?"

"No. I've searched the floor. I can't find him." She added, "I'm sure he's here somewhere, though."

The minister marched toward the hallway, brushing past the nurse. Chris followed. It was still early, and the hospital floor was deserted aside from them. Johan's room was at the end of the hall, the last room before the Exit sign over the stairway. The door was open. Magnus pushed past the curtain, calling his son's name softly as he entered. Chris heard the minister inhale sharply. The bed was unmade, but it was empty.

"He may be with Olivia," Chris suggested. "Let's not panic."

"I'll check," the nurse replied.

She hurried up the corridor toward Olivia's room, but Magnus threw open the door of the small closet, where empty hangers dangled on the wooden rod. "No, his clothes are gone."

"You think he left?" Chris asked.

"He must have gone down the back stairs."

The minister went to the window near the stairwell and examined the dark parking lot below them. There were only a handful of cars there in the early morning hours. He pointed at a section of the lot bathed in the glow of a streetlight. "My car is gone. I parked next to that light. He took it."

"Did he say anything to you?" Chris asked.

Magnus shook his head. "The last thing I did was tell him about Ashlynn and the baby. He was stricken. I never should have told him." He murmured to himself, as if praying, "Johan, what do you think you're doing, son? Don't be a fool."

31

Kirk Watson deposited Lenny at the Indian monument half an hour before the scheduled drop.

The eastern horizon was pink. A cardinal sang from the bare trees and flew past Lenny in a flash of red. He hiked up the cracked gravel road from the highway with binoculars slung around his neck. The road led to a park on the shallow hillside, dominated by an obelisk of rough gray stone. Huge trees dotted the open lawn surrounding the monument. Once, when he was really bored, he'd read the historical marker. The monument honored a pioneer victory in a long-ago frontier war, when Dakota Indians surrendered to a Minnesota colonel and released hundreds of farmers they'd held captive. If Lenny had been an Indian, he would have warned them, *They'll kill you anyway, guys.*

He sat down on a park bench to watch the highway traffic going in and out of Barron. Two sets of headlights stared from the predawn gloom in the east. The bass growl of the engine told him the first vehicle was a semi. He raised his binoculars and focused, watching the truck draw closer. As it roared past the entrance road to the monument, he could make out its distinguishing characteristics. The trailer was white, mostly unmarked, with numbers painted on the side like a code. Kirk had told him once that a lot of the unmarked trucks were military, carrying secret payloads. The truck headed west, doing at least seventy, and he wondered what was inside.

Behind the truck, the other set of headlights didn't move. A vehicle was parked on the shoulder a mile away. Lenny couldn't identify the car, and he couldn't remember whether it had been waiting there as he hiked from the highway. He wondered whether someone could have followed them. The headlights watched him like unblinking eyes, and as two or three minutes passed, his fears grew. He was getting ready to warn his brother when the headlights winked out, and he saw the red flicker of taillights as the car reversed direction. It disappeared, turning south on one of the long farm driveways. He breathed easier.

His phone rang. It was Kirk.

"You've got a semi heading west," Lenny said. "Nothing funky."

"Soon as you see our guy, you call me, right?"

"Right."

"Then you tell me when you spot him heading east again. I want to make sure he's not playing games with us."

"I know, I know. Don't worry."

"You see anything that smells like a cop, you call me."

Lenny thought about the car parked on the highway, but it was long gone. "Got it."

"Keep your eyes open, Leno, and don't fucking fall asleep."

"I won't."

He hung up. It annoyed him that Kirk didn't trust him, no matter how many times they had done drops in different parts of the state. He knew what he was doing. Even so, Kirk was right. When you assumed you were safe, when you stopped looking for a trap, that was when the steel jaws clamped shut.

Fifteen minutes passed slowly as he sat on the bench with his chin cradled in his hands and the binoculars swinging below his neck. Traffic in the early morning was light. He didn't spot many cars in either direction. The cardinal kept him company, flitting between the lower branches of the trees. In the long gaps when the highway was deserted he stared at the obelisk, which reminded him of the arrowheads you could dig up in the fields around here. Every now and then he heard noises in the trees behind him, and he looked around nervously, as if the Indians were massing for an attack.

He was alone.

Five minutes before seven o'clock, he spotted the mark. He knew the vehicle; he'd tracked it before. The customer was right on time, like always.

He punched the speed-dial button for his brother's phone.

"Yeah?"

"He's coming."

Lenny hung up. He had nothing to do but wait. It would take five minutes for the customer to get to the drop zone. He'd check his mirrors, make sure he was alone, and pull onto the shoulder. He'd open his driver's door and toss the bag over the hood into the north-side fields. It would be over in seconds; he wouldn't stay any longer than necessary. He wouldn't wait to see who showed up, because curiosity could kill you. No, he'd do a U-turn and head back, probably going even faster, because he'd want to pretend like the drop had never happened.

It would be ten minutes before the SUV passed the monument again, heading back toward Barron. Lenny needed to know the mark was gone before Kirk went for the cash. They'd never had a customer go rogue, but it could happen. They'd never had the police run a sting, but it could happen.

Lenny kept his eyes on the highway. Three minutes passed with no traffic. There was no sign that the car was being tracked by the cops. Everything was going smoothly.

He dialed Kirk again. "Nobody on his tail."

"Keep watching."

Lenny slapped the phone shut. He lifted his binoculars and zoomed in on the empty road.

In the next instant, he was airborne.

Two hands grabbed him under his shoulder blades and yanked him bodily off the bench. He flew backward, seeing the crowns of trees over his head. He fell hard in the wet grass. Someone landed on his chest, punching the air from his lungs, and he wheezed, unable to catch a breath. He blinked in terror, recognizing Johan Magnus on top of him. He struggled, but the strong football player kept him pinned like a squashed bug. Johan grabbed the leather strap of the binoculars and tightened it. Lenny choked and clawed to get free, but he couldn't squeeze his fingers between the strap and the skin of his neck.

"Was it Kirk?" Johan hissed into his ear.

Lenny twitched. His legs jerked like jumping beans. He tried to beg, but he couldn't make a sound. His eyes went blind, and he heard a roaring like a train.

Johan loosened the strap. Lenny spit and gasped as air rushed back into his lungs, but when he tried to get up, Johan piled a fist into Lenny's jaw. His head snapped into the mud. Johan twisted the strap, and Lenny felt the blindness again, the roaring, the blackness sinking like a shroud over his brain.

The strap came free, and he inhaled in a rush. Tears streamed from his eyes, and he squeaked out a plea. "Stop."

"Was it Kirk?"

Lenny shook his head, crying, gasping, saying nothing.

"*Was it Kirk?* Did he attack Olivia?"

"Please. Please."

Johan slapped him. Lenny felt the impact like stinging wasps.

"I swear I will choke you again," Johan told him.

"*No*, don't, don't!"

Johan bunched Lenny's shirt in his fists and yanked his torso off the ground. He shook him like a doll. "Did Kirk attack Olivia? Was it him?"

Lenny's head bobbed. "*Yes*," he croaked.

"Were you there, too?"

"I called—I called for help. *Please*."

Johan dragged Lenny to his feet. The older boy towered over him, and his face was red with fury. Lenny cowered, expecting another blow. Instead, Johan grabbed Lenny's arm and belt and threw him across the bench. Lenny tumbled over it and crashed down on his knee in the dirt, where he lay terrified, not moving. Angry footsteps sloshed through the wet grass as Johan stormed away. Lenny pushed himself over onto his stomach. His neck burned where the leather strap had chewed into his skin. Shivers of pain knifed up and down his spine. He bit down, and his teeth didn't align. He pushed his tongue around his mouth and tasted blood. He collapsed onto his chest, crying.

He heard his phone ringing on the bench, but he didn't answer it. He couldn't get up. He couldn't face Kirk.

He didn't see the SUV passing the monument on the eastbound route toward Barron.

A minute later, he didn't see the SUV turn around and speed back toward the drop.

The phone rang and rang. Leno didn't answer. Kirk hung up and dialed, hung up and dialed, hung up and dialed. Nothing. His brother had gone silent.

"Pick up, you worthless fucker!" he screamed in his closed-up truck. "Answer the goddamn phone, Leno!"

His blood vessels pulsed. He climbed out and delivered a ferocious kick to the front tire with his boot. Breathing hard, he sank back against the hood and drummed his fist against his chin. He could see the splash of bright red in the field. The backpack. The money. He told himself there was nothing to worry about. The customer had made the drop and run away with his tail between his legs. This one was just like all the others. No cops. No traps.

Even so, if Leno didn't answer, that meant there was a problem. The safe thing to do was get out of there, but if he left, someone else would stumble onto the backpack and steal his money. He wasn't going to let that happen. No way.

Kirk eyed the highway. He saw no cars, and the world was flat enough here that he had at least a minute of safety before anyone else could reach the drop. If he moved now, he could grab the backpack and be gone. He wouldn't head back toward Barron. He'd use the dirt roads and leave Leno at the monument with the dead Indians. Fuck him.

He got into the pickup and drove fast. He kept his eyes on the highway. At the intersection, he spun the truck around, pointed back toward the dirt road heading north. He got out, leaving the door open, and jogged through the rutted field. He left boot prints; he didn't care. The backpack was thirty yards from the highway shoulder. He reached it and and tore open the zipper, confirming the wads of cash inside. Throwing the strap over his shoulder, he ran for his truck.

He heard the roaring engine of the SUV before he saw it. He was still in the field when the truck rocketed past the drop site.

It was him.

The bastard had turned around. He'd come back to find him.

The SUV was going so fast that the man's face was a blur, but it was enough for them to see each other. Their eyes met, from the speeding vehicle to the field. Kirk recognized him, and he recognized Kirk. The game between them was over. The engine on the highway gunned as the bastard accelerated. The SUV would be gone in seconds.

Kirk couldn't waste time. He had to get out of here.

He retraced his steps to his pickup then shot north. He made random checkerboard turns, keeping his eyes on his mirror. No one followed him. He glanced at the backpack and wondered if there was a tracking device inside. Was that it? Maybe it didn't matter where he went or how fast he drove; maybe they were behind him, watching him like a blip on a screen. He pulled onto the shoulder, dumped the contents of the backpack onto the seat, and sifted through the money. He saw no obvious electronic devices, but he knew that meant nothing. The feds were clever.

He waited in the middle of nowhere. The roads shot like arrows in every direction. The fields were empty. When ten minutes passed and he was still alone, he decided that the sirens weren't coming. Whatever the trap was, it hadn't closed around his neck yet.

So what was it all about?

Maybe his prey simply wanted to know who'd been taunting him and needed to put a face to the childish voice on the phone. If so, he'd succeeded. He'd stripped away the mask, and they were both at risk now, both exposed. They could each destroy the other's life, but only by giving up their own.

Kirk's mouth curled into a sour frown. He didn't like not knowing.

What happens now, Daddy?

32

Hannah put her arms around their daughter when Chris brought her home from the hospital. Olivia was six inches taller than her mother, and the girl bowed her head to rest on Hannah's shoulder. There had been awkwardness between them for three years, but mother and daughter had both declared a truce. When Olivia went upstairs to her bedroom, Hannah's teary eyes followed her. Chris sensed his ex-wife's flood of relief at having her daughter safely back home.

He waited until Olivia closed her door upstairs. "The counselor says she's strong," he reported. "She takes after you."

"I don't feel very strong," Hannah said. She wiped her eyes, as if she felt guilty about letting her emotions overrun her.

"She'll be okay. Really. It will just take some time."

"I know." Hannah reached out and put a hand on his shoulder. With her, the simple touches went a long way. "Do you want me to make breakfast for us?"

"That would be great."

She glanced down at herself. She wore a plain terry robe, and her face was without makeup. Her feet were bare. "I need to shower and dress first. Can you wait?"

"Sure. I'm sorry I kept you up late."

"No, I'm glad you called. It was like old times."

"Take your time," he said. "I'll wait."

"Why don't you come up and talk to me?"

She padded up the stairs, and he followed behind her. Her bedroom was at the end of the hall, and she went into the bathroom to start the shower, leaving the door ajar. Her voice carried over the noise of the water.

"Are you staying at the Riverside Motel?" she asked.

"That's right."

"It's a dump, isn't it?"

He laughed. "Oh, it's not so bad. The owner's a decent guy. He tries hard."

Hannah poked her face around the door. "Why not stay here with us, Chris?"

He was so surprised that he had nothing to say. Hannah picked up on his hesitation.

"I'm sorry," she added. "Please don't feel obligated."

"No, I'd like that. Are you sure I wouldn't be getting in your way?"

"Of course you would," she said, smiling again.

Her face disappeared, and he heard the shower door open and close. He studied the bedroom, which was nothing like the modern room they'd shared in the suburbs. The furniture was secondhand oak, its stain fading. The queen bed had a hand-made quilt thrown casually across the duvet cover. She had pictures of Olivia on her dresser at every stage of the girl's life. There were other, older pictures, too. Hannah's parents. Her brother in Ohio. There was even a picture of Chris, but it wasn't one he found particularly flattering. He was younger, unshaved, wavy-haired, with a grin a mile wide. That was the man she'd chosen to remember.

The pipes of the shower went silent. He heard Hannah's voice again. "What do you want for breakfast? Bacon and eggs, I suppose."

He stood beside the door and called to her. "I've been steering clear of the good stuff lately. Some cereal and fruit would be fine if you have it."

"I have homemade granola."

"Great." He added, "What does Olivia usually have?"

"Bacon and eggs. Who does that sound like?"

"She's lucky she got your skinny genes," he said.

"You're getting pretty skinny these days, too, Chris. I told you that you looked great, didn't I?"

"You did. Thanks."

"I admire your willpower. I suppose it's a lot easier without me nagging you about it."

"I don't recall that," he said.

"Liar."

He laughed.

"I hope Olivia makes a more understanding wife than I ever did," Hannah added.

"Oh, I don't know. She's a lot like you. That's a pretty good start."

"Remind me to warn her future husband," she said.

"I said Olivia would make a good wife," Chris replied, chuckling, "but I never, ever said you would make a good mother-in-law."

There was no reply from inside the bathroom. He was afraid she had taken him seriously.

"Hannah?"

He still heard nothing. Seconds ticked by.

"Hannah, it was a joke." Chris nudged the door open but remained on the threshold. "Are you okay?"

She was there, but she was silent.

"Hannah, I'm coming in."

He took a step into the bathroom. Steam hung in the air, making the small space warm and close. Hannah stood in front of the pedestal sink, holding it with both hands. She was naked. Water droplets clung to her bare skin. She'd removed the wig she used in public, and her skull was bald and smooth, paler than the rest of her body. Her back was familiar to him, her curving spine like train tracks. He saw the scar on her shoulder from a childhood burn and the inside of her knees where she liked to be kissed.

She sobbed quietly.

She stared at her face in the mirror as if it were the face of a stranger, and she cried with her shoulders trembling. Tears ran like shower water. He came up behind her and said nothing; he laid cool hands on her neck and eased her backward into his chest. Her mouth fell open as she tried to breathe. He caressed her bare head with a gentle touch, turned her around, gathered her up in his arms, and felt her cling to him, pouring out her despair.

"I'll never see it," she murmured, her words barely audible. "I won't be there."

He knew what she meant. Olivia married. Thanksgiving dinners. Grandchildren. The future.

"You will."

She stared up at him, her eyes laced with red. "Look at me."

"I am. You're beautiful."

"Don't lie to me."

"I don't lie. I'm a lawyer."

She laughed through her tears.

He tilted her head with a finger on the underside of her chin. He cupped her neck with his other hand. He leaned in and kissed her, a kiss lasting only a second, a kiss that was like thousands of other simple kisses they had shared together in their lifetimes. And yet it was different. It was like their first kiss. It was their most important kiss.

It made her cry harder and push him away. "You don't have to do this. You don't have to pity me."

"Are you kidding?"

He pulled her to him and kissed her again. He was conscious of her bare skin under his hands and her wet torso trapped against his chest, and he quickly grew aroused. She responded, too. They didn't lose themselves in their passion; they knew who they were. They weren't kids, and they weren't newlyweds. They were a not-quite-young divorced couple in the middle of a world going crazy, and for a moment, they needed an escape.

She helped him peel off his clothes, which were wet now, too. She led him to her bed, guiding him with an arm around his waist. They didn't hold hands. She was saying she needed him; she wasn't necessarily saying she loved him. It didn't matter. They laid on the bed together, and he let her lead, descending on him, pinching her mouth shut to keep her cries muffled. That was the way parents made love, in hushed silence behind a closed door. She bent forward, her petite hands on his chest, her small breasts swaying. Her face was different without her long hair caught in the sheen of sweat on her cheeks, but her mouth was just as he remembered, forming an oval as it fell into a breathless smile. Her eyes were the same, too, wide open as she neared climax, not letting go of his stare. It had always been the most intimate, erotic sensation of his life, making love to Hannah with open eyes.

When they were both spent, when she lowered herself onto him with her face in the crook of his neck, he had a fleeting thought about what would happen next between them. She must have had the same doubts, but neither wanted to spoil it by talking. Her breathing grew steady as she drifted into sleep. He was content to hold her. He tried to stay awake to treasure the sensation, but he realized he was weary to the point of exhaustion, and he slept, too. It was the most restful sleep he'd had since he'd arrived in St. Croix.

Olivia lay on top of the covers, staring at the ceiling. She was conscious of all the places where her body hurt. When she moved, she was reminded of what they'd done to her. Her skin bore their marks. Even so, she refused to think about it. She didn't care about herself or about the ugly bruises. Those would fade and heal. Instead, she thought about Ashlynn in the park. That was the injury that would always be with her. That regret would never go away.

She imagined Ashlynn on the corner of the bed, alive, luminous, still maddeningly beautiful, the way she would have been right now if Olivia had driven her home.

"You left me," Ashlynn reminded her, with sadness in her voice.

Olivia said nothing, because Ashlynn was right. It didn't matter that she was angry and jealous at this girl for taking Johan away. It didn't matter what secrets Ashlynn had kept. She'd asked for help, and Olivia had rejected her. That was what Olivia had to live with. That was the person she'd become, someone who deserted a girl who desperately needed her help.

"You left me," Ashlynn said again.

She never said anything else. It was always the same. *You left me. You left me. You left me.*

Olivia closed her eyes, and when she opened them again, Ashlynn was gone. Her guilt tunneled a mile deep. All she could think about were ways to make it stop. Stupid ways. She went to her open closet, staring at the clothes arranged neatly on the rod. On the far back of the closet shelf, she spotted a slim gold box. She brought it to the bed and removed the top. The box contained a silk men's tie. Three years ago, she'd bought it as a gift for her father, but in the wake of the divorce, she'd never given it to him.

She draped the tie over her fingers, stretching the soft fabric. She pushed her pink lips together with such force they turned white. She looped the tie around her neck, just to see how it would feel. Taking both ends, she pulled it tighter, until the pressure began to hurt. It would have to be much tighter. She would have to knot it so she couldn't pry it loose with her fingers. A knot on one end. The other end tied to the clothes rod.

Olivia went to the full-length mirror on the closet door. The flaps of the navy-blue tie hung down her T-shirt.

You left me.

She took the fat end of the tie in her hands. She stared at her face and imagined it purple, her tongue swollen, her eyes bulged out like a boxer dog. Hideous.

She heard Kimberly's voice in her head, and she knew what her friend would say. "Don't you dare, Livvy."

Olivia sighed, knowing that Kimberly was right. She couldn't do it. She wrapped the fat end over the skinny end and pushed it over the loop on her neck. She tucked the flap back into the knot and adjusted it so that it was perfect. It was just a tie now, not a noose. She stuck out her tongue at herself, and then she stripped off the tie and threw it back in the closet.

Olivia heard a sharp *ping* on her bedroom window. Sometimes a bird flew into the glass. Sometimes the wind blew acorns against it. She glanced toward the river, and as she watched, it happened again. A rock struck the window and bounced away. Someone was down there, throwing stones to attract her attention.

She knew who it was, and her heart raced. She ran to the window and saw him hiding in the trees on the riverbank, waving at her.

Johan.

Olivia threw open the window, but she thought better of calling to him. She didn't think her parents would want them talking to each other. Instead, she made her usual escape, clinging to the gutter, jumping to the ground. The fall hurt this time. She ran for the trees, and before she could say a word, he pulled her toward the riverbank, where they were invisible from the house. He reached out and held her fiercely.

"Those bastards," he whispered. "Are you okay?"

She could feel him quivering with rage. When he took her elbows she had a chance to look at him, and he wasn't the Johan she knew. It wasn't just the cuts and welts on his face. His eyes were different. She didn't recognize him.

"I'm fine," she said. "Really, it's fine."

"You're lying."

She was, but he didn't need to hear the truth. "Don't worry about me. How are you?"

He shrugged, as if his own injuries were nothing. "It was Kirk," he said. "Him and the others. They did it."

"Big surprise."

"I made Lenny tell me."

Olivia looked at his hands, where the knuckles were bloody. "Johan, what did you do?"

"Nothing compared to what I'm going to do."

She'd heard that hatred in the voices of other St. Croix boys, but never from Johan. "Don't take this on," she told him. "Please. It's not your fight."

"Yes, it is. I've listened to my father for years, but he's wrong. You can't just take it. You can't lie down and let them kick you. Sooner or later, you have to fight back."

"You'll get hurt or you'll get in trouble. That won't change what happened."

"I don't care. I can't take doing nothing. Look at what they did to you! Look at what they did to Ashlynn!"

"Nothing you do will bring her back or make this go away for me. You're only going to make things worse."

Johan sank to his knees, and Olivia squatted to meet his gaze. When he spoke, his throat was tight with grief. "She was pregnant, Olivia."

"I know."

"The baby was going to die. Our baby. She had to have an abortion."

"I heard. It's awful."

"It's their fault. All of them. Florian. Mondamin. Kirk. Barron. I have to do something."

"What are you going to do?" Olivia asked.

"I'm going after Kirk tonight. With him gone, the feud will collapse. It'll be over and done."

"*No*. For God's sake, Johan, do *not* do that. I won't let you."

"I'm doing it for you. And Ashlynn. And Kimberly, too."

"All you'll do is throw your life away. I don't want to lose you, too."

Johan got up and pulled her with him. "I tried peace. I tried turning the other cheek. Look what it got us. I'm not lying down anymore. I'm fighting back."

"I'll tell your father. I'll tell the police. They'll stop you."

He grabbed her and shook his head. "Don't."

"Damn it, Johan, I will. This is crazy."

"If you still love me, don't tell anyone. Don't tell them what I'm going to do." He kissed her, as if he knew she couldn't resist him, and whispered, "Please."

She tried to hold him, but he ran along the riverbank without looking back. He was swallowed by the woods, but she could still hear his footsteps trampling the brush. She stood by the water, torn with indecision. She told herself that he wasn't really serious about Kirk. He wouldn't do it. Not Johan. He would be like her, thinking crazy thoughts and finally pulling back before it was too late.

His eyes said something else. His eyes said murder.

She had to stop him.

33

CHRIS AWOKE TO A BUZZING NOISE, LIKE AN INSECT FLYING AROUND HIS FACE. He opened his eyes, momentarily disoriented. He was alone in Hannah's bed, and the house was filled with the greasy, seductive aroma of frying bacon. The buzzing noise was his phone vibrating in the pocket of his pants, which were now neatly folded on top of Hannah's dresser instead of in a heap on the floor where he'd left them.

Naked, he climbed out of bed and retrieved his phone. He found a text message from Michael Altman on the screen.

I need to see you. MA.

Chris texted back to the county attorney. *One hour in your office?*

He took a shower and re-dressed. Downstairs, he found Hannah at the stove, with an apron over her work clothes. Olivia sat at the butcher-block table, pushing around a runny egg on her plate and chewing a piece of crisp bacon. His ex-wife nodded her head at Olivia and gave him a meaningful glance. He understood. What had happened between them was a secret from their daughter.

He sat down at the table, and Hannah put a mug of coffee in front of him and a bowl of granola. Olivia's face was dark, as if her mind were far away. Her leg drummed restlessly like a piston under the table.

"You okay, Olivia?" he asked.

His daughter didn't look at him. "Yeah, fine."

"You sure?"

She gave him a smile, but it felt false. "I'm sure."

He didn't push her. She'd been through enough. If she needed time, he wanted her to have it.

Hannah sat down between them. She gave him a tiny, embarrassed smile that their daughter didn't see. They ate mostly in silence, but he realized how much he had missed their morning routine since the divorce. It was like the old days in Minneapolis, each of them getting ready to go their separate ways.

When he finished, he put his bowl in the sink and kissed his daughter on the head. She hugged him around the waist, and it felt good.

"I'll walk you out," Hannah told him.

She accompanied him to his car. It was a gray morning, promising more rain. They lingered on the sidewalk, aware of the awkwardness between them and not sure how to make it better. He thought about kissing her, but he didn't. They were acting like teenagers again.

"That was nice," Hannah said finally.

"Yes, it was."

"It's been a long time for me," she added.

"For me, too."

Hannah smiled. "Oh, sure, likely story. What's a long time for a guy? A month?"

"A year and a half," he told her, "and even that was a stupid one-time bar fling."

"Really?" She looked surprised, but then she shook her head, as if she were mad at herself. "Sorry, it's none of my business. I don't know why I'm talking like this. I never expected this to happen between us."

"Neither did I."

"Everything that's going on. The cancer. Olivia. I just—"

"You don't need to explain," he said.

"It was a stupid mistake."

"Was it?"

She looked uncomfortable. "I'm not saying I regret it, but we don't have to make a big thing out of it, do we?"

"Maybe we should."

Hannah reached for his face, but she pulled her hand back. "Think about our situation, Chris. We have enough to worry about with Olivia. We don't need to add more complications right now."

He nodded, but he wasn't happy. "That's true."

"I'm sorry."

"No, you're right." He nodded at the house. "Do you want to rescind your invitation?"

"About staying here? No, you should."

"What do we tell Olivia?"

"We tell her that it will be easier if you stay in the house. She doesn't need to know what happened between us."

Chris didn't think it would be easier for him, being around Hannah after they'd made love again, but he didn't object. He opened his car door, and before he climbed inside Hannah embraced him. She held on longer than two friends would. When they broke apart, the flush on her face suggested that she was conflicted about their relationship, too. He drove off without saying more, but he watched her in the mirror, and she followed him with her eyes until he was gone.

Things were already complicated.

He headed north on the lonely highway toward the courthouse in Barron for his meeting with Michael Altman. When he arrived at the grand old building on the hill, he found the county attorney waiting for him on a bench among the empty flower urns. Altman had his black trench coat draped over his arm and his fedora planted neatly on his head. His black glasses were pushed to the end of his nose, and he had his mobile phone extended at the end of his arm. He squinted, trying to read.

"Mr. Hawk," Altman said. "I need coffee. Do you mind?"

"Not at all."

Altman slid his phone into his suit coat pocket. "These little screens are a conspiracy of the young. I'm sorry I won't be around to enjoy it when the current generation turns fifty and their eyes give out."

Chris laughed. The county attorney bounded off the bench and led him down the terraced steps toward the town's main street. He struggled to keep up with Altman, and he was convinced that the older attorney would outlive most of the younger generation. They went across the street to a dive called Jack's that smelled of beer and stale smoke. Altman waved at the bartender and slid into a booth covered in torn red vinyl. Chris sat opposite him. They were the only customers inside.

"This place is old Barron," Altman said, laying his fedora on the table. "Pre-Mondamin. It's been around since before I became county attorney. They water down their beer so much they could sell it as Dasani, but I've got a soft spot for the place. That, and they make morning coffee so strong you can chew it."

Without being asked, the bartender dropped a steaming mug in front of

222 • BRIAN FREEMAN

Altman and stared at Chris with a question mark on his face. Chris shook his head.

"You wanted to see me?" Chris asked when the bartender was gone.

Altman blew on his coffee. "I hear you've been busy."

"You could say that."

"The sheriff says you dropped off bloody clothes belonging to Johan Magnus."

"That's right."

"So Johan was in the park that night. I'm impressed. Do you think he killed her?"

Chris thought about Glenn Magnus. *I hope we're both right.* "I don't know, but he had a motive. Ashlynn dumped him when she got pregnant. She had an abortion. He could have lost control when he found out."

Altman sipped his coffee and used a napkin to wipe the mug and the table. "I'm not sure a jury will see Johan as a killer. I'm not sure I do, either."

"There's as much evidence to suggest that Johan killed her as there is to suggest that Olivia killed her. Your airtight case just sprang a big leak."

The county attorney smiled at him over the top of the coffee mug. "I'm used to defense attorneys blowing smoke, Mr. Hawk. You're trolling for other suspects, which is fine, but the evidence still points squarely at your daughter."

"I reviewed the evidence the police gathered," Chris added. "Something else doesn't make sense."

Altman lifted an eyebrow. "What's that?"

"Ashlynn didn't have a laptop. It's not in the inventory of personal possessions, either in her car or her room."

The county attorney frowned. "That's a little odd, I'll grant you."

"I can think of a few reasons why the police didn't find it. One, Ashlynn got rid of it herself before she arrived in the ghost town. Two, it was taken from her, either before or after the murder. Three, Florian and Julia removed it from her room prior to the police search."

"Why would they do that?"

"Maybe because there were things about Ashlynn they didn't want anyone to find."

"Or maybe Olivia took the laptop herself," Altman said.

"Now who's blowing smoke?"

Altman smiled. "Exactly what do you think was on Ashlynn's laptop that makes it so important?"

"I have no idea. E-mails? Calendar items? A history of websites she visited?"

"I'll talk to Florian," Altman said. "There may be an innocent explanation. Her computer may be at school or somewhere else in the house."

"Maybe."

Altman put his mug down and folded his hands together. "I understand your interest in conspiracy theories, Mr. Hawk, but let me explain something to you about the men and women who serve on juries in this county. They're not fools. They're solid, hardworking Christians with a lot of common sense. If you think you can misdirect them, you're wasting your time. If you really want to help your daughter, tell her to come clean, and we'll see what we can do for her."

"She didn't kill Ashlynn."

Altman sighed. "Mr. Hawk, I don't like to see a sixteen-year-old girl spend the rest of her life in prison, no matter what she did, but at the end of the day, my responsibility is to Ashlynn Steele. I knew that girl well. I'm not going to let her death go unpunished."

"There were other things going on in Ashlynn's life. There are other possible motives for her murder."

"Like what?"

"Vernon Clay," Chris said.

He expected another dismissal from the county attorney. *You're chasing ghosts.* Instead, Altman pursed his lips with concern and eased back into the booth. He studied Chris with a new curiosity. "Why bring him up?"

"I didn't. Ashlynn did. She was asking questions about him before she was killed."

For the first time, Chris saw a crack of doubt in the man's eyes.

"You're sure about that?" Altman asked.

"I am."

"Who was she talking to?"

"I'd rather not give you a name right now, but my source is reliable. Ashlynn talked to him directly."

"Is it someone at Mondamin?"

Chris said nothing.

Altman drummed his fingers on the table. "Vernon Clay left town years ago. Do you have any actual evidence that Ashlynn's interest in him had something to do with her death?"

"No, but I don't have her laptop."

"Ah, yes, of course. The mysterious laptop. I like how you tie things together. So what do you want me to believe? You think Ashlynn was poking around in her father's secrets because of Vernon Clay, and she learned something that put her in danger?"

"Maybe. If she kicked the hornet's nest, who knows what flew out?"

"Do you have any theories?"

Chris leaned forward across the table. "You tell me, Mr. Altman. I get the feeling you know something you're not sharing with me."

Altman shrugged. "This is your party."

"Is it? A few minutes ago, I was spouting conspiracy theories. Now you're pumping me for information. I'd like to know why."

The county attorney fingered his coffee mug. "First answer another question for me, and then we'll see. This reliable source of yours, did he mention anything about this man who calls himself Aquarius?"

"No."

"Ashlynn said nothing to him about Aquarius?"

"Not that I know of. I think he would have mentioned it." Chris studied Altman with suspicion. "Why? Did you discover evidence that Aquarius might have been involved in Ashlynn's death?"

"We've found nothing like that."

"Then why bring him up?"

Altman's face was pained. "Aquarius is a separate investigation, Mr. Hawk. I'm afraid I can't share any information with you."

"It was separate. Now I'm not so sure. If you have any reason to believe there's a connection between Ashlynn and Aquarius, you owe me the truth about it." Chris frowned, and suddenly he understood. "You think Aquarius may be Vernon Clay, don't you? You found something to tie them together. That's what this is about."

The county attorney gave a tiny sigh. "All I can tell you, Mr. Hawk, is that we'll know soon enough if that's true."

"What do you mean?"

"Aquarius," Altman said. "We've found him."

34

THE RESPITE WAS OVER. THE RAIN CAME AGAIN.

Chris listened to the splash of the wet streets under his tires as he drove north. The downpour sent everyone in Barron inside, leaving the sidewalks deserted. It was as dark at noon as it would have been at dusk. He stopped at a red light, and sheets of water pelted his windshield like machine-gun fire. He could see gray waves blowing from west to east, pebbling the dark surface of the river.

The parking lot of the Riverside Motel was a lake. He stopped in front of his corner room, where a waterfall spilled from the overflowing gutters. Getting out, his feet landed in a deep puddle, soaking through his socks. He unlocked the door and went inside. Rain thundered in a drumbeat on the roof. He didn't have much to pack. In two minutes, he threw what he had inside his suitcase, returned to his Lexus, then dumped the bag inside his trunk.

He kicked through standing water to the motel office and found Marco Piva in a flimsy folding chair under a large vinyl picnic umbrella, a beer bottle in his hand, as if it were a summer Sunday. He wore a white undershirt, and his thick black chest hair curled over the V-neck. His heavy arms bulged out of the sleeves. He had a paper napkin spread out on his lap, and he was eating a capicola sandwich.

Marco held up his beer bottle, saluting him. "Mr. Hawk. Join me, please."

Chris ducked under the shower of rain falling from the edges of the umbrella. "It's not much of a day for a picnic, Marco."

The squat motel owner waved his hand dismissively. His skin was damp, and his wiry salt-and-pepper hair was wet. "Rain is nothing. I love the rain. This is a gorgeous day."

"If you say so." He pointed at an empty chair next to Marco. "Are you expecting someone?"

Marco shrugged. "You."

"How did you know I was coming?"

"I didn't, but here you are. My wife always used to set an extra place at our dinner table, just in case someone showed up. She did that every night of the week for more than thirty years."

"How often did someone arrive?" Chris asked.

"Not once!" Marco chortled.

Chris sat down on the rickety folding chair. Marco reached into a cooler of ice and offered him a dripping beer, but Chris shook his head. "Too early for me," he said.

"How about half a sandwich? This is my favorite meal. I ship in my sausage from Chiaramonte's. Some things in life I refuse to do without."

"It smells amazing, but no thanks."

Marco took a large mouthful of his sandwich. The crusty bread made a loud crunch as he bit into it. A dollop of brown mustard leaked out of the corner of his mouth, and he wiped it up with his finger.

"I saw you packing your bag," he said. "Are you leaving me?"

"That's right." Chris handed him his motel key, and Marco shoved it into a pocket. "My ex-wife and I decided it would be easier if I stayed at her place. That way I can be close to Olivia."

Marco winked, and his jowly face brightened. "Close to your wife, too, eh?"

"I think she wants to be friends again. I'm not sure it's anything more than that."

"You sound like you'd like it to be something more," he said.

"In a perfect world, sure."

"Who says anything has to be perfect?" Marco asked. "God screwed up the world the first time, didn't he? You screw up, you try again. I'd love to have one more fight with my wife, just so we could make up."

"I thought you were soul mates," Chris said, smiling.

"Oh, lovers argue better than anyone else, you know that. I'd scream at her that she worked too hard, she traveled too much. She'd scream at me that she hated what I did, she hated the risks. Then we'd drink wine and have sex."

"That does sound perfect."

"See? You're a smart man, Mr. Hawk. Of course, the key to a happy marriage is to marry a woman who's much smarter than you are. Fortunately for us men, that's easy to do."

Chris laughed. "True."

"Why did you and your wife split up? You sound like a love match. I hope you didn't cheat on her."

"No, nothing like that."

"I didn't think so. You strike me as a man of honor, Mr. Hawk." He added, "So what was it between you?"

"If you ask Hannah, she'd say I forgot my priorities."

"Is that true?"

Chris watched the rain, and he acknowledged the reality for the first time. "Yes, I guess it is."

"Then change them."

"I'm here," he said, "but I'm not sure it's enough."

"Well, what are you willing to give up to get her back? Have you asked yourself that?"

"Three years ago, I didn't see why I should give up anything at all," he said.

"And now?"

"Now, I think I'd give up just about everything to have what we had."

Marco calmly ate his sandwich and swallowed down his beer. "Sometimes that's what it takes. Of course, the past is long gone. You can only build something different. Life changes, my friend."

"Are you a motel owner, or are you a marriage counselor?" Chris asked, smiling.

"I'm just a busybody," Marco said, his mouth full. "My wife isn't around to offer advice, so I have to fill in for her." When he swallowed, his face grew serious, and he reached out with a fist and thumped it on Chris's knee. "Me, I would give up everything, too, if I could have my wife back. I don't have that choice, Mr. Hawk, but you do. Grab it."

"It's her choice, not mine."

"Or maybe she's waiting for you to reach out to her. Someone has to extend a hand, you know?"

Chris stood up. The rain was as strong as ever. Even in the mild air, he felt a chill. "I'll keep that in mind."

"Do that."

"It's been a pleasure, Marco, but I have to go." Chris shook hands with the older man. "I know where to come if I need advice."

"Truly, the pleasure has been mine, Mr. Hawk. I wish you good luck in all things." Marco held the handshake without letting go and added in a dark voice, "Speaking of choices, I assume you did not burden yourself with revenge against those who harmed your daughter."

Chris remembered standing outside Kirk Watson's window. "I almost did."

"God doesn't punish us for things we *almost* do."

"I still have your gun," Chris said. "Would you like it back?"

"My gun? I have no idea what you're talking about." Marco winked and whispered, "You keep it, Mr. Hawk. You never know when it will come in handy."

"Thanks."

Chris left the motel owner sitting under the umbrella with his beer and the last bites of his capicola sandwich. He walked past the line of red doors toward his car. Most of the motel rooms were empty, but he heard a loud television blaring in one room and an even louder couple making love in another. Everyone had different ways of escaping the rain.

Before he climbed inside his Lexus, he saw that he'd failed to latch the door of his own room. The wood was warped, so the lock didn't always catch. The door hung six inches ajar. He crossed through the curtain of water off the roof and reached for the knob to yank the door shut. As he did, he saw the weak glow of a lamp on the end table.

He was certain he'd turned it off as he left.

Chris pushed at the door with the toe of his shoe. The rusting hinges groaned in protest as it swung open. Cautiously, he stepped through the opening, smelling dampness and something else.

Perfume. He recognized the aroma. He'd smelled the same sweet cloud once before, on the steps of a box home on the streets of Barron.

Chris went inside. The forty-watt bulb under the lampshade left the room semidark with the curtains closed. Someone was waiting for him in the shadows. Tanya Swenson sat on the end of the motel bed.

35

"How did you get here?" Chris asked her.

Tanya was soaked to the bone in a blue T-shirt and jeans. Her arms hugged her chest. "There's a place in the woods where you can pull off the highway and park. Johan showed it to me."

Chris switched on the motel room heater. The fan had a loud rattle. "You look cold. Pull the blanket around you."

"I'm okay."

He checked outside to make sure they were alone, but he left the door open. "So you visit Johan when he's working here?"

"Sometimes. It's boring making beds, you know, so I keep him company."

"What do you talk about?"

"I don't know. Stupid stuff. Like how much I want to get the hell out of this place after school."

"You don't like it here in Barron?" Chris asked.

"Duh. No."

"Why is that?"

"You want a list? There's nothing to do. The boys are all jerks. The girls treat me like shit."

Chris sat down, leaving as much space between them as he could. "Johan isn't a jerk," he said.

"No, he's great."

He watched her face. "You like him, don't you?"

"Why do you care?" Tanya asked defensively.

"I was just wondering. I can hear it in your voice."

"It's dumb. It's a crush. It's not like he'd ever look at me that way anyway. He says with Kimberly gone, I'm like his little sister."

"That's sweet."

Tanya rolled her eyes. "It sucks. I don't want a brother, I want a boyfriend."

"Yeah, I get it." He added, "How'd you feel about him dating Olivia?"

"I didn't care."

"You weren't jealous?"

"So what if I was? It didn't change anything."

"Did he tell you when he broke up with her?"

"Yeah. He was afraid I'd be pissed because we were friends."

"Were you?"

Tanya shook her head. "I knew she wasn't his type."

"Who was? Ashlynn?"

"I guess. Miss Perfect." She frowned. "That was mean. Ashlynn wasn't the typical rich blonde bitch. I liked her."

"Did you know that Johan and Ashlynn started dating after he split with Olivia?"

"No."

"You never saw them together? Johan said she came to the motel to see him."

"They kept it a big secret," she insisted. "I only found out when everyone in town started talking about it."

"Why didn't Johan tell you?"

"I'm sure he figured I'd tell Olivia, but I guess she found out anyway. I told you there was something going on between her and Ashlynn."

"Friends keep a lot of secrets around here," he said.

Tanya squeezed the comforter of the bed under her fingers. "It's a small town. If you want to keep something hidden, you don't tell anybody. Johan dating Ashlynn? People would have been all over that."

"Did you hear that Johan went to the ghost town that night? Olivia went to see him after you called her."

"Yeah."

"Do you think Johan could have killed Ashlynn?"

"No way."

"You sound pretty sure."

"He'd never do anything bad to a girl."

"Sometimes people do bad things in the heat of the moment."

"He wouldn't hurt her. Not Johan."

Chris glanced around the motel room at the faded wallpaper. Rain splattered over the threshold onto the beige shag carpet. "He's missing, Tanya."

"That's why I'm here."

"Do you know where he is?"

"No."

He heard the crack in her voice. "Are you sure?"

"I don't know," she said again.

"Has he been in contact with you?"

The girl hesitated.

"Tanya, you came here for a reason. Do you know what Johan is doing?"

"He—he called me a little while ago."

"What did he want?"

"If I tell you, you'll tell the police. I don't want him getting in trouble."

"You don't want him to get hurt, either. What did he want?"

Tanya kicked at the carpet with her sneaker. "He wanted to know if my dad kept any guns in the house."

Chris closed his eyes. "Damn it."

"He said he needed to find one fast."

"What did you tell him?"

"I told him no," she said. "I told him not to be an idiot."

"Did he say what he was planning to do?"

"It's not hard to figure out. Sooner or later, he's going to show up at Kirk Watson's house."

Chris got up from the end of the bed. "I need to call the police about this."

Tanya grabbed his arm. "Wait."

"We can't wait, Tanya. We have to stop him."

"There's more."

"What is it?"

The girl clamped her mouth shut. Her face was white, as if she were about to jump from a bridge. Chris sat down next to her again. He put a hand softly on her shoulder, not wanting to spook her. "Does your father know you're here?" he asked.

"No. He said I shouldn't talk to you."

"Did you tell him about Johan looking for a gun?"

"No."

"Why not?"

"Because he wouldn't do anything. He's terrified something will happen to me. He doesn't want me involved in any of this, but I can't sit here and do nothing. If Johan goes after Kirk, Johan's the one who will get killed."

"Why is your father afraid something will happen to you?"

"Kirk already went after me. That was the warning."

"Warning?" Chris asked.

"Not to say anything."

"About what?"

Tanya hesitated. "About Ashlynn."

"What about her? Please, Tanya, you need to tell me what's going on."

"Dad says it's nothing. He still thinks Olivia killed her."

"You don't?"

"I don't know," she said. "At first, that was the only thing that made sense. Now I'm not sure."

"So who do you think it was?"

"I have no idea," she insisted. "How would I know?"

"Was it Kirk? Did he know what was going on between Ashlynn and Johan?"

Tanya shook her head. "No, no, it doesn't have anything to do with that."

"Then explain it to me."

The girl scrambled off the bed and knit her hands together in front of her chin. "I sat next to Ashlynn in a religious studies class. We'd talk sometimes. She wasn't what I expected."

"How so?"

"I thought she'd be stuck-up, but she wasn't. She was actually pretty lonely like me. She'd stopped hanging out with the Barron gang, and the St. Croix kids all hated her. I think she figured it was safe to talk to me, because no one from Barron wanted me around because of the lawsuit. We got to know each other, but she said I shouldn't tell anyone we were friends. Especially Olivia. I thought it was because Olivia was so anti-Mondamin, but now I guess it was because of Johan, too."

Chris waited. He was afraid if he said anything wrong the girl would shut up, and he badly wanted to hear what she had to say.

"A few months ago, she pulled me aside after class, when all of the other kids were gone," Tanya went on. "She was acting weird. She wanted to make sure no one saw us."

She stopped and chewed her fingernail. She went to the doorway and looked outside, and then she closed the door. The room got darker, and the blasting heat grew oppressive. Chris expected her to talk, but she remained frozen in silence.

"What did she want?" he asked her quietly.

"She wanted to get a message to my dad," Tanya told him. Her soft voice was hard to hear above the noisy heater.

"What was the message?"

"She was willing to—to steal stuff."

"Stuff?"

"Papers from her father's office. Mondamin documents. She wanted to help us prove that the company had been concealing things during the lawsuit."

Vernon Clay.

"Did you give your dad the message?"

Tanya bit her lip and nodded. "Yes, he said if Ashlynn really believed there was something illegal going on at Mondamin, she should go to the county attorney. Michael Altman."

Chris swore under his breath. He didn't like the possibility of a secret relationship between Altman and Ashlynn. He wondered what the county attorney would have done if Florian Steele's daughter arrived in his office with information against her father's company. Altman had already told him, *I knew that girl well.*

"Did she talk to Altman?" he asked her.

"I don't know. Ashlynn never mentioned it again. Not until the day before she died."

"She called you on Thursday night," Chris said. "The phone call wasn't about homework, was it?"

Tanya shook her head. "She said she had evidence now. She said Mondamin chemicals killed those people in St. Croix, and her father covered the whole thing up. She said she could prove it."

ROLLIE SWENSON'S BLACK HAIR SPROUTED WINGS AS HE MUSSED IT IN frustration. He slammed his office door and whirled around on Chris. "I told you that I didn't want you talking to my daughter without my permission."

Chris sat in front of Rollie's desk. "I'm sorry, but Tanya came to me. She wanted to talk."

"She's *sixteen*."

"I don't care how old she is. I'm not the police. If a witness comes to me with information, I'm going to listen to her."

One of the flaps of Rollie's yellow shirt had come untucked, and it dangled over the bulge of his stomach. He sat down behind his desk and grabbed an oversize cup that had a straw squeezed through the hole. He sucked up a mouthful of pop. When he was done he slammed it down, and Coke spewed upward through the straw and onto his desk. He let it drip onto the floor.

"You're going to get her killed," Rollie told him. "I am trying to *protect* her."

"I'm just asking questions."

"Don't play games with me, Chris. I know you're doing everything you can to save your own daughter, but I thought you'd respect me when I told you to stay away from Tanya. Instead, you took advantage of her."

"You lied to me, Rollie," Chris snapped. "Don't talk about respect unless you're prepared to be honest with me first."

"Okay. Fine. I lied. You'd lie, too, if you were in my shoes."

Chris stood up. "I'm done here. You can talk to Michael Altman and the sheriff about all of this."

He yanked open Rollie's door, but before he could leave Rollie bounced off his chair and intercepted him. The younger attorney pushed the door closed again. "Don't get them involved in this. Not yet."

"Why not?"

"Because I don't know who to trust."

Chris pointed at the empty chair. "Start over, Rollie."

Rollie's chin, which looked perpetually unshaven, was especially dark. There were circles under his eyes, and the caffeine wasn't helping to revive him. They both sat down again.

"Tanya told me that Ashlynn offered to get inside information about Mondamin," Chris said. "Did you meet with her?"

Rollie's fists gripped the arms of his chair. "Sure, I did."

"When was this?"

"Sometime last fall. November, I think."

"What did she tell you?"

Rollie shook his head. "Nothing we didn't already know."

"Meaning what?"

"Ashlynn suspected that her father was involved in a cover-up, but she didn't have any actual evidence."

"Did she mention Vernon Clay?" Chris asked.

Rollie's eyebrows went up. "Yes, she did. How did you make that connection?"

"A contact at Mondamin. Someone else Ashlynn reached out to."

"Well, you know we were trying to find him. We thought he might be our smoking gun."

"What did Ashlynn know about him?"

"That's the trouble. She didn't have any new information. She didn't know where he was or how we could reach him. She didn't have any details about what he might have done while he was at Mondamin. All she had was the same speculation that we had years ago. It was a dead end."

"So what was Ashlynn proposing?" he asked.

Rollie took another slug of Coke and wiped his face, which had a dew of sweat. "She told me she could hack into Florian's computer at home and copy his paper files. She thought she could do it at his office, too, without him finding out."

"What did you tell her?"

Rollie scowled. "What the hell do you think I told her? I said no. She was offering to violate civil and criminal statutes by stealing private company documents. If I'd encouraged her, I would have been disbarred, sued, and dumped in jail. I told her that if she had any specific information regarding a crime, which she didn't, she should take it to Michael Altman, not me."

"How did Ashlynn react when you said no?"

"She said she'd do it on her own. I tried to dissuade her. I told her not to go behind her father's back or break the law by taking anything that didn't belong to her. I also told her the truth, which is that we lost the litigation fair and square. A judge dismissed it. The scientific issues involving Mondamin and St. Croix—including Vernon Clay—were examined in detail by an outside expert who found no link between the cancer cluster and the actions of the company."

"Did you convince Ashlynn to stay out of it?"

"I thought I did."

"Did she contact you again?"

"Not until she called Tanya on Thursday night."

"What did she say when she called?"

"You already know. Ashlynn claimed to have evidence against her father now. She didn't say what it was."

"Did you talk to her yourself?"

"No, Tanya did."

"Did she tell Tanya anything else?"

"No. I don't know what kind of proof she supposedly had."

Chris leaned forward with his elbows on the desk and stared into Rollie's tired eyes. "Why the hell didn't you tell the police about this when Ashlynn's body was found? Why didn't you tell me?"

Rollie backed up in his chair, putting distance between them. He spread his hands. "I'm a lawyer, Chris, just like you. I share information on my terms. Not yours. Not Altman's. Not the sheriff's."

"What does that mean?"

"I already told you. My only concern is my daughter. Before I said anything that might put her in danger, I needed to know what was really going on. Ashlynn had already been murdered. For all I knew, Tanya was next."

"So you withheld critical information?"

"I wasn't sure the information was relevant at all. The evidence was overwhelming that Olivia killed Ashlynn. The police considered it an open-and-shut case."

"The police didn't know about the phone call," Chris said. "Ashlynn told Tanya she had evidence against her father the day before she was killed. Do you really think that's a coincidence?"

Rollie shrugged. "I have no idea whether Ashlynn had proof of anything at all. She was a kid. Who knows whether she really found anything?"

"If that's true, then why are you so afraid Tanya is in danger? Did something change between that phone call on Thursday night and now?"

Rollie's face flushed again. He pounded the desk. "Of course something changed! Kirk Watson tried to assault my daughter!"

"What makes you think that had anything to do with Ashlynn's phone call?"

"I know Kirk. I know what the son of a bitch is capable of, and I know he's mixed up with Florian."

"So talk to the police," Chris said. "Once the facts are out, no one's going to touch her."

"You don't know that. Besides, it's not that simple anymore."

"Why not?"

"It's not just about Kirk."

Chris watched Rollie's face and saw another side to his fear emerge. "What happened?"

"Someone else contacted me."

"Who?"

Rollie closed his eyes and squeezed his fists against his forehead. He looked torn with doubt. Finally, exhaling loudly, he opened the top drawer of his desk and removed a single sheet of paper. Chris saw the block printing and recognized it. He'd seen it before.

He thought about Michael Altman. *We've found him.*

"This was in my mailbox yesterday," Rollie said. He handed the paper across the desk.

TO THE ATTENTION OF

MR. ROLAND SWENSON

SAY NOTHING

SPEAK TO NO ONE

SILENCE WILL KEEP YOUR DAUGHTER ALIVE

SHE IS NOT PART OF MY PLAN

DO NOT FORCE ME TO DO

WHAT I WISH TO AVOID

MY NAME IS

AQUARIUS

37

THE POLICE CARS SURROUNDING THE BARN GLISTENED IN THE DRIVING RAIN. Their flashing lights made halos of red and blue. Rivers of brown water wound through the overlapping tire tracks toward the highway, and the swift-moving black clouds looked low enough to touch. The barn itself was weathered, with a rounded roof and patchy blue siding, and two winter ash trees waggled their bare branches overhead. There was a farmhouse nearby, with frilly lace curtains in the windows. The deserted farm was surrounded by miles of fields. The gravel road north of Route 212 wasn't far from the South Dakota border. Chris didn't think Rand McNally had ever mapped it.

He opened an umbrella as he got out of his car, but the wind bent the downpour onto his clothes. He approached a young cop in a yellow slicker at the crime-scene tape and asked for Michael Altman. The kid used a wet microphone against his face to squawk out a request for the county attorney.

Chris waited. He counted two dozen uniformed police and evidence technicians processing the scene at both buildings. They probably doubled the population in the ten square miles around the farm.

Aquarius had chosen well. No one was ever likely to stumble onto his remote lair.

The cop's microphone came alive with a growl of static. "Altman's in back," the kid told him. "Stay out of the barn."

Chris bent down under the crime-scene tape. Stretches of muddy tarpaulin had been laid out on the ground, leading toward the rear of the barn. Where the tarp didn't cover, the earth was like quicksand. As he passed the open door, he peered inside and saw technicians examining empty metal shelves and a rubber-lined floor. The interior was shockingly bright against the dark day. Otherwise, the barn itself was vacant.

He followed the tarp behind the barn. He found a brown Honda Civic hatchback parked out of sight of the road and an oversize metal garbage can with its lid open. A makeshift tent had been staked out close to the edge of the fields, and he saw the county attorney talking to two police officers.

Altman gestured at him.

"Aquarius is still a step ahead of us," the county attorney told Chris when he joined him under the tent. Rain hammered in a *rat-tat-tat* on the plastic. "He's already gone, but he was here recently."

"Do you think he's coming back?"

"I don't think so. The interior of the barn has been cleaned out. We've got spotters near the crossroads in case anyone heads this way, but I'm not counting on it. I don't know if he smelled us on his tail or whether he's getting ready for whatever the hell he's planning."

"Have you found any clues about what he's up to?" Chris asked.

"We're just getting started. It took us two hours to get clearance to go inside. We needed to make sure it wasn't booby-trapped. Whatever he was doing, he set up a generator and a lot of interior lights. He had a vehicle inside, and based on the indentations in the rubber floor, it was heavy."

"I don't like the sound of that."

"Neither do I," Altman said. "We're beefing up security outside Mondamin. I don't think this guy is faking. I think he's the real deal."

"So how did you find him?"

Altman took off his fedora and smoothed raindrops from it. He repositioned it carefully on his head and tugged on the knot of his trench coat. "I'd like to tell you we found this place through painstaking investigation, but in truth, we got lucky. So lucky that it can't be an accident. Aquarius wants us to chase him."

"You think he deliberately led you here?"

"I do. We lifted a fingerprint off one of the Aquarius notes and matched it to a graduate student in Ames who's heavily involved in the fringe environmental movement. He's been arrested at protests all over the Midwest during the last five years—including right here in Barron outside Mondamin. At that point, I figured we had him. He was Aquarius."

"He's not?"

The county attorney shook his head. "No, he's been in jail for six weeks. An Iowa judge finally got tired of this guy being arrested for vandalism, B&E, harassment, whatever, and decided to teach him a lesson."

Chris shrugged. "So Aquarius must be one of his furry friends."

"Yes, we began looking at people in the environmental organizations he's connected to, but the break in the case came from somewhere else. It turns out this activist has a night job at an Ames hotel. One of the things he does all the time is fix paper jams in the printer for guests who use their business center. Hence his fingerprint."

"How do you know the paper came from the hotel?"

"The Iowa cops showed him one of the Aquarius notes. He said there was no way it came from a printer at any of the environmental groups he worked with. They only use paper with a higher recycling use of post-consumer waste. I guess that means you can still see flecks of fecal matter from the toilet paper they reuse. Anyway, he said it looked like the standard office supply stock they use at the hotel."

"So you think Aquarius stayed there?"

Altman nodded. "That's right. At first, I figured Aquarius might be setting up this kid as a fall guy. Anyone familiar with the environmental movement knows his name and knows his fingerprints would pop in the system. Then we ran a guest list at the hotel for the past six months, and one name leaped out."

"Who?"

"Vernon Clay."

"So that's why it raised a red flag that Ashlynn was talking about him. You think Vernon is back?"

"Maybe, maybe not. Nobody at the hotel remembered him or recognized a description of him. If it's not Vernon, it's someone who knew we'd spot the name immediately. The address on the register led us right here to this farm. That's not an accident. He wanted us to find the kid, find the hotel, find the guest list. He made it hard but not too hard. He wanted to get our attention."

Chris looked at the Honda Civic parked behind the barn. "What about the car?"

"The Minnesota plates don't match the VIN. We're trying to trace it."

"If Vernon Clay really is Aquarius, has he been hiding out here?"

"It doesn't look that way. The house is largely untouched. He's been doing his work in the barn. The property belongs to the family of a widow who passed away three years ago. None of the kids are local. The place has been vacant since she died, and they haven't been able to sell it. Someone called them in December about renting it for a year and sent them a lump sum in cash. They didn't ask a lot of questions."

"Did you talk to Florian?"

"I did. He says there is no reason why Vernon Clay would bear a grudge against him or Mondamin."

"What about Ashlynn? Did you tell him that she was asking questions about Vernon Clay?"

Altman shoved his hands in the pockets of his trench coat. "I did."

"What did he say?"

"He said her mind had obviously been poisoned by Glenn Magnus and his son."

"It was more than that," Chris said. "She knew something."

"Is that a guess, or do you know that for a fact?"

Chris hesitated. He thought about Rollie and Tanya. "I'm not sure what I can say right now."

The county attorney didn't hide his annoyance. "I've kept you in the loop, Mr. Hawk, because you made a connection between Ashlynn and Vernon Clay at the same time that Vernon's name appeared in the context of our Aquarius investigation. However, the favor goes both ways. I expect you to share anything you know that might help me find this man. Whatever he's planning, the threat is real."

Chris had to make a snap decision, and he chose to trust Michael Altman. "Ashlynn told Tanya Swenson she had proof that Florian was involved in a cover-up connected to the deaths in St. Croix. This was the night before she was killed."

Altman's lips wrinkled with distaste. "What kind of proof?"

"She didn't say."

"So how exactly does that help me?"

"Aquarius knew about it," Chris said. "He sent a note to Rollie Swenson warning him to keep quiet. He threatened Tanya's life."

"Why didn't Rollie tell me about any of this?" Altman asked.

"He's scared for Tanya. He probably has reason to be. If Vernon Clay really is Aquarius, and if Ashlynn found him, then you have to admit it's a possibility that he killed her to keep her quiet."

"Let's wait to see how this plays out," Altman told him. "Right now, I just want to find Aquarius and stop him."

"Kirk Watson may know something," Chris said.

"Kirk's just a thug."

"Yes, but he works for Florian. Rollie thinks Kirk tried to assault Tanya to intimidate her into silence. There's something else, too. Ashlynn went out with Kirk a few times last fall, but Johan said she wasn't interested in him. It wasn't romantic. Now I wonder if she was trolling for information about her father and Mondamin. And maybe Vernon Clay, too."

"Kirk's not going to tell us anything. Not if it involves Florian."

"You may be too late anyway."

"What do you mean?"

"Johan Magnus told Tanya he was trying to find a gun. She thinks he's going after Kirk."

Altman closed his eyes and let out a slow breath in frustration. "It's Pandora's box in this town. Bad things are happening, Mr. Hawk, and I'm afraid that I'm not going to be able to stop it before we all get swept away."

"I'd like to know what Ashlynn found out about her father," Chris said.

The county attorney frowned, as if he were again debating how much to share. He walked away from Chris and spoke to the police he'd been talking to earlier. When he returned, he had a sealed plastic bag in his hand. "Did you say that Ashlynn told Tanya Swenson that she'd found proof connecting Mondamin to the deaths in St. Croix?"

"That's what she said."

Altman held up the plastic bag. There was a single sheet of paper inside. "Aquarius left us another bread crumb. We found bags of shredded paper in the garbage. It will take us weeks to figure out what it all is. However, there was one page in the middle of the pile that wasn't destroyed. This page. He obviously meant for us to find it."

Chris leaned closer to study the paper. The plastic was speckled with rain, but he could see that it wasn't a note from Aquarius. "What is it?"

"It's the cover page of a report prepared by a woman named Lucia Causey."

He shook his head. He'd heard the name, but he couldn't place it. "I'm not familiar with her."

"Lucia Causey is a Stanford epidemiologist," Altman explained. "She was the special master in the litigation against Mondamin. She wrote the scientific analysis that the judge used to dismiss the lawsuit."

LENNY WAITED UNTIL DARK TO RETURN HOME.

He hoped that Kirk's temper had cooled. It was obvious after he spent two hours near the Indian monument, nursing his bruises, that his brother wasn't coming back for him. He'd hitchhiked with a truck driver into Barron and spent most of the day playing video games at the pizza parlor on Main Street. His phone didn't ring. Kirk didn't try to call. That was ominous.

As night fell, he tried to bum a ride south, but no one was heading his way. He hiked in the rain. His jaw ached like shit; he thought it might be broken. He limped, too, with his right knee throbbing. The miles were slow and miserable. He stuck out his thumb when he saw headlights, but the drivers ignored him. He tried to stay under the shelter of the trees, but the rain found him anyway. After walking for an hour, he found himself shivering uncontrollably.

When he finally lurched down 120th toward the river, he found their house dark. Kirk wasn't home. He was glad he didn't have to face his brother yet. He unlocked the door and went inside, and he made a beeline for the bathroom in the hallway. He ran a bath, making the water as hot as his fingers could stand. As he waited for the tub to fill, he peeled off his clothes and left them in a soggy pile on the tile floor. Before the water reached the top, he dipped one foot into the bath, then the other. His frigid skin felt scalded. He sank to his knees, and the blistering water stung his genitals. He didn't care. He sank onto his back, wincing as the heat assaulted every cut and bruise.

His shivering subsided. He was warm again, burning and sweating. He closed his eyes. Under the water, he reached for his shaft and twiddled it until it grew hard, sprouting from the surface of the bath like a pink mushroom. He thought about Olivia as he masturbated. The mental image of her sitting on the edge of the tub as he jerked off sent him flying. He shot wriggling ropes of semen into the dirty water. Sticky strands stuck to his legs.

He was still breathing hard when the front door slammed like a cannon going off. Kirk was home. He heard his brother's wild voice bellowing through the house, and his intestines convulsed in fear.

"*Leno, where the fuck are you?*"

Lenny scrambled to his feet, white goo dripping from his deflated shaft. He clawed for a bath towel, but before he could wrap it around his body, Kirk kicked open the door so hard that the top hinge splintered and cracked. His brother filled the entire doorway. His long hair was loose. Beer smell burped from his mouth; he was wide-eyed drunk.

"Kirk, listen—" Lenny began, but his brother took two steps, grabbed him by the throat, and hauled him out of the tub. Kirk took Lenny's scrawny shoulders and threw him across the slippery floor. Lenny stumbled out of the bathroom, and his forehead cracked on the wall. He was hot and dizzy; he staggered forward, and his pizza and Mountain Dew evacuated his stomach, barely missing his brother.

Kirk took a fistful of Lenny's hair. He dragged him, naked, into the living room, and drove him face-first into the carpet with a knee in the small of his back.

"You useless fucking moron," Kirk hissed.

Lenny's mouth was sour with vomit. He tried to talk. "I'm sorry, man."

"Sorry? Who gives a shit if you're sorry?"

Kirk spun Lenny onto his back and leaned an elbow into his chest with a crushing pressure. Tears leaked from Lenny's eyes.

"Really, Kirk, I'm sorry, I'm sorry." He squirmed in pain. It felt like a knife driving between his ribs. "Johan snuck up on me, man. He kicked the shit out of me. There was nothing I could do. He made me tell him, man. I didn't want to."

"Tell him what?"

"About Olivia. About what we did to her."

Kirk swatted Lenny's head down like he was breaking a coconut. Lenny saw nothing but swirls of color. He thought he would throw up again.

"You worthless fucking piece of shit, get the hell out of this house and don't come back."

"Please, Kirk."

"*Get out.*"

His brother released him, and Lenny could breathe again, but each breath ached in his ribs. He pushed himself up on his elbows. Kirk stared at him as if he were a maggot in a bowl of rice. He'd seen Kirk furious before, but not like this. This was bad.

"I'll get some clothes," Lenny said.

"Forget the clothes. Get out. Now."

"Hey, come on, man."

Kirk's eyes were black with rage. Lenny scampered to his feet, feeling the world spin. He knew better than to protest again. He ducked backward, colliding with the front door. It opened, and he spilled outside into the fierce rain. The water felt like ice. He clutched the railing and descended the porch steps to the mud.

Kirk was right. He'd fucked up. After everything Kirk had done for him, he'd let him down again.

Lenny didn't know where to go. He was naked. He was cold. He was humiliated. He decided he would spend the night in the truck. Kirk would pass out soon enough, and Lenny could go back to his own bed then. In the morning, his brother would forgive him. The storm would break. It always did.

He hauled himself inside the pickup, which was parked in front of the garage. He didn't have the keys; he couldn't turn on the engine. He found a musty blanket behind the seat, and he covered his bare skin with it, curling into a ball. He squeezed his eyes shut. His body was shivering again, and the wool turned his skin into a scratching post. He yearned for sleep, but his pain and misery kept him awake.

He heard the rain firing bullets at the roof of the pickup.

He didn't hear the footsteps outside the truck.

Kirk stripped to his boxers and flipped the channels on the television until he found a Minnesota Wild hockey game. He couldn't concentrate. He was still too pumped with rage. Part of him wanted to follow his baby brother outside and beat the little fucker until he was a lifeless pulp of blood and bones. Cut him up, just like Dad, and send the parts floating down the river.

He drank another bottle of beer in two swallows. His phone rang. The caller ID was blocked, and he muted the television and barked into the phone, "What?"

There was a long silence and then a cool, familiar voice.

"It's me."

Kirk tried to unfog his brain. *Shit.* He didn't want to be drunk when he was talking to the boss. He didn't want to talk to him at all. Not now. He thought about hanging up, but you didn't play games with Florian Steele.

"Hey," he said, taking a breath. "What's up?"

"I'm hearing things I don't like."

"Yeah? Like what?"

"The police think they're close to tracking down this man Aquarius."

"So what?" Kirk asked.

"Do you know who he is? Do you know what he's doing?"

"Me? I don't have a clue, boss."

Florian was silent. The dead air felt tense. "I'm hearing a name I'd hoped never to hear again," he said finally.

"Oh, yeah? Who's that?"

"Vernon Clay."

Kirk gripped the phone with a slippery hand and listened to the rain outside. "Who's talking about him?"

"Apparently Ashlynn was before she was killed."

"No way."

"I was wondering where she heard about him."

"Hell if I know, boss."

"Did you go out with her?"

"Uh, yeah, we went out a few times. It was months ago." He added quickly, "I didn't touch her."

"I told you to *stay away* from her."

"She came on to me, boss. I figured you knew."

"She was trying to get information out of you, you idiot. What did you tell her?"

"Tell her? Nothing. Nada."

"Did you tell her about Vernon Clay?"

"Fuck, no. Are you kidding?"

Shit.

Kirk thought about his last evening with Ashlynn. He wanted a kiss. A squeeze. A fuck. Anything from that beautiful chick. They were drinking; he needed to get her wasted if he hoped to get anywhere near that amazing body. He figured out later that she kept pouring her beers on the ground when he went to piss. The more he drank, the more he bragged, hoping to impress her. *When your daddy has a problem, you know who he calls? Kirk, baby. Me and him are tight.*

She talked about how warm she was. She undid a couple of buttons on that churchy silk blouse of hers. He could see the swell of those perfect breasts. "Really?" she asked, with her big eyes and that smoky voice. "What problems?"

Vernon Clay, baby. Big problem.

"Swear to God, boss," Kirk went on. "I didn't say a word."

"The police have linked Aquarius to Vernon Clay through a name on a hotel registry," Florian told him. "They believe he's back."

"He's not."

"I'm having doubts."

"I told you four years ago the problem was solved."

"Yes, you did."

Kirk was getting angry. "What, do you think I lied?"

"I think for enough money, you'd tell me whatever I wanted to hear. Don't forget, I know all about your other disgusting business, too."

The vein in Kirk's neck throbbed. "You don't complain when it saves your neck."

"Vernon Clay," Florian repeated calmly.

"What about him? I'm telling you, he's not Aquarius. The police have it all wrong."

"I don't believe you."

Kirk didn't want to argue with the boss, but he was losing control. The frustrations of the day piled up on him. "What the fuck are you saying?"

"I'm asking if Vernon Clay *paid* you to help him disappear."

"Hell no!"

"Where is he?"

"You know where he is."

"Do I?"

"You want proof?" Kirk asked. "Is that what you're saying? I'll give you proof."

"I want to know whether Aquarius is Vernon Clay."

"He's not. Look, give me two hours, and meet me in the usual place."

"Why?"

"Because then you can ask Vernon yourself whether he's been sending fucking notes to anybody."

CHRIS SAT IN THE DESERTED PARKING LOT OF THE HIGH SCHOOL WHILE the rain poured over his car. It was supposed to keep raining most of the night, swelling the rivers and ditches. Temperatures were sinking. He waited in the cold with his engine and lights off, wondering whether George Valma would show up. The Mondamin scientist was fifteen minutes late. He thought about calling again, but as he opened his phone, he saw blurry headlights glowing from the residential streets of Barron. A white sedan crawled along the border of the athletic fields and pulled into the lot beside Chris. The linebacker-size scientist got out and climbed into the passenger seat of the Lexus.

"I appreciate your coming," Chris said.

George shook rain out of his gray hair. "This was a mistake. If anyone sees me with you, I could lose my job. I shouldn't have told you anything. I've got my kids to think about."

"I understand your situation."

George fidgeted impatiently. "So what is it now? What do you want?"

"Ashlynn found something," Chris said.

"What?"

"She told another girl she had proof that Mondamin was connected to the cancer cluster in St. Croix."

George shook his head. "She didn't. That's wrong."

"How do you know?"

"Because you can't *prove* something like that. Cancer doesn't work that way. You can have smokers who live to ninety-five and athletes who drop at twenty-six. God doesn't simply pick on the sinners."

Chris thought about Hannah, who had made all the right choices in her life and was now in a fight to stay alive. You could blame God. You could blame bad luck. It didn't change a thing. Cancer was a merciless enemy.

"Okay, you're right," Chris admitted, "but whatever she found, she was so horrified that she was willing to expose her own father."

"This involved Florian?" George asked.

"That's what she said."

"I don't know what it could be."

"I think you do, George. You think Vernon Clay poisoned the town of St. Croix, and Florian covered it up."

The scientist shook his head. "No."

"Vernon Clay was mentally ill. Obsessive. Delusional. Schizophrenic. That's the kind of man we're talking about, George. Pretend you're a mad scientist. If you got it in your head that you wanted to wreak havoc on a town, could you do it?"

The scientist nodded reluctantly. "Yes, someone with Vernon's knowledge of chemistry and access to hazardous pesticides could have done some bad things. He could have used any of a dozen different chemicals in quantities that would have been grotesquely dangerous. That doesn't mean he did, and even if he did, it doesn't mean that the contamination caused the cancers. Humans react in different ways to environmental toxins. It might have caused widespread illness. It might have had no effect at all."

"If he did, though, the truth would have been devastating in a courtroom. That would have been the end of Mondamin."

George shrugged. "You're the lawyer."

"Florian's a lawyer, too. If he discovered that Vernon Clay was involved in widespread chemical contamination, he knew he would have been at risk of losing everything. Having it exposed would have been devastating."

"Exactly. So why would Florian bankroll an independent investigation when he got sued?" George asked. "He wouldn't do that. He would have fought like hell to make sure no one got near Vernon Clay's land."

"Maybe he'd already cleaned it up. Maybe he knew there was nothing to find."

"You can't ever be sure about things like that," the scientist insisted. "With the proper equipment, an expert would have found evidence of dumping, particularly if it was as extreme as what we're talking about. You can't hide from the kind of technology we have today. Florian knows that."

Chris thought about Aquarius and the cover page of Lucia Causey's special master report. "On the other hand, if an outside expert ran all the tests and found nothing, that would quash the rumors once and for all. No more litigation. No more questions from the environmental agencies."

"That's exactly what happened," George told him.

"So maybe the special master screwed up."

"Impossible. Lucia Causey is a top-flight epidemiologist. She had state-of-the-art equipment at her disposal. If there was something to find, she would have found it."

"What if Florian got to her?" Chris asked. "What if he influenced her?"

"You're not talking about a hired gun," George protested. "You're talking about a tenured university scientist."

"No offense, but plenty of scientists are willing to be hacks for any lawyer who pays them. That's the reason the courts started coming up with ways to screen out junk science."

"I don't believe a scientist like Lucia would sell her soul," George replied. "I hear what you're saying about scientists whose conclusions are for sale to the highest bidder, but that's not her. Her track record isn't pro-defense or pro-plaintiff. She's independent. If she had a reputation for being one-sided, the judge wouldn't have picked her."

"Do you know Lucia well enough to call her?" Chris asked.

"To say what? 'Dr. Causey, this is George Valma at Mondamin. I was just wondering, did you take a bribe from our CEO and falsify the data in your report?' Do you think she's simply going to admit it?"

"No."

"Then what do you expect me to do? I couldn't help Ashlynn, and I can't help you."

Chris stared at the scientist. "Wait a minute. Ashlynn? Did she want to know about Lucia Causey, too?"

George shrugged his beefy shoulders. "Yes, she wanted to talk to Lucia. She contacted the epidemiology department at the medical school, and they wouldn't tell her a thing. Ashlynn asked if I would make the contact for her."

Chris remembered the records he'd reviewed from the girl's cell phone and realized he'd overlooked something important. *Stanford.* He'd thought she was pursuing college admissions, but the call meant something completely different now.

"Did you make the call?" he asked.

"No. I told her what I told you."

"George, this is important. Do you have any contacts at Stanford?"

"I have a college friend who's a visiting professor there."

Chris reached into the pocket of his coat and pulled out a phone. He handed it across the car. "Call him."

"Even if he transfers me to Lucia Causey, what am I supposed to say to her?"

"Ask if Ashlynn contacted her. Ask her what she said."

George waved off Chris's phone and slipped his own phone from the pocket of his pants. He checked his contact list and dialed. Chris heard a voice pick up the call on the third ring.

"Chester? It's George Valma calling. Yes, long time, I know. Right, I'm in small-town Minnesota now. Not exactly Palo Alto."

The two scientists made small talk. Chris grew impatient, but he waited without pushing George. Eventually, when his Stanford colleague asked what George wanted, the Mondamin scientist got to the point.

"Listen, Chester, I'm trying to contact a researcher at the med school there. I was wondering if you could look up her direct line. Her name is Lucia Causey. I appreciate it." George waited, and while he did, he covered the phone. "If Lucia calls Florian about this, you know what's going to happen to me."

"Blame me," Chris said.

"It's not that simple."

George's colleague came back on the line.

"Are you sure about that?" George asked. His face grew puzzled. "Let me give you the spelling." He spelled out the name of the epidemiologist, but moments later, he shook his head. "Okay, thanks, Chester. No, that's okay. I'll see you at the conference in May, okay?"

George hung up.

"Lucia Causey isn't in the Stanford directory," he told Chris. "She doesn't work there anymore."

"Where did she go?"

"I have no idea."

"Was she ever there to begin with?"

"You mean, was she fictitious? A fraud? No. She was there, and she left. She probably got a better offer. It happens."

"So how do we find her?"

"You mean, how do you find her? I'm sorry, Chris, but I've already stuck my neck out too far for you. I'm done."

Chris nodded. "Understood. I appreciate your help, George. Really."

The scientist opened the door. Rain poured through the gap onto the leather seats. George Valma slammed the door shut, causing the Lexus to shake. He got back into his own white sedan and drove out of the parking lot, leaving Chris alone.

Chris sat in silence as the taillights disappeared.

He didn't like coincidences. He didn't like the fact that a top-notch researcher had left one of the nation's premier research universities after completing the investigation at Mondamin. Lucia Causey wasn't Vernon Clay. She couldn't drop off the face of the earth. Someone at Stanford knew where she'd gone.

Chris opened his own phone and called directory assistance. He got the number for the Stanford Medical School, and when the receptionist answered, he asked for a transfer to the school's epidemiology division. He found himself directed to the Department of Health Research and Policy, where a secretary named Leanne answered the phone.

"Leanne, I'm trying to track down an epidemiologist named Lucia Causey," Chris told her. "She used to work in that department, and I was wondering if anyone there had forwarding information for her."

"I'm sorry, what was that name?" the secretary asked with a slight Georgia twang in her voice. "I only just started here, and I'm not real up on all the people yet."

Chris spelled the name.

"Okay, sure, hang on."

She put him on hold. He was patient for the first minute of silence, but the length drifted to two minutes, and then three. He knew he was still connected because of the music playing in his ear. After five minutes, he began to get concerned, and his concern grew when a different voice picked up the phone. The man on the line was all business.

"This is Dr. Naresh Vinshabi, how may I help you?"

Chris repeated his request and gave his name.

"May I ask why you're trying to contact Lucia Causey, Mr. Hawk?" the doctor asked.

"I have some follow-up questions about a report that she prepared as a special master for litigation in Minnesota."

"I see. I'm sorry, but I can't help you with that."

"Yes, I know that Dr. Causey isn't at the university anymore. I was hoping you knew where she went."

The Stanford doctor didn't reply for a long time, but Chris heard him breathing. "She didn't go anywhere," the man finally replied.

"What does that mean?"

"She's dead," he told Chris.

40

KIRK DROVE A SHOVEL INTO THE SODDEN EARTH.

The blade cut the soil easily, and he hoisted a heavy pile of mud into the air and overturned the shovel beside the hole. The pattering noise of rain beating on the trees covered the sound of his digging. Sweat and rain seeped under the neck of his tank top onto his chest. His arms and hands grew black with dirt. He worked at a feverish pace, driven by drunken anger.

He was two hundred yards from his house. It was as isolated a burying place as he could find. To be safe, he should have disposed of the body permanently, but he liked to have an insurance policy for certain jobs. If you burn a murdered body, you lose your leverage. He liked to have leverage when he was dealing with Florian Steele. *You want to fuck with me? Watch me fuck with you.*

Kirk had nothing to fear from Florian as long as he knew where to find Vernon Clay.

The hole got bigger and deeper. Groundwater oozed from the sides. When he was two feet down, he had to climb inside to reach the bottom. He didn't need to retrieve the whole body. All he needed was enough to convince Florian of the truth. Vernon was dead. Kirk had made damned sure of that. One bullet, right in the forehead, delivered by a gun that was deep in the silt of a swamp outside Mankato.

"You remember me, Vernon?" Kirk asked the black hole in the ground. "I'll bet you do. You asked me if I was from the CIA when I came to your door. That was funny. The CIA. I said, 'Yeah, they need you in Washington, sir.'"

Kirk leaned on the handle of the shovel and laughed into his arm. What a fucking hysterical line. He should have been a comedian. *They need you in Washington, sir.* After that, it was easy. Follow Clay outside, knock him silly with the butt of the gun, drag him here. Clay never woke up. He was unconscious when Kirk dropped him in the hole and fired the gun into his brain. Better that than to bury him alive. That was the kind of thing that could give you nightmares.

It was funny how the mind worked. You didn't always believe something even when you knew it was true. There was a part of him that was paranoid about what was really in the hole. He knew that he was within inches of Vernon Clay's body, but the deeper he dug, the more his drunken mind began to panic that something had gone wrong. Vernon had survived the bullet in his skull. He'd clawed his way out of the ground and escaped. He was out there, messing with all of them.

My name is Aquarius.

Kirk's shovel banged onto something hard. Finally.

He threw the shovel out of the hole onto the mountain of dirt. He reached for his flashlight and shined it at his feet. There he was. Vernon Clay, or what was left of him. His flesh had long ago been devoured by the dirt dwellers. Kirk squatted, wiped grime from the bones, and saw that he'd unearthed the dead man's hand and forearm. The bones were brittle. He levered the wrist bone under his heel and snapped the hand back. The entire hand broke off with a sickening crack.

"They need you in Washington, sir," he said in his deepest voice, and he started howling with laughter again.

He deposited the hand on the ground and hauled his body out of the five-foot-deep pit. His muscles rippled. He was dirty, wet, and cold, and he wanted a hot shower before meeting Florian. He thought about dragging his brother down here and making Lenny fill in the open hole, but he was still pissed enough that he might push the pussy boy inside and dump the mud on top of him. *Leno, meet Vernon.*

Kirk bent in the darkness for the shovel. He pushed around with his hands to locate the handle, but he couldn't find it. Annoyed, he shined his flashlight at the pyramid of wet soil and realized that the shovel was gone. He could see the long indentation of the pole, but it wasn't there now.

"What the fuck?" he said aloud.

His brain screamed a warning, but at the same moment he heard whistling, so close and loud that he thought it was the skeleton at his feet, blowing a tune through the remains of his teeth. He was wrong. He spun toward the noise, but he was too slow to duck or shout. The whistle howled in his ears, and the shovel blade whipped with the force of a speeding truck into the meat of his skull. He never felt it.

Chris figured that the death of a prominent university researcher would have made the news. He booted up his laptop, drove out of the high school parking lot into the residential streets of Barron, and he soon found an unsecured wireless network that he used to access the Internet. Parked on the street in the rain, with the dome light of the Lexus casting shadows inside the car, he ran a Google search and found an article with the basic facts.

Lucia Causey, 51, a professor and researcher in the epidemiology of cancer at Stanford Medical School, had been found in the garage of her Sunnyvale home one year ago. She'd connected a swimming pool hose to her tailpipe and rerouted the deadly exhaust into the front seat of her Accord.

Lucia killed herself.

Why?

That was what Chris wanted to know. Maybe her death was unrelated to the events in Barron, but he didn't like the fact that so many of the people who might have known what happened at Mondamin weren't around to talk about it. Vernon Clay was missing. Lucia Causey was dead. So was Ashlynn. What had she found?

Chris searched again, hunting for blog posts connected to Lucia Causey on the day after her death, when news would have broken across campus. Most of the results were inconsequential: expressions of disbelief or sympathy, questions about classes or research projects in which she'd been involved, discussions of suicide awareness and prevention, and a handful of religious diatribes. He tried again, changing his search terms, and found a mention of the scientist's death in a blogger's chat room called The Truth about Pesticide Poisoning.

What caught his eye was the handle of the chat room host. It was AMES_GREEN_GUY.

Another coincidence? The environmental activist whose fingerprint had shown up on one of the Aquarius letters lived and worked in Ames, Iowa. Chris loaded the thread, which mostly consisted of an online argument between the poster in Ames and a research assistant at Stanford who used the handle WUNDERLICH. He scrolled through the posts:

AGG: Sux for her kids, man, but hard for me to drum up sympathy for her. She was IPP.

W: She and her husband didn't have kids. What's IPP?

AGG: In the Pocket of Polluters.

W: Hey, slow down, green. You're wrong. She played it straight.

AGG: What about Mondamin? They got summary judgment in toxic tort lit thx to her.

W: That's one case. She wrote plaintiff-friendly reports, too.

AGG: Defense hack. The Mondamin thing smelled.

W: Shit, must be nice to see the world in black and white. There are bad actors, but you can't blame Big Chem for every lymphoma.

AGG: Wake up, wunder. Who writes big chex to the univ research depts?

W: Lucia was clean.

AGG: She offed herself. Feeling guilty?

W: STFU.

AGG: I'm just saying. You see it coming?

W: No.

AGG: So why'd she do it?

W: Who knows why anyone does that. You can be brilliant but screwed up. She had problems. Depression. Gambling.

AGG: She leave a note?

W: Don't think so. The whole thing sucks.

AGG: Cancer sux. Pesticide sux. Suicide is quick.

W: She HATED cancer.

AGG: Still sounds like guilty conscience 2 me. IPP.

W: She was my friend. She killed herself. FU.

There was silence from the blogger in Ames following the last comment. He didn't answer.

Chris tried to understand the implications of what he'd read. If the chat participant in Ames was the same man whose fingerprint had been found on the hotel paper, he obviously wasn't a fan of Lucia Causey. He'd also mentioned Mondamin specifically. According to Michael Altman, however, the Ames activist was in an Iowa jail, which meant he couldn't be the man who called himself Aquarius. It was another dead end.

He was about to shut down his laptop when he realized that the online chat on the pollution site spilled over to a second page. He clicked on the next page of the thread and saw that there was one additional post, but it wasn't from either of the two original participants. Instead, it was from someone new. The final comment was dated only two and a half weeks ago, long after the chat began.

Seeing it, Chris found himself frozen as he stared at the screen. The post was dated three days after Ashlynn called Stanford, and the poster had used her initials as a handle. AS.

There were too many coincidences now. This wasn't random.

He read what Ashlynn had written and realized she'd left him a clue, as if she were speaking to him from the grave. If it was Ashlynn. If it was true.

AS: Lucia didn't kill herself. She was murdered.

WHERE WAS JOHAN?

Olivia felt helpless without any way to reach him. She couldn't sit and wait as he threw his life away. When night fell, she knew she had to move quickly, and she knew where to go. She slipped out of her window, ducked through the wet streets of St. Croix, and borrowed a rusty Grand Am from the garage of one of her friends. She turned on her brights as she reached the highway. Her tires kicked up spray behind her like an ocean wave. Kirk's house was ten minutes away, and with each mile closer to him her terror climbed up her throat.

She parked on the shoulder near 120th. When she got out, a wave of rain slashed her chest. She ran for the dirt road, where she stopped and stared into the hole between the trees. It felt like descending into a monster's cave. She smelled the smoke of a log fire and a wave of pine. The wind was fierce. With her hands shoved in the pockets of her jeans, she took tentative steps into the darkness. Her feet sank into the ooze. Her hair became wet ropes on her face.

Branches from the dense woods scraped her face. The constant patter of rain drowned out the other noises of the forest, and she worried that if someone were nearby, she wouldn't hear them until their breath was on her neck. Her brain fed flashbacks from a horror movie, but it wasn't a movie. In the invisible night, she found herself back in the belly of the train car as the boys assaulted her. She remembered quick, stabbing reminders of what she'd buried in her mind. She felt the crush of their hands on her skin, holding her down. Her body rattled on the metal floor with hammering jolts of pain.

It's not real.

She wanted to go back home, but she couldn't.

She hiked step by step like a blind girl. When her knee collided with something hard, she stopped and pawed with her hands, running her fingers along wet steel. It was a car, parked deep in the soft mud under a canopy of brush. She reached into her pocket and yanked out a penlight on her keychain. It cast a feeble light, but it was enough to show her the make of the vehicle. She recognized it. The car belonged to Glenn Magnus.

Johan was here.

The car was empty, but when she laid a palm on the hood she felt the heat of the engine. He hadn't been here long. She still had a chance to catch him. She opened her mouth to shout his name, but she caught herself and bit her tongue to stay quiet. She couldn't let anyone know they were here. Even so, she felt his presence nearby, like a Wi-Fi signal connecting them. All her old feelings came back as strong as ever. Memories of the two of them in the cornfield last summer supplanted the black memories of the train car. She felt him holding her as they made love. Her first time. His, too, he said. His body was on top of her, and his heaviness was arousing.

Olivia walked faster. She needed to find him.

She reached Kirk's house steps away from the black river. It was flooded with light, but she saw no one moving inside. She recognized Kirk's pickup parked near the garage. He was home. Or was he? The stillness of the place bothered her. She expected the music of a party, or boys' voices, or the squeals of stupid girls who didn't know better. Instead, the house was as silent as a tomb.

She crept closer, exposed in the glow of the garage lights. If Johan could see her, she hoped he'd break cover and call to her. No one did. She walked past the truck to the front porch steps. Loose boards groaned as she climbed them, and she winced at the noise. At the front door, she cupped her hands by her face to stare inside the house. The living room lights were on, and the place was a mess. Someone had torn it apart. Two drawers of a file cabinet were open and had been emptied onto the floor, which was strewn with papers and photographs. A desktop computer lay on the floor; its metal side had been stripped open.

What the hell?

Olivia backed away and retraced her steps off the porch. At each window, she saw more signs of a frantic search, but she saw no one. Not Kirk. Not Johan. She reached the rear corner of the house backing up to the wilderness and the river. The window on the corner looked in on a small bedroom. She saw the high school textbooks on the laminate desk and figured that the room belonged to Kirk's brother, Lenny. He had a lava lamp, glowing with floating orange clouds. Dirty clothes covered the floor. There were posters tacked on the wall, all of naked porn stars. Front. Back. On their knees. It was disgusting.

On his bed, immediately below the window, she saw other photographs, too. Photographs of her.

Olivia felt violated all over again. She saw herself in the swimming pool at school. On the street outsider her mother's clinic. On her front lawn in St. Croix with Tanya. Wherever she'd gone, he'd been there with her. Spying. Lenny had been following her for weeks.

She recoiled from the window, and as she did, a hand clapped over her mouth from behind. Another hand snaked around her waist, and she felt dirty fingers on her bare stomach.

The touch of a boy's hand set her off like a bomb. She drove her elbow backward into her attacker's kidney, landing the blow so hard she thought the fleshy organ would squish out onto the mushy ground. She heard a yelp of pain and felt the hands loosen on her body. Free now, she spun, throwing her left fist, colliding with hard bone. It was the side of his skull. Another gasp. His hands flew in front of his face in self-defense. She shoved violently on his bare chest. His legs spilled out underneath him, and he dropped flat on his back. His body was a mucky stretch of skin; he was naked. She swung her leg to punt his groin like a football kicker, but he squirmed away and covered himself, screaming, "No!"

She focused on his face for the first time. It was Lenny. She looked around, expecting Kirk and the other Barron boys to charge her. No one did. The two of them were alone.

"Lenny, you bastard!"

On the ground at her feet, the boy wailed. "I'm sorry, I'm sorry. Olivia, I didn't know it was you." There was a dirty wool blanket near him on the ground, and he scrambled to cover himself. "Honest, I didn't know."

"Where's Kirk?"

"I don't know. He kicked me out. I fell asleep in the truck."

"Have you seen anybody else?"

"No, nobody. I told you, I was sleeping. Something woke me up."

Lenny struggled to his feet, clutching the blanket at his waist. His chest was scrawny, his arms like toothpicks. His eyes darted up and down Olivia's body, and she realized that her nipples were pointy and visible through the soaked fabric of her shirt. She folded her arms over her chest.

"How long have you been following me?"

His eyes widened. "What?"

"You've been stalking me, you creep. I saw the pictures on your bed."

"It's not what you think. I just like to see you."

"You're repulsive."

"I'm sorry. Really."

She watched him adjust the blanket around his waist and knew he was becoming aroused. She felt another urge to kick him between his legs. "Go put some clothes on."

"Yeah. Okay."

Lenny brushed past her. The touch of his shoulder made her fists clench. He squeezed his fingers under the sash and pushed open the window to his bedroom. As he climbed inside she looked away, not wanting to see his naked body. She heard him opening drawers, tugging out clothes. When he climbed outside again, he wore a flannel shirt and blue corduroys. He'd combed his wet, greasy hair back over his head.

Before he closed the window, she told him, "Show me the pictures."

"Huh?"

"The pictures you took. I want to see them."

He looked as if he wanted to run.

"Reach in and get them, Lenny. Now."

Lenny bent over the ledge, and he pushed together the photos on the bed into a messy pile. They were printed on ordinary copier paper, and he'd used a low-pixel camera on his phone. Most of the pictures were blurry. He handed them to her, and the rain began to soak into the colors immediately. The photos ran. The paper became flimsy mush.

She stared at each one, and as she did, she crushed it and threw it on the ground in anger. He'd been everywhere, hiding, watching. It wasn't just outside. He'd spied on her when she was in her bedroom, from a tree near the river. She saw herself sprawled on her bed, reading. Drinking pop from a can as she did homework on her computer. Some were at night, as she got ready to sleep. Her in a towel, coming out of the shower. Her in her shorty nightgown. One, so blurry his hands must have been shaking, showed her nude in profile.

Olivia slapped his face, leaving a pink palm print on his cheek. Lenny groaned but didn't say anything. He just stood there and took it.

She dropped the photos to the ground and began obliterating them under her shoe, but she stopped as she spotted a moonlit scene, so dark it was almost indistinguishable. Something about it screamed at her. She grabbed the pictures from the ground again. Frantically, she flipped through at least ten more photos, all apparently taken the same night. Most were too black or out of focus to see, but she found two that were bright enough to identify. In these pictures, she wasn't alone. Tanya was with her. When she looked closer, she saw someone else, too.

It was Ashlynn.

The photos were taken in the ghost town.

"You were there!" she shouted. "You saw us!"

Lenny tugged at his flannel shirt, which he'd misbuttoned in haste. "I was on the other side of the railroad tracks."

"Did you see everything?"

"Yeah. I thought you were going to shoot her."

"I *didn't*."

"I know. I saw you leave."

Olivia took him by the shoulders and shouted in his face, "You didn't say anything? You let them arrest me? You let Kirk and those bastards come after me? You knew I didn't kill her. How could you do that to me?"

"I—I don't know. I thought, like, if they tried you or something, I could be a hero, you know? I could come forward and save you."

"You *bastard*."

"I'm really sorry," he moaned.

"Did you see who killed Ashlynn?"

"No, no, I got the hell out of there. I left right after you did."

Olivia tried to decide if she believed him. She struggled to rein in her emotions. Everything she'd been through, everything she'd suffered, it all could have been avoided if Lenny had opened his mouth. "Was it you?" she asked. "Did you shoot her?"

"No!"

She folded the wet photographs and shoved them in her pocket. "You're going to talk to the police tomorrow, Lenny. You're going to tell them what you saw."

"Yeah. Sure. Whatever you say."

"You're going to tell them what Kirk did to me, too."

Lenny shook his head. "Oh, fuck, Olivia, you know I can't do that. He's my brother!"

Olivia stared closely at Lenny's face and saw for the first time that he had fresh bruises and dried blood on his skin. "Did Kirk do that to you? Is that how your brother treats you?"

"I deserved it. I'm a loser."

"You're a loser if you don't help me."

"Kirk's done everything for me. I'd be dead if it weren't for him."

Olivia knew she was on the losing end. Even if Lenny loved her, he loved his brother more. Or feared him more. "Where is he?"

"I don't know. Why are you here? What's going on?"

"I'm trying to stop something bad from happening."

"Like what?"

"Someone getting killed. Where is Kirk, Lenny? His truck is still here. If he didn't leave, where did he go?"

"I told you, I don't know."

"You said something woke you up," Olivia said. "What was it?"

"I think I dreamed it. It sounded like gunshots."

"*Gunshots*? From where?"

"In the woods near the river." Lenny covered his mouth with both fists. "Oh, fuck."

"Come on, we need to check it out. Do you have a flashlight?"

"Yeah."

Lenny slithered back inside the window to his room and emerged with a red Maglite. Olivia grabbed it from him and shot the beam toward the river. It lit up the streams of rain. She took his dirty hand and dragged him with her toward the woods. Where the trail dove into the trees, she spotted deep boot prints filling with water. She listened, but the spattering rain covered up every other noise. The river shouldered in front of them like a fat snake.

"What's down here?" she asked Lenny.

"Nothing."

She heard it in his voice. He was lying. She stopped and turned the light into his face. He put up a hand, covering his eyes. Rain poured on his acne and his cuts.

"Tell me," she said.

"I don't know. Kirk says he's got something big down here. He doesn't let me come with him."

Olivia led them through the mud. The river slapped against the bank beside them. She had no sense of how far they'd gone. She didn't like the idea that Kirk was out here somewhere or that she might run into him alone. She thought about switching off the light because it was a beacon for anyone else in the woods, but without it, she may as well have closed her eyes.

Snap.

She stopped so quickly that Lenny bumped into her. A twig broke under someone's foot. She swung the light off the trail, and she stifled a scream as the beam lit up a boy's face, no more than ten feet away.

There he was, frozen between the flaky trunks of two birch trees.

"*Johan*," she whispered.

His face was shock white. "Olivia! What are you doing here?"

He crashed toward her through the weeds. They felt like lovers as they embraced, the way they'd been in the summer. The light of the flashlight danced crazily. Behind them, Lenny was almost invisible in the night.

She read the terror in his eyes. "What's wrong?"

When he didn't answer, she studied him from head to toe with a flick of the light. His wet sneakers were splashed in red. So were the cuffs of his jeans. "Oh my God, Johan, what did you do?"

Lenny saw the blood, too. "*Kirk.*"

Johan took her hand. "We have to get out of here right now. It's not safe."

"*Kirk!*" Lenny screamed again. He grabbed the flashlight out of Olivia's hand, dove off the trail, and was swallowed up by the darkness. He shouted his brother's name over and over.

"Quick," Johan said. He had his own flashlight, and he switched it on. "We have to hurry."

Olivia felt a strange calm. "I have a car. We'd better hide yours, they're looking for it. C'mon, let's go."

They hadn't traveled twenty yards before she heard an anguished cry. It was Lenny, somewhere in the woods behind them. She didn't stop. She didn't ask Johan what Lenny had found, and she didn't care. The only thing that mattered was that they were together.

They kept running.

42

THE HOUSE IN ST. CROIX WAS EMPTY. HANNAH WASN'T HOME. NEITHER was Olivia. Chris stood on the porch with his hands on his hips. Water pounded on the metal gutters, and the wind felt like ice on his wet clothes. He was alone in the rain, with nothing but the gauzy orbs of house lights dotting the streets. The town felt abandoned.

He'd spent years in the city, surrounded by people. The empty land of the country had always scared him. Now he realized he'd been a fool. Being with Hannah, being with Olivia, had changed everything. The only thing that mattered was for them to be safe. With him. What scared him more than anything was the idea of losing them again.

He walked through the downpour to the St. Croix church. Inside, he called for Glenn Magnus, but no one answered. The downstairs lights were dark. He heard the vibration of the bells, humming in the wind. He checked the sanctuary, which was lit only with dim wall sconces, and he almost missed the single worshipper on her knees in the pew nearest the altar.

It was Hannah.

He didn't want to interrupt her, but he wondered what she said to God in her private thoughts. He'd never been a believer himself, but she always told him she prayed for him anyway. For him, for Olivia, for her family, for her town, for the women and children who had no one on their side. He tried to imagine whether she had added herself to the list now, but he didn't think so. That wasn't Hannah. She would pray for everyone else but not for herself.

He stared at the cross hanging over the altar, and the thought came to him unbidden. *Save her.* He didn't think anyone was listening, and he didn't imagine he was first on the list for answered prayers. He thought it again anyway. *Save her.*

Hannah felt his presence. She saw him at the front of the church, and her face lit up in a smile. When she saw him now, she didn't think immediately of the past, the pain, the breakup, the murder, the fear. For a millisecond, those things didn't exist, and she simply reacted with a brief, instinctive moment of joy at the sight of him. He smiled, too.

They met halfway in the aisle.

"You're late," she said. "I was worried."

"I'm fine."

She stared into his eyes as if she were looking for something. "You didn't go back there, did you?"

"Where?"

"To Kirk's."

"Of course not."

Her face softened with relief. "I'm glad. I didn't think you would."

"Why do you ask?"

Hannah hesitated. "We need to talk."

"I know. There's a lot I need to tell you. I may know what happened to Ashlynn."

She glanced at the doors to the sanctuary. Her eyes were nervous. "Tell me quickly. We don't have much time."

"Why not? What's going on?"

"They'll be coming soon."

"Who?"

"The police."

"Why?" he asked. "Is Olivia okay?"

"She's fine." Hannah pulled him gently into an empty pew. "Tell me what you found out."

Chris struggled to arrange his thoughts. "Ashlynn told Tanya Swenson she had proof that Florian and Mondamin were involved in what happened in St. Croix. She suspected her father of orchestrating a cover-up. Somehow it involved not only Vernon Clay but Lucia Causey, too."

"The special master in the litigation?" Hannah asked. "You think she falsified her report?"

"Florian has long arms," Chris said. "Lucia's dead. She committed suicide last year, but Ashlynn thought she was murdered."

Hannah shook her head. "What did Ashlynn find out?"

"I'm not sure, but I can think of two people who would want to make sure she didn't tell anyone."

"Who?"

"One is this man Aquarius. He left a trail that leads to Vernon Clay and Lucia Causey. If Ashlynn found out who he was, he might have decided to stop her from getting in the way of his plans."

"What plans?"

"That's the problem. Nobody knows."

"Who's the other?" Hannah asked.

"Kirk Watson."

She tensed and glanced at the closed doors of the church again. "Kirk's dead."

"*What?*"

She didn't stop to explain. Something made her bolt to her feet. Chris stood up, too, and he heard sirens wailing on the highway. It was just as she'd predicted. The police were coming.

"What's going on?" he asked.

Hannah pulled him toward the front of the sanctuary. "*Don't* say anything to them, Chris. Not yet."

They exited into the church lobby. Outside the glass doors, three squad cars from the sheriff's department screeched to a stop on the street. The sirens were loud enough to make him cover his ears, and then they cut off into stark silence. The light bars revolved on the tops of the cars. Silver rain blew sideways as officers in yellow slickers climbed out of the vehicles and headed for the church steps.

He saw someone else with them. A man in a black trench coat with a fedora. It was Michael Altman.

Chris and Hannah stayed in the lobby as the county attorney came inside from the rain. His face was dark. The police officers with him filed downstairs. Chris didn't think they were looking for the church party room. They were heading for Johan's apartment.

"Mr. and Mrs. Hawk," Altman said, dusting water from his hat. "You always seem to be around when I have trouble."

"What are you doing here?" Chris asked.

"I'm looking for Johan Magnus."

"Why? What's going on?"

"Someone murdered Kirk Watson this evening."

Hannah stiffened but said nothing. Chris found that his own heart was ice cold. He didn't care that Kirk was dead. He only cared about protecting Olivia. "How did it happen?"

"Someone hit him in the head," Altman said, "and then finished him off with two gunshots. One to the head, one to the genitals. Very personal."

Hannah covered her mouth. Chris felt queasy, too. Altman watched both of them carefully, studying their reactions.

"That sounds like someone with a grudge," Altman added. "Like maybe someone whose daughter had been assaulted recently."

"You think I did this?" Chris asked.

"I don't know, Mr. Hawk. Where have you been this evening?"

"Out."

"Alone?"

"Mostly." He didn't want to get George Valma into more trouble by calling on him for an alibi. He also hoped that the rain had long ago washed away any evidence that he'd been outside Kirk's window the previous night.

"Doing what?"

"Researching Lucia Causey," Chris said. "Check my phone records. You'll find that I've been making inquiries about her for most of the last two hours. You can probably get a track on my laptop Internet settings, too. I've been hooked up to a limited-range wireless network in Barron. Feel free to check it out."

"I'll do that," Altman said. "We found the murder weapon. It was a revolver. The cylinder had four spent casings, but only two shots appear to have been fired at the scene. Does that suggest anything to you?"

Chris knew what Altman meant.

"We think it was the same gun that was used to kill Ashlynn Steele," the county attorney went on. He frowned and asked pointedly, "Where's your daughter? I'd like to talk to her."

"She's in her room," Hannah interjected. "She's been there all evening. Whatever's going on, this doesn't concern her. Leave her alone."

She said it calmly and convincingly, but Chris knew it was a lie. Olivia wasn't in her room.

"What about Johan Magnus?" Altman went on. "Have you seen him?"

"No," Chris said.

"You told me Johan was going after Kirk. Did he try to reach you? Did he ask for your help?"

"He didn't."

"If he had, would you have tried to stop him?"

"Of course I would."

Chris could see the county attorney debating whether they were being honest. The man's frustration showed. "I need to find Johan Magnus quickly," Altman said.

"So you can pin a murder charge on him?" Hannah demanded. "Don't ask us to help you do that. Whoever killed Kirk did the world a favor."

"I'm trying to protect the boy, too."

"Protect him? Why? From what?"

"We got a call from Kirk's brother," Altman told them. "Lenny Watson told us Kirk had been murdered and where to find the body. He told us Johan was at the scene, covered in blood."

"You believe him?" Chris asked.

"It doesn't matter whether I believe him. That's not the point. When we got to the house, Lenny was nowhere to be found. He's missing, too, and we're trying to find him. In his 9-1-1 call, Lenny said he was going to avenge his brother. He's planning to kill Johan."

"Where is she?" Chris asked.

They were back on the porch of Hannah's house, out of the rain. Hannah left her red umbrella on one of the Adirondack chairs. She beckoned him inside. The house was warm and quiet. She took off her raincoat and peered through the windows at the church, which was still a hive of police activity. No one had followed them. No one was watching them.

"Is she here?" he asked again.

Hannah pointed at the closed door that led down into the basement. "She came to me for help. They both did. I wasn't going to say no, Chris."

"Jesus, Hannah. Tell me she wasn't at Kirk's house tonight."

She said nothing, but he knew that was exactly where Olivia had been. He opened the basement door. The light was off.

"Olivia, it's me," he called into the darkness.

He switched on the light and marched down the wooden steps beside the stone blocks of the foundation. Hannah followed him. It was cool and damp under the ground. In the open space, he saw area rugs spread across the hard floor and metal shelves lining the walls. Ductwork made a maze overhead. Mice had found their way under the house; he saw tunnels in the pink insulation.

A ratty blue sofa was pushed against the north wall. During tornado season, it was a place to wait out the storm.

Olivia sat on the sofa with her arm around the waist of Johan Magnus.

Both teenagers looked freshly showered; they wore clean clothes; their skin was pink. They had a blanket over their laps. Chris heard the bang of the drier; their clothes had been washed and were tumbling dry. Hannah had already helped them. She'd destroyed evidence.

Johan didn't say a word. He looked overwhelmed. Olivia, in contrast, looked in complete control. She was the strong one. The determined one. Her voice, when she spoke, was perfectly calm.

"Johan didn't do it, Dad," she told him. "He didn't kill anyone. He's innocent. Like me."

43

Florian Steele waited fifteen minutes, but Kirk never showed.

The park by the Indian monument was where they always conducted their business. Their relationship wasn't for public eyes. It was cash only. It was one on one. It was only at night. They met, they talked, they did their deal, they went their separate ways. He didn't like it, but he'd long ago made peace with the fact that every business needed a Kirk Watson to survive.

Kirk was Florian's problem solver. When Vernon Clay's insanity became a liability, he'd sent Kirk to deal with him. He'd hoped never to cross that line, but the scientist gave him no choice. Since then, Florian had slept soundly, convinced that Vernon was no longer a threat. Now he didn't know what to believe. If Vernon was alive, then Florian understood the danger. If Vernon was dead, then Aquarius was a mystery. His plans were unknown.

He remembered what Julia had said, *I think he plans to kill us.*

Florian checked his watch. He couldn't wait any longer. It was unlike Kirk to miss a meeting, and the more time that passed the more he worried about a trap. He drove out of the park onto the rainy roads. He kept his eyes on his mirrors, but no one followed him.

He called Julia to tell her he was on his way home. She didn't answer. She was probably in the shower, getting ready for bed, ignoring his messages. Since Ashlynn's death, she was always asleep when he came to bed. She hadn't let him touch her for days. Tonight, he would wake her up, undress her, make love to her, sweat passion out of her. He couldn't stand the emptiness of his life for another night. He was dead, and he needed to feel alive. If he could break the dam between them, they could both grieve like normal people. They could take comfort in each other. They could finally cry.

He dialed again. "Pick up, Julia," he murmured, but if she was there, she let him stew in silence.

Florian turned off the highway and followed the sharp incline of the bluff. The city, the river, the company were all in the valley below him. He reached his U-shaped driveway and saw that Julia had turned off every light in the house. She was leaving him in darkness. The gulf in their marriage pained him. It was hard enough to deal with the loss of his daughter, but it was even worse to do so alone. He wondered if Julia realized how much he still loved her. He wondered if she knew he had always been faithful.

He pressed the garage door opener and almost drove into the closed door. He pushed the button again, but the door didn't move. He studied the unlit house and realized that the power was out. When he looked at the rest of the neighborhood, he saw that lights burned everywhere but here.

Something else was going on, and he didn't like it.

Florian unlocked his glove compartment. He kept a Ruger 9mm pistol there at all times. Everyone knew who he was; everyone knew he had money. He couldn't take chances with pirates on the rural roads. He took the butt of the pistol in his hand, checked it, and got out of the car into the rain. He followed the flagstones on his walkway and reached his front door.

It was ajar. Rain and dirt streaked the crack of the opening onto the plush white carpet.

He pushed open the door with his shoulder. Inside, with no electricity, the house was absolutely still, and the air was growing cold. The security system was off. He couldn't see, but he could trace every inch of the house blind-folded. He led with the barrel of the gun and headed for the magnificent spiral staircase that climbed to the bedrooms.

Halfway up the steps, he called for her, "Julia!"

His voice, shattering the silence, sounded loud. He didn't care who heard him. If someone was here, they'd already seen his headlights as he arrived. They knew he was in the house. They knew where he would go to find his wife.

"Julia!" he shouted again.

She didn't answer, or she couldn't answer. He was terrified of what he might find.

Florian climbed to the landing. Their master suite was in front of him. Through the doorway, he saw a light winking at him. It wasn't one of their lamps; it was the flame of a candle. He thought for a moment that the dark house was Julia's idea of romance, but when he slipped inside, he found his fears realized. The bedroom was empty. His wife wasn't there. Instead, the candle teased him from her nightstand.

He saw a single sheet of paper on the polished oak beside the candle. A message.

Florian knew what it was. He knew who had sent it. He walked to the bed and stared down at the ivory wax melting into drippy streaks on the candlestick and forming a hot liquid pool at its base. The note on the nightstand was illuminated by the dancing flame, but he hardly dared to pick it up.

He thought, *Julia.*

He took the message in his hand, and he felt his entire world crashing down as he read it. First his daughter. Now his wife. There was nothing left.

TO THE ATTENTION OF

MR. FLORIAN STEELE

YOUR WIFE IS GONE

HER LIFE IS NOW IN MY HANDS

YOU CANNOT ESCAPE

YOUR OWN DESTRUCTION

YOU CANNOT SAVE

YOUR WORLD

YOU CAN ONLY SAVE HER

I WILL CALL YOU

AND YOU WILL COME TO ME

ALONE

MY NAME IS

AQUARIUS

PART FOUR

EVERY CREEPING
THING

LENNY SLEPT IN THE PICKUP OVERNIGHT. HE AWOKE AT THE FIRST LIGHT of dawn, freezing, his head pounding. He'd taken a six-pack of beer as he escaped the house, and he'd drunk more than he ever had in his life while sitting in the truck. The windshield was covered with tracks of frost. The rain had stopped, but water dripped from the tree branches and the hood was covered with wet, dead leaves. On the horizon, there was no sun, only steel-gray clouds. He was parked on the border of a state park west of the city. From his hiding place, he'd seen the lights of police cars coming and going at high speed on the county road. They were looking for him.

He was starving; he hadn't eaten since his slice of pizza at noon the previous day. He pawed through the junk piled in the backseat and found an unopened power bar. He ripped off the foil and ate it in three bites, choking on the gluey peanut butter. It only made his stomach growl, wanting more. He thought about stopping at a Holiday gas station for an egg sandwich, but he couldn't take the risk of being seen.

The truck smelled like smoke and beer. It smelled like Kirk. Daylight didn't change the night into a bad dream. His brother was dead. Kirk would never hit him again; he would never protect him again; he would never give him money and skin mags; he would never take him to the woods to shoot, or give him joints, or tell him stories about the girls he fucked. For years, Kirk had been the center of his world, and now he was gone.

Lenny sat in the pickup, and as the reality of his situation sank into his brain, he bawled like a baby. Snot dripped from his nose to his mouth and down the back of his throat. He coughed it up, hacking so hard that his lungs felt raw. He wasn't crying for Kirk. He was crying for himself. He was angry at the people he'd lost. They'd all abandoned him—every single person in his life. His mother, his father, his brother. All gone. He was utterly, absolutely, completely, forever alone.

He knew what Kirk would say to him, with a rap to his skull. *Grow some balls, Leno.*

That was right. He wouldn't run away and hide. He wouldn't be a coward and a pussy anymore. He would do what Kirk would have done.

He would make them all pay.

Lenny wiped his face and saw his reflection in the rearview mirror. Red-streaked eyes. Scraggly, unshaven beard, with hairs of different lengths on the point of his chin. A pus-filled white pimple bulging from the base of one nostril. The cut on his face was puffy; it was getting infected. His sallow skin looked like dishwater. He was a mess. Not handsome and powerful like Kirk. Not a clean-shaven blond god like Johan Magnus. It didn't matter.

He would make them all pay.

Lenny turned on the engine, and the big motor growled like a tiger. The radio blared Kid Rock. He checked the highway, but he didn't see any cops. It was early. Even so, he stuck to the back roads, past block-long towns and empty farms where you could count the people on your fingers. That was what Kirk would have done to give everybody the slip. *Stay off the grid and nobody will find you, Leno.*

Everywhere he looked, he saw water left by the storm. Standing water on the roads. Lakes across the cornfields. Ditches filled like swimming pools. Even without the rain, it was an ugly day, black and cold. A day for bad things to happen.

The ruts of the dirt roads hammered his kidneys, and he bounced in the seat. He reached over to the glove compartment and took out Kirk's silver wraparound shades. They cost two hundred bucks. No one touched them but Kirk. Lenny figured Kirk wouldn't care now, and he slid them over his eyes. The shades were a loose fit and the day was so dark he didn't need them, but when he checked his look in the mirror again, his teeth flashed into a crooked smile. He was cool.

He reached over to the passenger seat, where there was one can of beer left from the six-pack. He popped the top with his index finger, and some of the foam burbled out of the hole. He took a swig. It was warm, but he didn't care. He was feeling better. He had a plan.

It took him twenty minutes to twist his way down the complicated network of back roads, and he got lost more than once. He'd only been to Kirk's U-Stor garage three or four times, and the roads out here all looked alike. Same fields. Same dirt. No signs. Finally, he saw the driveway and the rundown double row of locked storage units behind the red doors. No one else was around.

Lenny parked in front of Kirk's garage and got out. He had a few swallows of beer left, and as he drank, some of it leaked down his chin. He was still buzzed from the overnight hours. His head swam. He heard the noisy squawk of a crow in a tall oak tree, and he could see the bird, big and black, perched on a high branch. It yelled at him and wouldn't quit, and the annoying *caw caw* made his headache worse.

"Shut the fuck up, bird," Lenny shouted. The crow didn't quit. It screeched louder, as if it were laughing at him. He found a rock on the ground and hoisted it at the tree, but his aim wasn't even close. The crow aired its wings defiantly.

Caw caw. It kept laughing.

Lenny spat on the ground. Damn bird.

He walked around to the tailgate of the pickup and squeezed his hand under the dirty bumper near the left rear tire. Kirk kept the locker key in a hidden magnetic case, rather than on his key ring. Fiddling with his fingers, Lenny found it and pried it off the inside of the bumper. He squeezed the case open, grabbed the key, and he undid the padlock on the metal door.

Lenny went inside, leaving the door open behind him. The musty garage was where Kirk kept everything he didn't want the cops to find. He saw the file cabinets with Kirk's records, his gun cases, and boxes of thumb drives and overstuffed folders spilling across his brother's desk. Kirk would come here, play Tim McGraw on his iPod, copy porn for his customers, and count his money.

Money. Lenny needed money.

He spotted the two-foot safe with the combination lock shoved against the rear wall. He squatted and spun the dial, entering the four numbers he'd memorized: 17-4-19-26. The door opened with a click as he wrenched the lever to the right. He spilled the heavy box forward, dumping the contents, and he whistled in delight. Stacks of cash, tied with rubber bands, littered the floor. Dozens of them. A fortune. He didn't stop to count; there must have been thousands of dollars here, enough to last him a year or more on the run.

He also saw a lone USB flash drive, no bigger than a stick of gum. It was labeled in thick letters with black marker: *Daddy.*

Lenny knew what it was, but he didn't care. Not now. He could deal with it later. He stuffed everything back into the safe and spun the combination lock. He lifted up the safe, grunting at its weight, and hauled it awkwardly in his arms to the truck, where he dumped the metal box on the floor in front of the passenger seat. He exhaled in relief. *You're rich, Leno.* He could go anywhere he wanted now. Mexico maybe. He could buy himself a brown girl and live on the beach.

First things first. He had things to do. He needed guns.

Kirk stored his rifles in a locked cabinet, and he kept the key in the top drawer of the desk. Lenny found it and swung the doors wide. He gasped in awe, studying the trove of weaponry. He smelled wood oil. Light bounced off the mirrored interior of the cabinet. He ran a finger down the black metal of the barrels, and his hands got sweaty as he fondled the sleek mechanisms of the rifles. He'd only fired two guns in his life, a bolt-action Remington deer rifle and a Ruger semiautomatic that was like an eight-inch penis. Kirk had taken him hunting north of Thief River Falls last October. Lenny hadn't made a kill, but he'd loved the deadly power of the weapons in his grip. Guns didn't ask if you were short or tall, strong or weak, brave or scared.

Lenny took the Remington into his arms, cradling the butt under his shoulder, aiming at the trees beyond the garage door. "Bang," he said, squeezing the trigger, hearing the empty click. In the desk drawer, he found boxes of gold cartridges gleaming like tiny rockets. He took the Remington and the ammunition and loaded it all in the pickup next to the driver's seat.

Handguns. He wanted those, too. Kirk had lots, stored on the metal shelves. You could never have too many. *They're like potato chips, Leno.* He found the Ruger he'd used when shooting targets with Kirk. He loaded the clip and shoved it in his belt. He didn't know if he'd need more, but he found an empty packing box and dumped the rest of the guns and clips inside, then carried the whole mess to the truck.

He had everything he wanted for now. He wasn't sure if he'd ever come back here. It was time to go, but he stood in the mud with the pickup door open and the garage door open and he couldn't move. He was frozen. The loneliness of the world landed on his shoulders again, making him feel sick and small. He could put on cool shades, he could load the truck with guns, but that didn't change who he was. He wasn't Kirk.

Over his shoulder he heard the crow, still taunting him from its perch in the tree. *Caw caw caw*, making his head throb. The bird knew his secrets and his fears. The bird wasn't afraid of him.

Lenny yanked the Ruger from his belt.

"Shut up!" he screamed again, but the crow only screeched louder.

He aimed at the tree and squeezed the trigger. The gun went off with a bang, making him lose his balance. The shot went off into the sky, nowhere near the bird, which spread its wings again as if to say, *Can't hit me, can't hit me.* He fired again, blasting away bits of bark. And again. And again.

The crow, bored with the game, flew away, laughing as it disappeared beyond the treetops.

"*What the hell are you shooting at, kid?*"

Lenny spun around at the voice behind him. He saw a man in his sixties standing near the pickup with his hands on his hips. The old man wore a Twins baseball cap, a Vikings sweatshirt, and camouflage pants. His boots were half-laced. He had a bushy salt-and-pepper mustache. His eyes were angry.

"Are you crazy?" the man went on. "Put that gun down."

Lenny had his arm extended, the barrel of the gun pointed upward at the tree, even though the crow was long gone. Their eyes met, his and the old man's. They were the only two people for miles around. Lenny didn't even know where the man had come from, but his car must have been parked out of sight behind the other row of storage units.

The old man glanced into the truck, and watching his face twitch, Lenny knew he'd seen the guns. Casually, the man shifted his eyes the other way, into the storage unit, where the gun locker with Kirk's rifles was open. His expression morphed from anger to worry. His voice got lower and softer.

"So what exactly are you doing here, son?"

Lenny swung the pistol and pointed it at the man's chest. "None of your fucking business, old man. Who the hell are you?"

The man raised his hands defensively. "Nobody, son. You just look like you could use some help. How about you put away the gun, and the two of us talk for a little while?"

Lenny marched on him menacingly, jabbing at him with the Ruger. The old man was six inches taller than Lenny. Everyone was taller than Lenny. "Get the hell out of here."

The old man stood his ground. They were six feet apart. "I have to be honest, you're making me nervous with that gun. I'd feel better if you put it down."

"Just get out of here! Go!" Lenny's voice quavered.

"Whatever you're doing, I think you're in over your head, son. Put that gun down, and let's talk about it."

"If you don't get out of here, I'll shoot," Lenny swore. "I will."

The man reached out his hand. "How about you let me take that gun from you? You don't want anyone to get hurt."

Lenny's arm shook. "Don't make me kill you."

The man took a cautious step toward Lenny. His mouth crinkled into a warm smile. "When you're a teenager, things can seem pretty overwhelming. I've been there. Then you get old, and you realize most stuff that you thought was important when you were a kid isn't important at all."

"*Stop!*"

"Let's talk about this, okay? You and me."

He took another step. His hand was inches from the gun.

Lenny's finger jerked. He didn't even want to fire, but he fired. The explosion rang in his ears, and the recoil shuddered through his arm. He watched the old man stutter backward, his hand over his chest, blood seeping through his knuckles, trickling down his skin and over his purple sweatshirt. The man's eyes were wide with disbelief. His face contorted in pain. He stumbled and sank to his knees. His breathing was ragged.

Lenny ran. He went wild with panic. He leaped into the pickup and drove, spinning the wheel so wildly that the truck nearly upended as he shot onto the highway. The passenger door flapped and finally shut itself. He twisted his torso to look over his shoulder, and he could see the old man on the ground. *Oh shit, oh shit, oh shit.* There was no going back now.

You just killed a man, Leno.

45

"DID MY SON KILL KIRK WATSON?" GLENN MAGNUS ASKED, HIS VOICE LOW. "Tell me the truth, Chris."

"He says he didn't."

"I know what he says. I know what the police told me. I want to know what you think."

Chris glanced at the porch, where Hannah sat with Olivia. Johan was hidden inside. They were out of earshot but he saw Olivia watching him, and her eyes reached out to him for help. It was a feeling he'd missed, the way she used to turn to him when she was a child. He'd never thought he would experience it again. His daughter needed him. She'd grown up, but she still needed him.

He'd interviewed Olivia and Johan separately throughout the night. Their stories matched. He didn't think they were lying.

"Johan admits he went there to kill Kirk," Chris said, "but before he reached the house, he heard gunshots near the river. He went to check it out and came across Kirk's body. He says he heard footsteps running in the opposite direction."

"What about the gun? It was the same gun that killed Ashlynn, wasn't it?"

"It looks that way."

"I've never doubted Johan in my life," the minister said, "but it's hard to know what to think. There was blood on his clothes after Ashlynn was killed. There was blood on his clothes now."

The two men stood eye to eye in the street. The minister looked shaken.

"He was honest about what he wanted to do," Chris said. "He was honest about trying to get a gun from Tanya. If he already had a gun, why would he bother calling her? I think if Johan killed Kirk, he'd simply say so. He'd be proud of it."

"That scares me, too. If he didn't do it, it's only because someone beat him to it."

Chris thought of himself outside Kirk's house. One by one, they had all come face-to-face with the devil. "Not necessarily."

"You said yourself he had murder in his heart."

"It's one thing to think about it, Glenn, it's another to do it. It's a lot harder than people believe."

"The police want to talk to him."

"I know. Get a lawyer first. In the meantime, don't let him say anything or answer any questions. Olivia says Johan wasn't wearing gloves. If he didn't swing the shovel, if he didn't touch the gun, they won't find prints. If he wasn't there, they won't find anything to prove he was."

"On the other hand, if he's lying, they'll know."

"Probably."

Magnus stared at the sky. Chris wondered if he was debating with God. If anyone had reason to question his faith, it was Glenn Magnus, who had already lost a wife and a daughter. Now his son was at risk, too.

"If he didn't do it, someone else did," the minister said.

"Olivia said someone searched Kirk's house," Chris said. "Whoever killed him was looking for something."

"What do you think it was?"

"I don't know, but my bet is that the killer didn't find it. If you find what you're looking for, you stop. I think whoever it was saw Kirk leave and ransacked the house. When he didn't find what he wanted, he went after Kirk and killed him. Then Johan showed up, and he had to bolt."

"If it's worth killing over, someone else may be in danger."

"Johan's already in danger," Chris said. "Keep an eye out for Lenny Watson. With his brother dead, he's out for blood. The feud's not over."

"Lenny isn't a monster like Kirk."

"No, but he's desperate. You don't know what he'll do."

Distantly, Chris heard music. He realized it was Hannah's phone, ringing on the porch. He watched Hannah answer, and only seconds later, his ex-wife hurried toward them. He realized, watching the minister's face, that they had something in common. They both loved Hannah.

"Who was on the phone?" Chris asked.

"It's a woman I've worked with at the center," Hannah replied. "She's an EMT in Barron. She responded to a 9-1-1 call, and she thought I'd want to know about it. There's been a shooting."

Chris found Michael Altman at the remote U-Stor facility outside Barron. The ambulance was gone, but the police presence surrounding Kirk's storage garage remained. The county attorney looked older, as if his inexhaustible energy had been drained. He stared into space, oblivious to his surroundings. Chris tapped on the window of the county sedan, and Altman made a weary gesture at the other door. Chris climbed inside. The engine was running, and the interior of the car was warm. Altman had a bulky laptop computer, an old model, open on his dashboard. The screen saver had come on, sending rotating swirls of color across the monitor. There were several file folders next to the computer and a plastic bag filled with computer thumb drives.

"You have an excellent network of spies, Mr. Hawk," Altman told him.

"Hannah does."

"Ah. Of course."

"How's the victim?" Chris asked.

"He lost a lot of blood, but he was able to call for help, and he was conscious when the EMTs arrived. The medical personnel think he'll survive."

"Hannah said it was Lenny Watson who shot him?"

"It looks that way, based on the description the victim provided. He's armed and dangerous now. That stupid boy, all he's going to do is get himself killed." Altman swiveled his head and stared at Chris. "I need to know where Johan Magnus is."

"He's at Hannah's house. His father is with him. He's safe."

"I don't appreciate your hiding that fact from me last night."

"I didn't know it when I saw you."

Altman frowned, but he dropped it.

"You don't look happy," Chris said.

The county attorney had sunken eyes. Like Glenn Magnus, he appeared to be in the midst of an utter crisis of faith. It wasn't anger or disappointment. It was devastation. Whatever the man had found in Kirk's garage had shaken him to the core.

"You would think that after the years I've spent in this job, I would have cultivated a cynical view of human behavior," Altman told him. "The strange thing is, I haven't. I'm a Christian, Mr. Hawk. I believe people are basically good."

"Actually, I agree with you," Chris said.

Altman reached for a file folder and handed it to Chris silently. Chris opened it, and he felt a weight land upon his chest, heavy and awful. With each page he turned, he felt nausea grip his stomach, he felt rage chill his heart, and he felt his soul release a silent, irrepressible scream. The images printed on the pages spoke of such depravity that he had a difficult time imagining whoever had done this was part of the same human race. The trouble was, they were. They walked the same streets. They breathed the same air. They looked like everyone else.

That was the horror Michael Altman was facing. How could you ever trust your neighbor again, when you knew that there were people on earth capable of this?

Chris closed the folder, and he closed his eyes. He steadied his breathing. "I'm sorry," he said.

Altman held up the bag of flash drives. "There's more. These are even worse. Videos. It's unspeakable."

Chris had a hard time conceiving of something that could be worse than what he had already seen. "I can't begin to explain it. I wish I could."

Altman held up another folder. "His buyers are numbered rather than named. The drop shipments go to post office boxes. We'll have to identify the customers one by one."

"They'll go to prison."

"Of course they will, but that's not the point. Look at how many people are on this list! These are people with family and friends. People who show a normal face to the world. People who profess to worship the same God I do and live by the same ideals." His voice was eloquent in its pain, disbelief, and desperation.

"Without Kirk's murder, you might never have found this place," Chris said. "Now you can put these people away."

Altman shook his head. "I could have gone the rest of my life without seeing the inside of that garage."

Chris studied the storage locker beyond the police tape. The cops were carrying out guns. "Someone ransacked Kirk's house. Do you think this is what they were looking for?"

"Possibly."

"I know you're searching for Johan, but I don't think he killed Kirk. He's not the one."

"Now that I've seen this, I think you may be right." Altman hesitated and then added, "There's something I failed to mention last night. Where we found Kirk's body, we found another body, too. A skeleton, partially unburied. Kirk had apparently been digging it up when he was attacked."

"Do you have any idea who it was?"

Altman shrugged. "The forensics will take a long time, but I can think of one person who went missing at an opportune time in the last few years."

Chris thought about it. "Vernon Clay."

"I'm not a gambling man, but that would be my bet."

"If he was dead all this time, then he's obviously not Aquarius."

"Yes, and if he's dead and Kirk killed him, I doubt Kirk acted on his own."

"Florian wanted him eliminated," Chris said.

"Again, that's a possibility. Not that I'm ever likely to prove it."

"So who is Aquarius?" Chris asked. "What's he planning?"

"I don't know, but I'm beginning to think there really has been a monstrous cover-up at Mondamin. Because of it, Aquarius seems to be bent on taking revenge against Florian and exposing his sins. The question is why and what he's planning next."

"Do you think Aquarius killed Kirk? Is that part of the plan?"

Altman turned his head toward Chris. "If he did, and if he used that gun, that means one thing."

"He started with Ashlynn," Chris said.

THE RATTLE OF THE VAN AWAKENED JULIA STEELE. THEY WERE MOVING.

She was blindfolded, but she could tell from the paler shade of darkness on her eyes that they had left the cold garage and were out in the daylight. The bumps of the road pummeled her body like tiny punches. Her seat was reclined. Her hands were tied securely and uncomfortably behind her back, but her feet were free.

She didn't know whether to be afraid. The man who had taken her from her bedroom had been surprisingly tender. He'd apologized as he tied her up. He'd asked about her comfort. When it was obvious she was cold, he'd taken a blanket and positioned it gently over her body. His voice wasn't cruel. Even so, she was a prisoner, taken against her will.

They'd spent the night in the cramped confines of the van. They were inside; she could tell from the quiet, and she'd heard the slam of a garage door. He'd been with her the whole time, in the driver's seat. He hadn't touched her. Despite herself, she'd fallen in and out of sleep, but whenever she awakened, she felt his presence beside her and heard him breathing. As far as she knew, he hadn't slept at all.

"Who are you?" she asked quietly.

He waited a long time before he replied. "You know who I am, Mrs. Steele."

"Aquarius."

"Yes."

"That tells me nothing," she said.

He was silent again. The truck rumbled on the road, but the pavement felt smooth, like a highway. She wondered where he was taking her. And why.

"Aquarius is the Water Bearer," he went on.

"I'm a Christian, not an astrologer."

"As am I."

"A Christian wouldn't do what you've done."

His voice remained measured and calm. "You're not a woman to offer lectures on morality."

"What do you mean by that?"

"You're married to Florian Steele," he said.

"So?"

"So he created something evil and immoral. I intend to destroy it."

"Florian has done great things," she insisted. "People who would have starved in this world are alive because of my husband. Is that a sin? Are you one of those anarchists who believe we can go back to the Garden of Eden by wandering around naked?"

"No."

"Then why do you have a vendetta against Florian?"

"Your husband took away my life, and now I will take away his."

Julia sucked in her breath. He said it with a matter-of-fact sincerity. "Who are you?" she asked again. When the man next to her was silent, she said, "You're not Vernon Clay. I'd recognize his voice."

"So you do know."

"What?"

"You know what Vernon Clay did."

Julia didn't want to pretend anymore. They had made a mistake, but she had never dreamed that God would make them pay and pay and pay.

"Vernon was insane," she told him. "Yes, it's true, Vernon spent years poisoning the groundwater near St. Croix. It was horrifying, *but we didn't know it was happening.* If you want to believe the deaths there were connected to the chemicals, so be it. When Florian found out about Vernon, he made sure it *stopped*. He got rid of Vernon, and he cleaned up the land."

"Then he covered up the truth. He lied. He cheated. He destroyed."

"What choice did he have? Let the company be wiped out by the actions of one deranged psychopath? Would that have been fair to the employees and their families? To the people of Barron? To the farmers?"

"He killed."

"Florian would never do that."

"You don't know him as well as you think. Or have you deceived yourself all these years?"

"*Let me go.* Stop this."

Julia struggled against her bonds, but they held her tight. She was angry now. She wanted to escape. She wriggled in her seat and tried to reach the door handle, not caring if she spilled out of the moving van onto the highway. She found the indentation in the door where it should have been, but the handle had been removed. There was no way out.

She sank onto the seat cushion, breathing heavily, kicking the underside of the dashboard in frustration. The man next to her didn't say a thing. He made no move to stop her.

"So why are you doing this?" she asked quietly. "Are you related to one of the children in St. Croix? If so, I am very sorry. It may mean nothing, but our hearts broke with every death."

Aquarius was silent.

Julia felt a shiver of fear for the first time. She realized that calm, tender men can also be deadly. "Tell me something. Be honest with me. Should I make my peace with God?"

"You mean, am I planning to kill you?"

"Yes."

"What you say to God is up to you, Mrs. Steele, but I have no intention of harming you. I need you to bring your husband to me, and then you'll be free to go."

She tried to decide if she believed him. She didn't think he had a reason to lie. Not now. Then again, this man was intent on violence and revenge. He would say anything if it meant getting what he wanted. "Did my daughter figure out who you were?" she asked.

"Yes, she did," he acknowledged. "She was a smart girl."

"So you had to stop her from exposing you."

She heard sorrow in his voice. "The only person Ashlynn wanted to expose, Mrs. Steele, was her father."

"That's a lie," Julia snapped, but she remembered the light under Florian's door in the middle of the night. She remembered finding Ashlynn at Florian's computer. What was she looking for? What did she discover? Julia realized that Aquarius was right. There were some sins you couldn't cover up. Sooner or later, they rose up to consume you.

It was as if he could see the workings of her mind. "You know I'm right, don't you?"

Julia said nothing. She felt the van drift to a stop. The world around her was quiet. She listened, and she could hear the hiss of the wind, but she didn't hear any other traffic. "Where are we?" she asked.

He didn't reply.

"What are you going to do?"

"You're a Christian, Mrs. Steele, so you know the Book of Genesis."

"Of course, but what are you talking about?"

"God looked around at the world he had created and saw that it was so corrupt, so evil, so wicked, that it was beyond salvation. He determined to destroy it so that humankind could start over."

The man who called himself Aquarius reached over and removed Julia's blindfold. She squinted at the light, squeezing her eyes shut. Even the gray day felt bright after a night of darkness. When she could see, she craned her neck to stare through the windows of the van.

She knew where they were. She didn't understand.

And then she did.

"Oh, dear Lord," she murmured.

Aquarius didn't react. He reached for his phone and dialed. "Mr. Steele?" he said when Florian answered. "You know who this is. It's time we met."

47

CHRIS WATCHED OLIVIA FROM THE DOORWAY OF HANNAH'S BEDROOM. His daughter had a pencil in her teeth, and her brown eyes were serious and focused as she tapped on the keys of the computer. A long strand of her hair came loose on her cheek, and she brushed it back behind her ear. She wore a baggy pink T-shirt over her skinny frame and cotton boxers. Her feet were bare. Staring at her, he thought what any father would think. She was the prettiest girl in the whole world.

He didn't say anything, but eventually she felt his presence and the pencil dropped from her mouth. She gave him a smile. "Oh, hey, Dad," she said and went back to her work.

It was a nothing moment that felt like everything to Chris. If you didn't pay attention to those moments, they were gone. He couldn't believe he had missed out on three years of those smiles, and standing there, he swore to himself that he would never miss out on any of them again. He would never spend a day of his life where he didn't tell his daughter how he felt.

He walked over and kissed her on top of her head. "I love you, kiddo."

Olivia stopped typing. She looked up at him strangely. "You okay?"

"Fine." Chris sat on the bed and took a picture of her in his mind, the kind of picture you deliberately try to remember for years. "So what are you doing?"

"Research."

"On what?"

"Cancer."

Chris frowned. "Oh."

"I don't like doing nothing. I like to fight."

"Me, too."

"I'm trying to think of the best way to kick cancer's butt. Like, do I become a doctor? Or a lab rat trying to find a cure? Or do I just get really rich so I can give away lots of money."

He laughed. "I think whatever you do, you will kick butt."

"Unless I'm in jail, huh?"

"That's *not* going to happen. Don't even think about that."

Olivia got up from the chair and sat down next to him on the bed. "Can I tell you something? I haven't said anything to Mom, but I've been thinking about it."

"Sure."

"I'm scared," she said.

Chris put his arm around her shoulder and pulled her close. "I know. It's okay. Remember, Mom's a fighter, too."

"It's bad, though, huh? She doesn't talk about it, so I figure she's trying to protect me. I wish she would just be straight with me. I know how horrible it can be. I saw it with Kimberly."

"Cancer's never good, but your mom is about the strongest person I've ever met. Except maybe for you."

His daughter spoke softly, her head buried in the crook of his neck, her chestnut hair swishing over his shoulder. "You still love her, don't you?"

"Olivia," he murmured.

"It's not like you're a great actor, Dad. I can see it in your face. So if you were in love with her, how could you let her go?"

It wasn't an accusation. It wasn't angry. She said it curiously, but there was another question in her voice. It was tucked behind the wall, unspoken. *How could you let* me *go?* She wanted the truth. She wanted him to be straight with her. He owed it to her to be straight with himself.

He thought about a million different excuses. A million different ways to rationalize the mistakes they'd made. It all boiled down to one thing.

"I always thought she'd come back," he said.

Olivia said nothing for a long time. "That's funny," she said finally.

"How so?"

"I think Mom always thought you'd come after her."

Chris laid his head back against the soft blankets of the bed and did his best not to let his emotions spill from his eyes.

"Guess we're all pretty stubborn," she said.

"I guess so."

"I suppose when this is all over, you go back home, huh?" Her voice was light. Her fear was real.

He nudged her head from his shoulder and stroked her face. "Whatever happens, Olivia, I promise you this. I'll always be there for you."

"That sounds good to me." She stood up again, and she stretched her gangly arms over her head. Her face clouded over. "It must have sucked for Ashlynn."

"What do you mean?"

"Knowing what kind of man her dad is. Knowing what he did."

"We don't know exactly what Florian did or didn't do, Olivia, but I'm sure he loved his daughter."

"Yeah, but she found something, right? That's what got her killed."

"Maybe. I think she discovered something about this man who calls himself Aquarius, but I can't figure out how she did it. She was researching Vernon Clay, but now it looks like he's been dead for years. She was researching Lucia Causey, and she's dead, too. If Ashlynn found something, she's smarter than all of us."

Olivia sat down at the computer again and limbered up her fingers like a pianist. "Well, let's see if I can retrace her steps."

"I did that," Chris said, "but without her laptop or her notes, I don't know what she found. She posted about Lucia's death, but she didn't leave much of a trail."

Olivia grinned. "No offense, Dad, but this is a job for a geeky daughter not a legal beagle. What did you do, run Google searches?"

"Uh, yeah."

"What else?"

"Well, I guess that was it."

She rolled her eyes at him. "Okay. Lucia Causey." She opened up a screen and ten seconds later she announced, "She's pretty. I mean, for being old."

"You got a picture of her?"

"Sure. She's on Facebook."

"She's dead," Chris said.

"Yeah, well, it's not like they go out and take the pages down."

Chris stared over Olivia's shoulder at a photograph of Lucia Causey. His daughter was right. Lucia was pretty—not just for being old. She was probably in her midforties at the time the photograph was taken. She had jet-black hair, a hawk nose, and a big, teasing smile. Her features were slim and elegant. "She reminds me of Sophia Loren," he said.

"Who?"

"Never mind. I thought you had to be friends with her to see anything."

"That depends on your privacy settings. Most people don't have a clue what's out there for strangers to see. You can usually find out where people live, what they like, who their friends are, that kind of thing." Olivia's fingers flashed on the keys. "Wow, she really liked Las Vegas. Tons of photos of the Strip. She stayed at the Bellagio and the Wynn."

"One of the guys on the chat site said that she had had gambling problems."

"Yeah, looks like she was a blackjack fiend. There are links to some sites about card-counting strategies and links to Atlantic City, Jackson, and a bunch of Indian casinos. She was pretty into it. Kinda weird for a brainiac, huh?"

"Everybody has their weaknesses."

"Let's see how bad it got," Olivia said. She typed again. "Here's her address in Cupertino. Nice that she's got a unique name. You can't miss Lucia Causey, huh? She didn't bother with unlisted numbers either. Anyway, let me get the county records for her house."

"I know how to do that, too, you know," Chris said defensively.

Olivia opened up a window with a maze of legal filings for the California property. "So what does this all mean?"

Chris studied the records. "It means she was on the verge of losing her home three years ago. The lender initiated foreclosure proceedings."

"And then?"

"Then the loan was satisfied. The lien was removed."

"You mean it got paid off?"

Chris nodded. "Yup."

"She was so far behind they were going to take her house, and then she paid off her mortgage?"

"You got it."

"Any idea how much?"

Chris reached across her to the keyboard and clicked on the lien satisfaction. "One point six million dollars."

"Son of a bitch!" Olivia clapped a hand over her mouth. "Sorry."

"No, you got it right."

"Where'd she get the money?"

"I'd like to know," Chris said, but it wasn't hard to guess the truth. The payoff had occurred only weeks after the Mondamin litigation was dismissed on summary judgment.

Olivia opened up another window. "I can't believe this woman killed herself. I wouldn't kill myself if someone dropped a million bucks in my lap."

"Ashlynn thought she was murdered."

His daughter frowned as she typed. "Well, the police sure don't think so. They say she committed suicide a year ago in her garage. One year ago today, in fact. Can you fake it so that it looks like someone sucked a tailpipe?"

"That's not exactly my line of work," Chris said. "I suppose people who do that sort of thing can make anything look convincing."

"So why would Ashlynn think it wasn't suicide?"

"I don't know. Unless she found something in her father's files."

"'Fraid I can't help you with that, Dad."

"Yeah." He kissed her again. "Thanks for your help, kiddo."

Olivia clicked back to Lucia Causey's Facebook profile and opened up a listing of her fan pages. "Hey, here's a reason to kill yourself. She liked *Real Housewives of Beverly Hills*. Yikes."

Chris laughed. "I prefer *NCIS*."

"Uh-huh, but you're also about a hundred years old, Dad. Let's see, she also liked *Keeping the House* by Ellen Baker, *Six Feet Under*, the Bay to Breakers race, Luciano Pavarotti, Pink Ribbons Project, sausage and peppers from Chiaramonte's, the Geico Gecko, Miraculous bras from Victoria's Secret, and the Sunol Regional Wilderness."

He pushed himself off the floor and headed for the bedroom doorway. "I kind of like that stupid gecko, too."

"Yeah, and I bet you're okay with those bras, Dad."

Chris chuckled. He was out of the bedroom and halfway down the dark hallway when he stopped dead in his tracks. Cold air breathed up the back of his body, from his heels to his neck, as if he'd found his path blocked by a ghost. Maybe he had. Maybe Ashlynn was with him in the house, whispering in his ear. He spun around and marched back to the bedroom, gripping the door frame with both hands.

"What did you say?" he asked Olivia.

"Miraculous bras?"

"No, no, before that. Something about a delicatessen that Lucia liked?"

Olivia checked the screen. "Sausage and peppers from Chiaramonte's. Why, are you hungry?"

Chris didn't answer. He knew. Ashlynn knew, too. It would have been simple for her to discover the truth. It had been laid out in front of him since the moment he arrived in town. Every conversation with his friend, his philosopher, should have told him what was going on. He'd been looking for a vast conspiracy, and the reality was so much simpler. The reality was about love and loss.

Is it better to do nothing in the face of injustice or do the wrong thing?

Aquarius had made his choice.

Chris realized Olivia had found something else, too, something that he had failed to notice as he ran searches in his car in the rain. Something terrible and important. "Did you say that Lucia Causey committed suicide one year ago *today?*"

"Today," she repeated.

He didn't say anything. He turned and ran.

48

FLORIAN DID AS HE WAS INSTRUCTED; HE TOLD NO ONE ABOUT HIS rendezvous with Aquarius. If he brought the police, Julia died. He went alone, but he didn't go without protection. The Ruger that he normally kept in his glove compartment was buried in the pocket of his wool coat. It was a cold day. He would keep his hands in his pockets, the way anyone would. All he needed was an opportunity to pull the trigger.

He didn't know who this man was, or what he knew, but he had no intention of letting him leave their meeting alive. This game ended today. Aquarius would be gone.

He listened to Brahms on the car stereo as he drove. The sound was so rich and vivid, it was as if the pianist were with him in the car, fingers meticulously unlocking the puzzle of the music. It calmed him. He remembered how much Ashlynn had loved this concerto as a girl. She'd acquired his taste for the classics at a young age. She would close her eyes and pretend to play, and when it was over she would bow, as if the audience were silently cheering her.

Ashlynn.

He wondered if it was true that she'd turned against him. He wondered how much she knew before she died. He hated to think that, in her last days of life, she would have hated him for what he'd done.

Florian passed the headquarters of Mondamin on the river as he drove north, but he didn't stop. The guards at the gate recognized his car; they waved at him. He tooted his horn in salute. The facility operated 24/7; it was never empty, never idle. A decade earlier, there had been nothing on that land. He'd built it all from his own sweat, his own vision. People's livelihoods depended on him. If Mondamin was at risk, if it was under threat, he was sworn to defend it. That was his job.

Ashlynn, try to understand.

If only she'd come to him and given him a chance to explain.

He continued into the dense wilderness. The meeting ground wasn't far. Trees on both sides leaned over the road, and he caught glimpses of the river winking in and out of the forest. For three miles, the highway was like a tunnel crossing from one world to the next, and when he finally burst into the open, he was at the county gateway. The Spirit Dam muscled across the water. The thick trees gave way to swaths of dormant park land tracking the giant lake. Ribbons of charcoal clouds stretched overhead in dark layers.

He parked on the Barron side of the dam and got out. He buttoned his coat and tugged up his collar. The wind off the water bit his skin. He shoved his hands in his pockets and marched onto the concrete bridge. To his left, the lake sprawled over a mile of erratic banks like a well-fed spider. Below him, winding toward the town, the Spirit River swirled in white foam as the dam squeezed a pulsing current through its gates into the narrow canal.

Florian saw a dark-blue van parked on the concrete deck. Its windows were smoked; he couldn't see inside. Its headlights blinked at him. Aquarius was waiting, but Florian didn't hurry. As he crossed the dam, he glanced in every direction to make sure they were alone. His fingers gripped the gun in his pocket.

The driver's door of the van opened. A man climbed out. Without his anonymous threats, and with his identity unmasked, Aquarius was an ordinary man. He was a stranger, but he wasn't scary. Florian didn't know him, but he studied him carefully, assessing the danger. The man was underdressed for the weather, with no coat. He saw no gun in the man's hands and no place where he could hide one. He wondered if the man was foolish enough to think that Florian would come unarmed.

He didn't see Julia.

They approached each other warily, like spies at a prisoner exchange. When they were ten feet apart, Florian stopped, and so did Aquarius.

"Mr. Florian Steele," the man announced. "I've waited a long time for this moment."

"Where's my wife?"

"First things first. I'm sure you have a phone. Please throw it in the river."

Florian reached inside his coat and slid out his phone from an inner pocket. He stood next to a steel railing. He flipped his phone into the whirlpool, where it disappeared.

"You came alone?" the man asked. "No police?"

"That's what you told me to do." His eyes darted toward the van and the lake. He listened, but the roar of the water through the dam was a thunder covering every other noise.

Aquarius smiled. "You're wondering if I'm alone. You're wondering if someone else is in the van with your wife. Or perhaps there is a sniper on the bank, with a crosshair trained on your head."

"Is there?"

The smile washed away. Aquarius headed for the passenger door of the van and opened it, and he helped Julia out to the bridge. His wife, usually as perfectly arranged as jewels in a store window, now looked fragile and pale. Aquarius took a pocketknife from his pants and cut the bonds that held Julia's hands behind her back. She stretched her fingers, restoring the circulation.

Julia's and Florian's eyes met. He tried to decipher her expression. He saw sadness and fear. Anger. There was sorrow, but no love. Her heart was dead to him. He realized you can't rescue someone from a cage you built yourself.

"Are you all right?" he asked her.

She said nothing. She brushed her tangled hair from her eyes.

Aquarius held out his hand to Florian. "Your car keys, Mr. Steele."

"Why?"

"I promised you I would free your wife. I'm keeping my promise."

"And me?"

"I thought it was understood, Mr. Steele," Aquarius said. "You're not leaving."

Florian wanted to laugh. The threat sounded hollow, but there was no hint of a bluff in the man's eyes. There was no mercy. He shrugged, extracting his keys from his pants pocket, throwing them across the short space. The man caught them and passed the keys to Julia.

"Go," Aquarius said.

Julia shook her head. "I'm staying."

"This doesn't involve you, Mrs. Steele."

"Go, Julia," Florian told her. "Get out of here. Please."

Her hesitation was eloquent. There needed to be words between them, but they were at a loss. She didn't want to hear him say he loved her. They were beyond that. She didn't need empty encouragement, and she wouldn't believe it. "I'm sorry," he said, because he'd brought them here, to this place, to this moment. It was his fault.

He looked for tears and didn't see any. Not Julia.

"I was wrong, Florian," she said. "God didn't want any of this to happen."

She hugged herself in the cold, and she hurried past him. He heard the tap of her shoes, *click click*, moving away from him, until her footsteps were covered up by the rumble of rushing water. He didn't look back; he didn't take his eyes off Aquarius. Seconds later, he heard his car engine on the other side of the bridge. She'd left him here, which was the only thing she could do.

She was safe.

"Now we're alone," Florian said. "Or do you have accomplices with you?"

"We're alone, Mr. Steele. It's just the two of us."

"That's what I wanted to know." Florian drew out the Ruger from his pocket and pointed it at the chest of the man in front of him.

He fired.

49

"Marco!"

Chris hammered on the door of the motel owner's house, which was a tiny cottage two hundred yards up the slope from the motel itself. The view down the river valley gave him a perfect vantage on the headquarters of Mondamin. It was easy to imagine Marco Piva here, staring each day at the company he despised, contemplating his revenge on Florian Steele for the death of his wife of thirty-two years.

Lucia Causey.

There was no answer. Chris was too late to stop him. He pushed heavily with his shoulder against the lock, and the door caved inward. The cottage smelled of garlic and browned beef. Opera music played softly on the stereo, but no one was in the living room to listen to it. He searched quickly from room to room. The formal dining room was set for two places, but dust had gathered on the plates and glasses. There was an unopened bottle of red wine on the table and a candle in the floral centerpiece with a box of matches beside it. He remembered Marco telling him that his wife had always set a place for a guest who never arrived. The house was a shrine to a woman who wasn't coming back.

In the kitchen, there she was. Everywhere. The oval dinette table overflowed with photographs. Chris recognized her from the Facebook photo. It was the beautiful Lucia Causey, channeling Sophia Loren with her wicked smile and low-cut dresses. Even in her fifties, her bronzed skin looked preserved by time, taut and attractive. This was a woman who peered into a microscope by day and danced in the bistros at night. This was a woman whose animal lust was obvious even in the still life of old photos. This was a woman who must have made her husband laugh, scream, bellow, cry, and groan with pleasure.

This was a woman who had been eaten by a demon. Gambling. A woman who had sold her soul to the devil to escape.

Florian.

Marco was in the pictures, too. A young man. An old man. Years of pictures. Eating, drinking, dancing, singing, playing, traveling, sleeping, waking. He hung on his wife as if she were his treasure, which she clearly was. One of the pictures showed them kissing on a crowded sidewalk in Rome, and their passion for each other was so obvious it made Chris want to run home to Hannah, sweep her into his arms, and carry her to the bedroom. That was how much Marco Piva loved Lucia Causey. That was the void in his soul that she left behind.

The man who took her away would suffer.

He found Marco's bedroom, which was small and dark. The heavy curtains were closed. The furnishings were in cherrywood. Religious icons in gold leaf graced the walls. He saw heavy metal crosses and paintings of Christ. Marco's bed was a twin, and he'd made it neatly before he left, creasing corners into the blanket and smoothing the floral drape on the pillows. A Bible lay open on the bed, and a necklace of silver-and-black rosary beads was spread across the pages. On the floor, he could see the indentations in the carpet of a man who had been spent hours in prayer.

Chris leaned closer to look at the Bible. Marco had highlighted the verses of Genesis 6:5 to 6:7.

And God saw that man's wickedness was great on the earth and that his imagination and thoughts were nothing but evil.

And God repented that he had created man on the earth and was grieved to his heart.

And God said, I will destroy man from the face of the earth, man and beast, every creeping thing.

"Marco," Chris pleaded aloud, as if the motel owner could hear him. "What are you doing, my friend? This isn't the way."

He followed the hallway to the cottage's second bedroom, which smelled of cigar smoke. Ash sprinkled the floor. Marco had fashioned it as an office, with a rolltop desk, an old leather chair, and oak filing cabinets so stuffed with papers that the drawers didn't close. There were photographs hung on the wall from Marco's decades with the police in San Jose. Marco in a perfectly fitted uniform, his expression serious, his badge gleaming. Marco in a row with other officers, all of them with their hands neatly folded behind their backs. Above the desk, Chris saw four framed graduation certificates, too. They were all identical, from different years over the past decade, all signed by the director of the FBI and the secretary of the army. Marco had gone through explosives training at the Hazardous Devices School at the Redstone Arsenal in Huntsville, Alabama.

Marco wasn't just a cop. He had spent his career in the bomb squad.

Chris felt his breathing quicken. He was suddenly conscious of every second that passed. He opened the drawers of the desk and piled papers in front of him, and everything he found made him sick.

Engineering diagrams.

Orders for electronics, tools, switches, wires, chemicals.

Web printouts on underground sources of explosive materials. Comparisons of yield. Bomb designs.

Photographs.

Marco had taken hundreds of photographs in a single location, and Chris recognized the innocent stretch of roadway, not even a hundred yards across. People who drove across it didn't even know what was built below them. It was no more than three miles away, upriver. It was the cork in the bottle controlling the flow of millions of gallons of water into the valley.

The Spirit Dam.

Marco had analyzed the dam in exhaustive detail. He'd taken close-ups of every gate, valve, and pipe. He'd obtained the structural blueprints and marked notes on the elevation, crosssections, and contour lines. He'd mapped the points of maximum stress. He'd studied the FEMA flood plains for southwestern Minnesota. He'd consulted with security experts and engineers by letter and e-mail, using his bomb-squad credentials to seek help from outsiders in assessing the risk of an IED to the integrity of the dam.

Instead, unknowingly, they'd helped him design a bomb to blow it up. Destroy it. Bring a wall of water down on every creeping thing.

Sometimes choices are easy. Sometimes they are hard.

Chris bolted through the cottage. He had to get to the dam. He had to stop Marco, but even as he ran, he knew in the pit of his gut that the effort was futile. Marco was already there. He had chosen his path of revenge. He was unstoppable.

As he passed through the dining room, with its odd settings of plates, crystal, wine, and flowers, he spotted a slim envelope tucked under one of the lace placemats. He stopped long enough to pull it into his hand, and he was startled to see his own name written across the envelope.

Marco was way ahead of him.

Chris opened the envelope and removed a single sheet of paper inside. He knew what he would find. It was a note of death, yet it made him cry. It was the last note from Aquarius.

TO THE ATTENTION OF
MR. CHRISTOPHER HAWK

IF YOU ARE READING THIS, MIO AMICO,
YOU KNOW THE TRUTH

I AM SORRY

WHAT IS DONE CANNOT BE UNDONE

SOON I WILL BE WITH LUCIA

SOON JUSTICE WILL BE MINE

I WILL PRAY THAT YOU AND YOUR FAMILY ARE SAFE

NOW YOU HAVE YOUR CHANCE

TO START OVER

MY NAME IS

AQUARIUS

50

Marco Piva staggered backward as the bullet tunneled through his body, splintering bone, searing and tearing muscle, and splattering blood, tissue, and skin across his back as it exited into the cold air and spent itself in the dead grass beyond the river. Inhaling, he felt knives cutting open his chest. He coughed, spraying red-tinged spit onto the white cotton of his T-shirt. Blood pulsed through the hole in his torso with the pumping of his heart. Even so, he managed to laugh. His lips folded into a smile. He'd expected deceit from Florian Steele.

"*Bastardo*," he whispered.

Florian kept the gun pointed at him. "Who are you?"

Marco focused beyond the agony of every breath. His T-shirt had a small breast pocket, and he slid out a photograph. It was partly soaked in blood now. He stared at his beloved Lucia, in one of the happiest times of their lives. A decade earlier, they had spent a month in his hometown outside Milan. For four weeks, they had gotten drunk and made love like teenagers.

He stared at her face. Her eyes making love to the camera. Her lips blowing him a kiss. That was the image of her he wanted to take to the grave. That beautiful memory, inked into his brain.

He handed the photograph to Florian, whose eyes flicked to the picture in confusion. It took him a moment to recognize her. She looked different in the lab, her hair pinned, her glasses on that perfect sharp nose. The scientist was all business. The wife and lover let her hair down.

"Lucia Causey," Florian said finally, remembering her face. He studied Marco, dying in front of him. "You're her husband."

Marco thumped his chest. "Thirty-two years."

Florian shook his head. "You crazy son of a bitch. This was never even about Mondamin? Hell, you should thank me instead of trying to kill me. I saved you, both of you. Your wife was gambling your lives into oblivion. You were going to lose everything until I came along."

Marco stabbed a finger at him. "You killed her."

"She killed herself."

"It was you," he insisted.

"What, do you think I sent someone there to murder her? You're wrong. You may hate it, you may not want to accept it, but your wife went into that garage all by herself and chose to end her life."

Marco gripped the bridge railing for support. His knees buckled, and he sank toward the ground, feeling dizzy. "I know."

"You know?" Florian demanded angrily. "If you know, then why the hell are we here? I had nothing to do with your wife's suicide!"

Marco bowed his head. He'd been expecting those words. The arrogance of the man was amazing. It was why he and his company were beyond salvation. Out here, unashamed, unaware of his fate, Florian Steele still managed to believe that he was innocent.

"Ashlynn knew," Marco whispered.

"*What about my daughter?*"

"She understood. She knew who you are."

Florian pointed the gun at Marco's skull. "What did you do to my daughter?"

Words came harder now. He was floating with the loss of blood. "She knew . . . you destroy . . . everything you touch."

"Ashlynn loved me."

"You can love . . . and you can still hate." He wrapped his left arm around the railing, holding himself up.

He'd loved Lucia. He'd hated her, too. He'd hated what the gambling did to her, how it had sent her spiraling into despair. He'd hated watching his beautiful wife devolve into someone he didn't know. The begging, the pleading, the threats, the screaming made no difference. She was in thrall to the disease. She couldn't stop herself, couldn't help pouring the fruits of their life down a pit of adrenaline and thrill.

Only one fragile lifeline kept her sane. Through it all, only one aspect of her life didn't succumb to the poison. Her work. Her research. Her integrity. Then Florian Steele took that away and left her with nothing.

Florian had found her in Las Vegas. He had followed her there. He enabled her like a common drug dealer. He gave her all the money she wanted to get her life back, and all she had to give away was everything. Everything she stood for. Everything to which she had devoted her life. Every value that made her who she was. She had to turn a blind eye to the poison she'd found at Mondamin, the horrific remnants of what Vernon Clay had done to the people of St. Croix. She had to pretend it didn't exist.

She had to lie. She had to betray families and children. All to save Florian Steele and his legacy of death.

Marco had begged her not to do it. Better to lose everything. Better to lose the house and start over. He knew where it would lead if she crossed that line. He knew that Lucia would never be able to live with what she had done. From that moment forward, every dollar in her grasp, every cell on every slide under her microscope, would be a voice accusing her. Convicting her. Sentencing her.

I had nothing to do with it!

Florian Steele could still stand there and proclaim that he didn't kill her. He could still protest that his ghost wasn't in the garage with Lucia as she connected the hose to the tailpipe and drifted out of her pain into a final, blissful unconsciousness. He could pretend that his entire world was not irreparably evil.

It didn't matter. The choice was made.

"Marco."

He heard his name as if through a fog. His chin had fallen against his neck, but he labored to look up. The voice came from downriver. He winced as each breath became thicker, and he followed the ribbon of the water with his eyes but saw nothing. The voice may as well have come from the clouds.

"Marco," he heard again.

He wasn't imagining it. Florian heard it, too, and hunted in the trees, as if another threat were waiting for him there. Marco saw. Christopher Hawk stood on the plateau of the riverbank, a few hundred yards away, calling for him. He was shouting, but across the space, his voice was faint.

"Don't do this."

Marco waved him away with a feeble brush of his hand, but he didn't know if his friend could see him. In his head, he thought about the distance. Chris was safe from the blast but not from what came next. He wished he had the strength to shout, *Get out of here. Go to your family.*

Get to high ground.

Marco watched anxiety bloom in Florian's face. The man really thought he had won, bringing his gun, firing before Marco could react. He thought it was all over. It had never dawned on him that this meeting was about something else altogether. Seeing Christopher Hawk, listening to the panic in his voice, Florian's face grew puzzled, trying to understand the urgency in the man's pleas. Suspicion washed over his features. Then fear.

He stared at Marco, who knelt in his own blood. He stared at the white water eddying below him, placidly flowing toward Mondamin and the town of Barron. He gazed across the highway at the giant lake, its water pushed well beyond its banks, swelled by the rapid snow melt and the raging rainfall of the past two weeks. The lake lay there as it did in every season, freezing, thawing, pushing, glistening.

Waiting.

Finally, Florian's eyes dissolved in terrible understanding. He saw the cargo van parked on the dam. He saw Marco staring back at him with no fear, and for the first and last time in his miserable life, he knew that punishment was at hand.

Marco uncurled his right fist to show him the trigger. It was such an inconsequential thing, a bit of plastic and wire, barely bigger than a postage stamp, with a white button to complete the circuit. Florian frantically raised the gun to fire again, and Marco squeezed his fingers closed. It was a race now between the shot into Marco's brain and the pressure of his hand on that plastic trigger, sending the signal, igniting the bomb. It took only a millisecond for the bullet to roar from the barrel of the gun and end Marco's life, but a millisecond is excruciatingly slow compared to the speed of light.

Before he could even fall, before he could feel any pain or hear any sound, Marco Piva and Florian Steele were both atomized.

The detonation lifted Chris off his feet and catapulted him onto the wet ground, as if he'd been slapped down by the hand of God. Lying on his back, he was deaf, dumb, and blind. He heard silence, he saw blackness, and his brain was cleared of everything except a single thought: *I'm dead.*

He wasn't.

Debris rained out of the sky, awakening him. The air was burnt, and a wave of heat passed over his skin. He found himself pelted by a spray of concrete shards, sharp as knives, peppering his body with bruises and cuts. A choking mist, sucked into his lungs, made him gag and retch. He squinted as dust assaulted his eyes. The trees above him swirled like a kaleidoscope, broken into colorful fragments. He squeezed his head to make it stop.

Chris pushed himself up on his elbows. He felt alone and adrift, bobbing in an endless sea. The world was oddly silent, except for a rumbling thunder that sounded miles away, like a storm blowing in from the horizon. He shouted a warning. He screamed two names over and over.

"Hannah! Olivia!"

He didn't hear his voice. He didn't know if he was calling for them out loud or in his head. It didn't matter. They were miles away and couldn't hear him.

His eyes spun in and out of focus, as if he were drunk. When they finally came to rest, letting him see clearly, the land looked invisible beyond the reach of his arms. There was no river, no dam, no road, no earth, no trees. The universe in front of him was a gray wall of dust and smoke, billowing, expanding, rising into the heavens, towering like a genie released from its bottle. He stood as the cloud enveloped him and coughed as he tried to breathe. His legs bent like rubber, and as he stumbled, he clung to the flaky trunk of a birch tree, cherishing the feel of something real and solid under his hands.

On the ground, his feet became ice. Then his ankles. He looked down and realized he wasn't standing on the riverbank anymore, because there was no riverbank. There was only the river. He squinted into the cloud, and as the dust separated, drifting into the air, he could see a stain spreading over and consuming the land.

Water.

Water churned white.

Water leapfrogging itself, erupting through a jagged, hundred-foot gap where the dam had pancaked into rubble. The thunder in his head was the near-bottomless reservoir, freed from its prison, cascading into the valley with astonishing speed, pouring out its guts like an open wound and drowning everything in its path.

Chris had only seconds to escape. He was already immersed to his knees. He splashed up the shallow slope toward his Lexus, parked on the shoulder of the highway. The river chased him, rising inch by inch at his heels. As he climbed into the car, fingers of water slithered onto the road like snakes. He fired the engine and roared into a U-turn, trying to stay ahead of the flood as it surged downstream.

He fumbled with his phone, driving one-handed, weaving on the road as his scrambled brain tried to right itself.

First he dialed 9-1-1.

Then he dialed Hannah. *"You have to get out of St. Croix right now."*

51

The emergency sirens wailed.

Olivia ran from house to house, pounding on doors in St. Croix, alerting their neighbors to evacuate. In the crisscross blocks of the town, she could see Johan, her mother, and Glenn Magnus on the same mission of mercy. No one asked questions. Living in a river valley, everyone knew the risks. Sooner or later, someone would tell them that the water was coming.

The variable was time. Most floods rose with the river in a matter of days as the winter snow melted. Now, with the dam gone, they had minutes. An hour. Maybe.

She heard car tires slipping and squealing on the roads as families headed east and west to outrun the river. She waited long enough at each house to make sure they took her seriously. No, she wasn't kidding; yes, they had to leave now. Some agonized, hemming and hawing over their possessions. What to take, what to leave. It was hard, knowing there might be nothing left when you came back.

If you came back.

Some put up no fuss at all. She knocked on the door at Loren Werner's house, and the eighty-six-year-old widower simply told her to calm down and catch her breath and talk slowly. She explained, and he nodded, took his car keys from a bowl near the door, and walked with her back to the street. He patted her cheek, climbed into his 1981 Cutlass Supreme, and waved as he drove away. That was that. He didn't look back at the house once.

In half an hour, Olivia raised the warning with more than twenty houses. She found herself on the eastern edge of the town, across from the cornfields and the water tower, where the railroad tracks paralleled the southbound highway. From her vantage, she saw a speeding stream of traffic escaping from the lowlands of Barron. They'd moved fast. She wondered how many got out and how many were already trapped on their roofs. The lucky ones on the bluff over the town were probably saying prayers of thanks as they stood on the cliff and watched the disaster unfolding below them.

Her phone rang, and it was her mother. "Olivia! You have to get home now." There was a glimmer of panic in her voice. They were running out of time.

Olivia jogged the river route back home, wanting to see how bad it was. She followed the railroad tracks to the bridge, where she used to meet Johan, and she got her answer. It was bad. The lazy creek had become a torrent. There was no gap anymore to jump from the bridge deck to the water; instead, the current swept an inch below the gray steel. Tree trunks pounded the bridge like missiles, shooting spray and splinters across the tracks. She heard wood crunching and cracking.

She ran along the trail behind the houses, and the ground was already soupy mud. She wasn't looking down at the water anymore. She looked out across a stretch of brown magma at her feet, rolling into swells. She covered her mouth in horror as she saw the water carrying debris from the town of Barron, hoisted on its shoulders like a trophy. She saw light poles spinning like tiny twigs, suspension cables from the pedestrian bridge, shattered window glass like shrapnel, and even a white Toyota Corolla doing somersaults in the current before being carried up the bank and dumped at the fringe of the cornfield.

"Wow" she muttered.

When she looked down at her feet, she saw the tentacles of the river had wormed their way through the mud.

She sprinted away from the trail to their house. She eyed her bedroom window and thought about all the times she'd climbed up and down the drainpipe and knew she'd never do it again. She followed the lawn to the front porch. Her mother carried a box of soup cans to their truck. When Hannah saw her, her face dissolved with relief.

"Olivia, where were you?"

"I wanted to check out the river. It's almost over the bank. We better roll."

"Run to the church and check on Glenn. I want to know what's keeping him. Then get back here right now."

"Where's Dad?"

"He's five minutes away. *Go.*"

Olivia ran across the street and up the swath of lawn to the church steps.

The white steeple towered over her head, with its bird's-eye view of St. Croix. She didn't see Glenn Magnus. The town swarmed like a hive as residents frantically loaded their vehicles to join the escape parade. She hunted for the minister among the faces, but she didn't see him.

She pulled open the church doors. "Mr. Magnus!"

There was no answer, and she called again. "Mr. Magnus! Hello!"

She heard a groan. The oak door to the sanctuary was partially blocked, and when she yanked it open she found Glenn Magnus prone on the floor. He groaned again and pushed himself up to his hands and knees. The back of his skull was matted with blood.

"Oh my God!" Olivia clung to the minister's arm, helping him to his feet. "What happened?"

His voice was weak, and he winced as he put a hand tenderly on the back of his head. "I came back to retrieve some things from the church. Somehow I hit my head."

"We better go," Olivia said. "Mom can help."

Magnus slung an arm around her shoulder as she helped him out of the church. The Hawk house was barely fifty yards away, but it looked far as they took baby steps. She was conscious of the water rising. It wouldn't be long before their routes out of town were blocked. When they were halfway to the house, her mother jogged to help them, and they made their way inside the house. Hannah settled Glenn into a chair and got a damp towel from the kitchen to dab at the back of his head. Johan appeared from upstairs with a box in his hands, and he quickly put it down as he saw his father in the chair by the door, his eyes closed.

"Dad!"

The minister gave his son a weak smile. "I'm okay."

"What happened to you?"

"I don't know. One minute I was in the church, and the next thing I knew, Olivia was helping me up. I must have slipped and banged my head."

Hannah interrupted them. "There's no time. We have to get out of here. Olivia, Johan, get the last boxes into the truck. That'll give Glenn a minute to rest. If Chris isn't here by then, I'll call and tell him we're leaving, and he can meet us on the bluff." She gestured impatiently at the two of them. "Hurry, let's go!"

Johan picked up the box again. Olivia grabbed another box from the kitchen table. They headed for the front porch and across the lawn to the truck. The river was over the banks. They splashed through an inch of water, as it rose before their eyes. The current was so fast and slippery they could feel it under their shoes, trying to knock them off their feet. She piled the boxes into the back of the truck and slammed the door shut.

On impulse, she threw her arms around Johan's neck. "I'm so sorry."

"What for?"

"For you, for Ashlynn, for everything. I was a jerk."

"I'm the one who's sorry, Olivia. I should have trusted you."

He knelt into her and she felt him holding her again, strong and familiar. She lost herself in those blue eyes and felt a surge of arousal as his face drew close and he kissed her. It started quietly, soft lips on soft lips, but all the months of loss and violence spilled out of them and became passion. Their tongues, their faces, their hands, their bodies pressed together, until they were molded against each other.

She knew they had no time. She was conscious of the river on her bare ankles. They broke apart, breathless, and before they turned toward the porch, she heard a strange *bang* that bounced around them in an echo.

"What the hell was that?"

Johan heard it, too. He looked around in confusion. "I don't know."

It happened again. *Bang.* The noise was everywhere and nowhere. She saw an odd splash inches from her feet, and ripples washed into curves in the rushing water. What the hell was going on? She took a tentative step toward the street, and then, beside her, the windshield of the Explorer suddenly shattered.

"*Olivia,*" Johan cried, "get down!"

Johan leaped for her, but she still didn't understand. As his arms reached her, she heard it again—*bang*—and this time Johan screamed. She saw a red stain bloom on his shoulder. His face contorted in pain, and he clasped his hand to his shirt. Blood oozed between his fingers.

"Johan, no!"

Olivia grabbed him around the waist and guided him toward the porch. He staggered, and red drops sprayed into the water. The bullets followed them, erupting in splashes on either side of them, chasing them back inside the house. Another window shattered as they scrambled through the door and slammed it shut behind them.

They were trapped.

The water kept rising.

In the steeple of the church, Lenny Watson stood among the litter of cartridge boxes and spent shell casings. From here, the highest ground, he could see the river coming for them. He didn't know what had happened, and he didn't care. He'd heard the explosion, and now, minute by minute, he watched the town of St. Croix sink into the water before his eyes.

There were no streets now, no pavement, curbs, or corners, just avenue signs jutting out of the rapids. Nearly everyone was gone. He'd let them go, but not Johan Magnus. Not him. Not Olivia, either. He didn't want to hurt her, but he'd watched them kiss, the two of them pawing each other like animals, and he'd started firing and firing and firing. He wanted to make it stop. He wanted to drive them apart. He wouldn't be humiliated, watching her with another boy.

This was what Kirk would do. His brother would be proud of him. *You're finally a man, Leno.*

He slid the barrel of the rifle through the slats in the steeple again. Each time he fired, the bells made a metallic vibration behind him, like church music. He aimed for another window in Hannah Hawk's house, and he squeezed the trigger.

52

When Chris was one block from the church in St. Croix, the Lexus floated off the pavement.

The flooded engine died. Dank river water filled the base of the car, and the sedan spun in a lazy circle. Chris stripped off his seatbelt, pushed open the door, and spilled out of the car into a foot of rushing rapids. The current shoved him to his knees. His silver car, driverless, rammed an oak tree and ricocheted away, bouncing downstream through the town like a pinball.

He didn't have time to grieve for his car. The river popped with an odd splash no more than a foot away from him. Simultaneously, the crack of a rifle shot blasted and reverberated in his ears. Chris rolled right, deeper into the water, and when he looked up at the church steeple, he saw a long gun barrel poking out through the louvers, aimed downward. He scrambled forward on his knees, and another bullet buried itself in the water and mud.

Chris ran, trying to stay on his feet. He reached the wall of the church, where he was out of view from the shooter above him. He was wet, cold, and dirty. His phone was gone, lost somewhere in the water. He reached around to the small of his back and found Marco's gun still lodged tightly under his belt. He slid it into his hand, but he didn't know if it would fire—not after the gun had spent time swimming in the swollen Spirit River.

Marco.

He'd had his revenge. Florian was gone. So was Mondamin. So was the heart of Barron. The trouble was that revenge knew no boundaries, and the river didn't stop its destruction at the city limits. It kept flowing, kept flooding, kept growing, carrying everything away in its path.

Chris stayed under the eaves of the church and followed the wall to the corner. Ahead of him, no more than fifty yards away, he saw Hannah's house, now an island in the deepening lake. Trees and street signs grew oddly out of the water. Behind one of the corner beams on the porch he spotted movement, and someone waved frantically and called for him in a high-pitched voice.

His heart stuttered. It was Olivia. She was in the last place he wanted her to be. He couldn't stop her or hold her; instead, he watched in terror as his daughter bolted from her hiding place and splashed down the front steps. She was in the open, coming for him. Another shot tunneled into the rushing river, barely missing her.

"Olivia!" he shouted, his choked voice carrying over the flood. "Get inside!"

She ducked behind the steps, but he could see her face and the pink flash of her T-shirt. Her hands gripped the iron columns of the railing. The water swirled around her. "It's Lenny!" she screamed back at him. "He shot Johan!"

"*Get inside!*"

"I can help. I can talk to him."

Another rifle shot dissolved in echoes. He didn't see the ripples of the bullet. As the crack died away, Olivia broke cover again. He frantically waved his hands to stop her.

"*No!*"

She froze in place. She glanced back at the front door, but she didn't move. "Olivia, get back! Get in the house!"

She looked panicked by the power of the rapids. He waved Olivia back to the house one last time and charged up the church steps out of the water. The river hadn't risen above the top step, and inside, the foyer of the church was dry and quiet. On his right, a twisting staircase led into the steeple. He ran for the stairs and climbed around the spirals toward the bell chamber, taking the steps two at a time. Marco's gun was slippery in his hand. There were no windows and no light in the square stairwell; he was blind. Above him, to his horror, he heard the blast of another shot, and in the close confines, the explosion stung his ears. He heard the singing of the bells, rattled by the echoes. He listened for what he feared—a scream from his daughter outside—and was relieved when he heard nothing.

Natural light beamed out of the gloom. The trapdoor in the floor was just above him. It was open. He squatted and climbed another step, high enough to glimpse the claustrophobic interior of the steeple. It was no more than ten feet square, with a low roof and an arched, slatted vent on each of the walls. Light streamed through the slats and made parallel shadows on the floor. The bronze bells and wheels occupied most of the space. He heard Lenny's feet shuffling and his panicked breathing. The boy was immediately to the right of the gap where Chris needed to climb.

Chris shoved his torso through the trapdoor in the floor. He led with the gun. Lenny stood there, aiming his rifle at Hannah's house. He wasn't even four feet above Chris.

"Lenny, *stop*," Chris called sharply.

Still holding the rifle, the boy grabbed a pistol from his belt with his free hand and shoved it in front of him, pointing at Chris. His eyes were wide, almost drugged. His gun arm quaked. "Get the hell away from me!" Lenny screamed. "I'll kill you!"

They pointed guns at each other. Neither would miss.

"Listen to me, Lenny. *Listen*. You don't want to do this."

"Shut up!" the boy shouted, waving the gun. "Get out!"

"I can't do that," Chris told him. "My whole family is trapped across the street. I need your help."

"Kirk's dead!"

"I know he is, but don't throw your life away over him."

The teenager shook his head. "It's too late. Don't you get it? I already killed somebody."

"No, you didn't. The man at the garage isn't dead. It doesn't have to end like this."

Lenny hesitated. "I don't give a shit anymore."

"I think you do." Chris let his gun hand go limp. Slowly, he laid the revolver on the floor of the bell chamber where Lenny could see it. He raised both hands. "I'm coming up, okay? Let's talk."

Lenny backed up, flush against the wall. He hadn't lowered his pistol or let go of the rifle. Chris climbed into the heart of the tower but didn't try to draw closer to the boy. Dust hung heavy in the streams of light, and old cobwebs dripped from the ceiling. The wind in the vents made a whistling noise, and the large, brooding bells sang a bass chorus. Lenny's face was streaked with dirt and blood, and it was split with shadows.

"Do you think I'm a coward?" Lenny asked. "Is that it?"

"I think Kirk was a coward. Not you."

"Kirk was a hero, man."

Chris shook his head. "No, he wasn't. He was a sadist, a bully, and a killer. I don't think you're like him at all, Lenny."

"He was my brother."

"Maybe so, but he did bad things, and we both know it."

"Don't talk about him like that!"

"You know what he did. You know what's right and what's wrong. I don't need to tell you that."

He took a step forward. Lenny cocked the weapon, and he froze.

"Stop!" Lenny demanded, his voice cracking.

"I just want you to put down the guns. You've seen what's happening outside, Lenny. You've seen the river. We're running out of time."

"I shot Johan," Lenny said.

"That's why we need to get out of here right now. He needs a doctor."

"I don't care about him."

"What about Olivia?" Chris asked. "Do you care about her?"

Lenny blinked in rapid succession. He cocked his head as if his neck were in spasm. "She hates me. She wishes I was dead."

"That doesn't matter. If you care about her, then you won't hurt her."

Chris watched fear and indecision play across the boy's face. He studied the small patch of dirty wooden floor between them and knew he could jump for him, but he'd probably take a bullet in the stomach as he did. Lenny was alone and had nothing to lose. He looked at the floor and saw that Lenny had an arsenal in guns and ammunition. The boy could hold out, firing, for hours if he chose.

They didn't have hours. They had minutes. He had to go.

"That's it," Chris said. "I'm done with you."

"What do you mean?" Lenny asked.

"It means I can't stand here trying to convince you that a real man would *help me.* You've got to make that decision for yourself. I have to get to Hannah's house. I have to get to my family. If you want to stay up here and shoot me, go ahead."

"I'll do it," Lenny swore.

"Go ahead. That's what Kirk would do, right?"

"Kirk wasn't afraid of anything."

"Good for him. Me, I'm scared, Lenny. I'm scared of losing my wife and daughter, and that's why I'm leaving. You do what you have to do."

Chris turned around. He tensed, awaiting a paralyzing shot into the center of his back. He could hear Lenny panting behind him, torn with doubt. He left him alone. He took the first step through the trapdoor without looking back, and he disappeared down into the black confines of the tower. Lenny didn't move, and he didn't fire. That didn't mean the kid wouldn't change his mind and use the rifle again while Chris was in the no-man's-land between the church and Hannah's house.

He reached the base of the stairwell, and his feet landed in icy water. The river had risen into the belly of the church. He kicked his way toward the doors and had to throw his shoulder against the glass to force it open. Outside, he stared in disbelief at the inland sea running wild over the town, chocolate brown, surging and tumbling over itself in deep swells. The water was thick with debris: chunks of concrete, whole trees, remnants of walls and windows carried from houses that had been eviscerated. The air bristled with the noise of impact, wood on metal, metal on wood. The short distance to Hannah's house was a minefield, virtually impossible to cross.

In the middle of that minefield, he saw something that made his whole body turn cold with despair.

No, no, no, what did you do?

On the street in front of the house, Olivia clung to the few dry inches of metal pole on a Stop sign protruding out of the water. It was a fragile life raft, and the sign flapped as the river roared by, threatening to peel away her hands and carry her downstream.

She saw him, and her voice erupted in a desperate scream.

"Dad!"

53

CHRIS SHOULDERED INTO THE WATER, WHICH ROSE ABOVE HIS WAIST, and the chill hit him like a thousand needles. The current was ferocious, threatening to launch him off his feet, but he realized that the worst danger was invisible, hidden underneath the surface. Branches, glass, and rocks punched and cut him as they whipped through the water, as fast and sharp as knives. He didn't have far to go to reach Olivia but the distance looked overwhelming. His main concern was that the swirling currents would sweep him past her, and he wouldn't be able to make his way upstream.

He eyed the flow of the water. Two branches of the river had joined here, rippling together in curves like ribbons, moving in different directions. Among the tumbling flotsam, he saw the lid of a garbage can spinning toward him and he snatched it out of the water. He tossed it like a Frisbee toward the trunk of a huge oak tree in front of the church, and as it landed, the lid swooped into a giant arch that carried it within five feet of the sign where Olivia was trapped. That was the route he needed. That was how to get close to her.

He couldn't walk. He swam. On the surface, he could see and avoid more of the debris flowing toward him. The river smelled as fetid and poisonous as a landfill, but he couldn't avoid toxic mouthfuls as he fought upstream. He felt as if he were swimming in place, taking strokes and getting nowhere. When he stopped the water carried him farther away, and he had to redouble his effort to make up lost ground. His heart hammered with the exertion, and his muscles screamed in protest. By the time he reached the oak tree, he needed to hang on to the low branches and rest. He felt as if he'd been in the water for hours.

"Olivia, are you hurt?" he called to her. The roar of the water made him shout, as if he were trying to drown out Niagara Falls. He choked and coughed.

His daughter shouted back, "I think my ankle's broken. I'm sorry, Dad, I thought I could help if I got to the church."

"Just hold on."

She had both arms wrapped around the quivering Stop sign. He could see she was tiring. He watched the water and knew she was in a place where the current was particularly strong. There was no time to wait. He braced himself against the tree trunk and launched himself into the rapids. This time, with the flow propelling him, he moved at startling speed, and he was practically on top of Olivia before he had time to react. He careened toward the sign, and he was afraid he would swoop past it. He kicked to his right and stretched his arm as far as it would go. The pole slapped his hand, and he clawed at it, curling three fingers around the damp metal. His body kept traveling, and as he was swept downstream, he felt his grip loosening, but then Olivia grabbed his shirt, and his body spun. He cocked an elbow around the pole, and he shoved two fingers into one of Olivia's belt loops, pulling her into his chest. She let go of the sign and hung on to him.

"Nice day for a swim," he murmured into her ear. He didn't want her to be scared.

His daughter laughed and clung to his neck. Her wet hair pushed against his face.

He had no idea what to do next, other than to hang on for both of their lives, but then he heard Hannah shouting and saw her in the first-floor window of the house, no more than fifty feet away. The river was immediately below the sash; she had to be up to her knees in water inside the house. She had a coil of heavy, white clothesline in her hand. She flung it toward him through the window, hanging on to one end, but it didn't travel nearly far enough. The rope fell in the water and washed away downriver. Quickly, she wound it back up before debris took hold of it and ripped it out of her hands.

"Are you in a lot of pain?" he asked Olivia.

"It feels like an elephant's standing on my left ankle."

"Can you put any weight on it?"

"No way, Dad, sorry."

"That's okay."

"I'm so stupid. I knew it was Lenny. I thought I could talk him down."

"He's too far gone. How's Johan?"

"Not good, Dad."

Chris saw Hannah in the window again. This time, she'd tied one end of the rope around the handle of a heavy white coffee mug. Inside the house, she wound up and threw the mug toward Chris. He reached for it, and almost grabbed it, but it fell six inches short in the water, and Hannah had to reel it in again, pulling the mug out of the water.

The metal signpost wobbled. It wouldn't last much longer under the assault of water and debris.

Hannah threw again. She threw like a World Series pitcher. She threw like a Super Bowl quarterback. The mug flew out of the window, hard and strong, unwinding the rope like fishing line. It overshot Chris by six feet, landing in the water and carrying the rope into his hands. He wound it around the pole and knotted it tightly. On the other end, Hannah secured the rope inside the house. She pulled as much tension into the line as she could, but it sagged and sat atop the water.

"Time to go," he told Olivia. "Can you pull yourself across with just your arms?"

"I think so."

"I'll make sure the knot holds. Go as fast as you can."

Olivia draped her left arm over the line and used her other hand to drag herself forward. Her legs fluttered invisibly under the water. He held onto her as long as he could, and then she was on her own, creeping closer to the window. She moved an inch at a time. He watched her hold her breath, and her body floated up like a cork. Floating, she moved faster. She was halfway home.

His daughter looked back over her shoulder. She gave him an encouraging smile.

Then she screamed, and her scream cut off into a gurgle as she was sucked under the water.

"Olivia!" he and Hannah shouted simultaneously.

She clung to the rope with one hand, her face trapped below the surface. Something was dragging her, trying to cart her downstream. He saw a thick tree bough breach the water, straining like a whale with the current, and a torn white bedsheet flailed behind it, wound around the wood and twisted into a knotted tail. When Olivia's leg kicked out of the river, he saw the other end of the sheet coiled around her broken ankle, trapping her in a tug-of-war. She thrust her face above the surface, gasped for breath, and cried in agony, and then she sank out of sight again, with only three fingers clinging to the lifeline. He saw blood as the rope ate through her skin.

Chris threw himself onto the line and scrambled hand over hand to pull himself toward his daughter. Behind him, the Stop sign squealed as the metal weakened and bent. Twenty feet along the rope, he reached her and dragged her head out of the water by the neck of her shirt. She spat water and croaked as she sucked air into her lungs. Her mouth made a huge O, and her eyes went wide with terror and relief. Her brown hair draped in tangles across her face. He had only one hand to hold her; the other was locked around the rope, keeping them from being dragged down into the river.

He couldn't go forward. He couldn't go back. He simply held on.

"Mr. Hawk."

Chris wrenched his head around as someone called him. They weren't alone anymore in the wreckage of the town, stuck in the flooded river. Lenny Watson was hanging onto the Stop sign. The water was up to the boy's neck.

"Mr. Hawk, tell me what to do."

"Olivia's ankle is caught," Chris said immediately. "You need to free it."

Lenny nodded. "Okay."

Kirk's brother abandoned the signpost and inched onto the rope stretched loosely like a snake on the water. Behind him, the knot held, but it looked fragile. Lenny half-swam, half-dragged himself to the middle of the rope. When he reached the two of them, he met Olivia's eyes, and Chris knew he was right. She couldn't hide that she hated him. Right now, it didn't matter. Her life was in his hands.

"Can you hold us both?" Lenny asked.

Chris nodded. "Make it fast."

Lenny clung to Olivia's clothes and floated down the length of her body. He grabbed hold of her legs as the water tried to whisk him away, and Chris saw Olivia's face contort in pain as her ankle twisted. Lenny braced himself with an arm around her knee, and with his other hand, he bent her left leg so that her foot was above the water. The sheet was wrapped several times around her ankle. He tried to unwind the cloth at her foot, but the tension of the heavy tree branch straining with the speed of the river made the wet, knotted sheet as taut as a high wire.

He scraped at it. He bit into the sopping fabric with his teeth. He couldn't tear it. Chris felt his arms going numb as he tried to hold onto both teenagers against the strength of the current.

Lenny reached into his back pocket, fumbling to remove something without losing it. It was a switchblade. He punched the button, and a sharp, fierce blade shot from the handle. With one awkward hand, he sawed at the cloth. Olivia's mouth clenched, and her eyes squeezed shut as every slash of the knife wrenched her ankle. Lenny bit his lip as he worked the blade, severing wet threads. When the damp sheet resisted, he stabbed at it with the point of the knife. The cloth frayed, stretched, and finally snapped apart. Olivia's ankle came free.

"*Yes!*"

The tree bough shot downstream, as if fired by a gun. Chris dragged his daughter toward him, and she wrapped her arms around the rope, breathing heavily. Her eyes were closed. Lenny clutched Olivia's jeans pocket and then her wet shirt to pull himself back to the rope. He closed the knife and tossed it into the water. Chris used his free hand to squeeze the boy's shoulder in thanks.

"Go," he told his daughter. "Hurry, get inside."

Chris watched Olivia swim her way along the rope toward the window. Hannah waited inside for her. The water had climbed nearly over the bottom of the sash. As Olivia reached the house, Hannah squeezed outside, grabbed their daughter under the arms, and pulled her through the frame. He felt himself start breathing again, seeing her safely out of the river.

"Come on, Lenny," Chris said.

He headed for the house, but when he looked back he saw that Lenny hadn't moved. The boy still clung to the middle of the rope, with the peaks and troughs of white water surging around him. He looked small, and in the midst of the flooded streets, he may as well have been the only person alive.

"We have to go," Chris called.

Lenny stared at him ten feet away. "I did it, huh?"

"Yes, you did."

The boy's face cracked into a smile. The smile froze there. It was his last expression.

Out of the depths of the water, a steel fence post surfed out of the waves, riding the river directly toward Lenny's head. It had the speed of a javelin, and it collided with his skull, cracking the bone. The boy's neck snapped sideways. Blood erupted from his hair. His eyes fell shut. His hand disappeared from the rope, and the water poured over his head, burying him under the muddy surface.

Chris stretched out a hand, but he was too far away to grab him. He watched the current take him away. When he saw Lenny again, the boy's body had made an X, facedown, riding the rapids fifty yards downriver. Lenny stayed afloat for ten seconds, but he didn't move. Then the undertow grabbed him, and he was gone.

54

As the river rose, there was nowhere to go but up.

They climbed from the first to the second floor. Hannah cried as a lifetime of possessions floated and sank, but they had no time to do anything but go higher as the water chased them up the stairs. From there, they climbed one at a time onto the overhang beyond Hannah's bedroom window. Hannah led. Glenn Magnus helped Johan. Chris carried Olivia piggyback. The minister climbed onto the roof and helped each of them follow, and then the five of them waited at the highest peak, overlooking the remains of the town.

The clouds broke apart into blue sky. Sitting atop the world, they found an oddly beautiful day waiting for them.

Hannah dialed 9-1-1. The circuits were jammed, and it took her four tries to reach an operator. She explained the urgency—one teenager shot, one with a broken leg, one man with a possible concussion. She gave their location. There was nothing to do but wait and hope.

Olivia lay next to Johan, keeping pressure on his wound, whispering into his ear. Her ankle had swollen into a multicolored mango fruit, and even a breath of air made her face scrunch up in pain. Glenn sat next to his son, holding his hand. The boy was pale and feverish, but he was conscious.

They were alive.

Chris straddled the gable. Hannah sat in front of him, leaning her head against his chest. He wrapped his arms around her and held her. From where they were, St. Croix looked like a town built in the middle of an ocean, occupied by nothing but treetops and roofs. There were no roads anywhere, not even signs; they were all submerged. Hannah stared across at the steeple of the Lutheran church, and Chris heard her whisper a prayer under her breath.

Twenty minutes later, they heard the throb of the helicopter.

Chris took off his shirt and waved to attract their attention. The gray behemoth steered from the north, dropping closer and lower, and finally hovered over their heads. He saw the logo of the Minnesota National Guard. The twin rotors of the helicopter were deafening, and he thought he'd never heard a more welcome sound. The whip of the downdraft made giant ripples on the river surrounding the house.

The side door of the helicopter slid open. A guardsman rode the harness slowly to the roof. He was young, no more than twenty-two, with cropped hair and a huge smile, the fresh-faced image of a soldier. Chris shook his hand, and the man's confident grip said everything. *Help is here. You're safe.*

The young guardsman checked each of them, and in less than a minute, he strapped Johan carefully into the harness and gave the thumbs-up to the pilot overhead. Slowly, twisting in the air, Johan rose off the roof and was gently pulled inside the belly of the chopper waiting above them.

The sling came down again, floating in the breeze.

Olivia insisted Glenn Magnus go next, to be with Johan. In less than five minutes, he was aboard, too. The sling came down, and Olivia was next. She professed to be scared to ride the sling alone, but Chris suspected she had other motives, too, like riding the harness strapped to the young guardsman. The two of them left together.

Chris and Hannah were alone, watching Olivia's hair blow, seeing their daughter smile. She was young. This was an adventure. He looked at Hannah and saw her hands over her mouth, tears streaming down her face. He put an arm around her shoulder and pulled her against him.

"You next," he said.

"No, you go."

"Forget it, Hannah."

She looked at him and smiled through her tears. They glanced at the sky. Olivia was halfway to freedom.

Under their feet, the house growled and moved.

"What was that?" Hannah asked.

The ground shifted beneath them like an earthquake, and they both toppled onto the roof. Hannah rolled away on the wet tiles, and he jumped and caught her leg as her torso spilled past the edge of the house over the water. She screamed, but he pulled her back and pinched his fingers against the gable, trying to hold on. He looked down at the river and knew it was eating away the soft land under the foundation, hollowing out the earth and filling it with water, creating stresses on the wooden frame that would rip the structure apart and pull it down piece by piece.

The house was dying.

"It's going to go soon," he said.

They looked toward the sky. Olivia was being pulled to safety inside the helicopter. Chris made a frantic downward motion with his hand. They needed the sling back on the roof. Fast.

The house belched out an awful grinding noise. It lurched, and he lost his grip. He clung to Hannah and dug in his heels on the slippery roof as gravity worked against them, forcing them down the sharp angle of the frame. There was no way to stand, no way to keep his balance. He heard wood and metal tearing.

Overhead, through the perfect sky, the harness descended inch by inch, foot by foot. He watched, willing it to come faster. The wind spun the sling like a pinwheel, dancing in hypnotic circles. He reached for it, and it teased him, blowing out of his grasp. It swung away and began to swing back. Below him, he heard windows shattering. The house was sinking.

He reached again. This time, the wind swept the harness into his hands.

He felt as if he were in a fun house, with the steep angle of the roof tilting under their feet. Awkwardly, like a clown, he stepped into one leg hole of the sling, then the other, and leaned into the harness. The red strap dangling from the helicopter was heavy and thick.

Hannah lay next to him, clinging to the roof. He reached for her.

"Take my hand," he said.

Take my hand.

In that moment, his life rewound. He took Hannah's hand and led her to bed in his college dorm to make love to her. He took Hannah's hand, lifted her veil, and watched the face of the woman who made his life worth living. He took Hannah's hand and heard the cry of their daughter for the first time as she made her way into the world.

He took her hand. He didn't need to say it, but he said it anyway.

"I love you."

She came into his arms. He lifted her up, slid her into the sling, facing him, and held on with a grip that said, *I'll never let go.* The cable above them went taut, their legs hung free, and they were airborne, rising, flying. Below them, with a lion's roar, the house split apart. Where they had just been sitting the roof opened up, beams breaking, floors caving, walls crashing. Hannah heard it, but she couldn't look down. She couldn't watch the river dismember generations of her past and wash it away. She buried her face in his chest. He witnessed the wreckage growing smaller as they rose, watched all the fragments fall, and by the time the strong hands of the helicopter crew pulled them inside, the house was gone. There was nothing to see below them but the river, rampaging over the valley like an uncaged animal.

55

CHRIS SAT IN A FOLDING CHAIR NEAR THE WALL OF THE HIGH SCHOOL auditorium. He drank a paper cup of Red Cross lemonade and ate a dry butter cookie. Cots and sleeping bags lined the glossy floor of the gym in neat rows. The school smelled of rescue. Vats of pasta and red sauce simmered on food trucks. Portable lavatories lined up like cheerleaders on the football field. He smelled the body odor and sweat of people crammed together in close quarters. No one cared; no one protested. Barron and St. Croix had become a single town of survivors. The feud was over.

It had been three days since the flood. The waters were slowly receding. He expected to see a dove carrying an olive branch, signaling that they could find land again. In its wake, though, the real scope of the devastation became clear: homes and buildings reduced to rubble or erased from the landscape, highways six inches deep in mud, hundreds of displaced families. Despite the loss, he'd heard not a word from anyone about giving up or walking away. In the Midwest, you prayed, you shrugged, and then you got to work.

He watched Hannah and Olivia. Hannah went from family to family, checking on their health, explaining the relief services that were available. Olivia, her foot in a cast, balancing on crutches, managing to play with young children in the gym by bouncing an inflatable beach ball from boy to girl in a big circle. He saw Glenn Magnus, too, comforting those who had lost everything.

Losing everything felt lucky to the people in the gym. If there was a miracle, it was that the losses were limited to homes, possessions, memories, and jobs. Florian was dead. Marco was dead. Lenny was dead. Everyone else had escaped with their lives.

"Mr. Hawk."

Chris saw Michael Altman standing over him. He almost didn't recognize the county attorney, who wore a bulky wool sweater and corduroys rather than his usual crisp business suit. He didn't have his fedora perched on his head, and his graying hair needed a comb.

"Mr. Altman," he said.

The county attorney sat down next to him. His hands were on his knees. He followed Chris's eyes to his ex-wife and daughter in the auditorium.

"I'm relieved that you and your family are safe," Altman told him.

"Thanks."

"I understand Johan Magnus is recovering in a hospital in Granite Falls."

"That's right. When Olivia's not here, she's there."

"I've been watching your wife and daughter. They seem to have a boundless energy. They've helped a lot of people."

"Them and the volunteers who dropped everything to come here from around the country. It revives a little of my faith in human nature."

"Mine, too."

"I'm sad about Marco Piva," Chris admitted. "I genuinely liked him. I'm horrified by what he did, but I can't bring myself to hate him. Losing someone you love can eat away your soul."

"Speaking of Marco," Altman murmured.

Chris frowned. He knew what was coming. He'd been thinking about it since the flood. He'd known it wasn't over since he learned that Marco Piva was the man known as Aquarius.

"I have a problem," the county attorney continued.

"Yes, I know."

"I'm reluctant to bring it up in the current circumstances, but I felt I should discuss it with you. Regardless of what's happened, this disaster doesn't erase that a murder was committed."

"That's true," Chris said.

Altman looked pleased that Chris wasn't fighting him, but his face was uncomfortable.

"I was prepared to believe that Aquarius murdered Ashlynn Steele," the county attorney went on. "Whether it was part of his vengeance against Florian, or whether Ashlynn simply discovered who he was as she poked into the affairs of Vernon Clay and Lucia Causey, I really thought the girl's death was different from what I originally believed."

"I believed that, too," Chris said.

"However, I didn't know at the time that Marco Piva was Aquarius."

"No."

"Marco didn't kill Ashlynn," Altman said. "You realize that, don't you?"

Chris said nothing. He knew it was true. He knew Marco was innocent, at least of that death. In a way, he was glad. Even if Marco had destroyed the towns of Barron and St. Croix, even if he had deliberately blown up himself and Florian Steele, he hadn't been cold or cruel enough to stare a beautiful young girl in the face and shoot her in the head. He wasn't that kind of man.

"Johan was with Marco at the motel until after midnight on the Friday night that Ashlynn was killed," Altman said. "He left when a plumber arrived, and I found the Barron plumber who got the emergency call. He confirmed that he spent most of that night working with Marco on the pipes in the motel room. And drinking Chianti, too, I gather."

"That sounds like Marco."

"You know where I'm going with this, don't you?"

"I think so," Chris said.

"It means we're back where we started. There are still only two explanations for Ashlynn's murder. I don't like either answer, but I'm left believing that Olivia really did kill Ashlynn, as it appeared from the beginning. Or Johan Magnus did."

"Lenny Watson was in the ghost town that night," Chris said. "He was following Olivia. He saw her walk away. Ashlynn was alive."

"Unfortunately, Lenny is dead," Altman said. "He can't tell us what he saw."

"I know. What about Kirk's murder? The same gun was used in both crimes. How do you explain that?"

"You know I can't rule out the possibility that Olivia shot Kirk," Altman told him. "She certainly had a motive to do so. Or it's possible that she gave Johan the gun, so he could do it for her."

"Or Johan had the gun himself all along, because he picked it up in the ghost town that Friday night," Chris said. "Right?"

"Yes. That's possible, too. I'm not saying I've made up my mind what really happened. We'll be running forensics, and hopefully that will shed light on the truth. I just thought you should know that I'm not dropping the case. It's my job. I'm not going to let a girl's murder go unpunished."

"I never thought you would," Chris said. He leaned his back against the gym wall and closed his eyes. He was tired.

"Obviously, this will all take months," Altman said. "Off the record, it may never go anywhere. I can assess reasonable doubt as well as any jury, and you have my word I won't bring a case unless I believe the evidence supports it."

Chris opened his eyes. "Have you talked to Julia Steele since the flood?"

"Julia? No, I haven't. Why?"

"I have," Chris said.

Altman waited in puzzled silence. Chris could see the question in the man's eyes.

"You've always been honest and open with me, Mr. Altman, and I appreciate it. The voters around here put a fine man in charge. However, in this case, you're wrong. Olivia didn't kill Ashlynn. Neither did Johan. They were just three teenagers caught in a love triangle."

"Teenage emotion can be overwhelming. And dangerous."

"Yes, it can, but that's not why Ashlynn was killed."

"I'd like to believe you, Chris. Really, I would, but the evidence doesn't point any other way. Marco didn't do it, so either Olivia or Johan must have pulled the trigger. No one else even knew Ashlynn was there."

Chris shook his head. "Not true. Someone else knew."

Altman thought about it. "Well, all right, Tanya Swenson knew."

"That's right," Chris said. "She called Olivia from her home that night, and they talked about the fact that Ashlynn was still alone in the ghost town. Alone and alive. Tanya knew."

56

When Chris saw Tanya go inside the high school, he went out into the frosty air and weak sunshine of the late afternoon. The smell of the river was oppressive, even on the bluff. Rollie Swenson was alone. He sat on top of a green park bench, staring into space. He wore a Windbreaker and a baseball cap, and his shirt was untucked under his jacket. His gray pants were stained, and his shoes were caked with dirt. Like everyone else, Rollie was homeless.

Chris sat down next to him. "Hello, Rollie."

The other attorney didn't take his eyes off the horizon. He took a bite of a chocolate doughnut. "Chris."

"Terrible days."

"Yeah."

"How's Tanya?" he asked.

"Stronger than me," Rollie said. "She's been spending a lot of time with Olivia again. It helps her to have a friend."

"I know. I'm glad."

They sat in silence. Rollie finished the doughnut and licked his fingers.

Chris found himself growing angry the longer they were together. He was angry about everything that had happened to Olivia. Angry about the waste, the loss of life, the loss of innocence. Angry about the ripples that had destroyed the lives of so many others.

"Did you know Marco Piva?" he asked Rollie.

"No, I didn't."

"I did. It was a tragic thing. He was a decent man."

Rollie snorted. "Decent? You're kidding."

"No, it's true. Decent men can do abominable things."

Rollie gave him a strange look and didn't reply.

"I wonder what I would have done in his shoes," Chris said. "Florian blackmailed Marco's wife, exploited her weakness. The guilt she felt must have been unimaginable. After all, she met the parents in St. Croix, right?

She talked to them. She saw what had happened to their children. The ugly, slow, awful deaths."

"Yes, she did," Rollie said. "She interviewed all of them."

"She could have given them comfort and closure, and instead she covered up what had been done to them. In the end, she couldn't live with the lie. It destroyed her. It destroyed Marco, too."

"Am I supposed to feel sorry for him?" Rollie asked.

"No, I'm just saying, it can't be easy, living your life in the grip of a horrible addiction." He shoved his hands in his pockets and shook his head. "Florian was a master of manipulation. He was like that in law school, too, finding people's pressure points, twisting the knife. I wonder how long it took him to find Lucia and figure out how he could influence her. I guess most people have dirty secrets if you know where to look."

Rollie stared coldly at Chris, and then he checked his watch. "I should go find Tanya."

He began to climb off the bench, but Chris stopped him with a firm hand on his shoulder. "One thing bothers me, Rollie. Ever since I found out the truth about Lucia, I couldn't understand how Florian could be so sure that the judge would pick her to be the special master in the litigation."

"I imagine he approached her after she was selected," Rollie said.

"Florian? No, he was much smarter than that. He only agreed to have a special master appointed because he knew Lucia Causey would write a report exonerating Mondamin. He would never take a risk on the judge picking someone who couldn't be compromised. I checked her property records. Lucia started getting money shortly after the lawsuit was filed. Florian had her in his pocket from the beginning."

"They fooled everyone. It was a good plan."

"Yes, it was, but only if the judge actually selected Lucia," Chris said. "Of course, if the plaintiff and the defense put the same name on their lists, it was a lock that the judge would pick her. I know why Florian put Lucia on *his* list of special-master candidates. She was the one he wanted. So I'm curious. Why did you put Lucia on *your* list, Rollie?"

Rollie's eyes were dead calm. He was a lawyer, unfazed by cross-examination. "She had the credentials. There aren't many epidemiologists with the expertise to handle a project like that."

"It was just an accident? A coincidence?"

"It must have been."

Chris shook his head. "I don't think so. Florian didn't bet the future of his company on a coincidence."

"I don't know what to tell you, Chris. I used freelance researchers to provide me with names for my special-master list. Maybe Florian got to them."

"Maybe so." Chris let the silence linger. "You know, something else has been bothering me, too."

"What's that?"

"It's the note that Aquarius sent you," Chris said. "Aquarius warned you to keep quiet. He didn't want Tanya talking to the police about what Ashlynn had told her. About her digging into her father's secrets. About the proof she had."

"So?"

"So why would Marco think that Tanya knew anything at all?"

Rollie hesitated. "Ashlynn must have told him."

"No, Ashlynn called Tanya on the night before she was killed, remember? She was in Nebraska. She never made it back home. There's no way she told Marco."

"Maybe she said something to him while they were in the ghost town," Rollie said.

"You mean when he killed her?"

"Exactly."

"I thought that, too. It made sense when we didn't know who Aquarius was, but now we do. The trouble is that Marco didn't kill Ashlynn. He had an alibi. He wasn't there."

Rollie frowned. "Well, he found out somehow. He was afraid that Tanya knew enough to expose him."

"Actually, I don't think Marco knew anything about Tanya."

"Then why did he send me that note?"

"That's easy. He didn't. The note was a fake."

"A fake? Why would someone go to that trouble?"

"Not someone, Rollie. You. You faked the note. You needed a reason for Tanya not to tell anyone about Ashlynn's phone call. You needed to be able to explain why you didn't tell the police about that call. Aquarius gave you the perfect excuse. You were afraid your daughter was in danger."

"What are you saying, Chris?" Rollie asked, but he knew. He couldn't hide it.

"I'm saying that the phone call from Ashlynn was your worst nightmare."

"That's crazy."

"Is it? I'm trying to imagine what was going through your head when Ashlynn called. Did she only talk to Tanya, or did Tanya give you the phone? It must have been a shock. Here was Ashlynn talking about her father covering up Mondamin's role in the deaths in St. Croix, and she says she can *prove* it now. Did she give you any specifics? Did she mention Lucia Causey? I bet she did."

Rollie's face was stone. He said nothing.

"Poor Ashlynn," Chris went on. "She thought she was telling the one man who could help her. She thought she was giving you a chance to go back into court and be a hero for the people of St. Croix. She was willing to betray her father and expose his corruption, but she had no idea that exposing Florian meant exposing *you*."

"Exposing me?" Rollie asked impassively.

"Florian didn't just blackmail Lucia," Chris said. "He blackmailed you, too."

"You have no idea what you're talking about."

"Yes, I do. It must have seemed so simple. So safe. All you had to do was put Lucia Causey on your list for the judge. One little betrayal. No one would ever question it. Like you said, she had the credentials."

Rollie scratched the stubble on his chin with his thick fingers. He didn't look at Chris; instead, he stared across the trampled mud of the field. Finally, his lips folded into a small smile. "It's a shame you're not a trial lawyer, Chris. You'd be good with juries. You really know how to tell a story. Hell, I almost believed it myself. Then I remembered. This is the man who would do anything to protect his daughter from a murder charge. He'd lie. He'd destroy reputations. Don't play those games with me. You're shooting in the dark. You don't know a damn thing."

Chris leaned closer to him. The proximity made his flesh crawl. "I know about the sick shit that Kirk Watson was selling you, Rollie."

The young lawyer froze. He looked like an invisible man who suddenly realized the world could see who he was. Chris saw a glimmer in his dark eyes of what it had been like for the man to live two separate lives, one in public, one for his private desires.

"Kirk told Florian you were one of his customers, didn't he?" Chris said.

344 • BRIAN FREEMAN

"That was the leverage Florian had. It must have been devastating when he came to see you. The litigation was your shot at redemption, wasn't it? You thought you were doing something noble for once in your life, but your addiction poisoned it like everything else. Did Florian humiliate you? Did he treat you like a criminal? If you didn't play along with him, you'd be arrested, exposed, disbarred, destroyed. Everyone would know what kind of man you really are. Including your daughter."

Rollie's chest heaved. He ginned up his outrage. "You better stop spreading this slander before it gets you into big trouble," he said. "You have no evidence. No proof."

"Is that what you were looking for at Kirk's house?" Chris asked. "Proof? Were you trying to find the evidence he kept against you? When you didn't find it, that's when you killed Kirk."

"This is a pointless game, Chris. You're not going to win. Even if there were something to find, it's buried under four feet of silt somewhere in Iowa now."

"You think you're free?"

"I think the flood wiped the slate clean. That's what floods do."

"Not for everyone. Not for a monster like you."

Rollie stood up and yanked the brim of his baseball cap down on his face. "Don't pretend you know anything about who I am. You don't."

"No, you're right, I don't," Chris snapped. He stood up, too, his emotions spilling into his voice. "I don't know how any man could be *aroused* by staring at things that would make most people stab out their eyes."

"We're done here," Rollie told him. He zipped up his Windbreaker. "You're wasting my time. Like I said, you have nothing."

Chris slid a tiny flash drive out of his pocket and held it in his fingers for the other lawyer to see. "Did you think Florian wouldn't keep a copy?"

Rollie stared at the sliver of metal. "What is that?"

"You know exactly what it is."

"Don't think you can bluff me."

"It's not a bluff," Chris told him. "I've seen the video, Rollie."

"You're lying."

"Kirk didn't leave anything to chance," Chris went on. "He videotaped the porn as he put it in the envelope, so everyone would know exactly what was inside. He used that ugly polka-dot envelope you can recognize a mile away, too. He videotaped the address as he wrote it down. PO Box 24321 in Ortonville. He videotaped the envelope going in the mail. And then you, Rollie. He filmed you picking up the envelope at the post office like a kid on Christmas morning. He had you in close-up. You know what the sickest part was? It was obvious you had an erection. It turned you on just thinking about opening up another shipment of that filth."

Rollie squeezed his eyes shut and said nothing. He heard the box number, and he knew he was done. Everyone knew. There was no escape. The weight on his soul was so great he could barely breathe.

"Julia gave me the video," Chris told him. "With Florian dead, with the truth exposed, she had no reason to keep your secret anymore. Not when she realized it was you who killed her daughter."

Rollie opened his eyes again, and Chris saw the completeness of his destruction. His life was gone, emptying into a vacuum. The door to hell was open.

"*How could you, Daddy?*"

The voice jolted Rollie like an electric shock. He spun around, as if expecting to see the devil. Instead, it was Tanya Swenson, screaming at her father.

Tanya stood behind the bench. Her Westie dog squirmed in her arms. Olivia, on crutches, stood next to her. Hannah was there, too, her arms folded across her chest, her face impassive in its fury. So was Michael Altman, accompanied by three police officers.

His daughter's words, and the look of disgust in her eyes, cut Rollie like the slash of a blade. His mouth fell open. His face twisted into despair. He was choking. Crying. The only emotion more powerful than his self-loathing was how much he loved his little girl, but even that love hadn't been enough to save him. "Baby, you don't understand."

"*How could you?*" she said again.

Chris saw Tanya's face, and her tears couldn't mask the truth. She'd known. She'd always known. He wondered if that was why she'd come to him and told him about the phone call. She wanted justice for Ashlynn. She wanted to end the suffering once and for all. Even if it meant losing her father.

"You overheard Tanya talking to Olivia on the phone that Friday night, didn't you?" Chris asked Rollie. "You heard what they'd done, where they'd been. That was your chance. You knew Ashlynn was alone in the ghost town."

Rollie was silent.

Chris looked at Tanya, who squared her shoulders and wiped the tears from her eyes. She was done covering for him.

"I saw him leave," she said. "I was in my bedroom. I heard the car. He came back an hour later. I didn't say a word. I pretended I didn't know."

Rollie's head sagged. He stared at his lap, as if the worst punishment was hearing what he'd done from his daughter's lips. He could see the future. How she would grow up despising him. How she would see the demon he saw in himself every time he looked in the mirror.

"Ashlynn was probably excited to see you," Chris said. "She thought you'd come to rescue her."

"I just wanted to know what she'd found out," Rollie murmured. "I didn't go there to kill her. I figured she had suspicions, that was all."

"But she had more."

Rollie nodded. "She knew what Florian had done. She had proof. It was all in her laptop. She knew everything about Lucia. She'd copied phone records, bank records, travel records from Florian's computer. She'd found e-mails between them. She knew about all of it."

"Except you."

"Except me," he said.

He looked up at his daughter and reached for her, but Tanya recoiled. She turned and ran away, making wet footprints in the grass, sprinting for the school. He watched every step until she disappeared.

Altman nodded at the cops, who took Rollie off the bench and handcuffed him. He was in a daze and didn't resist. One fat tear trickled onto his cheek. It was followed by another, and another, turning into a flood. He looked as if he would rather be on the bottom of the river, buried like the ruins. They had to help him walk as they led him away.

Chris watched him go, thinking about fathers and daughters. Husbands and wives. Florian losing Ashlynn. Julia losing Florian. Tanya losing Rollie. Marco had it right. *Life changes, my friend.* One moment it was in your hand, and the next it was slipping away.

The county attorney turned to Olivia and put a hand on her shoulder. "I made a mistake about you, Miss Hawk. I falsely accused you of a terrible crime. I apologize."

Olivia shook her head. "I made a mistake, too. Mine was worse."

"You're sixteen," Altman told her. "I hate to break this to you, but you have a lifetime of mistakes ahead of you. I think your parents will tell you that the thing about mistakes is learning how to live with them."

The county attorney winked at Chris, and he marched after the police officers with the precise steps of a soldier.

When everyone else was gone, it was just the three of them in the field. Chris. Olivia. Hannah.

The sun vanished, searing the clouds with streaks of orange. The air got colder.

They were a family torn apart and brought back together. They'd lost everything and won everything. Chris had exactly what he wanted now; he had what he'd come here for. His home in the city had never been a home without them. Out here, they had nowhere to go and nowhere to live, and somehow, it didn't matter to Chris at all.

He cupped his daughter's face, and they bent into each other, forehead to forehead. He felt lucky. He felt saved.

"I should find Tanya," Olivia said. "She's going to need help."

"Go."

His daughter kissed his cheek. "Love you, Dad."

"I love you, too."

Olivia eyed both of her parents, and she got a silly smile as she watched them together. For a moment, she could have been ten again, their little girl, not a young woman who had already had her heart broken and grown up too fast. She was happy. Chris realized his daughter had learned something that it had taken him decades to figure out. When something good happens, you don't ask questions. You just smile and hold on tight.

Hannah stood beside him as Olivia hobbled toward the school to find her friend. He felt her fingers curl around his as she took his hand. They both knew. They both felt it. She didn't ask if he was staying, if he would be there for her, if he would be there for Olivia, if they could rebuild themselves along with the towns. It was understood. No questions. Smile and hold on tight.

Maybe they had months. Maybe they had years. Time was a funny thing. He didn't care. He wasn't going anywhere. Right there, holding onto Hannah, he felt time freeze as solid as the winter ice until it didn't move at all.

JOIN BRIAN'S COMMUNITY

You can write to me at brian@bfreemanbooks.com. I welcome e-mails from readers and always respond personally. Visit my website at www.bfreemanbooks.com to join my mailing list, get book club discussion questions, read bonus content, and find out more about me and my books. You can also join me on Facebook at www.facebook.com/bfreemanfans.

ACKNOWLEDGMENTS

The towns of Barron and St. Croix are fictional, so those of you who enjoy using Google Earth to follow my locales won't find them on a map this time. However, most of the scenes in the book are based on real places found in southwestern Minnesota—towns such as Montevideo, Granite Falls, Ortonville, and Hazel Run. The Spirit Dam was inspired by the Lac Qui Parle Dam over the Minnesota River.

I'm very grateful to the team who has helped me navigate the last few years of significant change in the publishing industry. This includes my international agents Ali Gunn and Diana Mackay and my US agent, Deborah Schneider, as well as co-agents around the world who have helped me bring my books to readers in many countries.

In the publishing world itself, I am especially grateful to my new UK colleagues, David North and Charlotte Van Wijk of Quercus, for their enthusiasm and support in launching Spilled Blood. I have been delighted to work with a tremendous new team at Sterling/Silver Oak, including Nathaniel Marunas, Jason Prince, Kim Brown, Leigh Ann Ambrosi, Anwesha Basu, Katherine Furman, and Elizabeth Mihaltse. Their commitment to me and this book has been sensational every step of the way.

A special thanks, too, to Isanti County Attorney (and longtime reader of my books) Jeff Edblad for his help on juvenile legal proceedings in Minnesota. Any errors or dramatic license in such matters are, of course, totally of my own making.

I've been privileged to enjoy the support of a very loyal cadre of readers around the world. I'm grateful to my advance readers—Marcia (who never lets love get in the way of helpful criticism!), Matt and Paula Davis, Mike O'Neill, and Alton Koren—for their insights and advice on the earliest drafts of this manuscript. I also want to thank the Italian readers at Corpi Freddi—especially Marco Piva—for many years of dedication to me and my books. These "cold bodies" have warm hearts!

Marcia and I are fortunate to have dear friends to help us through the roller-coaster ride of the writing life, including Barb, Jerry, Matt, Paula,

Keith, Katie, Terri, Pat, Gary, Sally, and many others who open their hearts to us. My parents, my brother, and his family have been supportive of my career in so many ways. They are far from us in distance but always close to us in spirit.

Finally, readers who have followed me from the beginning know that the most important words in each book are the first two: "For Marcia." For twenty-eight years, she has been my wife and best friend, and I'm always grateful to her for sharing this ride with me.